# Resurrecting Harry

## Constance Phillips

**Resurrecting Harry**
**Constance Phillips**

ISBN 13: 978-0692422151
ISBN 10: 0692422153

Editor: Sheldon Reid

Cover artist: Kim Jacobs – Calliope-designs

This book is a work of fiction. The names, characters, places, and incidents are products of the author's imagination or have been used fictitiously and are not to be construed as real. Any resemblance to persons, living or dead, actual events, locale or organizations are entirely coincidental.

# Dedication

This book is dedicated to my grandmother, Chris Martin, who showed me that each day is a gift and should be lived to its fullest extent.

# Chapter One

For Harry Houdini, failure wasn't an option.

Being closed into the old steamer trunk didn't faze him, not even when the familiar sound of a padlock clanking in place echoed in his ear. When water began to seep through the seams, most men would panic, but years of experience pushed down the instinct. He knew his faithful assistant and wife, Bess, had slipped into the spotlight to distract the crowd and raise the tension, just like they'd practiced for hours and performed dozens of times.

While the fans anticipated the worst, he took a slow and measured breath and prepared for several minutes without oxygen.

Harry focused on his center from behind veiled lids and used every last bit of strength to extend his legs. The side of the trunk he'd carefully loosened the night before popped off, and the water now rushed in. With cuffed hands, he felt along the lid, guiding himself out. His hooked pinky swiped the key from beneath his tongue, but the metallic taste remained.

Lifting his legs, he made short work of the shackles binding his ankles and then arched his back, reaching toward the surface. In seconds, the cuffs securing his wrists fell away too.

All that was left was to break the surface and claim his reward. The roar of the crowd and Bess's loving arms were the only two things that thrilled him more than defying death. Her and his fans gave him the drive to succeed.

Light faded away, as if rain clouds covered the sun or as if he was sinking further away from his destination.

His world spun like a child's top. A pulse thumped in his ear and molten-hot blood pumped through his veins. Pure adrenaline fueled the glimpses of his past, which flashed by like the slides his brother, Theo, showed after every vacation. But Harry wasn't watching the events unfold; he relived the memories over and again.

The spinning stopped. He now hung upside down, wrapped tighter than a Christmas present. His Chinese Water Torture Chamber, a straitjacket and the stage of the Orpheum Theatre; Harry might as well be safe at home in bed. He'd free himself from the binds as soon as he pushed his shoulder out of joint.

With a pop, this faded to white too.

Always trapped. Never escaping. No reward.

The spinning continued, like a phonograph record.

Shivers raked his body. In the distance, he could hear a doctor offering comfort and explaining to a sobbing Bess that hope was lost.

Harry saw nothing, just shuddered and listened. Icy water enveloped him; his neck rested on the frosty cast-iron tub. No matter how many times he relived it, he still believed his infection would clear and the fever would break. He may have stood in the shadow cast by the angel of death, but he still denied the inevitable. A burst appendix destroy the great Harry Houdini, master escape artist and expert showman? Never. When the lights fell on his final performance, something grander than illness would extinguish his flame.

Swallowing hard, he fought the quiver in his lips and tried to call out for Bess. Her touch to his cheek would provide the needed strength. The only vision that ever played out completely: he whispered her name and watched his own chest rise and fall for the last time.

*Spinning. Spinning.*

The cold vanished, his pain dissipated, but the mental torture never ended. Over and over he experienced his greatest challenges, but not the successes. Never completing an escape and returning to Bess's embrace kept him lonely and devastated. What had he done to deserve such torment, and for how long would this agony continue?

Harry always believed in ashes to ashes. When his heart stopped, his mind would too. Anything else seemed impossible, but now he knew different. This was Hell.

But what of the fire and brimstone ol' man Thomas used to preach about on the corner?

As a child, Harry's sainted mother would rush him past Seventh and Main where the elderly man testified to the world. She'd whisper passages from the Torah and remind him his main concern should be this life. Despite his mother's dislike for the reverend, he taught Harry a valuable lesson that would stick with him his whole life: give people a show.

Would it disappoint the preacher to know that, despite what the scriptures said, Hell didn't torture the body with never-ending fires, but focused on the mind? Harry knew this was worse.

His stomach heaved to and fro. Bile bubbled in his gut and pushed its way up, burning his throat, but the relief vomiting would bring never came.

*Why won't the spinning stop?* Maybe because he allowed it to continue. Change comes from within. That's how he lived his life: for every action, a reaction. Why should death be different?

No more complacency.

He tightened his muscles and stretched his body as taut as possible. "STOP!"

*Spinning. Spinning.* As if he was embedded on a reel-to-reel film and someone had pushed rewind, but he was through being held at someone else's mercy. Again, he ordered an end to the torture.

The loud clank of rusty gears grinding together sounded, and he felt whatever force kept him tied to this existence snap. His body plummeted and his arms thrashed; pleas turned to screams. Maybe there *was* something worse than the status quo. Falling faster now, he tensed his muscles and braced for the agonizing pain of hitting the ground.

Soft and comforting instead, like slipping into a feather bed and wrapping up in a patchwork quilt, he felt ground beneath him. And serenity. An end to his anguish? He opened his eyes and wondered if he'd see anything but his past. White padding adorned the walls and the floor, like he'd seen in those mental hospitals he toured while concocting his straitjacket escape.

But Harry wasn't crazy. He was dead.

The air shifted; the temperature rose. Sweat replaced the goose bumps that covered his arms. A body? Harry touched the flesh to make sure it was real. The image of a floating soul now shattered by this reality. Hot, humid air burned his lungs as he leaned against the wall and looked up into the ice-blue eyes of a stranger who loomed a good foot taller than Harry and was wrapped in tight, black leather like the blacksmiths he'd known in his youth or the cowboys he'd first met out west. Long, black hair veiled the stranger's face. He lit a cigarette and threw his head back, inhaling deeply and giving Harry another look at those bizarre eyes. A shiver rode his spine. "My God."

A bubbling laugh erupted from the giant. "Not bloody likely.

# Chapter Two

Harry struggled to keep the rattle out of his voice. Anxiety might tarnish his legacy and whoever this leather-clad giant was, he wouldn't know the Great Houdini trembled inside. "Then who are you?"

"Jaden." The look that brightened Jaden's face as he inhaled on the dangling cigarette could only be described as pure rapture.

Harry braced, expecting to be choked by the smoke, but instead a sweet aroma filled his head, turning his stomach. "You're the one who's been torturing me for so long?"

"Time means nothing here. For those who love you, eleven months have passed. Your life choices controlled your experience here, but that's over. Your future is up to me." Opening his eyes, the man gave Harry a long, level look. "On your feet."

Everyone expected more of Harry than they did the average man. Why should Jaden be different? Eleven months of anguish and he expected Harry to be none the worse for wear. Determined to keep the larger-than-life perception alive, he pressed his back against the padded wall and slid himself up, surprised to find his legs strong, even though his insides felt like sticky oatmeal. "What is this place?"

Jaden's face remained stoic. "You do know you're dead. Don't you?"

Indeed, but hearing it from someone else's lips didn't ease the blow to Harry's stomach or the tightening in his throat. He bit his lip and nodded.

"Where do you think you are?" Jaden paused for a beat, but then continued. "Oh, yes, Erich. You don't believe in anything after mortal death. Oops! How embarrassing for you? No wonder you're confused." Jaden's deep laugh erupted again.

A hundred or more questions raced through Harry's head, but for some reason he focused on that name. With something so simple, Jaden stripped away the celebrity and identified what was hidden beneath. "No one's called me Erich in years."

That wasn't the exact truth. In the throes of passion, Bess would call him by his given name, but that was intimate and only between them. This beast couldn't know about that.

"But it *is* the name your mother gave you?"

A simple truth, but one that Harry had guarded, the same way he protected anything that might detract from his image. "How do you know that?"

Jaden's body sagged, but it took little away from his intimidating presence. "You're beginning to sound like a broken record. I've told you all you need to know about me. We need to discuss you and process you to the next phase of your existence."

With a snap of Jaden's fingers, Harry's world tipped sharply to the left. He began to fall. Just as sudden, his balance righted, and they stood in a smoke-filled pool hall. Jaden's lanky frame bent over the table as he lined up a corner shot with his cigarette still hanging from his lips.

"An afterlife? Isn't this Hell?" It had to be. Even if Heaven existed, it wouldn't include leather-clad angels shooting pool. But then, that image didn't fit any traditional description of an underworld either.

Through a hearty laugh, Jaden said, "Wrong again. What? You're not having fun? Think of this as Ellis Island: your mortal life being the country you were born in, and your eternal ever-after being the land of opportunity. I'm the one who decides if you can pass through or not. Your actions determine my decisions, not only for you, but for Bess as well."

"Leave Bess out of this!" If the way he lived his life dictated his present, so be it, but why should Bess pay for his mistakes? He'd endure any imaginable pain to save her from experiencing one moment's worth.

Despite his plea, Jaden's focus remained on the stupid pool balls. A goofy grin turned his lips and lit his eyes. With a smooth stroke, the end of his stick hit the cue ball and propelled it into the yellow one, driving it into the pocket. "As in life, the choices you make now affect the ones you love as much, if not more, than they do you."

The rhythmic pounding in Harry's chest raced; his hands clenched. Diving across the pool table, he reached for Jaden's shirt, but another shift in reality landed him like a rock on the slate. Each ball assaulted a different part of his rib cage, causing him to gasp for air. "Don't threaten Bess!"

Jaden spoke with no emotion, as if they were talking about the weather. "I'm not the one who's put her in danger."

Reaching for Jaden again, Harry only grabbed air. A tremble crawled over his skin as he realized the pool table had vanished and he stood on his feet again. Jaden's backlit frame filled the opposite end of a long, white corridor. Whether utilizing sleight of hand or manipulating lights and shadows, Harry was used to being the one who delivered a false sense of reality to his audience. He needed to keep his focus or he'd fall prey to this master magician.

*Don't torture me with my own life anymore. Anything but that.*

Not even a moment after claiming Bess was the only thing he valued, Harry put his own fate first, making his previous defense ring false. At least he hadn't said it out loud. "Do what you want. Throw me into a pit of fire, but keep your filthy hands off Bess. Hurt one hair and I'll—"

In another snap, the distance closed. Harry stood mere inches from Jaden.

"What will you do, Erich?"

Every muscle of Harry's brand-new body tensed. It's not like he was in a position to help her. He was, after all, quite dead. Anger, regret, fear and pain swirled in his head, making him dizzy. An unexplainable force squeezed in from all sides, extracting the air from his lungs.

"Don't make me repeat myself. It makes me angry," Jaden said. "Your unexpected death forever altered Bess's life. Your time with her so changed her outlook on the world, she's lost without you."

Bess was the shining light in Harry's life. He'd loved and cared for her, protected her. He wanted to lash out at Jaden for even hinting that Harry had hurt her, even though he knew the giant could obliterate him based on their size difference alone, but the mystical force immobilized him.

"Conflicting messages. You taught her mediums and spiritualists who claimed to speak with the departed were con artists, but you also told her your love would find a way to break the barriers of death. You set her up to spend the remainder of her life pursuing a message that, according to you, she can never receive. Is it fair for you to rest in peace while she spends her final days chasing your non-existent ghost?"

The power that gripped Harry released. He fell back a couple steps and put a virtual wall between them. Jaden denied it, but Harry knew the Devil himself stood in front of him. Who else would torment him with such a preposterous idea? He'd taught Bess death was final. She understood the reasoning behind the contradictions and knew better than to hope for him to speak to her from beyond the grave. Jaden lied. He manipulated and tortured. That's what this was, just a new form of suffering Harry would have to endure for a life of pandering and profiteering.

"What, my friend, would you sacrifice to save Bess from your Hell?"

"My life." The answer spilled from his lips. The truth, but preposterous. How could he give what was no longer his?

"I'm more interested in your everlasting soul." A twinkle sparked in Jaden's otherwise cold eyes.

Harry stepped into his stage persona like most people would slip into a jacket. It didn't matter that his stomach quivered. He tipped his jaw slightly up and to the right. "I don't believe in such things. Remember?"

"That's what I thought. You're more worried about saving your own skin than preserving Bess's happiness."

That snapped Harry's attention to Jaden. *A lie. Wasn't it?* "If I don't believe in life everlasting, will sacrificing it mean anything?"

Jaden turned away from Harry, and the pool table reformed. Jaden leaned against it, giving the game more of his attention and concern than their conversation. "What do you think the last eleven months have been about, if not your soul?"

*Have I really spiraled that long?* Not possible. And why? The obvious reason would be punishment. But for what? "I'm guessing you're the man with all the answers."

"No. Just one of his ever-faithful servants." Jaden stepped up to line up another shot.

Harry's closed fist bounced against his thigh. He would spend an eternity tormented by this beast if that was the fate he'd created, but his angel deserved mercy. Reaching out, he pulled the ball from the table. With Jaden's follow-through, he fell against the mahogany rails. His head snapped and their eyes met, the frosty blue replaced with a glowing fire-red. "This is a bind you cannot escape with a pick or sleight of hand, and it's not a predicament your golden tongue will chatter your way out of."

A pain radiated in Harry's jaw from clenching it so tight. "What do you want from me?"

The table evaporated. Jaden closed the distance with one step. "I want nothing. The question is, Erich, what do you want? Will you do everything you can to keep Bess from chasing your ghost into an early grave? Can you risk your eternity to shorten her stay in purgatory?"

*Not my angel.* The thought of Bess having to live through the same torture he'd experienced sucked the breath from his lungs. But... "Bess wouldn't do the things you describe."

Jaden's large hand came toward Harry. He tried to move away, but his feet remained still, as if they were bound with shackles. An ice cold tremor coursed his body with Jaden's touch. Harry tried to push the giant away, but Jaden's hand remained glued to Harry's forehead. As if Jaden tried to retaliate, the ice turned to fire and a ripping, tearing pain centered itself in Harry's chest and branched out through his body. He dropped to his knees in surrender. A gut wrenching scream escaped from deep inside.

Even though Jaden's palm no longer touched Harry, the overwhelming grief still pulsed through his veins, as if it mingled with his blood. His body fell forward, and he braced himself on his forearms as he dropped to the sawdust covered, wood floor. White hot tears scalded his cheeks.

"That's the problem with love. When it runs so deep, its demise can cripple and destroy," Jaden said.

"Make...it...stop." Harry gasped between waves of pain.

"Only you can do that."

"I'm dead!" The pain was rooted so deep, he wasn't sure if it belonged to him, Bess, or worse, a combination. She was the only thing dying cost him. Nothing else mattered in the same way. His soul didn't miss the house, the money he'd accumulated, not even the admiration of his fans or the prickly praise of the press. Only her. The mere thought of Jaden toying with her locked his jaw and tightened his stomach.

"I can give you a brand new life if you use it to save her."

If Harry knew one thing for sure, anything too good to be true was just that. He welcomed a challenge, but not if Bess suffered the consequences. "And if I fail?"

"You pay with your life."

Curiosity pushed down the throbbing heat and cutting pain. "Explain."

The grit between his legs and the floor melted into something soft and cushioned. The honky-tonk faded, and the padded room they first met in came back into focus.

Jaden's leer loomed from above. "You, Erich, with no outward traces of Harry, can be given a life in Bess's proximity. Your sole goal: convince her to stop chasing your ghost. If you succeed, you can grow old in that body, even with her if the fates allow. But, if Bess holds her séance on the anniversary of your death, she'll draw your spirit from its new home, and you'll be condemned to the afterlife you don't believe in."

"The same torture I've endured at your hands?"

"No. Nothingness. A dark void so vast that the sinking never ends. An eternity of deprivation."

Jaden's description should have deterred Harry, but he'd gladly risk that fate for another chance at a long life with Bess. Harry doubted Jaden could devise a penalty harsh enough to keep him from trying. After all, it had been love at first sight the first time around. How would his soul being encased in a different body change that? It would be simple again.

"Despite what you think, she won't recognize you on sight as the man she loved," Jaden commented, as if Harry had conveyed his own thoughts aloud.

*Of course she would.* Their love lived and breathed with a life of its own. It was more than the sum of them, it consumed them. Hers would recognize his, regardless of the body it was wrapped in or what Jaden believed. "I have one month to convince Bess not to hold a séance, and I can have a second chance at a life with her? The only barrier is she won't recognize me?"

"And you cannot tell her the simple truth. If you do, it's an automatic failure, and a win for me."

Jaden had no concept of their love. "But when she recognizes me, then can I tell her the truth?"

"If the day comes that she believes with all her heart you are Harry wrapped in new skin, then you may confirm it. But, Erich, you remember the woman you fell in love with. You don't even know the one your contradictions have destroyed." Again, Jaden spoke to Harry's thoughts instead of the words he'd vocalized, cementing the idea the giant was omniscient.

"Why are you giving me this chance?" Not that Jaden's answer mattered. He'd already decided to take the wager and deal with the repercussions later.

"Not important. The question is: Are you man enough to save her?"

"What do I need to do?"

"Just agree to the terms."

****

Time heals all wounds. What a load of hooey!

Bess tugged hard on the desk drawer and freed it from its confines. Dumping the contents on the dining room table, she sifted through the odds and ends, looking for the small, black book Harry called his bible. It held the phone numbers of preferred service providers and notes on everyone they'd ever met. Since he'd died, she learned Eli could mow the lawn, but he never trimmed or fertilized it. Jeffery charged a fair price to take care of the storm windows and screens twice a year, but would he know how to fix that ancient, fuel oil furnace? It'd been coughing and hacking like Uncle Ralph with his emphysema for weeks. In the middle of the night, the monster gave up the fight and puttered its last breath.

The Santa Ana winds were blowing this morning, but they wouldn't last. Fall would give way to winter and the furnace was long overdue for service. She wished Harry would have kept his word and replaced that clunker last year. Instead, he hid everyday necessities as if they were treasured secrets, and made it so hard for her to go on alone.

"Damn you for always living in the moment!" She picked up a pen and tried to scribble on a worn, yellow notepad. As she suspected, no ink. She tossed them both in the garbage. A laugh spilled from her as the items clanked against the metal. Cold and empty, just like her life.

What she'd give for one more day with him.

When Harry died, it was like she had forgotten how to breathe, but that came back in time and she'd figure out how to take care of this too. She had no choice but to go on, praying he'd find a way to keep his most important promise.

*I'll return to you, if at all possible.*

She pressed her fingers to her eyes. No time for tears, let alone sobs. Only four weeks remained until the first anniversary of his death and the séance to call forth his spirit. There was so much left undone, including choosing the venue and a medium. For years she'd been Harry's faithful assistant, but now she ran the show. He needed her more in death, and she'd succeed no matter the cost.

A knock on the back door, just off the kitchen, drew her from her thoughts. She pulled the curtain aside and smiled at Gail Cooper.

*Don't you let that harlot in, Bess. You know she's just a well-dressed con-artist.*

Gail and Martin had cut Harry, but they'd been a blessing since his death. If Harry knew how much they'd helped, he'd forgive Gail, right? A cool breeze from the open window brushed against Bess's neck, arguing with her. To him, Gail's actions were unforgivable. He'd hate her in his house. Bess opened the door anyway. "Good morning. You're out early."

"Is it too early to be calling?" Gail's blonde hair was perfectly set, and her cheery blue eyes shined like the morning sun, but neither her eyes nor the actual sunrise were enough to lift Bess's spirits today.

"Heaven's no, I've been up for hours." She opened the door wider, trying hard to be hospitable. "Come, sit down and I'll pour us some coffee."

Gail followed Bess to the kitchen and took a seat at the table. "I headed over just after the nanny left to take the kids to school. I wanted to catch you before you left for town. I know you like to run your errands on Monday mornings."

*Children...if only Harry and I had been so blessed.*

Retrieving two cups from the cupboard, Bess filled them and then joined Gail at the table. "If it wasn't for that stupid furnace, I might already be gone. It quit working overnight."

"Oh dear. It's been one thing after the other with this house hasn't it?"

Bess swept her hand over the clutter. "I still can't find Harry's little book. Eleven months, you'd think I'd have stumbled across it by now."

"Now don't you fret, Bess. I'll have Martin send Joseph over this afternoon to take a look at that furnace and anything else you need repaired."

"That's nonsense. Joseph is studying to become a doctor. He has more important things to do then clean and repair my furnace."

"He's Martin's student," Gail corrected in a familiar disapproving tone. The same one she often used in reference to the protégée. "If you ask me, he should be more grateful for the opportunities Martin gives him. There isn't another facility or physician who would take one of *them* on as a fellow."

"Do you mean Cabazon tribe member?" So many held Martin's second wife under scrutiny, but Bess tried not to judge. Even though, at times like this, Gail made it difficult not to agree with them.

"Martin gives him so much. The very least Joseph can do is help one of our dear friends."

Bess wanted to accept the offer. It'd be one less worry. It wasn't that she didn't want Joseph to help. He was someone she'd grown to trust in the past few months. When Bess volunteered at the hospital, she and Joseph had shared many conversations about herbal remedies and native healing methods. But, Harry's imagined voice whispering in her ear and the need to start standing alone confirmed her refusal. "That's not necessary. Now, you didn't come by to listen to me whine."

"I just wanted to drop these off." Gail offered up a sterling silver flask and leather bound book.

The weight of the container surprised Bess. "What is this?"

"Some of Martin's homemade, blackberry brandy. You said you were having trouble with the meditation I've been teaching you. A sip or two will help open your mind to the other side."

*Bess, my angel, it's so important that we keep our minds clear and our body fit for the stage. Alcohol compromises both.*

Harry's words rang in her mind as if he were in the room with her. She always felt him next to her, helping her with every decision. But it was past time to stop that. Wasn't it? "Thank you, Gail. You've been so helpful. Your training will be the key to Harry's success. I'm sure."

"A successful séance is going to be so much more about you than him. His spirit simply exists. You'll be the one in control, not him. You need to learn how to let go of your own thoughts and concerns, open yourself to the universe and let those on the other side invade your body. Let Harry use you to deliver his messages. Read the book. It was a great help to me."

For the first time, Bess looked closely at the cover. *The Principles of Nature, Her Divine Revelations, and a Voice to Mankind* by Andrew Jackson Davis.

*Tomfoolery!* Harry's voice echoed on the wind. She could see his face all crinkled up at the mere thought of her reading it, let alone praying she learned a way to hear his voice for real, instead of just in her daydreams.

Bess bit her lip. Harry would hate her discussing their act with Gail, but if she couldn't lean on a friend, then who could she trust? "You know that Harry and I worked a spiritualist con in the early days?"

Gail frowned. "You aren't the only ones, Bess. But just because spiritualism *can* be faked, doesn't mean it's not real."

"I suppose you're right."

"Now that didn't sound very convincing. What's the matter, honey?"

*It's a con game. Once you know how it's done, it's easy as pie and as lucrative as sin.*

Bess tried to close out the running commentary, but he was so much a part of her life and ignoring his influences was like cutting off her arm. "Harry was brilliant and a very quick study. It didn't take him long to learn how to con a grieving loved one. He and I performed the illusion quite effectively for a long time."

"Some people prey on the grieving, but some are true, spiritual mediums. I know Harry thought I manipulated him, but you forget he asked me to try and contact his mother, not the other way around."

"That's the point, Gail. A lot of people do things while they are grieving that they normally wouldn't." And Bess knew that all too well. She'd found comfort from two people Harry had declared nemeses. "It devastated him to lose his mother. The way he took care of her, you'd think he was the parent. She lived a full life, but it was still too short for him." It marked the beginning of his search for a *true* medium. That obsession—and Gail's falsehoods—ended Harry's long-time friendship with Martin Cooper and Gail too.

And now look at her stumbling down the same path and hoping against hope that her husband could find a way to do the one thing he believed impossible.

"You're still defending his actions." Gail exhaled as if Bess was a hopeless cause. "Of the two, you are the strong one. Harry is going to need someone at that séance whom he can use, someone who is completely open to his state of being. You can't serve him if you lose faith."

Bess twisted her wedding ring. Roseabelle—their code word for believe—was engraved on the inside of it. Where another man would have declared his love, Harry asked for her undying faith. He'd want her to believe that he could escape any confine, physical or mental. No, not want. He'd demand it of her.

Not knowing what to say, Bess nodded. She knew that because of the coded message sealed in an envelope in her safe she couldn't be the medium at the séance, but she couldn't share that detail with Gail and risk losing her coaching. Bess needed to learn everything Gail offered if there was any hope of Harry coming to her alone before the big show. If Harry was able to reconnect with this world, he'd deliver only that message.

Maybe it was selfish of her to want the Great Houdini to put her above his public, but after everything she'd done for him, and all the pain she'd lived with since his death, she deserved it. She'd tell Gail the truth soon, but not while there was still time to contact Harry alone.

# Chapter Three

Steamy, thick air kissed Erich's cheeks, and his head rolled back on his shoulder. He embraced as an old friend the breeze he once cursed. Different than the dream state he'd been tied to for so long, real flesh encased his spirit. The body he sensed with Jaden gave form and had a sense of touch, but not with this intensity or clarity.

He was alive.

In the past, Harry might have ducked into one of the shops that lined the street for some shade, but Erich refused to escape anything this new life offered.

According to Jaden, Harry died eleven months earlier, making this a lovely September day, despite the Santa Anas. He didn't have to look up the block to see the small deli he and Bess frequented to know he stood in their old Laurel Canyon, California neighborhood. The scent of fresh pastries and frying chicken permeating the air confirmed it.

He found his bearings and turned toward the house. Four short blocks now separated him from the only love he'd ever know. With one goal in mind, he quickened his pace and headed for their home–and her. Rounding the corner, he collided with a woman, causing her to drop her purse and spill its contents across the narrow walk.

Erich knelt and a sharp pain stabbed his right side. His instinct told him to cradle it and investigate the cause, but the sooner he scooped the wallet, keys, coins and pens into the brown leather bag, the sooner he'd be with his beloved. He inhaled sharply and the pain subsided.

The sunlight reflected off a silver band wrapped in a broken chain. He instantly recognized it and his heart seized. Jaden *really* gave him his life back! As Erich slid his fingers over the etching, his throat closed around mounting tears.

*His* ring!

The sterling silver felt cool to his touch. He dropped the handbag and started to unravel the chain, needing to return it to his finger and reclaim his life.

"Excuse me, young man. That is my property."

Bess's voice stole his breath. But the words? *Young man?* He fine-tuned his focus beyond the ring and centered it on his flesh: smooth and soft, no lines of time and no calluses. Just how young was he?

So, that's the way Jaden played his games. No catches, indeed. An age difference would be a challenge, yes, but he welcomed it. The thrill of fighting against the odds and winning gave him a high–similar to the way others described a stiff drink or a good cigar. Harry didn't know for sure if those were good comparisons. He always resisted both activities, opting instead to keep his body pure and fit for the stage, but they felt right.

"Return the ring and the necklace to me this instant!"

Bess's voice sliced the air. Her bitter tone sounded as sweet as a songbird's call. Erich lifted his head bit by bit in order to make this moment last. The first time Harry laid eyes on Bess remained etched in his mind, and this memory would sit next to that one in honored glory.

"Bess." Her name slid off his tongue.

Hypnotized by her dark eyes, he scooped up the purse and offered it to her as he stood.

"That's right. Doesn't make you clairvoyant because you know my name. My husband—God rest his soul—made sure it would never be forgotten. Now, please. His ring."

A jagged, icy edge laced her voice. Coupled with her closed off stance, it cut at his new flesh. What happened to the sweet woman of his heart?

Despite Jaden's warning, he'd believed their eyes would lock, and much like the first time, love would blossom like lilies on a spring day. Instead, she demanded he give her back the symbol of their undying love. Nothing could hurt worse, even though his rational mind knew she couldn't recognize him. Not so soon, anyway. The connection he'd put all his faith in was broken like the delicate chain.

He laid the jewelry in her out-stretched palm. A familiar energy pulsed between the point where their hands touched, proving to Erich that not even time and death could alter what they'd once shared. Bess must have felt the same sensation. It was too strong to be ignored. She had to see something in his eyes and hear something in his voice.

He willed her to grab on to the connection between them, not knowing if she sensed it. "Here you go, Angel."

Her jaw locked. Though laugh lines etched her cheeks, reminding him of the love and joy they'd shared, no other traces of happiness remained on her face. For the first time, he understood Jaden's warning. This wasn't *his* Bess. Not anymore. The passage of time and depths of her misery could be mapped in the wrinkles at her temples and reflected in her cold, brown eyes.

"If you would be so kind as to return my handbag, I'll be on my way."

The way she treated him like an outsider shook him off balance. Of course, in this body, he was a stranger. His knees trembled. His head went light. *It's just not possible.*

Not wanting her to hear the tears constricting his voice, he silently offered the leather bag and stepped aside. He stumbled back and leaned against the brick wall, letting it hold his weight as she whisked around the corner. His heart belonged to her, and she held the string, dragging it behind her as she walked away.

The very first time they'd met, he spilled his drink on her dress, but she'd accepted his apology and, in no time at all, became quite taken with him. He had expected that warm, flirty smile and knew somewhere inside she'd never mistake him for anything but the love of her life. Yet, she had.

Why had he unraveled the chain from his ring? Because inside he was still Harry and that ring belonged to him. To her, those actions made him look like a thief. Instead of moving forward, his first encounter with Bess had set him back. Instead of building trust, he now had to regain it.

"I think we'll call that strike one."

*Jaden.*

He also leaned against the same wall. His leather outfit had been replaced with blue-grey flannel trousers and a white dress shirt, but the clothes didn't help him blend into the surroundings. Still tall, still thin, the same ice-blue eyes that shone like no other. This man—if that's what he was—would never appear normal in this world.

Erich's shoulders dropped. "You've set me up for one last round of torture before you sentence me to my never-ending Hell. Why don't you just be done with it now?"

"Giving up was never Harry's style."

Jaden's comment seemed off the cuff, but struck as if it were a blow to the chin. In life, he never once abandoned something he believed in. Was this different because it was hard? No. He had faced many obstacles in his short life, and the only one he ever failed to conquer was his own health. He owed Bess that same determination regardless if Jaden was right and his contradictions had made her into this cold, empty being. "I'm still me. No matter what you've done to my face."

"If you still believe that at month's end, the whole wager will be for nothing."

He'd never be ashamed to call himself Harry Houdini, despite Jaden's disgust. Because of his hard work, everyone knew who he and she were. "How can I not be me? That's impossible."

"This is not a game or one of your illusions. What you feel and how you act must come from your heart or it means nothing."

"If this isn't a game, why the bet?"

Jaden's chest rose and fell, and his lanky body shook with his sinister laugh. "I didn't say we couldn't have a little fun with it now."

How dare he amuse himself with his and Bess's pain? The agony of returning his ring and watching her walk away hurt like nothing he'd experienced in all his years of death defying acts. Not even the months he'd spent tortured by Jaden cut more. If Bess hurt even a fraction of what he did, Erich would do anything to save her. If only he knew where to start.

"I'd put myself in a place where she can't ignore you."

Jaden could read his mind. Erich was positive now. Despite the invasion into his private thoughts, Jaden's words made sense. He'd have to find some way to become part of her life—not as the man he once was, but as who Jaden had made him.

"There is a wallet and an ID that no employer would question in your back pocket."

As Erich twisted to retrieve it, pain shot through his side. He spun back, but Jaden had disappeared. No real surprise, he hadn't been much help so far.

Alone, he investigated the throbbing to find a six inch wound bound with stitches. He wasn't a doctor, but he'd seen enough injuries to guess this one was only a few days old. Another obstacle? Or was it a veiled reminder of the appendix surgery Harry received a few days before he died?

More of Harry's memories rolled through Erich's mind like a movie. Harry had been in such agony the last several days of his life, but refused to let anything stand in the way of providing for Bess or pleasing the fans who had spent hard-earned money to watch him perform. If Erich were to take a page from his book, this fresh incision was no cause for concern.

His attention back on the billfold, he stroked the fine leather. Even when he'd been able to afford it, he'd never have spent the money on such a luxury. Flipping the wallet open, he rummaged through the pockets until he found the papers Jaden spoke of and then read the details of his new identity: Erich Welch, born in 1902. That made him...twenty-four.

Less than half the age Harry had been at death. Half Bess's age.

No wonder Bess had called him a young man. It was going to be hard enough to get her to give anyone other than Harry a second look, but someone so young? Near impossible.

****

Safe inside the deli, Bess's walls fell. The strong face she reserved for the public evaporated. Grief enveloped her like the darkness of being closed in one of Harry's trunks or the seemingly endless nights since he'd died. So much for a crisp, new start, free of those memories.

Unclenching her hand, she looked down at the sterling ring and fingered the broken chain. It should still be on his finger, but in the last moments before they closed the coffin, her eyes fixated on the memento and her heart demanded she keep it. The chain, an anniversary gift from Harry, kept the ring close to her heart until it had snapped a week ago while she worked in the flower garden. She felt naked not having the comforting weight of the ring brush against her chest, but avoided dropping the chain off at the jeweler. Too much pain to discuss with strangers and way too precious to let out of her sight, she closed the symbols of their love in her fist, unable to let go of him or their past.

And *that man* might have stolen them. As quick as the thought flashed through her mind, Bess dismissed it. If he'd intended to take the jewelry, she wouldn't have been able to stop him. Besides, his eyes were too kind and his smile too sweet for him to be a ruffian.

And he'd called her "Angel." Just like Harry.

Was that some kind of confirmation that moving forward was the right choice? Or was she looking for signs where none existed? Even so, the young man refused to leave her thoughts.

*Goodness, he's just a child.* And she was married. Or had been. Even if almost a year had passed, her heart still belonged to her husband. She had no business noticing how attractive the stranger was.

"Are you all right, Bess?" Will Johnson, owner and operator of the Courtyard Deli, stood before her. He wiped his large hands on his stained apron and looked on with a father-like concern.

"Oh yes, I'm fine."

When he offered her his plump arm, Bess took it, allowing him to guide her to the corner booth in the back of the restaurant. "You sit right down, sweetheart, and let me bring you some coffee and a sweet roll."

"I don't know what I'd do without you to fuss over me."

"Aren't you lucky? You don't have to find out." He scurried behind the counter, pouring her a cup of coffee and picking the largest pastry from the display case.

"Since I'm your only customer at the moment, please pour yourself a cup and come sit with me." Part of her made the long walk to the deli at least twice a week out of habit. So many mornings she and Harry would wake up early, make the leisurely stroll and spend the morning enjoying the fresh coffee and baked goods while reading the paper. Another part of her kept the ritual alive because she feared the alternative: closing herself in the house and letting the walls suffocate her. The grief became bearable when her friends were around.

"I can sit for a few minutes, little lady." Will wedged himself into the seat across the table. "I'm worried about you. You look like you saw a ghost."

Maybe she had. Or maybe it was more like that déjà vue stuff she read about in dime store novels. Bess didn't believe in either, but running into that man on the street made her feel just like she had the day she'd met Harry. She set the ring and chain down on the table. "I bumped into a man on the street and my purse spilled."

"Are you hurt?"

"I'm fine. I just feel so scattered. So alone."

"But you're not."

Harry's memory and the imagined voice whispering in her ear weren't real company, and her friends only filled the void in short spurts. Unable to speak around the lump choking her throat, she nodded.

"Is that Harry's?" he asked, pointing to the ring.

"I should have buried him with it. That's what he would have wanted."

"All Harry ever wanted was to see your smile."

"Hmph!" She scooped the jewelry off the table. "Material things were more important to my husband. The act, the fans, the money and what he could buy with it."

Will scraped his jaw with the back of his hand. "Oh, I see how it is. You're in one of these moods again. You know he wanted the nice things for you."

The ring and tangled chain slipped from her hand and clattered against the table. "I'd rather have him."

"I know that. That's why these are so important to you. It keeps him close. He'd like that." Will picked up and examined the broken end of the chain. "How did this happen?"

"It got caught on a rose bush while I was weeding. I need to stop by the jewelers."

"If you'd like, I can take it home tonight and try to fix it."

His kind offer touched her heart. "Thank you, I'd like that. And so would Harry."

"So what brings you into town today? Just the usual errands?" Will set Harry's ring in front of Bess before he pulled himself from the booth and retreated behind the counter.

"I need to stop at the grocery store and the drug store. And I need to find someone who can fix that blasted furnace."

Will stabbed a few buttons on the cash register until the drawer slid out. He dropped the necklace into one of the compartments and then pushed it shut. "What you need to do, is have that thing replaced. It's been nothing but one headache after the other for you."

"I don't know anything about buying a new furnace, or who I would have to install it. Goodness knows I haven't chosen repairmen well."

"Or maybe you can't bear to let go of anything that belonged to Harry, no matter how much danger it's putting you in."

Bess clicked her tongue against the roof of her mouth, trying to hide the fact that Will had zeroed in on the truth. "Bothersome, maybe, but I don't believe that furnace has me in harm's way."

The bell sounded above the door. A young couple entered and approached the counter. Before tending to the customers, Will gave Bess all his focus. "I'm not so sure about that. Let me ask around for you and see what I can find out."

# Chapter Four

As Erich opened the door to the deli, the scent of fresh brewed coffee and hot cinnamon permeated the air, reminding him of home. Whether he and Bess were here in California, back in Brooklyn, or in any city that they performed in around the world, simple rituals like quiet time to drink coffee and read the paper had been the foundation of their married life. More than a building or a city, any moment Harry shared with Bess was home.

With a sideways glance, he saw her sitting alone in the corner booth, a large white mug and small plate with a half-eaten roll pushed aside and forgotten. Her eyes were locked on the pages of the book cradled in her hands. How could Bess not even notice him when she was his whole world? He fought the desire to go to her and make some excuse for acting so weird before. Instead, he approached the counter, holding the help wanted sign he'd pulled from the window. He resisted the urge to call the owner by name. "Excuse me, sir. I see you're looking for kitchen help."

"I am." Will wiped his hands on the bottom of the apron before offering to shake Erich's. "I need someone who can bus tables, do dishes and make deliveries. It's hard, physical labor. You think you're up to it?"

Without Harry's thoughts and memories, Erich might have been insulted, but with them he knew Will shot from the hip and laid everything out in the open. Harry never shied from hard work and kept his body in peak physical form. It was a necessity of his job. But what of *this* body? Would it respond and react in the same way just because Harry's thoughts and knowledge filled Erich's head?

From the fit of his clothes and bulk of his arms, Erich guessed he'd have the same strength as before. Along with Harry's worldly knowledge, he'd conquer anything put in front of him. The throbbing incision in his right side might be an obstacle, but he'd persevere. He didn't have another choice. If working here got him close to Bess, he'd endure any pain. "I promise I'll do all you ask and more."

"You don't look familiar. You new around here?"

He wanted to remind Will of the dozens of conversations they'd had at that very counter. Instead, he heeded Jaden's warning: better to effect change as someone else rather than a ghost. "Just got to town. I'll also be looking for a place to stay."

"If I give you the job, I'll expect you by five every morning, and you'd work until everything is cleaned up from the lunchtime rush. Fifty cents an hour is the wage, plus the tips you might earn on deliveries."

"That sounds fair." The salary was inconsequential. Erich needed this job if he were to meet his goal. From behind the counter he'd watch Bess, talk to her and connect with her. Regardless of how hurt or jaded she'd become, an undeniable bond existed between their spirits. All it would take is a little time. If he let go of that notion he might as well let go of her. He'd do neither.

"Say I decide to hire you, when can you start?"

"Is right now too soon?"

The portly elder laughed. "Why don't you tell me your name first?"

Erich swallowed the urge to answer "Harry Houdini" and instead stated the name adorned him by Jaden. His tongue tripped over it, and it rang foreign in his ear.

"I like your spirit, Erich. Why don't we give today a try and see how you work out? There's a clean apron on the back of the kitchen door and a sink full of dirty dishes."

"You'll see, sir. I won't let you down." Erich's chest swelled with pride in a sought-out-task completed, even if this was just another mundane job. Harry had done more than his share of manual labor and knew this kind of work left him feeling confined.

Stepping behind the counter transported Harry back to his childhood. Then, he'd been forced to work to support his family. The instinct to flee uncoiled itself in his stomach, but so much more than a loaf of bread lay in the balance this time. He wasn't working to feed his family; this was about reclaiming his wife and his life.

Tackling a sink full of coffee-stained cups and syrup-covered plates didn't allow him to interact with her. "If you'd like, I could tend to your customers. Refill coffee and water, maybe bus tables."

Will shook his head and grabbed Erich's forearm, leading him into the kitchen. As the door swung to and fro across the threshold, Will spoke in a low, firm voice that Harry had never heard. "Mrs. Houdini likes her solitude. You'd do best to remember that. I'll tend to her needs. You take care of the dishes."

Erich pivoted to the sink and began tying the apron strings behind his back with swift, yet smooth movements. He appreciated the friendship and loyalty to Harry that motivated Will's actions. If any other man tried to hit on his Bess, Harry would want Will there ready to throttle him. But Erich wasn't any other man, and Will's presence didn't deter, only irritated.

Erich scrunched his nose at the odor rising up from the pile of breakfast dishes. Busboy was a long fall from master escape artist, and he had no intention of spending a moment more than necessary in this role. All it would take was time and the right choice of words for his angel to see through the facade and recognize him as Harry. Until he achieved his goal, though, he'd have to play this little game.

Filling the appropriate sink bays with soapy water, rinse water and sanitizer, he picked through the dishes, washing only coffee mugs until he had enough to fill a large brown tray. A deep breath braced his lacerated stomach muscles as he lifted the tray and pushed the door open with his back. Setting the mugs on the counter, Erich ignored the other patrons in the diner and zeroed in on Bess sipping her coffee, but her eyes never left the book. When she unceremoniously licked her finger and turned the page, Erich's gut tightened. Oh, to hold her close and inhale the scent of her skin.

Physical need: one more thing to add to the list of sensations lost to his post-life body and regained in this new flesh. One more thing he'd never again take for granted and would move Heaven and earth to reclaim.

Swallowing his ache, he squatted down and began putting the cups on the shelf. This vantage point blocked his view of Bess, but her presence still called to him. He wrestled down the undeniable craving, knowing that if he pushed too hard or too fast it would only set off her defensive instincts.

The bell above the door sounded, announcing another customer, who Will greeted with a hearty welcome. "Erich, bring a fresh cup of coffee for Sergeant Fisher and one of those pecan rolls."

The officer took a stool at the counter, patted his stomach and laughed. "I'll take the coffee and a turkey sandwich. Let's skip the pecan roll today."

"Look at this?" Will laughed, patting the officer's back. "Trying to act like *he's* got to watch his weight."

"If I ate all the pastries you pushed my way, my uniform wouldn't fit." Fisher spun the stool toward Erich. "Just a cup of coffee and the turkey sandwich, please, on rye."

As Erich filled the order, Will continued his conversation. "Are you going to eat here, Stanley, or take it back to the station?"

"I was planning on sitting right here, if that's okay."

Will's fingers tapped against the counter. He shifted his weight. "Of course. I need to run across the street for a few minutes. Can you keep an eye on the place for me?"

"Not a problem."

*Finally! A chance to interact with Bess.*

Erich watched Will cross the street, dodging between straggling shoppers and the occasional car meandering down Main street. He delivered the order to Stanley, and then turned back, picking up the coffee pot and setting his sights on the corner booth. "A refill, Mrs. Houdini?"

A curt nod gave him permission, and he began to pour. She closed the book and gave him her full attention. "You won't spill it on me, will you?"

*Like our very first meeting!* His stomach lightened and spirits lifted. Maybe she did find him familiar. "Not if I can help it."

"It'd be a perfect distraction. Maybe give you another chance at my husband's ring."

If the short, choppy lilt didn't speak to her anger, her tone rang loud and clear. He leaned against the opposite seat of the booth and tried to explain. "It wasn't my intention to steal it. Why would I even try while standing right in front of you? It's ridiculous."

"My husband could steal your wallet while you were staring him dead in the eye. I know more than you might think about sleight of hand." She straightened her back and lifted her chin, self-assured and defiant.

God how he missed moments like these. Erich set the pot on the table and leaned against its edge. "Something tells me the great Houdini had a little more honor than to steal a man's wallet."

Bess cocked her head to the right and smiled. She tried to hide it, but he could see she also enjoyed the developing tit-for-tat. "But what of you, Mr. Erich Welch? Are you a man of honor? Or should I have warned Will that you have light fingers?"

She was teasing him now; her smile proved that. His guard fell, and he began to trust in the implicit soul-connection between them. "I may be clumsy or excitable. I often leap without thinking, but I'm not a thief."

Something darker wiped the hint of joy from her face. Her eyes shifted from him to the window. "I know all I care to about impetuous men."

Too much pain resided in her voice. Bess and Harry's life and love should be something she celebrated, not mourned. Separation hurt. He missed her in the same way he'd miss his beating heart. More than a joy, he needed her to breathe, but the pain didn't darken his memories or fill him with regret. Why did it do that to her? "You know what I think? Doing something impetuous might be just what you need. What do you say? Let me take you to dinner?"

Her eyes crawled up and down his body, evaluating him. She was putting Harry's lessons on reading people to good use. Erich's pulse quickened, but then being near Bess always did that.

She shook her head and laughed, mocking his joy. "Why would you do such a thing?"

*Because I love you, Bess.* "I'm new in town and want to make friends."

"With an older woman and a widow to boot?" Back again was the doubtful cynic.

"With a beautiful, spunky woman."

"Flattery may breed a fool, Mr. Welch, but I won't be swindled."

"I have no intention—"

Her waving hand cut him off. "I heard you tell Will you don't even have a place to stay. You have more important concerns than a frivolous dinner with me."

His lip curled between his teeth. As much as he enjoyed playing cat and mouse, she'd checked him with reality. Even if she agreed to spend time with him, the few coins jingling in his pocket wouldn't buy either of them more than a cup of coffee, let alone a meal for both.

Erich was about to suggest a walk in the park–something they could do on his limited budget–but was interrupted by the sound of a rubber ball hitting the tile floor. It brushed against his leg, and he bent over and picked up the ball.

A small boy with dark, disheveled hair and big brown eyes ran up, tugged on his pant leg and reached up to him. After returning the toy to its rightful owner, Erich patted the child's shoulder. His mother mumbled a thank you as she bustled by them, guiding the child out of the diner.

With the distraction out of the way, Erich tried to make headway with Bess, when the bell sounded again. Erich froze. He'd been caught doing the one thing he was warned against. Will's voice filled the room. "I'm paying you to wash dishes, Erich."

"I was just taking care of your customer," he replied, rounding the corner.

"Mrs. Houdini's coffee is just fine. Mr. Hanson is waiting for you at the hardware store. I just bought a cot. I figured until you can save up a paycheck or two, you might be just as comfortable sleeping in the store room. I'd have brought it back myself, but the clerk had to get it down off the top shelf. Go on. Pick it up."

And just that quick, one problem was solved. Not having to pay for a room would give him more assets in his pursuit of Bess. Most would have found Will's offer of a place to lay his head strange, but Erich knew it wasn't out of the norm. Harry's soul was littered with memories of the man taking in and nurturing abandoned kittens and helping the less fortunate. Will considered Erich just another stray. "That's very kind of you. Thank you."

The gruff man's eyes narrowed, but he nodded. "Thank me by doing the job I hired you to do."

Erich returned the pot to the warmer. The clank of glass hitting the metal reminded him some things are fragile and need a gentle hand, like forging a relationship with Bess. Pushing too hard and too fast would only cause any chance of success to shatter. He was a stranger in her eyes and needed to remember that.

As he untied his apron, he heard Will say to Bess, "I asked them about your furnace. The guy they recommended is out of town for a week."

"Oh dear," she replied. "I really didn't want to take Gail up on her offer. She and Martin have done too much for me already, but I'm running out of options."

*That god-forsaken furnace. And Gail Cooper?* If there were two things Harry could count on it was that old thing breaking down, and that wolf in sheep's clothing taking advantage of the situation, but he knew an opening when he saw it. "I know my way around a furnace, Mrs. Houdini. If you'd like, I can take a look at it."

She sized him up with curiosity. The scrutiny might have offended some, but it filled him with pride. She remembered Harry's lessons about the cheats and liars and wasn't going to walk down any blind path. "That's just what I need, for you to blow up my house."

Even with her refusal, he couldn't help but laugh. She may be dead serious, but then she didn't know it was really Harry she refused and chastised. "The house I used to own had a dinosaur of a fuel oil furnace, Mrs. Houdini. I spent more hours than I care to mention repairing it. And look. Not one burn or scar."

He offered his hands as evidence. Bess continued to stare at him without speaking, weighing his offer and considering her choices. After a long pause, she said, "Thank you, Mr. Welch, I just don't think so."

"They're waiting for you across the street," Will reminded him once again.

Erich thought better of defying his new boss for a third time, so with a short nod, he stepped away. Once outside, failure crept around him like a heavy blanket. Harry had experienced hardships, but winning over Bess had been simple back then. Sure, she had been tenacious, but never so crass. Their love had a way of pitting them as a team against the world. No wonder she raged skepticism against strangers. Without him, she must feel so alone.

Still, her fire warmed him, even if she meant it to burn.

Erich worked the problem over in his mind. Changing tactics, a skill he'd fine-tuned throughout his life, now came easily. He'd have to first focus on Will. Keeping his job was paramount in order to have any connection to Bess, no matter how slight.

At the hardware store, he pulled open the door as he turned back toward the diner, wondering if Bess would even be there when he got back. The small boy with the red ball caught Erich's eye.

The toddler bounced his prized possession against the brick building, catching the toy as it rolled back, repeating the game over again. The door handle slipped from Erich's hand. The tot's exuberance demanded his full attention, something he hadn't allowed himself to give while in Bess's presence. Erich recalled countless memories of nieces and nephews and brothers and sisters. Only the innocent could enjoy something so simple.

Again the ball ricocheted off the walk and against the building, but this time it skipped by the child and into the street. As the boy followed, Erich scanned the area for his mother to warn. Not finding her, he retraced his steps.

The child, oblivious to everything around him, chased his toy. Erich's stomach knotted as the worse-case-scenario played in his mind. He called out, "Stop! Don't move!"

Ignoring his scream, the toddler continued his quest. A horn sounded. A quick look up confirmed a car was barreling straight for the little one, who had picked up the ball and was now heading back toward the safety of the sidewalk. Without a doubt, the horrific scene in Erich's head was going to become a tragic reality.

He darted off the curb and leapt to grab the boy. Both tumbled toward the opposite walk. Panicked screams erupted in his ears. Pain flashed through his side. Spitting dirt from his mouth, Erich gripped the boy tighter. "Thank Heavens!" he muttered just as a woman ripped the child from his arms.

"What are you doing to my baby!" the frantic mother cried.

"He darted into—"

"Are you okay, Joey?" She wept, cradling the toddler to his chest. "How dare you!" Her anger fell on Erich as if he had hurt the child or attempted to grab him for some nefarious reason.

He pushed himself to a sitting position, ready to defend himself, but Bess jumped between the two of them. She stretched her muscles taut, trying to look larger and more imposing than her five-foot-two-inch frame. "Him? How dare *you*? That child is just a toddler, and you weren't watching him! Mr. Welch just saved your son and you have the nerve to accost him?"

"I-I-I-" The reality of the situation hit the woman. Anger dissolved to guilt as she broke down into sobs.

Now Bess loomed over him, offering a hand. "You're a hero, Mr. Welch."

Behind her, onlookers gathered, including Will. Impressing Bess hadn't entered his mind, but her smile—*that* made him feel like the most special man in the world. He accepted her help and basked in her admiration. He wanted to lose himself in it, or capitalize on Bess having dropped her walls, but the sobs of the woman cradling her little boy kept his focus where it belonged. "Ma'am. It's okay. He's safe. That's what's important."

She picked her head up and looked at Erich through strings of tear-soaked brown hair. "It was my fault for turning away. I shouldn't have yelled at you."

Erich could see Bess's anger crack, if only just a bit as she flipped her attention to the young mother. "You hold him tight, Miss. Children are precious." Bess then looked back to him. "Thank Heavens for you."

Erich braced his throbbing side and tried to mask his pain. "Any man would do the same, Angel."

"Everyone else couldn't be bothered," Will said, stepping up to them. "You were the only one to notice and anticipate—"

Erich shook off the adulation and put a hand against the boy's back while wrapping an arm around his sobbing mother. "It's all right, Ma'am. All that matters is he's okay."

A stream of thank-yous poured from the woman's mouth. Not knowing what else to say, he retreated and started walking up the block.

"Where you going?" Will asked.

"The hardware store, to pick up the cot."

"Nonsense!" Will answered. "You go inside and have a cup of coffee. Catch your breath. I'll go get the cot."

With a nod, Erich started for the diner. Taking slow, deep breaths, he tried to control the fire burning in his side. Suddenly, Bess stood in front of him.

"I've been thinking about your offer," she said, her eyes planted on his. "And I've decided to accept. If you're still willing, can you come by after work and look at my furnace?"

"Sure thing, Angel." Finally, his inroad! He'd be jumping for joy if not for the pain ripping him in two. Erich hobbled through the door and into the kitchen. Bracing against the sink, he pulled the shirt tales from his pants and noticed the blood stains. Lifting the fabric away, he saw that one of the stitches had split open, causing blood to ooze from the wound.

He picked up a white towel, wet one of the ends and pressed it to his stomach, swallowing the scream that pushed at his throat. The pain didn't crush his spirit, though. Tonight he'd be in his home, with his wife. If the cost for that was a single ripped stitch, he'd pay without question.

# Chapter Five

"Damn it!" A loud clank reverberated through the dingy basement as the wrench slipped from Erich's hands. A high-sulfur odor overpowered him. Holding his breath, he reached around the large metal box, hit the reset button and scratched the wooden stick-match against the floor. When the flame jumped to the furnace's pilot, a sigh escaped his lips.

Even being home again could not temper Erich's regret. Harry hated the furnace, knew it was on its last leg, yet never took the time to install a newer model. How surreal to be in his house, doing the same things he did in his past existence, but to still be a stranger to the one person who mattered the most. Once he won Bess's heart, he hoped this new reality would feel less like a dream.

He slid his hands over his thighs and then looked down. Soot smudges now covered the dirt and the tear in the knee, a remnant from his tumble in the street. Exactly what was he supposed to wear to work in the morning?

With an idea in mind, he returned the tools to the rusty old box and carried it up the stairs. He found Bess hovering over a pot on the stove. "The furnace is fixed, Mrs. Houdini."

She met him with a warm smile. Relief loosened the muscles of her face and neck. She looked softer, more like his loving wife. "I don't know how to thank you, but I hope a home-cooked meal will at least be a start. Dinner is nearly finished. Please stay and eat."

The invitation was more than he'd hoped for and made him second guess the request he'd set his mind on. Would he seem greedy? Without another option, he'd have to take the gamble. "I'd appreciate a good meal, thank you, but I was wondering if you'd allow me to use your shower. Between the soot from the furnace, the grease from the diner and the dirt from the incident in the street—"

"Oh my. Of course. Just up the stairs, you'll find a bathroom halfway down the hall and on the left. Clean up first, and then we'll eat. Oh, and bring me back those clothes. I'll wash and mend them. It's the least a hero like you deserves."

A grin played across his lips. Praise from Bess thrilled him, but deep down it was also embarrassing. "I did what any man would, but I am grateful for the help. I'm just not sure I can accept it."

"Why?"

Harry Houdini blush? Sure enough his cheeks were warming. "I don't think you want me sitting around your house in the suit I was born in."

Her mouth dropped, and her eyes opened wider. A few seconds later, her words followed in a short, choppy cadence. "Well, then, when you go back to the diner you can change. I'll pick them up next time I come into town."

"You don't understand. The clothes on my back are all I own." The whole thing might be funny, if it weren't true. The levity of the situation drew another memory of the dire straits Harry had grown out of. By the time they'd finally found fame, he'd sworn to Bess and himself they'd never again know poverty, yet here he stood, depending on the kindness of others for his most basic necessities.

A dozen questions or more play across her face, but mere seconds later she announced her solution. "Hanging on the left side of the closet in my bedroom are some of Harry's old clothes. Pick out two or three outfits."

He gave thanks and rounded the corner, climbing the steps. In the bathroom, he peeled the shirt from his body and looked at the incision. Red, swollen and mangled, some bruising now framed the cut's puffy edges. He'd have to clean the area well and try a little harder to be mindful of it.

It was all worth Bess's change of heart, though. Cuts healed, and this one would too.

On a hunch, he opened the medicine cabinet and found Harry's razor still sitting on the bottom shelf. Next to it was a small tube of Burma Shave. Standing in front of the sink, he rubbed the cool shaving cream against his cheeks. His reflection was such a contrast from the man he used to be, and it twisted his stomach into knots. Every so often, he'd let his eyes drift close, refusing to accept the image staring back at him.

Dark hair replaced with blond, blue eyes for his brown and that only scratched the surface. His face was thinner, longer and none of the pieces that made up his appearance seemed even close to real. No wonder Bess hadn't been drawn to him or connected with him. He couldn't even find a way to accept the face as his own.

In the shower, warm water soothed his flesh and the aching muscles beneath. He rolled the bar of soap in his hands. Frothy foam bubbled from the bar, dingy from the dirt it pulled from his hands, and the unmistakable powdered scent filled his head. Some things hadn't changed a bit: same sterile tub, scrubbed clean with Clorox bleach; same soft, white Ivory soap. He wished the smile he loved still graced Bess's lips more often, and he ached to return to her loving embrace.

Once out of the shower, he wrapped a towel around his waist and padded down the hall to the bedroom. Welcomed by the flowered scent of the perfume he bought Bess on each and every one of their anniversaries, it didn't feel strange to open the closet and flip through the wardrobe. The pants and shirts still hung exactly as Harry left them before he and Bess left for their last trip: a series of performances that ended for him in Detroit, Michigan. Except for his stage clothes, they were nowhere to be seen. His trunk sat in the corner, covered with a thin layer of dust. Erich wondered if she'd packed the costumes in there.

He stood in his home, yet was a stranger. And though it was only tiny things—like the stage clothes—that seemed different, each change ate at him.

*What to wear?* He slid his fingers down the sleeve of the blue cotton dress shirt. Or maybe he should pick the simple white one?

"Eleven months is a long time to hold on to anything. Isn't it?"

Erich didn't have to look to know Jaden stood behind him at the ready to probe his psyche. "You think it'd be better if she threw my things away?"

"Not yours. Harry Houdini's," Jaden said, his voice cool and firm. The reminder put Erich off balance. "You are no longer that man."

In some ways, a distinction between the two seemed absurd. Every single one of Harry's memories breathed inside of him, as if the period of time since he'd been hospitalized and received this new body was just a long, twisted dream. In other ways, the distinction made perfect sense. Everything from Bess's unknowing stare to an old friend treating him like a suspect stranger distanced that life, as if it had belonged to someone else.

But now—in this house—Harry's voice screamed at him from deep inside to reclaim his life. He touched the shirts again, Jaden's warnings bouncing around in his mind like a ping-pong ball.

"Is there a right choice?" he asked out loud, trying to remember if Bess had ever expressed a preference.

"To see you in either is going to cut her to the bone."

"Then why did she offer them?"

"It isn't that complicated. In your previous life, wouldn't you have given the clothes off your back to a man brave enough to dash into traffic to save a small child? Every action and every choice she makes is dictated by what Harry would have done."

Jaden spoke the truth. Harry would have applauded the bravery and done just as Jaden suggested. Following that gut instinct, Erich selected the light blue shirt and slipped it on, wincing at the pain the movement caused. "Why is this body marred with the incision from Harry's surgery?"

"You like that? I thought it was a nice touch." Jaden's laugh sounded yet again, causing acid to bubble and press up from Erich's stomach. The Houdini image was his hard-earned prize, and it offended him that Jaden mocked it.

"Why do I think it's there for a reason?"

"You're a smart guy. No one can deny you that. Everything in life has reason, value, consequence and repercussion."

"Repercussion. Saving the child burst a stitch. Punishment for a good deed?" Erich asked, frustrated by Jaden's typical avoidance techniques.

"Wrong. That was a consequence. Just because something is right doesn't mean it's always easy. Repercussion will be how it affects you."

"Pain?"

Jaden sighed and shook his head. "Too narrow a focus. I'm rather disappointed. I expected you'd visualize the future more."

The endless stream of riddles made Erich's head light. He had once enjoyed games like this, but having experienced death, the frivolity seemed pointless. He started buttoning the shirt. "What comes after pain? Either healing, more pain or death? Are there repercussions to death?"

Jaden's hand touched the center of Erich's back. An instant flash of fire shot through his body, dragging him to his knees. His head arched back and pain contorted every muscle. Not the physical, like when the stitch had torn in two, but the pain of a heart ripping to shreds, of drowning in grief.

In his mind, the slideshow of images, like those that played during his months of death, flashed in front of him. Only this time, he wasn't inside his own mind's eye. He looked on from above at the scenes, but the overwhelming sense of loss and the desperate grip at hope that compelled people to visit Harry and beg for that last moment of contact with their loved ones consumed Erich and ate away at his soul.

"Any touch to another's life alters their course. You've already effected a change in Bess just by being here." Jaden's words echoed in his mind, and Erich fought against the power coursing his body and constricting his muscles. "You haven't lost free will, but I implore you to remember the reason you entered that body to begin with."

The power consuming him left as quickly as it had impaled him. His body collapsed, and Jaden disappeared. An eerie silence exaggerated the emptiness, not only of the bedroom, but within him. Yes, death had repercussions. Maybe not to the lifeless body, but to everyone that person touched.

He pushed himself to his knees, trying to piece the images together with Jaden's words and decipher his warnings. Like a robot, he slipped into a pair of black pants and started for the door just as Bess came running into it.

"What happened? It sounded like something fell."

"Something did. Me."

She eyed him curiously, and he searched for the right words to explain. But what logical excuse could he give? His feet wet from the shower? That didn't make sense; the floor was carpeted. "What can I say? I'm clumsy. No harm. No foul. Nothing's broken." He tried to smile, hoping to ease the raw bundle of nerves he'd been since he collided with her on the street.

She nodded, accepting his excuse, but her stare lingered on his face for a moment. "I always liked that shirt on Harry, but it looks better on you. The blue matches your eyes."

Bess then pivoted away and started down the steps as if the comment meant nothing, not knowing how much it divided him. Of course, he liked that she noticed his eyes, but Harry's soul panged with jealousy that she looked at the smallest of detail in another man.

Oh, the irony. She would have to fall in love with another man to save both their lives.

****

*Those eyes. That strong jaw.* Bess shook off her stare and set the bone plate in front of Erich. Her heart sank to her quivering stomach. Harry was her first, and she'd vowed he'd be her only. Yet, here *this man* sat, and a piece of her was reaching to him for no other reason than her sleeping libido had awakened.

Erich's eyelids fluttered, and he seemed to be taking in the scent of fish, potatoes and corn. Sliding the napkin from the table to his lap, he said, "I can't thank you enough. This is so much more than I expected to be eating tonight."

"A man who works hard deserves a good meal, and thanks to you that little boy–" He'd asked her to put the deed out of her mind, and she should try harder to respect that. But what might have happened if Erich hadn't been so observant and selfless?

She loved Harry, as much as any woman could love a man, but she'd never use selfless to describe him. Erich had proven himself to be self-sacrificing twice.

*Is that why I find him so appealing?*

"That doesn't make you responsible for me," Erich said. "But I'm grateful for any kindness." Erich's cheeks pushed back with a smile that lit up those eyes she was trying to ignore.

She forced her gaze to the hastily prepared meal that he savored, and she asked the question that had circled her mind since he had said he only had the clothes on his back. "Are you running from something, Mr. Welch? The law, perhaps?"

He coughed on his tea and kept his focus on his plate as if the food fascinated him. "Why do you ask such a thing, Mrs—"

"Call me Bess. Because you showed up out of nowhere with nothing, not even enough cash to pay for a room."

Another bite of fish disappeared after Erich chewed it more thoroughly than needed. "Running away from something isn't really my style, but sometimes the need for change is overwhelming." His fork scraped the plate, reminding Bess of her niece. The child often picked at her food when she spun a tale, and Bess swore she could see the wheels spinning in Erich's head. As if every word was chosen with delicate purpose. "A death separated me from the one I loved. I was in this place where standing still just wasn't an option anymore. Like if I didn't change something, everything, I'd just cease to exist."

"So you just got on a bus with nothing and no direction?"

"Something like that. What did you call me before? Impetuous?"

"Maybe foolish is a better word."

The playful smile returned to his face. "Don't you ever do anything spur of the moment?"

"Not in quite some time." Order and familiarity were two things that kept the gears moving and made going from one day to the next possible. Things that happened without warning, like the furnace breaking, threw her off balance. Those moments reminded her just how alone she was. Grief was another thing she had in common with Erich. "Sorry that you've lost someone you love. I know that pain too well."

"It was quite unexpected. And at times, more than I think my heart can take. But I try to remember the good times: the laughs, the smiles and the unexpected joys."

Each quality Erich mentioned stabbed at a different piece of Bess's aching heart. How could such happy words recall such pain? She tried to think of the joy she shared with Harry, but more often than not, ended up feeling desolate and alone. Never happy. She pushed her chair away from the table and picked up her dishes, taking them to the sink. Within seconds, she could feel him behind her and smell the fresh scent of the soap from his shower. "Did I say something wrong?"

She dropped the dishes—too far by the sound of the rattle—and started filling the sink. "No, Mr. Welch—"

"Erich."

"That was Harry's given name." *Why did I say that out loud?* Because it'd been flashing in her mind like a bright, stage light since she'd heard him tell it to Will that morning.

Harry's parents had immigrated to the states when he was young, and neither ever lost their heavy Hungarian accents. Their native tongue caused them to focus more on the vowels than the harder sounds. So, when his mother would call him home from playing, his name came out "air-ee." To neighbors and friends it sounded more like Harry than Erich, and eventually that was what the entire world came to know him as.

She didn't have to look behind her to know Erich loomed close. A heat rolled off him and called to her. Spinning toward him, a familiar urge to slide her hand up his chest swelled inside, but this wasn't Harry. Standing in the same room and not touching him was always an exercise in restraint, but for those same sensations to roar to life with a stranger felt sacrilegious at best.

"It's obvious you miss your husband very much." The distance between them tightened as Erich stepped closer. He lifted his hand, reaching toward her.

She braced herself for the embrace or kiss she desired. Instead, he reached behind her, turned off the water and stepped back. Her chest expanded. She wouldn't have this conversation with Erich. Couldn't have it with such desire clouding her thoughts. Instead she focused on the menial chore and tried to drown her lust in the dishwater. "Excuse me, it's getting late. I'd like to finish up these dishes so I can tend to your clothes."

A touch grazed her shoulder, adding fuel to the fire burning inside her. "I thought we were having a nice dinner. If I said something to offend you—"

"You didn't."

"Let me help you—"

She laughed. Even to her own ears it sounded small, like a nervous child's. "Silly. Haven't you done enough dishes for one day? You must be exhausted."

His hand fell away. Once again, an almost strangling pressure lifted from her chest. She sidled past him to the table and collected his dishes.

"Whatever I said, I'm sorry, Angel."

The mug fell from her hand, hitting the table with a crash and spilling tea, just like the wave of grief that splashed over her heart. Hearing Harry's pet name for her come from another's lips would never feel right. "Damn it all!" She tried to contain the emotions twisting her gut into knots, but the tears spilled down her cheeks anyway.

Erich was there with the dishtowel, wiping up the mess. "Bess, please, sit down. Take a moment."

"Don't call me, Angel. Just don't. And I can do the dishes. I'm not fragile." Her stiff posture reinforced the defensive wall Bess hid behind. She refused to take his pity or comfort, but her knees gave way. She lowered herself to the chair.

He squatted in front of her and cradled her hands. "I'm sorry, Bess. I didn't mean to upset you. I reminded you of Harry. Didn't I?"

Even if she wanted to, Bess couldn't deny the truth. He squeezed her hands again. A sense of comfort wrapped around her like her favorite wool sweater. "It's not your fault. Some days are easier than others. This one was hard, so many memories."

"Believe me. I understand." He refilled her cup and set it in front of her. Without saying a word, he drizzled a bit of honey into the mug. Another example of how observant he was. He'd paid attention to how she liked her tea. "Just sit her for a few minutes and compose yourself. Leave these dishes to me."

Her lungs expanded and slowly deflated as she tried to find her center. The hot tea passed her lips and soothed her. She could hear the water splashing in the sink and feel Erich's presence behind her as if they were tied by a pair of Harry's shackles. *Harry would never...This has to stop!*

The ongoing comparison between her husband and this man was unhealthy. Almost as much as the way she asked Harry's ghost advice on every decision she had to make. It was past time to bury the dead, let him have his peaceful, final rest. She needed to look at Erich—and everyone she came in contact with—on their merits, not how they ranked on the "what would Harry think" scale.

She shared a commonality with Erich, like Martin he knew firsthand what it was like to lose a lover and companion. Unlike her, both men seemed to move beyond the pain with ease. Maybe Erich could help her learn to live without Harry?

# Chapter Six

Bess paused at the entry to the hospital ward. Of the ten beds in the room–five on each of the long walls– only half of them were filled. Even though Harry had spent his final days in a private room, under a physician's constant care, the antiseptic smell always took her straight back to the past October. She set the tray of homemade brownies on the small table to the left of the door and crossed to Joseph who was changing the bandages of a burn victim that she'd come to know during his weeks of treatment.

She brushed her hand against his ankle as she moved to where he could see her. "How are you doing today, Edwin?"

Though Joseph was using a gentle touch to clean the wounds, she could see the extent of the pain on the patient's face. His hands twisted the blankets as he grimaced. "Not good, Mrs. Houdini."

Bess sat on the edge of the bed and pried Edwin's fingers from the blanket. "Grip my hand, and look in my eyes," she directed. When he did, she gave him a kind smile. "Now, tell me how that wife of yours is doing? She and I keep missing each other here."

She was well aware that caring for the young couple's three children kept Edwin's wife's visits short and not as frequent as they would like. Bess also knew that anything that would distract him from pain would be welcomed. It was one of the reasons that kept her coming back to the hospital week after week to visit with the patients. Anything she could do to help someone else kept her mind focused on everything she still had instead of what she'd lost in Harry.

"The misses is just fine." Edwin spit the words through clenched teeth. He squeezed her hand so tight that her flesh turned white. "Hopefully they send me home, or these bills are going to do us in."

"Don't you worry about anything but getting better."

Bess had been volunteering at the hospital the day three of Edwin's coworkers had carried him into the hospital. He'd been in the utility room of the factory when a malfunctioning boiler had left the man with third degree burns on his arms, neck and the right side of his face. It was just the kind of work-related accident she'd always feared Harry would succumb to, and she'd bonded with the man from minute one. Anything she could do to assist him in his recovery made up, in part, for not being able to help her husband pull through his illness.

"It won't be long now," Joseph said. "You're healing nicely."

Bess gave a sideways glance and noticed Joseph rubbing an ointment from a small glass jar instead of the salve she'd witnessed Martin using the week before. "Is that a new treatment?"

Joseph began wrapping the arm with a clean bandage. "It is, in fact, an ancient remedy. We've been using it for a few days, and I'm quite pleased with the results."

Edwin rolled his head toward the door. "Did I smell your famous brownies?"

"You certainly did." She patted his hand. "As soon as Joseph is all done with you I will bring you one."

"I think I'd likely starve if it wasn't for you bringing us such good home cooking."

As Joseph carefully laid Edwin's arm back on the bed, Bess found her feet and released the man's hand. "You exaggerate. I know full well that they are treating you well."

"The treatment, maybe, but not the food."

"I need to talk to Dr. Cooper," Joseph said. "But I suspect you'll be able to go home by the end of the week. Now, I want you to lay back, close your eyes and get some rest. Mrs. Houdini knows the patients can't be given any outside food until the nurses check your prescribed dietary requirements and clear it."

Joseph walked to the foot of the bed and motioned for Bess to follow him.

"Hopefully when I come in next week, you'll have already gone home, Edwin."

"From your lips to God's ears, Mrs. Houdini."

Bess patted his hand again, before meeting Joseph. Together they walked toward the door, and she waited until they were out of earshot before speaking. "Why do you put me in these predicaments? You know how Martin feels about you using untested treatments in the ward."

"I will not apologize. It is my calling to heal. Since I've begun using my ointment, the patient's burns have been healing at an accelerated rate. His family needs him at home, and I'm helping him get there. Are you going to tell Dr. Cooper?"

She inhaled sharply and crossed her arms in front of her chest. "No. No, Joseph. You're secret is safe with me." She turned and walked toward the small table, grabbing the back of the chair to support herself.

Joseph's hand grazed her shoulder. "Mrs. Houdini? Are you all right?"

She shook her head. "It's been a very emotional couple of days."

"You've had your mind on Mr. Houdini lately. Haven't you?"

There was no point in trying to keep it a secret. She nodded. "Yes. It's silly. It's been almost a year."

"Grief doesn't keep time, nor do the spirits. He is heavy on your mind, because your soul feels his absence."

She turned and smiled at the man. Maybe Joseph was pandering to her. It wasn't unusual for people to try and please her simply because of her celebrity, but it did ease her pain to hear someone say they believed that her soul was tied to Harry's. "You are a good man, Joseph. I wish my Harry and I had known you then. I do believe you might have been able to do what those doctors in Detroit couldn't."

"I would have been honored to help him and you. Unfortunately, time doesn't move backwards, and there is no way to solve for the past's injustices."

"Amen," she whispered. A moment later she straightened her posture and reached for a smock hanging on a hook next to the door. I'm not here to wallow in my own pain. I'm here to help others. What needs to be done?"

Bess set the last lunch tray on the cart outside the ward and wiped her hands on the tails of her smock before checking her watch.

"My dear Bess, I heard rumors you were here today."

Recognizing Martin's voice immediately, she turned and greeted him with a warm smile. "No tall tales, it's true."

"It's so gracious of you to come week after week and volunteer your services." Martin bent to give her a hug. "Gail mentioned to me over dinner last night that you were having problems with that old furnace again. Are you sure you don't want me to send over a repair man?"

"Thank you for the offer, but I took care of it yesterday. I hired that nice young man who's working for Will now. He fixed it straight away."

Martin's eyebrows furrowed. "Who's this?"

"Erich. Erich Welch. He's new in town."

Martin looped his arm in hers and led her away from the doorway. "You need to be careful, my dear. It's not safe for any woman to be bringing a stranger into her home, add your fame to the equation—"

"I'm well aware of the dangers, and I've learned the hard way that not everyone is trustworthy, but I do have faith in Erich."

"Well, well. I'm planning to meet Gail for a cup of coffee at the deli on my mid-day break. I'll have to check out this Erich Welch for myself."

"This is perfect. I have business in town, and I was hoping to discuss another matter with you and Gail together. May I intrude on your break?"

"It's no intrusion at all, and I know Gail will be pleased to see you. Can you meet us in an hour?"

"Yes. Now, I have one more question for you."

Martin arched his eyebrows in question.

"I want to take care of Edwin's bill. Who do I see about that?"

That fatherly concern that Martin tended to take with her showed itself as his lips narrowed to a think pink line. "Edwin? The burn victim?"

"Yes."

"You have no responsibility for him, Bess. And he's been here for weeks, it will be quite expensive."

"Which is why I want to take care of it. Now who do I see?"

He took her elbow and led her away from the door to the ward. Martin lowered his voice to a whisper, but his tone was still hard as steel. "Mr. Fricano in accounting—but it's not up to you to take care of everyone who's in need. I know that you got quite a nice settlement from Harry's insurance policy, but I'm concerned that you're going to shoot right through it with this careless benevolence for others."

"It's not a matter of charity. That's not why I want to do this." Bess knew that Martin made a valid point. Still, she couldn't fight the urge to do what she could to help those who needed it most, especially when they were sincere like Edwin. Like Erich. "It's what Harry would want, Martin, and you're not going to talk me out of it. I'm going to go up and talk to Mr. Fricano right now. I will see you at the deli in an hour."

# Chapter Seven

Erich wiped the sweat from his brow with the sopping wet dishtowel. The kitchen reminded him of a sweatbox. The dishwater, hot enough to redden his hands, didn't help matters. The heat dampened everything from his clothes to the outer walls of the walk-in refrigerator.

Will had propped open the back door, hoping to get some air circulating, but it only made matters worse. The sweltering breeze blowing in from the back alley smelled of the overflowing garbage cans just outside the door: unnaturally sweet, like rotten fruit.

He dipped the rag back into the bucket of bleach water and continued washing down the aluminum prep trays. The kitchen sparkled, and he tried to ignore Harry's voice asking how long had passed since the kitchen had been treated to such a scrubbing. He and Bess might have not eaten here so often if they'd known cleanliness wasn't one of Will's strong suits.

Erich washed the chemicals from his now cracked flesh and wandered out to the dining room, longing to find Bess in her favorite booth.

Now early afternoon, the late lunch stragglers were filing out of the deli, and the tables were covered with dirty dishes.

"Erich," Will said over the clatter, "Start a fresh pot of coffee and then grab a dishpan and start clearing tables."

He wiped his hands on the end of the apron and picked up the pot, still distracted by the lack of Bess's presence. As soon as his shift ended, he needed an excuse to call on her. Yes, he'd made progress, but they were only small steps. Keeping the momentum going was essential to winning his bet with Jaden, and therefore, to regaining his life.

The bell rung above the door, and his head spun to it, hoping. Her laughter as she greeted Will filled the room, and in response Erich smiled his first real smile of the day.

"Have a seat, Bess," Will called out. "I'll bring you over a pastry straight away. Erich, take Mrs. Houdini fresh coffee as soon as it's finished brewing."

"Sure thing," Erich answered. Will's request was a huge step forward. He trusted Erich to associate with Bess: another pleasant after-effect of yesterday's good deed. He never would have willed such an incident or hoped for a child to be in danger, but his ability to avert a tragedy had elevated him from scrutinized stranger to new friend.

*So, don't mess it up, blockhead.* If he did, getting the trust back would be ten times more difficult than gaining it.

"Oh no. Nothing to eat today, but I will take the coffee, Erich. Actually, make it three. Martin and Gail Cooper should be here any moment."

Hovering over the coffee pot, Erich kept his back to Bess so that she couldn't see the scowl that veiled his face. Erich wondered how those wicked con-artists wormed their way into her good graces.

Harry had a theory. Gail took advantage of grieving hearts, used them to bolster some sort of fame for herself. Sure, he'd trusted her to try and contact his deceased mother, and her true colors had shown as bright as those neon lights he'd first seen in Paris. Through that incident, Harry also gleaned Martin wasn't the friend he once believed.

How could Bess have forgotten that? *Please, don't trust them, Angel.*

Despite his internal plea, Bess greeted Gail and Martin with the type of warm hugs that should be reserved for old friends.

Erich's heart pounded faster; his temple throbbed. Once, Harry had trusted Martin without question or boundaries, as a kindred spirit, but that changed because of Gail. Harry now wanted as much distance between Bess and Martin as possible. Harry's rage boiled inside Erich as if it had all happened yesterday.

Grabbing the coffee pot from the warmer, he rounded the counter and approached. He didn't speak as he filled their cups, only listened. He needed to know what the Coopers wanted from Bess so he could develop a plan to make sure they never got it.

"This will be a small gathering like my beloved husband prescribed," Bess said softly. "Harry will make his way back to me and this world, if that is possible, delivering the same message I've tucked away in our vault at home."

Martin shifted his weight in the seat, and his eyes darted toward his wife. Silence loomed between them. Gail studied Martin's face as if she knew what he was thinking.

Erich was sure. The two of them were up to no good. His eyes darted back to Bess. Surely, she saw the tell-tale signs of mischief those two displayed.

Gail gave her attention back to Bess. "I really wish you'd told me about this coded message. All these months, I've been training you without one word about this? Bess, this throws a big wrench into that plan. You can't be the seated medium."

"I realize that." Bess's posture loosened. Her shoulders dropped. "I apologize. I was being selfish. I wanted to learn, so that Harry might contact me before the séance."

Gail wrung her hands on the table as she scowled. "I do understand that, and if I'm to be honest I had selfish reasons for wanting to help you. I hoped teaching you might undo some of the damage Harry caused to my reputation."

Now filling Gail's cup, Erich had to fight his—no, Harry's—reaction to the accusations. As if he were somehow responsible for the lies she told. Whatever the public now thought of Gail, she deserved. Defending the man whose soul breathed inside him might satisfy the spirit, but could very well damage the progress he'd made with Bess. So, he bit his lip and moved on to Martin's cup.

"I thought as much," Bess answered. "And that's why I've decided to ask you to take the honored seat. Would you serve as medium, Gail?"

"Bess!" Martin said. "You know that as much as Harry adored the spotlight and the drama, he will not show. He may have loved to escape the inescapable, but will not give credence to the very spiritualists he cursed, especially Gail. Anyone who believes differently is a fool."

"This world holds so little for me now that Harry is gone, but I believe in our love and his word. He promised to come back. If it can be done, he'll get the message through. If he fails, I'll forgive him." Her words may have shown conviction, but her trembling hands and the slight tilt of her jaw told Erich just how much uncertainty existed beneath the surface.

"I want to do it," Gail answered as she straightened her spine. "Bess is right. Harry's commitment to her will outweigh any distaste he had for me."

Erich stepped away from the table, but continued to eavesdrop as he leaned against the counter. Martin had unraveled the heart of his plan—no one would ever falsely claim to have contacted him in death, the way many spiritualists—including Gail—claimed to converse with his dead mother. No one would steal his spotlight with lies. He'd made sure of that.

But Gail, in all of her arrogance, believed she could come away from this the victor. That Harry would really allow her to ride his coat-tails to fame?

*But if Bess holds her séance on the anniversary of your death, she'll draw your spirit from its new home and you'll be condemned to an afterlife of vast darkness.*

Erich's heart ached as if Jaden were squeezing it tight between his massive hands. Those words rang over and over in Erich's mind. How could he use the séance to prove Gail's dishonesty? He was mandated to flat-out stop it.

"Remember why you are here," Jaden had said.

To save Bess was the only acceptable answer. Erich had become so caught up in reclaiming Harry's life, that he'd forgotten his first and foremost goal: getting Bess to abandon the séance.

"You said a small gathering, Bess. You want no press or theatrics?" Martin asked, drawing Erich's focus back to the conversation.

A Cheshire-cat smile curved her lips. "I said we'd honor Harry; of course there'll be theatrics and publicity. He wouldn't have it any other way." She pulled a paper from her purse and unfolded it. Laying it on the table in front of Martin, she smoothed it with her hands. "I just came from the newspaper, where I ran this advertisement."

Martin's eyes scanned the page. The color faded from his face. "Have you really thought this out, Bess? Offering a $10,000 reward to the person who can deliver the message is inviting a long line of crazy and greedy people to your doorstep." He flipped his attention to his wife. "This could easily become a circus, Gail. I don't think it's a good idea to associate with it."

Had Hell frozen over? For the first time in a long time, Erich agreed with Martin. He caught Will's eyes on him and realized his eavesdropping was clear. He grabbed a dishrag and began washing down the counter without losing focus on the conversation.

"Martin, I believe in Harry." Bess's tone was whispery but filled with metal. "If this can be done, he will come through. If not with Gail, then someone else."

"So, not only do you accept every word he said as fact, but you believe all that malarkey the papers printed about him too?"

"That will be quite enough!" Anger dotted Bess's expression. "I won't allow anyone to speak ill of Harry."

The distaste in his one-time-friend's voice hung heavy in the air and stung as if it were a slap. Martin was entitled to his anger. Yes, Harry publicly called Gail a fraud, but this was different. He'd never lied to Bess and thought she understood the premise of the coded message. It was only meant as a defensive measure against those like Gail who'd manipulated Harry's grief, plain and simple.

Still, Bess's reaction made him proud. He appreciated her loyalty and respect. She may have accepted some level of friendship from Martin and Gail, but she wouldn't let them tarnish what existed between her and Harry.

Martin reached across the table and gripped Bess's hand. "I'm sorry, my dear. I just wish you'd see the simple facts. Harry preached that every spiritualist— including Gail—was a fraud. The man I knew would never readily admit he was wrong."

"All that tells me is that you didn't know him the way I did. He made a promise and will do all he can to keep it, and I think he'd enjoy the irony of Gail being the medium."

*Don't do this, Bess.* Erich had ignored Jaden's warning and entered into the deal to be close to her, even for just one more day. He'd hoped to feel her body pressed to his and taste her glossed lips once more. Hearing the certainty of Bess's conviction, Erich realized Jaden was right. He had to put an end to this whole mess.

If he let Bess reach for Harry the way she, Gail and Martin now planned, every bit of the soul that gave Erich life would slip away. In his second death, the promise Bess thought Harry made would never be fulfilled. Jaden hadn't been wrong yet. Certainly, his prediction for her future was also correct.

The séance could not happen.

His life depended on it, but so did hers. Not her ability to live and breathe, but the way she lived. She deserved a life of her own that was tied to keeping Harry's memory alive.

Will's voice pulled him back to the diner, even though he spoke to Bess and the Coopers. "The last thing I want is to push the three of you out the door, but it's time for me to lock up and call it a day."

Erich swallowed a smirk. Many a day Harry and Will had sat at the counter, talking well into the evening hours, even though the shop closed at three o'clock on the dot. Often their conversations centered on Martin's flamboyant arrogance. Will must've been sick of Gail and Martin's conversation with Bess too.

Several silver coins fell from Martin's hand to the tabletop. "I trust this will cover my bill and Mrs. Houdini's." He then crossed the short distance between him and Erich, extending a hand. "I don't believe we've been introduced. You must be the Erich that Bess has been talking about. I'm Doctor Cooper."

A matter of habit and good manners, Erich took Martin's hand and shook it firmly. "Erich Welch. I hope they're kind things that she's said about me."

Martin laughed. "Of course, it was good. Come, Bess. We'll give you a ride home."

The laugh struck Erich in a condescending way, no matter how Martin had meant it, and as he reached for Bess's arm, a rage bubbled up from Erich's gut. He wanted to push Martin aside and lay claim to Bess, or at least protect her from the faithless scoundrel.

*His wife? Harry's wife?* Was there a distinction? The questions made his head spin. The biggest part of what drove Erich's desire for Bess was Harry's memories of their past, but somehow, it was more than that too.

Only because it was better for the long-term goal, he kept his hands at his side and his thoughts to himself.

Bess waved off Martin's suggestion and his hand. "I found my way here. I can find my way home. I've been doing it with and without Harry for quite some time."

The bells above the door rang like a joyous celebration, marking Gail and Martin's exit, but also like church bells at a funeral. Watching Bess leave with the Coopers—the last people on the planet he wanted her to spend time with—was a death knell all on its own.

"Mr. Welch!" Will's booming voice shook his attention from the door. "Where's your mind, son? I called your name three times."

"I'm sorry. I was thinking about Mrs. Houdini and those people she was with." Erich's words sounded acidic to his own ears, even though he tried to hide how he really thought. As far as Will was concerned, Erich had no basis to dislike Martin.

"You're right to be concerned."

"So, you don't think too much of that doctor, either?"

Will shook his head slowly and then walked behind the counter. Opening the till, he began counting down the register and putting the day's profits into a dingy, canvas bag. "I used to think he was harmless enough. Arrogant and a little foolish, maybe, but not malicious."

"But now?"

He shook his head. "All this spirituality taradiddle. Bess is still in mourning and Gail is taking advantage of that. From my perspective, she doesn't care how much it hurts Bess, as long as the name Gail Cooper ends up carrying all the weight and respect she believes it deserves. Harry wouldn't like what those two are doing, not one single bit."

Erich nodded and leaned against the door frame. As he watched, Bess stood on the corner, conversing with the couple. "That poor woman is lost, and they are only leading her further astray."

"I used to think Harry exaggerated the intentions of those two, never believed they were acting spitefully, but now, watching them with Bess, I have to wonder." Will paused, scraped his hand across his jaw. "Do me a favor. Make sure she's always treated like a princess in here. It's the least I can do for my old friend."

# Chapter Eight

Bess waved as Martin and Gail pulled away in the shiny, new Studebaker. In a muted red, it was one of the first cars she'd seen that wasn't classic black. Some might say the color was ostentatious, but then flashy described Gail to a tee, and it was no secret Martin enjoyed showering gifts on his second wife.

Ten years had passed since Martin's first wife, Louise, had died. Bess had never known the other woman, but Martin and Joseph spoke of her often. Both of them described her as very different from Gail. Sort of like how Erich was different from Harry, yet he stirred the same emotions in her.

But when you looked beyond the physical, Erich wasn't all that different from her husband.

As the car rolled out of sight, Bess wrestled with the argument playing out between her heart and mind. Her house was in a state of disrepair and as much as she wanted to be a strong, independent woman, home maintenance fell outside her comfort zone. Erich had quickly fixed the furnace and did the dishes, even after a long, hard day at the deli. He didn't shy from work and was polite enough.

But to repeatedly ask the same man—an unattached man at that—into her home seemed disloyal to Harry, and she couldn't help but think she was only inviting gossip. People in this town talked. Gail was evidence enough of that.

*I'm not inviting Erich in as a lover.* Yes, she was lonely; the empty space beside her in bed kept her awake at night, but now wasn't the time to fill the void with another body. She wasn't like Martin. For her, it might never be the right time.

Bess sighed and brushed a stray strand of hair from her eyes. The blood stains she'd found on the tails of Erich's shirt were none of her business. She shouldn't be prying, but he was injured in some shape or way. The moment she'd laid eyes on the red blotches, the same motherly instinct that pushed her to volunteer at the hospital week in and week out had risen up.

The part of her that took over when she'd looked into his eyes could hardly be described as maternal.

Harry had always told her to follow her heart, but would he feel the same way if he knew the way it fluttered every time she looked at Erich?

A firm decision in mind, she pivoted and walked the few steps back to the deli. She pulled on the door handle, but found it locked. She peered through the window and expected to see Will wiping down the display cases or sweeping the floors, instead it was Erich who maneuvered the broom over the worn tile.

Hoping she'd made the right decision and wasn't following lust down a dangerous back alley, she knocked on the glass. He looked over his shoulder and moved toward her, leaving the broom to rest against one of the tables. A quick twist of the deadbolt allowed her access.

"Did you forget something, Bess?" His tone was warm and inviting. Was he happy to see her again?

"No. I—" The words slipped away. Standing next to this man turned her mind to mush, which was ridiculous. Someone her age should have a better handle on her emotions. Then she remembered the stained shirt. She'd risk being labeled meddlesome to know. "I wanted to apologize. I promised you that I'd launder your clothes and return them to you today."

"Don't be sorry. I'm grateful for your help and the clothes you gave me."

"I'll get them mended once I get home. I would have done so last night, but I needed to soak your shirt, what with the blood stains."

His face fell. He hadn't meant for her to learn of whatever injury he was trying to hide, that much was obvious.

"I probably should have mentioned that when I rolled in the street to push the child away..." He rocked his weight between his heels, searching for the right words.

"You cut yourself?"

"No." Erich paused, and his eyes flickered back and forth. Harry would say he was using the moment to prepare a lie, but she'd seen his selflessness in saving a child and didn't believe that. "I tore one of my stitches."

She clutched her purse tighter "Stitches? But why?"

"I had surgery not too long ago."

She stepped closer and reached out, but just as suddenly, she stopped. "Goodness. What in the world are you doing carrying dishpans and jumping in front of cars?"

He chuckled and dropped his gaze to his shoe. "As you pointed out, I impetuously came to a new town without more than two dimes to rub together. As far as yesterday goes, any man..."

"You shouldn't be embarrassed for saving that child."

His hands found his pockets as his shoulders folded in. "Stop! Bess. Don't make me out to be a hero just for doing the right thing."

*Modesty. Had Harry been modest a single day of his life?* As much as the dichotomy intrigued Bess, she bit her tongue. Why was the vow to stop comparing those two proving difficult to keep? "If that's your wish, I won't mention it again. That's not the reason I came back anyway."

His eyes widened, and he stepped forward. "No? Then why?"

"I had a favor, but now that I know you're recovering from surgery, it seems too much."

Twisting and fidgeting like a restless child, Erich didn't seem to be in pain. "I promise you I'm fine. Almost fully recovered. Now tell me, what is the favor you need?"

She waved her hands in front of her face. "It just wouldn't be right to ask, while you're still healing. My friend Martin is a doctor. You should have him look at your incision."

Erich's fingers curled into tight fists. "There isn't any reason for that. Whatever it is that you need me to do, I promise I'm man enough to take care of it."

A rush of warmth touched her cheeks, and she looked away. He probably spoke of his well-being, but his declaration of virility had sent Bess's thoughts in an inappropriate direction. He'd ruffled her feathers in a way that Harry had only been able to do. "Oh dear, Mr. Welch. I-I-I it's not a question of your manhood."

He chuckled as he stepped closer. He must have noticed her fluster, and now he was trying to set her at ease by getting back to the question of the hour. "Please, Bess, what do you need?"

"You did a good job with that old furnace last night, and I'm sure you noticed it wasn't the only thing broken in the house. I need someone who can help with maintenance, and you need a place to stay. I thought we might be able to trade services." As soon as the last words spilled from her mouth, she second guessed them, but it was too late to turn back now.

A huge grin showed his straight, white teeth. "You want me to move in with you?"

"I have a long list of home repairs I need done in exchange."

"It sounds like a good deal for both of us," he answered. "If you want to wait while I finish sweeping the dining room, I can walk you home."

She nodded and settled herself in a booth. "This is nothing more than a friendly exchange of services, mind you. Two friends, helping each other out."

"Of course." Erich felt like dancing as he picked the broom back up and returned to the task Bess had interrupted.

*I'm going home with Bess.*

She could disguise it all by calling it "mutual favors," but he knew the bond between their souls was being rebuilt. He'd convince her to forget the séances and the Coopers in no time flat.

He finished his chores, put away the cleaning supplies and then took a napkin from the metal holder on the counter, scribbling on it with a pencil he found in the pocket of his apron. "Will's gone for the day, but I can leave him a note in case he beats me here in the morning...to let him know that I found a place to stay."

He laid his hastily written explanation next to the cash register and left his apron on the hook on the kitchen door before crossing the dining room and holding the door for Bess. On the street, he twisted the key in the lock, not an easy task with the excited tremor in his hand.

The moment he'd been longing for—escorting his wife home—had arrived. He offered his arm and waited for her to take his elbow.

Her eyes narrowed as she twisted out of reach, continuing up the street without him.

"Bess! What's wrong?" He caught up to her and tried to take her elbow.

She deflected his advance and pivoted to him. "I thought I was clear that this is a business arrangement. I'm a widow and have no desire for a companion." She dropped her voice to a harsh whisper. "What would people say?"

"I don't really care! I only offered you guidance and stability." He stepped back, but couldn't help thinking of that old adage about protesting too much. Did this harsh reaction mean she was attracted to him? If so, she tempered it with equal amounts of guilt.

She crossed her arms in front of her chest. "You are in my employ, maybe a friend, but certainly nothing more than that."

"Of course," Erich said the words he guessed she wanted to hear, even though he didn't feel them. He doubted she meant hers either. Everyone knew tough-as-nails Bess, but she had a vulnerable side that she'd only displayed to him. If she knew Harry's soul lived in his body, she'd let him close.

He'd give anything to have her hand glide into his as they walked together and hear her admit she hungered for his touch as much as he did hers, but he also knew she'd never be unfaithful to Harry or his memory.

When making deals with Jaden, he'd never really considered what it'd take to make her trust him. He'd been so certain that instant connection they had always shared would reignite itself. Her offer of a room gave him hope that she felt something for him. Her reaction to his arm told a different story. But which one was a true reflection of her feelings?

"It's a preposterous idea any way," Bess snapped. "A man your age should be focused on finding a wife and having children. Family. That's what's most important in this life." She clamped her mouth tight and pursed her lips. Walls visibly crumbled and the too familiar grief took their place.

Erich wondered if she held Harry accountable that they'd never started a family. He knew the answer to the question he was about to ask. He was well aware of the pain not having children caused, but to Bess, Erich shouldn't have a clue. "Did you want children?"

"My husband would have been a wonderful father. Yesterday...that child...Harry would never let a toddler get out of his sight like that woman did."

Why hadn't he connected these dots yesterday? When he allowed himself to think about it, he now knew the answer to the question he asked, "Is that why it affected you so much?"

Bess stopped at the corner and waited for a car to clear the intersection before starting across the street. Only when they were on the other side did she continue. "Being deprived of something makes you see the world's inequities a little clearer." Her matter-of-fact tone did little to hide the jealousy that kept her words sharp as knives.

"Children are fast. It wasn't the mother's fault." No matter how true the words, Erich knew they wouldn't change her feelings. Harry believed their lives to be full, but knew how much Bess longed for what they'd never had.

"If she had to go just one day without, I bet she'd keep a tighter hand on that precious baby."

"You think Harry understood that?"

She didn't answer, but continued walking up the street. To resist the temptation to touch her again, he pushed his hands in his pockets and matched her stride. She continued a moment later by saying, "Family was important to Harry. His parents and siblings, mine too, he held them all dear. We used to believe we'd be blessed when the good Lord saw fit. Sometimes I wonder if he withheld his gift because our focus was so firmly placed in our work."

*We?* Even though she made it sound like they both held some responsibility, he knew better. Harry constantly drove the two of them further, always wanted more fame. Did Bess know he only wanted it to provide for her and that someday family? Erich suspected she shrouded Harry's desires with a "we" for the benefit of the stranger she thought he was. For so many years, he'd clung to the notion they'd one day be blessed. In her mind, his drive was the sin and never experiencing the joy of children its punishment.

Erich opened his mouth to defend Harry, but thought better of it. Any attempt to explain the feelings brewing inside him would seem cheap and insincere. He wanted to comfort her, but she already refused his touch once. Still, he couldn't let her grief lay there open between them and not say anything. "I know I've just met you, but I think you'd have been a wonderful mother."

A soft smile played across her face. Why did those words from a stranger mean so much? Having touched something, he continued. "There are mysteries and pains to the world that cannot be explained. I'm so sorry you had to endure even one."

She nodded in his direction and looked away. Even so, he caught a peek of her eyes, shiny with tears. He wanted to kiss them away, but if she'd gotten so angry at the offer of his elbow, she'd throttle him for even trying.

He'd pushed enough, maybe said too much. Getting Bess to trust him was going to mean walking a fine line, just like the tightrope he'd learned to master at a young age. It would just take time and patience, but he'd overcome this too, even though his time was limited.

They paused at the end of the drive, and she motioned to the house. "See what I mean?"

He'd noticed the previous night major maintenance had been ignored, but things look different at dusk. Zeroing in with a focused eye in full daylight, he was seeing the true extent for the first time. The lawn was overgrown. One of the shutters hung by a single bolt. Some shingles were missing from the roof. The wood siding could stand to be painted and, the bushes were overgrown. "You didn't exaggerate."

"Mr. Houdini knew who to hire to care for such things. I've had people offer their services, but it's difficult to decipher who means well and who only wishes for a piece of his legacy. And then there are those who will either charge too much or do shoddy work."

"So, why do you trust me? You barely know me."

"Observation. You work hard, and you have integrity. In a crisis, you do the right thing." She paused and closed her eyes, stepping from him as if she needed to hide from her words.

*His integrity?* It was a start, and one he'd cling to. He only had thirty days—no, twenty-nine—to get close enough to convince her to call off the séance. Not as easy of a task as he'd first thought. She'd embraced the notion Harry could escape any confine, even death, and part of her believed he'd deliver the message to her this Halloween.

Her already broken heart would shatter if he didn't. Convincing her to abandon this search for Harry's ghost would mean letting the legend rest in peace. Failing to change her mind would keep the Houdini name untarnished—with her in control of the séances, no one could untruthfully claim to speak to his ghost—but it would keep her pleading for an answer that would never come. Could he sacrifice what Harry had spent his whole life working for, a fame that never faded, or was the quest Jaden gave him doomed to fail? What once seemed like a crisp, clean decision was now blurred by love and conviction.

Erich knew the first step to gaining Bess's trust was to complete her list of chores. She'd assigned them as a test of his true spirit, and he had no intention of failing. Once he won her favor, he could turn his sights to the séance. His mind set, he made his way up the cobblestone walk to the shed.

"Where are you going?"

"To get a ladder. I thought I'd begin with the broken shutter before it's torn completely from the hinges. Then, if there's still daylight, I'll start trimming the lawn."

"Where do you *think* the ladder is?"

He cursed internally. He'd have to remember not to make himself too much at home, even if it was *his* house. "I don't think you keep it in the kitchen. The shed seemed probable."

Bess took her measure of him. She'd asked him to come here, but he could hear hesitation in her voice and see uncertainty in her eyes. "Of course. But can you handle the ladder and the shutter?"

"I accepted your offer, didn't I?"

She circled her fingers over her own stomach. "But your incision. I didn't know you'd had surgery."

"I'm fine, Bess. The tumble in the street broke a stitch, but I'm all right." Had his voice sounded convincing? He didn't feel the words, but what could he say? Any admittance of pain might cause her to change her mind, and he needed to stay. He'd made progress. There was no way he'd let some minor aches unravel it.

"Are you sure?"

"I am."

She nodded once, accepting his assurance, though he could still see reservation in her eyes. "I'll start dinner. Come eat when you've finished the shutter."

Now to live up to his word and complete the repair without further injuring himself. On their walk home, he'd learned that Bess had lingering doubts and resentment from her life with Harry, or maybe she was angry he'd left her to live alone. Regardless, Erich wouldn't let her down the same way.

The shutter proved to be an easier fix than he first thought. He replaced a few screws and put the ladder away within twenty minutes. Starting for the front door, he changed his mind and reversed his path. A hired hand would enter through the kitchen. As much as it hurt, that was all he was to her at this moment. Angering her with inappropriate behavior wouldn't help their relationship progress, so walking on eggshells and remembering his manners were the orders of the day.

With each step he took, he added another item to the long, mental checklist of what needed to be done, surprised that so much could go by the wayside in a few months.

Approaching the southwest corner of the house, the smell of smoke hit his senses. His eyes darted around the yard, and he wondered if one of the neighbors had lit their fireplace. As he stepped on the wooden deck, the scent grew stronger, and he realized it was coming from inside.

Seeing black smoke billow from the cast iron pot on the stove, Erich called out for Bess. As he pulled the screen door toward him, it hit the hook lock and snapped back closed. He called her name again.

It wasn't like Bess to abandon the kitchen while she was cooking. Preparing food was an act of love. She held the responsibility of nourishing her and Harry dear and always worried something like this would happen if she neglected her duties.

He tapped his foot as he waited for the clack of her shoes against the hardwood and the sound of her skirt bustling around her legs. The smoke billowed up, black as coal, and there was no time for caution or concern for manners. His hand against the frame, a quick, hard jerk ripped the hook-and-eye lock away, and the door broke free.

Inside, he grabbed a towel off the counter, pulled the pot from the stove and turned off the gas. The water had evaporated, and the beginnings of a soup stock blackened the bottom of the pan. With a twist of the faucet, the water popped and sizzled against the cast iron. He lifted his arm to shield his face.

The smell of charred chicken and vegetables filled the air, but the crisis was averted. His mind flashed to the reason. Was something wrong with Bess? He pushed open the swinging door between the kitchen and the living room to find her in the rocking chair. Her head rolled back on her shoulder, she was motionless.

His heart dropped to his stomach like a cinder block. On the table next to her, the radio blared but not on any station. Static rattled the room. How could she sleep with all of the racket? Erich fell to his knees in front of her and picked up Bess's hand, calling her name. "Wake up, Bess."

She startled awake, pulling her hand from his and rubbing her eyes. "What happened?"

"You fell asleep with the stove on!"

"Oh dear, supper!" She tried to jump up, but he gripped her arm and guided her back down.

"It's burnt, but it's you I'm worried about. You're very pale. Are you sure you're okay?"

She shook her head and flipped her attention to the radio. With a spin of the knob, the static silenced. "There's a technique in that book that I was trying to mimic. Instead of going into a trance, I must have fallen asleep."

*A trance?* Communicating with the departed! Was she really so fixated she might have burnt the house down around her if he wasn't there? "You must be deaf to be able to sleep through that clamor."

She pointed to the book on the table. "It's not just noise. Spirits have been known to use empty radio frequencies for communication." She shook her head as if trying to brush away the cobwebs. "Gail said the brandy would help clear my mind, but I'm afraid it just makes me sleepy."

He picked up the flask off the coffee table and sniffed the opening. "Brandy? How did you get this with prohibition?"

"My friend, Martin. He makes it himself." She motioned for him to move away. "Let me up. I'll see if I can salvage dinner."

"It's ruined," he said to her retreating frame, working to keep the disappointment clear from his voice, even though it soured his stomach. Bess had ignored Harry's lectures on the importance of a clear mind and body and found hope in foolish stunts. It didn't matter how farfetched success seemed. She also treaded a dangerous slope by listening to the Coopers, but a desperation that he'd never known in her while he was Harry pulsed inside her.

"I'll come up with something," she mumbled.

A master of making full meals out of a scrap of this and a piece of that, he didn't doubt she would, but his stomach was the last thing on his mind. Bess's fall—head over heels—into the world of spiritualism, a world Harry had tried to convince her was nothing but a huge con-game that damaged not only her spirit, but her body and mind, troubled him more.

Erich picked up the flask and sniffed it again. The scent almost knocked him off his feet. Much stronger than the occasional wine she used to sip now and then, it was no wonder it had knocked her out cold. Martin was to blame for this near tragedy, and there was no way Erich was going to let him get away with it.

He lowered himself to the rocker she'd just vacated and surveyed the room. An open pack of cigarettes sat next to an ashtray full of butts and ash. Had it not been the stove, she could have fallen asleep with a cigarette burning. Harry always hated that disgusting habit, and for years she'd abstained, but he was gone and grief consumed her. He could hardly blame her for a vice or two.

But alcohol-induced trances and listening to radio static? What spiritualist games was she willing to play in hopes of connecting with Harry once more? If she would only look with her heart instead of her eyes she'd see he stood right in front of her.

This séance needed to be stopped, and it wasn't about winning a bet with Jaden or holding Bess in his arms anymore. It wasn't about preserving his image and his legacy. He needed to save Bess.

# Chapter Nine

*What if Erich hadn't been here?*

Would the house have burnt to the ground around her while she slept? With each rhythmic clink of the butcher knife hitting the wood cutting board, Bess's eyes blinked. Though she tried to immerse herself in slicing the tomato and onion, she couldn't shake the images of just how bad it could have been. What if she hadn't invited him into her home?

Erich Welch and his appearance on the street yesterday had been like an anchor, something steadfast she could cling to as life tossed her around like a ship on stormy seas, but Bess questioned her compulsion to trust him. They'd only just met and there was the age difference, but there was also a familiar ease with Erich she didn't understand.

In other ways, he was like a hurricane force wind, spinning her emotions until she was dizzy. He changed everything by awakening the part of her heart that had died with her husband and forcing her to question the devotion she'd vowed to one man. It was wrong. She should be distancing herself from him instead of making excuses to be close. Even if it was the *real* reason she'd asked him to stay. Lucky for her, she'd acted on that impulse.

Bess could feel him standing in the doorway, his eyes focused on her as she pushed the sliced vegetables to the edge of the cutting board.

The silence becoming more than she could bear, she kept her attention focused on the meal, but said, "At this late hour the best I can come up with is some sandwiches and coleslaw. It's not fresh, I made it yesterday."

"That's fine," Erich answered. "I don't expect you to work your fingers to the bone for me."

She gripped at the counter as a wave of dizziness washed over her. Her body weaved to and fro on unsteady knees. A couple sips of brandy shouldn't make her feel so wobbly, but add in her stretched thin emotions, and it was as if she'd drank the whole flask. "I promised you a meal—"

"And you're providing one." He paused and again the silence loomed like a chasm between them. Something she wasn't sure either of them could cross. "I broke the hook-lock. I'll stop by the hardware store after work and pick up everything I need to fix it."

"I'll leave money on the table."

"Nonsense. I broke it. I'll take responsibility."

"You're being ridiculous. What you did saved me and my house." She stopped making the sandwiches and pivoted, looking at him for the first time. She'd been right to avoid him. Every aspect of him was strong and made her oh so weak. "Thank you."

"Anyone in my shoes would have done the same."

She could tell he meant the words he said, but knew from experience that true heroism was in short supply in this world. Few men put the welfare of others before their own. "Seems you've been saying that a lot lately, Mr. Welch."

"I thought we had this all sorted out and you were going to stop with this mister nonsense."

"We have," she said, returning to the meal preparations. Calling him by her husband's given name was just too painful, even if no one had called him anything but Harry for years. It was more than just the name, though. When Bess looked in Erich's eyes, she had to struggle against that unexplainable pull, drawing her away from the life and love she knew before.

Bess swayed, her vision blurring to white. She gripped the counter again. A few moments alone, without his masculine scent and imposing presence clouding her senses would make a world of difference;

give her time to clear her head. "Did you want to take a shower before you eat?"

"I'm fine, Bess. Are you?"

She couldn't stop the laugh, not because what he said was funny but ironic. Up until eleven months ago, she'd been a caregiver to most, but in the time since Harry's death every bit of her reality became twisted and mangled. Just when she thought she was moving forward, her reality shifted again. Fate, or whatever ruled the universe, dropped things like her uncanny attraction to Erich and the way she'd passed out cold in the living room on her. "It's just what my life's become."

"Chasing Harry's ghost?"

She almost missed the whispered, tender words, but they pricked at her flesh. "That seems a little absurd now. Doesn't it?"

"I don't think so." He took two steps closer to her, but then stopped.

Did he feel it too, this big void between them, pushing them apart? Absurd! She imagined the cavity same as the magnetic pull. How could both forces be working between them, let alone either one? How could she feel such desire, yet need the distance? "Honoring someone you've loved for most of your life—"

"Is fine, but that's not what you're doing." Erich pushed his fingers through his hair and exhaled a haggard breath. "You're so stuck in what was that you can't even imagine a tomorrow."

The force of his accusation pushed her back a step. What was he trying to say? That she wasted her time being true to Harry? "Are you insinuating I should just forget my husband?"

"No! I'm sure that's impossible, but it is time to move forward."

Her brows rutted together and her jaw set. "I didn't invite you into my home to preach to me—"

Erich bit his lip, tried to find tactful words to say and then spoke them with a weight and purpose. "I'm not the kind of man who's going to hold my tongue if I think I can help."

"When it comes to honoring my husband's memory, I'll ask you kindly to do just that. I know better than anyone what Harry would want me to do."

Stumbling toward the chair, Bess reached out to grab the back. Erich leapt forward and wrapped one arm around her shoulders while taking her elbow with the other. "Are you okay?"

"Just so woozy," she mumbled, her words running together and her voice soft.

"I think you need to lie down. No doubt your head is swimming from the brandy." Erich's strong arms wrapped tight around her, and her head found his shoulder. His comforting voice caressed her ear. So right, yet...She braced her hands against him and firmly pushed back, leaving a dark, empty hole where her heart had just fluttered. "I only had a couple of sips."

"It's hard to tell with anything homemade. It could be stronger than what you're used to, or tainted—"

She shielded her face with her hand, abruptly stopping him. "I trust Martin. He wouldn't give me anything that wasn't safe." As another wave of nausea hit her, she reconsidered. "But you could be right. Possibly, it is stronger than I'm used to."

"Go rest in the living room while I finish making these sandwiches."

She smacked her hand against the table in defiance. "Erich! I promised you I'd provide the meals."

"And you are. Everything is ready. I just have to put it together. Please. Take a moment to collect yourself."

The weight of the world settled in, and she couldn't argue, didn't even want to. A few moments on the couch might be just what she needed to unburden her heart. Once again, she conceded and allowed Erich to save the day, wondering if a pattern was developing.

****

The hours at work passed at a glacial pace. Bess didn't visit, and without the distraction Erich could only count the minutes until quitting time. Now that he had a place in her house, he didn't need the job. It had served its purpose and brought them closer together. Resigning seemed like an obvious decision, but he knew it would set him back. He'd look lazy, a trait both Bess and Harry had frowned upon.

Erich explained to Will that he needed to pick up a few things at the hardware store for Bess, and was granted an advance on his first week's pay. It wasn't a lie. Not really. He did have to fix the lock. Will didn't need to know she'd left plenty of money for Erich to buy what he needed for the chore. Nor was it any of Will's business how badly Erich needed antiseptic and bandages to tend to his wound. He also kept to himself just how the incision had grown from a tender annoyance to downright painful, swollen and oozy.

After the deli closed, he rushed through the hardware and drug stores, purchasing the needed items before making a beeline for home. Anxious to see Bess again, he didn't care if her greeting was warm or cool. As long as he could be with her, it didn't matter.

Instead, he found a note on the kitchen table telling him she was napping and prescribing a list of chores. The living room smelled of stale cigarettes. No doubt she'd spent the day chain smoking and reading the book on spiritualism that was now abandoned on the end table. All in the name of honoring Harry. Yet again, he was seeing with his own eyes how accurately Jaden had painted the picture of what her life had become. A truth he'd denied and a reality Harry had caused. A wave of nausea bubbled up from his gut as guilt settled in the void.

In the guest room, he found a stack of shirts, pants and undergarments—all from Harry's closet and dresser. Thankful for the gift, despite the fact they were his belongings in the first place, he put them in the chest, dressed his wound and began shortening the list of chores she'd given him.

He fixed the lock and then began pushing the hand-powered mover to and fro through the overgrown lawn. Up and down over the uneven terrain, he often had to stop and move the large rocks that littered the lawn to the edge of the flowerbeds that surrounded the house. He also noted the patches of weeds that had taken up residence in his absence. If the herbicide usually stored in the shed was gone, he'd have to pick some up in town.

He'd hoped Bess would venture outside to keep him company, or at the very least bark some orders at him. Time in the evening air would do her a world of good, but he didn't have a clue how to invite her without angering her. He wondered if she'd been drinking that brandy Martin gave her. Instead of napping, maybe she was passed out? Harry screamed at him from inside, ordered him to go check on her, but Erich knew she'd set boundaries for a reason. He'd respect them. For a little longer, anyway.

Erich hosed off the blades of the lawnmower and pushed it back to the shed. His body ached, but the hard work felt good—he was blessed to be alive. Jaden's torture had focused on mental anguish. Erich remembered sensing heat and cold in the afterlife, but it didn't compare to the sun beating down on him and the cold water splashing up and hitting his face. A ladybug crawled up his arm. He paused, enjoying the tickle and then brushed it back into the grass.

Erich now understood that how his soul and his body experienced sensations were very different. What he'd wagered—his afterlife—hadn't meant all that much to him in the moment, but now that he'd experienced life again, giving up a body seemed too much to endure.

As he set the lawn mower in its proper place, Erich noticed a wooden cabinet. It had escaped his attention earlier and had to be a recent purchase. He reached to open it and found a padlock dangling between the two bar handles. Upon closer inspection he discovered the lock was one of Harry's favorites, used in numerous escapes. He could pick it blindfolded—and, in fact, quite often had. All he needed was the proper tools. If not his set of master keys or his picks, a needle, sewing pin, or hair pin would do the trick. Turning back to the work bench, he started rifling through the draws, looking for anything suitable.

Harry's memories, his very soul, pulsed inside with each beat of Erich's heart. Was it even possible for him to use those memories to accomplish the skills Harry had worked tirelessly to learn? There was much more to picking a lock or escaping shackles or a straitjacket than the mental know-how. In this moment, nothing seemed more important than proving those skills were not as dead as his previous body.

Finding a hat pin, of all things, in the bottom of the drawer, Erich faced off against the lock. That piece of him that was all Harry stood tall inside, filling the void, making his head swell and swim. Squatting so he was on eye level, his fingers began their manipulations, driven by the memories of a past life. Pride welled as the lock popped open in just a handful of seconds. "My, my, I do believe that's a new record," he said in a voice that was more boastful and more Harry's than the one he'd grown used to. The lock fell away from the handles.

With his curiosity driving him, Erich moved to his feet and began to open the door. From behind, an arm extended forward, slamming it shut. Bess's stern voice pierced the previous silence. "What do you think you're doing, Mr. Welch?"

*So, I'm back to being Mister?* Erich searched for any excuse other than the truth. He spun to face her. "I was looking—"

Cool liquid drenched his face and hair, running down and soaking his shirt. His eyes began to burn, and he licked his lips. She'd thrown lemonade in his face.

"What's in there isn't for your eyes or pockets. The lock should have been your first clue to that."

*Dear God, what have I done?* She was right. No excuse would pacify her now. He picked a lock to rifle through her things! If he were in her shoes, he'd be just as angry, if not more so. Harry would have tossed him off the property by his shirt collar, and goodness knows she was inclined to do as Harry would.

*The weed killer?* That was a legitimate excuse, but a lie just the same. Harry's possessions felt like his, but she'd think he was certifiably crazy if he said that. He hadn't meant harm, but lying would be purposeful and hurtful if discovered. Was there any way to make light of the situation? "Thanks for the drink. It would have been more refreshing when I was working in the blazing sun." He wiped his face with the sleeve of his shirt. "What's not important enough to be kept in the house but so valuable you have to lock it up anyway?"

She set the now empty glass on the work bench and with a firm hand to his shoulder, pushed him aside. After examining the front of the cabinet, she replaced the lock. "Not that it's any of your business, but Harry's museum is under construction in Pennsylvania. They've already taken possession of the larger props, but asked me to hold on to the smaller items until they are ready to display them."

His life on display? So, *that's* why his props and stage clothes weren't in the house. A sense of pride coursed him. "You trust a feeble padlock that has been compromised hundreds of times to protect—"

"Who says it's been compromised at all? Maybe it's brand new."

*Really?* She was going to argue with him on this? Bess didn't have a clue who she was up against or that he could be just as stubborn and spirited as her. He pushed his way between her and the cabinet, tipping the lock and showing her the scratches on the face. "Even a master escape artist leaves a trail."

Her eyes narrowed. He had no doubt if it were possible, she'd shoot daggers at him. "Don't be flip with me, especially about Harry. It doesn't matter if the lock was brand new or fifty years old, it's a lock all the same. Why would you think it was proper for you to go nosing around where I clearly didn't want you? If I can't trust you to respect me or my property—"

He regretted eroding her trust, but twisted his heel against the dirt floor and held his ground. New body or not, he'd played a game similar to this with Bess more times than he could count. "I'm sorry. Picking the lock was wrong, but I assure you it wasn't malicious. I wasn't going to take anything."

"Like you weren't going to steal Harry's ring?"

The blood whooshing through Erich's veins reminded him that such a fine line existed between passion and frustration. As always, when she stood tall and challenged him, his desire for her raged. "Are we really going there again? I told you then I was curious. I was curious now."

"Curiosity killed the cat, don't you know."

"Especially if it runs into someone wielding a glass of lemonade. You could put an eye out with the ice."

Was that a smile that curved her lips and a twinkle that touched her eyes, only to fade just as fast? How many past arguments ended with roars of laughter, followed by a loving embrace? If he could touch her with humor, would romance follow? Before he could try, her posture tightened. "You're lucky I wasn't swinging a bat. I have every right to protect Harry's property from thieves."

"I wouldn't steal from you, Bess. And it's quite impossible for me to steal from–" He stopped himself short of blurting out the secret eating at him. Who would have thought it'd be so hard to be a guest in his own life—Harry's life. Where did Harry end and Erich begin? The line just wasn't clear anymore.

"You think because my husband has passed, his property is up for looting?"

He gripped her shoulders, encouraging her to look in his eyes. To Hell with Jaden's warnings and threats. The connection that had always been there between the two of them still loomed, he could feel it. She'd recognize it. "Look in my eyes, Bess, and you'll see the truth. You'll see Ha—" Erich's throat constricted tight. He tried to push forward, say the name, but with each attempt his stomach turned and his throat burned. *Damn Jaden and his games.*

"All I is see when I look at you is a stranger, a rogue. I can't even imagine how angry Harry would be to know you were trying to steal from him."

"Harry's gone. It's not his property, it's yours. I'd never steal from you—or anyone—Bess. My crimes are being nosy and acting on stupid impulses. I apologize for that."

Her body softened in his grip, and he resisted the urge to pull her tighter, though it tore his heart in two.

"You're here for him—or his memory—aren't you?" Bess asked.

Erich wasn't exactly sure what she accused him of, but there was only one reason he was here, and it wasn't for himself. "No."

Tears veiled her voice. "I can see it. In your eyes, there's a fire so strong, so bright. Harry's the only other person I ever saw with such a determined gleam. You're driven. You get what you want."

The profound sadness in her voice knocked him off balance, and he released his hold on her. He'd never thought those to be bad traits, but both her and Jaden described them as sins. "Are you telling me Harry had flaws?"

"Of course he did. He was human." A wistful smile showed itself. "I loved my husband, but that drive is what took him from me. That desire to put the show above us. He's gone because for days he denied my pleas to see a doctor. His last good breath was given to his legions of fans, and I'm left to keep aflame the fire that burned my life to the ground."

*Is that how she saw those last days?* Yes, he was sick, but he never guessed he was anything close to dying. It all started with those students. They'd challenged his claim that he could take any punch to the stomach without giving him time to brace for their blows. Had it been so ludicrous to blame them for the intense pain, even though somewhere deep inside he knew more was going on?

Even if money was no longer the issue for them, old habits die hard. Doctors were a frivolous expense, especially since he thought he had a touch of flu that would soon pass. "I doubt he knew how sick he was."

"His appendix had burst. The doctors said the pain must have been unbearable for days. I begged him to cancel shows, but the roar of the crowd called louder."

Nothing could be further from the truth, and her accusations pushed the air from him like those sucker-punches. How could she think he valued anything more than her?

The more she told him, the further she drifted away. Her face became a vacant slate, as if showing one emotion would crack the rock-hard pretense she showed the world. "I swear he was able to manipulate that insurance company from beyond the grave. They paid out on the double indemnity clause of his policy. Ruled it was work-related even though the doctors said his own ignorance caused his death. *That* is the fire I see in your eyes. Nothing matters more to you than you."

Good news wrapped in the worst kind. She recognized something and identified it with Harry. Maybe her soul called to his, but Bess's didn't much care for him anymore. Harry had no idea the pain he'd caused, and Erich had no basis to explain it or make it pass for her. "I like to consider myself a driven man, but about everything else, you're wrong." With nothing more to add, he walked to the far corner of the shed and picked up a pair of trimmers. "I'm going to tend to the hedges before supper, if I'm still a welcome guest in your home."

"How can I let you stay? I don't trust you."

Her words spun him back, and he stepped toward her. Pleading with her went against every instinct Harry ever lived by, but what did he have left? "I'm sorry I've breached your faith in me. Give me a chance to prove myself."

She swallowed hard and looked him up and down. He could see her indecision. "You've made headway with the chores, but we've barely scratched the surface of what needs to be done. You're welcome to stay on, but if you forget your place just one more time, I will have no choice but to ask you to leave."

Words escaped him, so he acknowledged her statement with a single nod and returned to his work. Earning his bed and meals would win respect, the rest he'd sort out later.

Back in the yard, the sun was beginning to droop in the sky as the evening waned, but the Santa Anas were blowing again, scorching everything it touched. He'd never remembered them burning for so long with such intensity. Dropping the clippers to the grass in front of the shrubs, he peeled the soaked shirt off and began to lift the cotton undershirt. It occurred to him if Bess saw the bandage beneath seeping blood, puss and now soaked with lemonade, she'd try to nurse him. The similarity between this wound and Harry's condition would cause more pain. Instead, he lifted the t-shirt away from his skin and tried to ring it out, even though the acid and sugar had permeated the bandage and burned the open wound.

Bending back at the waist, he let the hot breeze dry his flesh and pleaded to the empty skies to heal her heart and ease her pain.

A chuckle erupted from low in his gut. For three days, he'd walked this plane with Harry's spirit, and Erich now did something Harry would despise. He *prayed* that Bess's soul would find healing.

# Chapter Ten

Bess let the screen door slam behind her, stomped to the sink and peered out the window. How was it possible to want to strangle someone and kiss them at the same time? The inexplicable attraction was primal. Maddening. Yet, it refused to be ignored.

Now, she watched as he stood with his back stretched out and his face pointed toward the waning sun. So in tune with everything around him, like Harry, but Erich blended in with his surroundings. He coexisted in way that felt spiritual, whereas Harry was always guarded.

Why didn't she throw him out of the house? Twice she'd caught him eyeing her property. Still, a small voice whispered to trust him. Erich had no idea what was in the cabinet. Gardening tools would be a logical assumption.

*What am I doing? Why am I making excuses for him?*

He'd admitted to being in the wrong. So, why did the idea of sending him away pull at her heart?

*Hold me up, baby. Let me know you're still here.*

Had she really sunk to begging a ghost? If only she could hear his voice again, it would give her the strength to continue pursuing his dream. Just because Harry was gone didn't mean the spotlight wouldn't shine bold and bright for The Houdinis again, and she only had a little over three short weeks to prepare for his return. Erich was a distraction, pure and simple. A diversion that could cost her everything she and her husband had worked so hard to obtain.

Erich's words in the shed reverberated in his ears: *It's impossible for me to steal from Harry; he's dead.* He didn't understand what was at stake.

So black and white. So misguided. So painful. And exactly what Harry would have said.

Her husband's voice disappeared from her mind the moment she'd met Erich. The running commentary ceased to play, and she guessed at Harry's will instead of feeling it with conviction. He'd want her to keep their dream alive. *Wouldn't he?*

Martin had spoken of loss, grief and finding love again, but she'd never imagined it would happen to her. Her misery seemed boundless, but that changed in a snap when Erich appeared out of thin air. Maybe this was simply lust.

The mere thought caused her stomach to churn with guilt. Her long marriage and Harry's devotion deserved more than eleven months of mourning. The legacy that he'd worked to build—that he'd given his life for—shouldn't fade away from anyone's mind. Definitely not hers.

When she examined the facts, she had no other choice. Her preparation for the séance had to come first. If Erich continued at his current pace, the house would be in order by the end of the week. She'd push him on his way and set her mind and heart back where it belonged.

Through the window, she saw him heading for the house. Having put the tools away, he'd be expecting dinner, and he might not accept her drooling over his chiseled abs through the thin veil of his drenched t-shirt as an acceptable excuse for the delay. She wiped her sweaty hands on her skirt and opened the refrigerator.

The screen door squeaked, announcing Erich's entrance. She called to him, "I'll have supper for you in thirty minutes."

His large hand gripped her shoulder. She didn't want to look in his eyes, but she allowed him to spin her toward him. "Bess, I just wanted...needed to express again how sorry I am. Please, believe me. It was mischief, not theft on my mind."

What was she supposed to say? She couldn't tell him it was okay. It'd never be all right for him to grub through Harry's things or invade her privacy. So then why couldn't she shake the urge to curl up against his shoulder and feel his arms wrapped tight around her, protecting her from the storm of emotions tearing her apart? The sight of him drove up her blood pressure and made her palms sweaty and sticky again.

She fought her desire with the image of him picking the lock. Even if he didn't look a thing like Harry, the way his body moved, his focus and his drive all touched parts of her only Harry ever had before.

"All I ask is that you respect my privacy from this moment forward."

His hands clasped, the fingers tapped against each other. Did all grown men fidget like naughty boys or had she been unlucky enough to find the only two?

"Of course. Seeing as I have some time, I think I'd like to shower before dinner."

Deflecting her stare, she waved him off. As he left, her craving became a longing. Part of her belonged to him. It didn't make any sense, but was true nonetheless. Bess now knew that pushing Erich out of her life was not only the right thing to do, but what had to be done if she had any chance of getting Harry back.

****

In the shower, a cool spray washed the sticky sweat and lemonade from his body, but it did little to ease his aches and pains. Erich didn't mind much, though. The stiff, sore muscles were a stark reminder of what was at stake. Life was about how a person lived, not what was acquired. He'd never forget that or take life for granted again.

It didn't matter if Bess was screaming at him or dousing him with drinks, those moments were more beautiful and active then what he'd experienced in Jaden's hands on the other side. Too bad it could all slip away if he didn't find a way to get through to her.

Still, for fleeting moments when their gazes locked, he swore she reached for him. When they shared a laugh or he touched her, he sensed that she knew his soul was Harry's, but those brief seconds never lasted. They always faded.

He patted his wound dry, swallowing the screams each touch unleashed. He poured peroxide over the loose, tattered stitches and watched it bubble, gripping the counter and biting his tongue to shield Bess from the truth. Instead of healing, his flesh was turning dark red, and a yellow puss oozed from beneath the black threads. If there were any hope of a recovery, he'd have to find a way to rest and keep lemon and sugar away from it. Now was the worst possible time for Bess to lose faith in him. He'd have to work twice as hard to regain her favor.

Dressed in clean clothes, he returned to the kitchen, walking in just as Bess set the two plates on the table. Each plate contained a few slices of corn beef, some rice, a spoonful of peas—probably picked from the garden—and a slice of homemade bread so fresh from the oven the butter melted into it. His stomach rumbled, and his mouth watered in anticipation.

"Good timing. Come eat while it's still hot."

They sat at the same table, but Bess kept her eyes focused on the plate and the conversation to a minimum. Answering Harry's call to open the lock had closed the doors with Bess that Erich had struggled to open. His spirit deflated. He wanted to push and tried steering the conversation to the weather or how much he'd accomplished, but each question or comment was met with the shortest, starkest reply.

His gut told him to fall to his knees and confess the whole truth about who he was and the deal with Jaden. Then he'd take her in his arms and escort her to their marriage bed, but he knew the reality. Not only was it against Jaden's rules, but the brute had made admission impossible. If Erich attempted again, Jaden might claim victory and call him back. Easing his conscious wasn't worth losing a moment with Bess.

So he stood and took his dishes to the sink. He heard stones kicking up in the driveway and saw an old black pickup truck approaching the house. It didn't match anything from Harry's memories, and Erich wondered who would be calling at such a time.

"It seems you have a visitor."

Bess brought her dishes to the sink and peered out the window. "It's Joseph. I wonder what he wants." She washed her hands and dried them on the dishtowel hanging from the drawer handle before going to greet the man at the back door.

Unwilling to leave Bess alone with the stranger, and more than a little curious as to why he was entering his house, Erich filled the sink with soapy water and began cleaning up the dishes.

Bess greeted the man warmly, inviting him into the kitchen. "Can I get you a cup of tea, Joseph?"

"No, thank you, Mrs. Houdini. I didn't come to be trouble. I just wanted to drop this off for you." He offered her a large canning jar filled with green leaves.

Bess took it, holding the jar up to the light and examining the contents. "What is this?"

"The leaves from a black currant vine. Steep them in boiling water with dandelion greens for a quarter hour. The resulting tea will help you make peace with your troubled heart and that restless soul that haunts you."

Bess reached for Joseph's hand and squeezed it. She then motioned to a chair. "What did I ever do to deserve your kindness? Please, you went to so much trouble to share your remedy with me. Sit and tell me more about it."

Joseph reached for the back of the chair, but hesitated and tipped his ear toward the ceiling. Letting his eyes flutter closed, he seemed to be giving himself over to his surroundings. He then straightened and walked toward Erich with an outstretched arm. "You are ill, son."

Erich resisted the urge to cradle the wound on his stomach. How did this man know he was injured? "No. I'm fine."

Joseph put his hands up between the two of them starting at mid-chest level. He then raised them up and lowered them, mumbling to himself so softly that Erich couldn't decipher the words. "Your body is broken and your soul is lost. Both hope to find a home here, but the road is long, and the terrain uneven. You must find sure footing if you hope to unearth peace."

Having washed the dishes and properly cared for the leftover food, Erich picked up the dishtowel Bess had discarded and wiped his hands. "I appreciate the diagnosis, but you're wrong. I'm fine." He flipped his attention over his shoulder. "Good night, Bess."

"Yes, yes, I must leave too, for you will be in need of my services soon, and I must prepare. Good night, Bess."

Erich retreated to the guest room. It was bad enough that he had to sleep alone, not only would he be tortured by his memories and Bess's new spin on their past, but now he had the weird ranting of the madman to process. If there was anything that Harry was not, it was transparent to those around him. To have this stranger see clear through his injured body to Harry's tormented soul unnerved Erich and the ghost living within.

He was positive sleep would prove impossible, but the instant his head hit the pillow, consciousness slipped away. Images of how Harry's choices in life had devastated Bess filled the void.

"This body is not yours. It is merely a loan. Continue to step on the wrong path and it will be mine once again."

Not his voice, but it rolled up from the same place his conscious would. Jaden spoke in a hushed whisper, raising goose bumps on Erich's arms. The life that resided in his body's shell was wrapped in something cold and wet, lighter than a quilt but heavier than mist.

A long stone pier on a cool foggy night materialized, and he could see a lighthouse in the distance. It was the New York/New Jersey shoreline, but not really. This was a dream, and Jaden controlled his experiences. In those images, he found himself face-to-mid-chest with the hulk of a man, this time dressed in a flowing white robe.

"You sent me here to heal, but all I do is hurt," Erich said.

"Just because you possess the power doesn't mean you're using it right. Remember how many hours of persistent patience it took before you were able to pick your first lock?"

He was tired of Jaden's mind games. The more time he spent with Bess, the more he learned about her battered heart. Jaden's callous competition wouldn't give her closure. Erich wasn't sure anything or anyone could. Why in the world had he accepted a challenge where his wife's heart, mind, and quite possibly her soul lay on the line? "Are you comparing Bess to some cold piece of metal?"

"No. I'm saying anything worth having is worth fighting for." Disappointment resided in Jaden's eyes, and Erich had to turn his focus away. Whether it was a crowd of strangers or a dear friend, Harry didn't accept failure as an option, yet that's exactly what he was doing. "I expected so much more spunk from you. You've taken every blow like you don't want to succeed."

The will to fight for Bess wasn't the problem. He'd go to the ends of the world for her. He just didn't have a clue how to turn her head. They'd come together so easily the first time, there was no chase. No great pursuit. Only love. He didn't need the desire; he needed a lesson in chivalry.

Erich stepped away from Jaden and continued walking through the thick fog, feeling it cling to him as if it—and he—were real and not just an illusion. "My arms ache to hold her."

"Then why don't you claim her?"

Erich's fingers curled to a tight fist. Jaden knew what he faced, but prodded at him anyway. "She can't see the man inside, because she's haunted by the ghost. I didn't want to believe you, but I caused that pain."

"Grief ravages the heart and mind, tainting everything it touches. For some its stay is short, forced away by memories of love and joy. For others, grief takes root and strangles out anything positive."

"The same could be said for anger." The answer to grief would be to soothe her, but she felt so much more. Heartbroken from loss, yes, but burning with rage for the choices he'd made. How could he reconcile the two? She now believed Harry had picked fame over her and manipulated the truth to substantiate her claims, like saying he refused a doctor's care because of the fans.

"You knew you were sick." A moral compass, Jaden spoke the simple truth.

"I did."

"You knew it was serious."

"Not deathly!" And that was fact. Wasn't it? Erich tried to access the memories, but for once, his recollection of the past was as murky and clouded as the mist that surrounded them.

"Harry's death resulted from ignoring the cries his body made. Now you, Erich, are faced with the same dilemma. You can choose for Bess or choose for Harry, but not both."

Acid bubbled in his stomach, and his shoulders constricted. Right. Wrong. Repercussions. Consequences. "I already chose Bess. That's why I'm here!"

"I'm not interested in the words of someone who sells illusions. I'm interested in the actions of a man who puts others before himself."

In an instant, the cold mist, the stony pier and the lighthouse vanished. Erich stared at the wall opposite his bed in the Laurel Canyon bedroom. He could hear a blood curdling scream in the distance. It sounded like some poor bastard was being ripped apart. The agonizing and sharp tones pierced his ears, slowly growing louder, until he realized it was coming from his mouth and the depths of his gut.

The pain ripped through his abdomen, debilitating and obliterating. His hands went to cradle his stomach, but with the touch a deep, burning pain flashed through him. His back arched, and his skull smacked the headboard.

More agony. Too much to bear.

Control slipped away with the tears cascading down his cheeks unchecked. His hands curled up in the twisted sheets, and he prayed for some sort of relief.

The door to the room flung open, and Bess rushed to his side. Kneeling on the bed, she ran her cool hand over his forehead. Her normally porcelain skin was ghost-white, and he wondered if it was a mirror-reflection. Had Jaden placed him on death's door?

"Heavens, you're burning up."

"The...it...hurts..." His body trembled as if he were in an ice bath instead of the bed, but he knew the chills were a delusion of the fever.

"Erich, shhhh, lay back. I'm calling Joseph. No arguments."

She wrapped her arms under his neck and leg and struggled to lay him back down. Something inside him lurched. Despite the pain, her touch soothed him. He noticed her hair, freed from its daily binds and hanging in dark curls around her shoulder. He regretted that he hadn't felt the softness of those curls against the palm of his hand or his chest once more.

As she swept from the room, the pain grew, dragging another scream from him. He gritted his teeth and tried to control the agony with slow, deep breaths.

*You bastard, you promised me thirty days. Instead you're going to make her live through this again.*

He waited for an answer he knew Jaden wouldn't deliver. His ominous warning against stepping on the wrong path echoed over and over. This journey was about choices. In order to save Bess, he'd have to make the right ones. Did that mean if he let her call the doctor, all would be fine? It didn't matter. In Bess's eyes he saw her fear and memories of Harry. She was taking control. History wouldn't repeat itself on her watch.

# Chapter Eleven

Bess scurried into the room, placing the basin on the nightstand. Her hands swirled in the water, and ice clanked against the bowl's metal sides. Lowering herself to the side of the bed, she placed the cloth to his head. The shivers raking his body intensified. "Joseph is on his way."

"Thank you...for helping." His teeth chattered around the words. He pushed his hand to her knee. The soft satin against his hand comforted him almost as much as her touch to his flesh.

"What am I going to do? Let you die in this bed?"

Real concern intermingled with the lines of passing time on her face. She refreshed the towel, and then returned it his forehead. "Forgive me, Mr. Welch, but if I'm going to control the fever, I need to get these blankets off of you."

*Mr. Welch?* Were they back to formalities or was she establishing distance?

She let the quilt pile around his feet, exposing the soaking wet boxers and thin tank top that clung to his flesh. Her eyes caressed their way up his body. Or he was just delirious from fever. Did she feel something more than concern for a fellow being?

That was too much to wish for, but Erich gripped on to hope. He may have started this journey believing a single day in her presence would satisfy his longing, but the thought of leaving her again, knowing the pain Harry's death had caused, hurt more than any surgical wound.

She crossed the room and flipped on the window fan. Another chill crawled up his spine, lifting him off the bed in a wave. He reached for the blanket, but didn't have enough strength to grasp it. His eyes fluttered closed as he forced her name through dry, cracked lips.

The return of the damp cloth to his forehead snapped him back to the moment.

"Don't worry. I won't leave you like this." Her gentle touch brushed his cheek. "I do believe you're cooler."

"C-c-c-cold." Erich gripped her forearm, believing she possessed the power to anchor him to this life.

"It's the fever. Joseph is going to be here soon, and you're going to be fine." Her words echoed those she spoke while keeping vigil at Harry's deathbed, right down to the rattled tone. She feared he would die. Erich knew reliving those last moments would only deepen her despair. Instead of saving Bess from her future, this would condemn her to it.

"Mrs. Houdini?" The accented, male voice called from the bottom of the stairs.

She pulled herself from the bedside. "We're upstairs, the room at the end of the hall." Coming back to Erich, she said, "He will know what to do."

Joseph might not be a traditional doctor, but he was a medical student. Harry's will stirred inside, insisting he didn't want anyone associated with Martin and his wife in this house. He may be a fine physician, but the bad blood clouded reason and tugged at Erich harder than logic. "D-d-d-on't...want...any...d-d-doctor..."

"Then it's a good thing I'm not one. I've been expecting your call."

Erich rolled his head to see the man with dark skin and silky, black hair. "But you...work...at the...hospital...with Martin."

"That doesn't mean I agree with all of his practices."

"That's why I called you. I don't want to offend Martin—especially since he's been such a good friend—but I want a different outcome than Harry had, and I think you can provide that."

Joseph tossed a tan canvas bag on the foot of the bed and moved up the opposite side that Bess hovered over. "Tell me what's going on."

Bess said, "He woke up screaming in pain and trembling. I think it's his appendix."

Placing his large, red-brown hands on either side of Erich's face, Joseph looked deep in Erich's eyes. "Thank you, Mrs. Houdini, but now let Mister—"

"Welch. Erich Welch," she answered again.

Joseph shot her a daggered glance that must have hit its mark, because this time, she stepped back. He returned his focus to Erich, who opened his mouth even though he wasn't sure how to answer.

The pain-ravaged words came from someone else. Jaden perhaps? "My stomach...Surgery...ten days ago...appendix."

"Yet, you tried to tell me you were in perfectly fine health." Joseph lifted the soaked, tank-top from Erich's stomach and pulled away the bandage. He tried to steal a look, but the shirt blocked his view. Judging from the expression on Joseph's face, the incision must have been as ugly as it was painful. "I'm going to need you to boil some water and bring me clean, white towels."

"I'll get them straight away. You can help him. Right?" Bess laid all hope at the faux doctor's feet.

"I will do my best."

Joseph scored points for not giving false expectations. If Erich's agony was a gauge, he'd be in the grim reaper's shadow soon. Another wave of pain coursed his body, this one more intense than the last. Erich tried to access Harry's memories, compare this pain to what Harry experienced before dying. How could he trust a mere medical student to save his life when a team of doctors had failed to save Harry?

"It looks like you've ripped some stitches and the incision is infected."

This guy was brilliant. Huh? Erich didn't need medical instruction to know that. "I've been trying to care for it."

Joseph's eyes darted up to Bess. "Put the water on to boil and bring him a glass to drink. I need to clean up the incision and repair the stitches."

"Maybe this...isn't a...good idea." Erich choked out the words in short gasps.

Bess was halfway out of the room, but his objection called her back. "You will do exactly what he says without one word of argument."

"Please, Mrs. Houdini. If you want me to treat him, I need the items I asked for." Joseph ignored the brewing struggle for power, and his words pushed her on her way. He then focused on the task-at-hand and began pulling objects from his bag, laying them out on the bed. "Now, Mr. Welch, do you want to tell me exactly what happened? Where did you have this surgery and why didn't you stay in a hospital until you were fully recovered?"

Erich couldn't tell Joseph the wound was the mark of a previous life or that three days earlier his spirit had been Jaden's whipping boy. Expecting Jaden to take over again, he parted his lips, but no words came. So, he said the first thing that popped into his mind. "I couldn't pay. I can't pay."

"Don't worry about the expenses. I want all bills sent to me." Bess spouted her orders as she rustled back into the room, setting the glass on the nightstand and handing a stack of towels across the bed.

Joseph took the offering, but mulled over her words as if he were a dog with a bone. "You can't put a price on healing. Those who know how are obligated by the spirits to serve. The boiling water?"

"It's coming." Bess's face mirrored the confusion bouncing around in Erich's head. Did Joseph just say there would be no charge for his treatments? Noble, maybe, but not at all aligned with Martin's philosophy on life.

"What I'm going to have to do is open up what's left of these stitches and irrigate the wound. If you like, I can mix some herbs with the water that will help you manage the pain."

Intense and stabbing, Erich's agony took center stage. Everything else happening in the room annoyed, but didn't distract. But what if he slipped and said something he shouldn't while in an altered state? Jaden's control would keep him from admitting to being Harry, but it wouldn't stop him from saying something painful to Bess. He needed his wits about him to protect what was left of his relationship with her. "I don't want any drugs."

"But the pain." Joseph said nothing more, as if the fragment were enough to change his mind.

Bess returned, carrying the cast iron pot by the handle with potholders. "You do what is necessary to make him well." Her voice quivered and tears glossed her eyes. No doubt this experience had put her right back in that Detroit hospital several months earlier. At least this time, Joseph kept her busy with idle tasks. Erich suspected it was the real reason Joseph continued to send her up and down the steps. Back then, all she could do was sit and watch, with no control over the outcome. Was that why she held on to her guilt so tightly?

With her help, this scenario might have a happy ending. Maybe then she'd release the past. There was no other choice. If he died here on this bed, she'd have to relive the same horrible nightmare, the same way he had in purgatory. Erich gripped the sheets, fighting the agony and swearing to never give up the fight. For Bess's sake, he'd do what was asked and fight the infection. "Do whatever you have to."

Joseph opened a small, brown bottle and dumped its contents—a greenish-brown powder—on to a small piece of cheese cloth he'd pulled from his bag. He pulled the four corners up and tied them, before placing the formed ball into a clay mug and dipping it into the boiling water. Handing the concoction to Bess, he said, "Make sure he drinks it all. It will dull his pain without altering his mind."

Taking another clay bowl from his bag, he filled it from the pot and immersed several metal instruments. He then opened a brown vial, closed his eyes, whispered a short phrase in his native tongue and dripped a few drops on top of his tools.

When the medicine man placed the first towel on his midsection, white-hot pain radiated out from the gaping slice in his abdomen, consuming every inch of him. Erich's back arched, and he cried out.

"This is barbaric. Isn't there anything more you can give him?" Bess's voice cracked as she slid a trembling arm under his neck and took the towel from his forehead, refreshing it in the cold water, and replacing it with a gentle touch as if she knew her contact was magnified tenfold by the pain.

"Not here. If he wants anesthetic, he needs to go to the hospital."

"No! No hospital. I'll be all right." Erich swallowed and focused on controlling his reactions for Bess's peace of mind.

"I have some of Martin's brandy. Would that help?" She asked. With Joseph's nod, Bess fled the room again.

"No brandy. Just do what you must. Please." Harry's disdain for tainting his body with alcohol reverberated inside him, even if it would ease the pain. But as the moments passed, Erich wondered why he should hold Harry's ideals steadfast. Would a few sips of brandy change all that much? Doctors had used alcohol medicinally for decades, trusted it to help their patients. Maybe he should trust others to do the right thing. Easing Bess's fears was the least he could do after everything Harry had put her through.

Joseph lifted the towels, examined the flesh beneath and applied a clean layer to Erich's flesh. "It is my hope the heat will not only soften the stitches, but draw out the infection and take the swelling down. If I were you, I'd take advantage of Mrs. Houdini's offer and use these next few minutes to numb yourself."

Erich rolled his head on the pillow and fought all the sensations pounding at him: the intense pain, the memories of dying, Harry's life philosophy and Jaden's ominous warning of wrong turns and missteps. "You could never understand what it's like."

Returning to the room, Bess poured from the silver flask into a glass tumbler. "I thought I made myself clear. You're going to do exactly what Joseph tells you."

Through vision blurred from by pain and tears, Erich focused on her face and found concern and pain mixed in equal proportions. He could fight to keep his body pure of alcohol and honor the man he once was, but comforting Bess was more important. He needed to act like a man and give her control. He nodded and tried to lift himself to accept the offered drink.

Bess supported his neck and placed the glass to his lips. "Not too fast. Just sip."

Bitter blackberry fluid hit his tongue, and he struggled against the urge to cough it back up. Joseph poked at Erich's wound. He was aware of the pain, but somehow Bess's soft caress made everything else seem distant.

"Another sip, Erich." The nurturing look in her eyes as she scanned his face, looking for signs of improvement, touched him in a way nothing else could. With her leaning in so close, he stared at the dark curls framing her cheek and remembered Jaden's warnings about choices. Harry had made his based on pride and ego. Erich needed to carve a different path if he wanted a better outcome.

Accepting a third sip, his focus diminished. His limbs grew heavy, and his mind clouded as his body collapsed. Maybe it was too late to make better choices than Harry had. Just maybe he'd already made too many missteps. Or was it a mixture of the brandy and the tea stealing his consciousness?

He struggled hard to stay alert. He needed this moment in Bess's arms to sustain him. If Jaden was dissolving their bargain, pulling him back early for some misguided misstep, he'd fight for every last second close to her. He opened his mouth to speak her name, but lost the battle.

Everything went black.

****

Memories flooded Bess's mind as Erich's body collapsed in her arms. She'd cradled Harry in her arms, stroking his hair and kissing his brow, in the same way until his body turned ice-cold. Rage filled her heart, permeating the void her one true love had left behind, and she had cursed God for taking him away.

Now, looking down at Erich's limp, lifeless body, those emotions rolled over her again. They ebbed like a tidal wave searching for a shore to crash on, and she doubted she'd be left standing when the full impact hit her. She brushed Erich's jaw; something she wouldn't dare do while he was awake, no matter how much he or her heart begged. This illness drew another parallel between him and Harry, and her unexplainable yearning would no longer be denied.

His flesh still burned with fever, and she guided him down, resting his head on the pillow before going to Joseph's side. "What can I do?"

He didn't look up and continued cutting away the old stitches. "I need no assistance. He needs you to take the wet clothes off of his body and wash him down with cool water."

Bess blinked. There was no way that she'd just heard Joseph right. For a man of medicine, one human form might resemble another, but for her, nothing could be further from the truth. At least her feelings for Erich weren't as obvious as if she'd advertised them like the kid with the sandwich board outside the dime store. Joseph wouldn't have asked her to undress Erich if they were.

Still, it needed to be done. Bess picked up a clean washcloth from the nightstand and dipped it into the ice water. She began with his forehead then slid it down to his cheeks and neck. She returned the cloth to the ice water and then wiped it over his hair, following with her fingers.

*This isn't Harry.* She repeated to herself over and again. *It will end differently.* Erich wouldn't die on her. Couldn't.

"Do you have any sage?"

Joseph's odd question pulled Bess out of her thoughts. "Sage? Yes, but why?"

A restless spirit resides in these walls. He is tied to you and will not leave by his own choice. If you like, I could try to help him find his peaceful rest, but he is stubborn. I will need the help of burning sage."

Bess looked around the room, as if she could see what Joseph felt. Some might think he was a ranting mad man, one who'd drank too much of Martin's brandy perhaps, but she'd felt what Joseph talked about. Harry's spirit was tied to her. He was with her, trying to find a way to communicate, just as he'd promised. "No, do not exercise Harry from the house. He may stay as long as he sees fit."

"Excuse me, ma'am, but do you make this choice for you or for him?"

His question was fair, and his point taken. She wanted Harry's spirit with her, because the idea of him really being gone seemed too much to endure. If she were putting him first, letting him go would be more compassionate.

"Regardless, for now I want to focus on Erich. When he is well again, we can discuss Harry." She abandoned the cloth and the ice water and set her focus on pulling the soaked, cotton undershirt from his body.

Because of the brandy or the fever, his limbs were dead weight. It took all her strength to complete the chore, but one glance at his broad shoulders, firm abs and lean arms and Bess was the one who needed an ice bath. A flush burned her cheeks, and her mouth went dry. The little voice reminding her she needed to nurse him to health was pushed silent by images of those muscular limbs wrapped around her body, holding her tight. She wondered what it would be like to have his long, slender fingers teasing her flesh.

She missed the way her husband held, comforted and thrilled her most. She shouldn't be thinking about doing those same things with this virtual stranger: a man who'd breezed into town and her life just a few short days ago and blatantly tried to steal from her. A man who reminded her in many ways of the one true love of her life, but was also just as different.

"Joseph! Bess!" Martin's voice called from the bottom of the stairs, pulling Bess back to the moment. She answered his call. A moment later, the sound of his heavy stride on the steps and down the hall announced him to the room.

He went straight to Bess and brushed his hand against her shoulder. "Oh, thank Heavens. When the maid said Joseph answered a call from you, and then left with his medical bag, I feared you'd taken ill."

"She called me to tend to her hired hand," Joseph said.

Martin twisted toward his student and then flipped his attention back to Bess. "He's confused, right? You really called for me, didn't you?"

Bess stammered and searched for the right words to explain, but Martin had turned his attention to Erich. Stepping closer to the bed, Martin glanced at his watch as he gripped Erich's wrist. Taking his pulse, perhaps. "Where do I know him from?"

"He works for Will at the deli. I offered him room and board in exchange for doing some repairs around the house."

Joseph picked up where Bess stopped. "When I got here, he was burning up with fever. Stitches from a surgery were ripped, and the wound infected."

"Why didn't you take him to the hospital?" From the fire in Martin's eyes, Bess could tell this wasn't the first time Martin had called Joseph's judgment into question.

"He refused, and it wasn't necessary." Not giving Martin any of his focus, Joseph continued to go about treating Erich in his own way.

Martin slipped off his suit jacket and pulled the white cotton gloves from his hands. Joseph had said

Martin and Gail had been away from the house. Based on Martin's fine clothing, she guessed they'd gone into the city to a fancy restaurant or maybe the theater. Glitz and glamor was Martin and Gail's way.

Guilt pinged inside Bess's chest that Martin had left Gail's side and ruined their evening. Nights alone together were too precious not to be savored.

Especially since Bess wasn't about to put her faith in medicine this time around, not when it had failed her before. "You should go back to Gail."

"Nonsense. I am a doctor and this man needs my help." Setting the garments on the dresser, Martin went to Erich's side and lifted the towel. "We must close the incision."

"The infection is not gone." Joseph's tone stayed level as he took the towel from Martin's grip and returned it to Erich's stomach.

An animalistic sound reverberated from Martin's throat, and he poked his finger in his student's face. "You can't leave an incision open."

Joseph glanced up at the other man, but seemed undeterred by Martin's presence. Stepping between Martin and the bed, Joseph continued his treatment. "If you seal the wound, where will the infection go?"

Martin grimaced and stepped back to the dresser. Looking at the instruments Joseph had arranged on a white towel, Martin picked up one of the several brown vials, read the label and tossed it back down, shaking his head. "What is all this? Why didn't you bring my medical bag?"

"I had no use for it." For all of Martin's rage, Joseph stood self-confident and unwavering in his actions.

Martin's eye twitched, and his hands clenched and unclenched against his thigh. "I'm not going to argue with you. I'm the doctor here." To Bess, he said, "I need to take this man to the hospital."

Harry died in a hospital. "Joseph says it's not necessary. Erich is doing better."

"Well, since I wasn't here from the beginning I can't speak to that, but he's had a recent surgery and now an infection. And he's a stranger, one of Will's strays. I just think it's best for everyone concerned if we put him in my car and take him to the hospital. Get him out of your way."

Joseph said, "He shouldn't be moved."

Martin dug the heel of his boot into the wood floor. "It's unfair to ask Bess to care for him."

Bess closed her eyes and tried to think despite the infantile arguing. These two should be working together to help Erich, not fighting over whose methods were best. "It's my choice to have Erich here, and my decision if he stays or goes."

"He needs more treatment than I can give him here, Bess. He'll receive better care in the hospital from doctors." In Martin's eyes, Bess saw complete sincerity, but a cloud of doubt still hovered. She couldn't forget how modern medicine had failed her and Harry.

"Moving him now will only injure him more." Joseph's words earned him another death-glare by Martin.

Martin lunged forward and Bess stepped between them. "I think we should do as Joseph says and leave him. He's resting comfortably and doing better."

Martin placed the back of his hand to Erich's forehead. "He's not sleeping. He's passed out. The fever is still very high."

"It's coming down," Joseph said.

"From what? Have you been taking his temperature? Recording your findings? Charting your treatments?"

"Those are your ways. Erich asked me to treat him in my way. We've bathed him, given him fluids, licorice root and thyme to control the pain and fever. I've applied heat to the incision, pulled away the old stitches and irrigated the wound. I'll irrigate it again, and then pack it with a bran poultice."

"There is no way I can allow you to pack an open, infected incision with bran." Martin's words came through gritted teeth. Bess had no doubt he would physically remove Joseph before allowing that treatment. She stepped forward, took Martin by the arm. "Why don't we give his ways a chance? What can it hurt?"

"It could cost this man his life," Martin said. "These are savage treatments, Bess. They're not medically proven."

"They have worked for centuries among my people."

"And those doctors in Detroit," Bess continued, "with all their proven cures, couldn't help Harry. Erich's illness is similar. I have been talking to Joseph, watching him at the hospital. That is why I called *him*. I think it's best if we let Joseph finish what he's started."

"This is not the same," Martin pleaded with Bess, but then flipped his attention to Joseph. "You are taking advantage of a grieving widow who doesn't understand medicine. She hasn't had the training I've given you. I've defended you to my colleagues and the board at the hospital, but I can't defend this. It goes against my oath to heal. If you don't tend to this patient the way I've taught you, you can pack your things, leave my house and go back to the reservation."

"That is fine with me."

Martin turned to Bess. "Erich's life is in the balance, sweetie. You're really going to leave it in Joseph's hands?"

"You can't promise me you can save him. I put my faith in doctors once before, and they failed me. I can't make that mistake again."

She'd expected shock in Martin's eyes. No one would have known by the hours she spent volunteering at the hospital that she'd become so distrustful of medicine. What she didn't expect was the anger.

"That's not fair, Bess. You can't blame the doctors because Harry was a stubborn fool who refused medical treatment until it was too late."

Did Martin have point? God knows Harry was tenacious. Erich, too, for that matter. Why was it up to her who treated Erich or where he went?

Because just like with her Harry, the patient couldn't speak for himself. Then again, Erich had. He'd said no doctor and no to Martin, but had allowed

Joseph to treat him, even followed his prescriptions. "I'm sorry, Martin, but I need to do what Erich would want, and he said no hospitals. I want to give Joseph's treatments a chance."

Martin lowered his gaze. "If he dies in that bed, Bess, don't come crying to me." He turned to the dresser and picked up his jacket and gloves. "I want you out of my guest house by tomorrow, Joseph. Your fellowship is over."

****

Bess straightened the quilt over Erich's body, running her hands over the fabric, smoothing out the wrinkles, even though she knew that did nothing to help his illness. Joseph had changed his dressings, reapplied the ointment he made from various herbs and plants in her kitchen, and Erich hadn't stirred a bit. In fact, he remained deathly still, just as he had for the last day. "Wouldn't you think he'd be waking up by now?"

Joseph stepped up to her side. Crossing his arms, he studied Erich's face. "Sleep allows the body to put its full focus on healing. It is good. He is getting well."

"He's not nearly as warm as he was."

"Still, the fever has not broken. That is cause for concern." He paused, studied Erich's face a little more, before touching his forehead and then stroking his hand and examining his finger nails. "Some licorice root tea is in order."

"He can't drink unless he's awake."

"His body can absorb the fluid without him being awake. Just as you've been rubbing ice cubes to his lips to keep him hydrated, we can soak a cloth with the tea. Rubbing his lips and drizzling a few drops at a time will give his body fluid and the healing properties of the licorice root. We should freeze some too. May I have use of your kitchen?"

"Of course. But I don't have licorice root. I wouldn't have known what to do with it before I met you."

"I will look through my things that Dr. Cooper had delivered. Hopefully, he had the good sense to send my supplies." Joseph turned from the room and started down the steps.

Bess followed. "Why is it that Dr. Cooper and the others at the hospital don't want to listen to the decades of experience you and those who taught you have? I've seen your treatments work."

Joseph shook his head and shrugged his shoulders. "There was a time the doctor did have faith in my people's ways. You remember that he sought me out to treat dear Louise."

Bess watched as Joseph rummaged through the cardboard boxes on her kitchen table. Martin had Joseph's life at the Cooper estate packed up and delivered to her doorstep that morning. "It was tuberculosis that took Martin's first wife, wasn't it?"

Joseph bowed his head and closed his eyes. A moment later, when he continued his search, she could see those same eyes were glossed with tears. "A cruel illness that slowly and painfully drained the life from a once vibrant flower and generous soul."

"I wish I had known her. To hear you and Martin talk, she was lovely."

"She would have thought the same of you, Mrs. Houdini. In fact, in some ways, you remind me of her." He stopped digging in the box, and a smile turned his lips. Pulling up a small jar, he showed it to Bess. "I used to make Louise licorice root tea. It gave her many more good days than she would have had with Dr. Cooper's treatments."

Bess reached out and brushed her hand against his shoulder. "Thank you for sharing these treatments with Erich."

He nodded once to her but then shuffled toward her stove. Taking a sauce pan from where it hung on the rack, he filled it with water. "We are all given a calling, Ma'am, a purpose in this life that will be a catalyst for lessons to the soul. Mine is to heal, when possible."

Bess watched as he put a few pieces of the dried root in the water and turned the flame on under the pan.

"You know so much about all of these treatments. Who taught you? You're father?"

Joseph chest heaved with a heavy sigh as he picked a wooden spoon from the drawer and gently stirred the water. "My calling was not his. When I was ten-years-old my mother left me with the healer in our tribe. I would stay with him for days and days and days, watching him caring for the weak and the ill in our tribe. I would spend weeks at a time with only him and his patients. Every now and again I would go spend a few days with my own parents, but from that moment in time that my healing gift was revealed to me, I became my mentor's son, not my father's."

Bess laid a hand in the middle of his back, "I'm sorry."

He tipped his head to her. "Why does that story make you sad? I answered my calling and am living my purpose. Had I not been trained by other healers, Dr. Cooper would not have chosen me to care for Louise. Without those events, I would not be here helping your friend. Each experience led to the other. Every one of them has left its mark on my soul and teachings in my heart."

"But what about your family? Didn't you miss them?"

"At times." Joseph paused, his eyes locked on the brewing tea. He circled the wooden spoon through the water tapping the edges of the pan. "But the bonds of family are not defined by blood. In our communities—the tribe—we are all of one. Each uses the gifts we are given to serve the whole. If more communities were like that, I think there would be less suffering in the world."

Bess reached up into the cupboard next to the stove, bringing down a glass pitcher. "You are a very wise man."

# Chapter Twelve

Bess knocked on the solid oak door and let her gaze follow the scent of snapdragons and aster floating from the manicured flowerbeds off the porch. She chuckled at the image of Gail caring for the plants. Gardening wasn't her style.

The Coopers had a gardener to tend to the landscape and a nanny to tend to the kids, emphasized by the lack of toys and bikes Bess would expect on the lawn of a house with three children. Bess surmised the kids were just another of Gail's possessions and nothing more.

Somehow, the cold and clinical atmosphere reminded Bess of what her life had become since losing Harry. It might have been just the two of them, but they were a family, and their home—no matter what house they resided in—overflowed with a love that they had no problem displaying to the world.

A deep breath steeled Bess's nerves. She should have called Martin two nights ago after he stormed out of the house, or at the very least phoned the next morning, but her mind wouldn't sway from Erich and his care. Only today, when his fever broke and the danger passed, did she dare to think of anything but him.

How shameful that an argument between two grown men had escalated to such a level. How infantile that Martin had all of Joseph's possessions dropped on her doorstep the following morning. That was men for you, though. Bruised egos caused them to act more like kids. Still, there was enough blame to go around. She'd hurt Martin's feelings by putting her faith in Joseph, and she wasn't above apologizing to the good doctor for that and making the first move to repair the damage to her friends' relationship.

"Bess? What are you doing here? How did you—" Martin looked over her shoulder, searching for a car, perhaps.

"I called a cab. I wanted to talk to you, smooth things over. May I come in?"

He stepped aside, giving her access. "By all means. How is that young man doing?"

Bess hadn't expected concern for Erich or a warm welcome, but she probably should have. Martin had always been a good friend despite his feud with Harry, and she was embarrassed that she let Joseph's complaints over the past two days of Martin's over inflated ego sway her perception. A pent-up breath escaped. "Much better."

"Good. I'm glad to hear it. Come, let's find Gail, and I'll have the cook make us a pot of tea."

She held him off with a wave of her hand. "First, I owe you an apology. I was rude the other night."

His chuckle lit up his eyes and filled the room. "No, my dear. I don't blame you for your decision. Given all you've been through, I even understand it. Joseph, however, is another matter."

"He only did as I asked. He wanted to help."

Moving back a step, Martin shifted his weight and narrowed his eyes. "This isn't a new fight for the two of us. If he's going to be a student of mine, proper medical care has to come first."

Joseph had told her the battle between native healing and modern medicine had been a long struggle between them. He'd even expressed relief that this chapter of his life had come to an end, and he seemed excited to be returning to the reservation now that Erich's ordeal was over. "He's a good man. Very selfless and interested in healing others."

"I do not argue that point. He's been in and out my door for ten years now—comes back, asks for training only to leave when we butt heads over a patient. He should have insisted that young man be moved to a hospital. He left me no choice but to end his fellowship. This time, it's for good."

"But he did so much for Louise!" Bess hadn't meant to scold. She knew Martin had fought the hospital board for the right to teach Joseph because of the care he'd given Louise, and he didn't need Bess recapping the clash or the pain.

"I will be forever grateful for the pain management he provided, but how much do I owe in return?" Martin's shoulders fell, reminding Bess of the connection between them. They'd both loved and lost.

"I'm sorry, Martin. I know what a difficult time that was for you."

He forced a smile, but it was an obvious mask. Despair could be seen in his flat eyes. "Through everything, Gail has been a rock. Having our lives together interrupted by those memories is painful for her. She doesn't deserve to live in Louise's shadow."

Was it really that simple to close the door to the past for a new lover? Both Martin and Gail had encouraged Bess to do the same thing: release Harry and begin to live again. Easy to say; impossible to do. "But it isn't fair to you for Gail to dismiss your past."

"She doesn't do that. But, how is it right for me to live for what was? Gail deserves my total devotion. She sees him as Louise's care giver and my loyalty to him as a commitment to someone who is gone. It's time to dissolve the arrangement with Joseph. I only wish that he would have taken advantage of the opportunity to take real medicine back to his people."

Bess wondered if it was the loss of his first wife, Gail's hurt feelings, or a disappointment in Joseph that caused the pain that edged Martin's eyes. She suspected all three played a part.

She realized that Erich's presence in her life had been a catalyst for Martin to lock the door to his past, and thought about what Joseph had said about how the events in his life were strung together with purpose. Was her connection to Erich more meaningful than the accident on the street that had brought them together?

"I didn't want to cause a problem. I only wanted to help Erich."

"I know you don't want to hear this, my dear, but if your hired hand is doing better, it's by luck alone. Now, please, can we just let it go? Gail's in the back garden, and I know she's been nervous you might hold all of this against her."

"I'd do no such thing."

****

Erich could hear voices whispering, like the sound of way-off locust singing at dusk, only it was black night. He couldn't move his body despite the torture. Certain words he made out: infection, abscess, danger, dying.

What a cruel twist of fate if Jaden took his life in this way, in this bed. Why give him a chance to save Bess, only to put her through the exact same pain? Even if she didn't connect him to Harry, and didn't adore Erich in the same way, it was obvious the similarities were affecting her. He waited for the beast to show its face and ridicule him for causing the woman he loved more pain.

Jaden didn't come. Sleep did.

He thought a mere moment passed before his eyes fluttered open, but the sun beating through the west window told him different. Hours had passed. At least a day, maybe more. He reached for his right side only to have his hand pulled away. Joseph stepped into his line of sight. "What are you trying to do?"

Finding his throat dry, he swallowed and then tried to joke. "Just checking to see if I'm still alive."

"It was touch and go, but you've turned a corner." Dropping Erich's hand back to the bed, Joseph lifted a china cup from the nightstand, offering it to Erich. "This is a licorice root tea. It will help with the infection."

He looked around the room, wanting Bess to confirm what the pseudo-doctor said. "Where's Bess?"

"She went into town to pick up some supplies and run some errands for me. She'll be back soon. In the meantime, you should drink this."

Erich scrunched his nose and cowered back from the bitter scent. "I thought you were trying to make me better. There's no way I can keep that down."

Even though Joseph couldn't have stood more than five foot five, he locked his stance and rested a hand on his hip, spreading his shoulders and filling as much space as he could. "If you don't keep up with the treatments, the infection will return."

The noxious fumes clenched his stomach. Erich tried, but failed, to suppress a cough. "No way had that helped."

"Mrs. Houdini has seen me work and has faith in the ways of my people. If she were here, she'd tell you to listen to me."

That much was true, but it didn't mean he trusted this stranger. Erich had allowed himself to follow Bess's lead and consumed the brandy, only to have lost consciousness. "How long have I been asleep?"

"You've been in and out for two days. At times I wasn't sure you'd pull through, but your fever broke last night, and we closed the wound this morning."

So matter-of-fact, but it was probably easy to talk about dying if it was someone other than yourself doing it. But two days? How had he let another forty-eight hours of sand slip through Jaden's magic hourglass? Bracing his hands against the mattress, he pushed himself into a sitting position. He swallowed the moans that gurgled from his gut. "I've never been the type to rest on my laurels and sleep to excess. There's too much living to be done and time is short."

"I suppose that's true for those who only have one life to live, but when a single soul stacks its many lives upon each other, well that's a different story. Isn't it?"

Erich's heart plummeted. No way that this guy saw through Erich's gifted body to Harry's soul. That second sight might be the foundation of one of Harry's schemes, but it didn't exist in reality. "Most learned medical types don't believe in reincarnation or souls."

Joseph gave a slight nod and pushed the fine china cup at Erich again. "And anyone who has felt Mother Earth's fingers dance against their spine knows that believing only in what you can see and study under a microscope is foolhardy."

The tea passed over his lips. Cold. If Bess brewed it before she left, then she'd been gone a while. Erich's existence might prove Joseph's prophecies, but the piece of him that was still Harry refused to publicly give credence to any part of spiritualism. Denying Harry, Erich could do, but he was here to get Bess to give up the séance. Agreeing with the medicine man about the notion of an everlasting soul might backfire when it came to that fight. "I don't believe in such nonsense."

"I find that interesting from a soul as old as yours." Erich cocked his head in question, and Joseph continued. "A body: flesh, bones and blood aren't what's alive. They only encase the spirit. A body dies and the spirit takes a reprieve, comprehends the lessons learned, and then finds a new body to contain it. Yours has walked this earth for many more years than your youthful flesh would indicate."

A shiver crawled Erich's spine, but not from the fever this time. Joseph wasn't the first person he'd ever encountered who believed in an afterlife or the concept of many lives. Heck, it was the foundation of the spiritualist movement and at the heart of the cons Harry and Bess had run. Harry might want to argue with Joseph but he spoke with a quiet certainty. Erich knew what the medicine man saw in him was true.

"If it can't be seen or studied how can you know its existence with such confidence?"

"I've been blessed with a gift. My eyes see beyond the flesh. Your soul is quite old and very conflicted."

Had everyone in the whole damn world started claiming they talked to the dead? Maybe Joseph was working with Martin, trying to manipulate Bess, but to what end? Erich decided to dig a little and see if he could unearth what Joseph was up to. "Let's pretend for a minute you're right. If spirits never die, then they'd all be really old."

"Some eventually retire to a higher plane, when they've learned all this life has to offer. Others are born new. The root tea will help your body fight the infection, but only if you drink it. The scars you carry deeper, however, I'm not sure how to heal those."

"I think I'll be just fine." Erich tried to sound upbeat and ignore the conflicts in his own heart and the lessons Jaden had subscribed. He forced another sip of tea. *For Bess.* She needed him here, if for no other reason than to protect her against Martin and his merry band of spiritualists.

"Perhaps. Your body needs more time in bed. Soon, though, you can tend to your soul."

He heard Bess's footsteps in the hall and excitement thrummed through him. His conversation with Joseph instantly forgotten, Erich craned his vision over his shoulder, wanting nothing more than to look into her eyes.

She bustled into the room, shifting the overflowing bags in her arms, but stopped suddenly and smiled at him. "Look at you, up and awake."

Her bright smile brought forth his own. He'd say it made the fight worth it, but the past two days were such a blur he barely remembered anything, let alone the battle. Just patches of her touch and concern through a wispy white fog. "I'm feeling much better."

"Thank Heavens Joseph knew what to do for you." She carried the bags to the dresser. "I think I found everything on your list. What I couldn't find in the market, Gail provided."

"I'm surprised she helped you," Joseph said.

Bess paused in front of Joseph and took his hand in hers. "I went to the Cooper's and had a long talk with Gail and Martin. I explained how I asked you to treat Erich and you were only doing as I requested. I tried, but Martin is unwilling to continue your fellowship."

"That was unnecessary, Mrs. Houdini. I told you I was at peace with my new path."

"You're a good man. You saved Erich's life, and you shouldn't be punished for that. You've already refused to let me pay you, so I had to try to set things right with Martin." Bess gave Erich her attention. "Do you remember meeting Martin and Gail in the deli earlier this week? They've been most helpful this past year."

Erich gritted his teeth. Even if he hadn't remembered, Harry's memories burned bright in his mind. "I think so. The blonde with all the sparkling jewelry and the tall, dark-haired man with shifty eyes."

Bess shook her head and stepped back. "Shifty eyes. Really? He's a good doctor and a trusted friend. It's because of him that I know Joseph. Without him, you'd most certainly not be sitting there now with the strength to complain. He saved you."

Her offense to his statement confounded Erich more. How and why had Martin become a god-send in her life? As for Joseph... "I'm grateful for the treatment, but as far as the hocus-pocus stuff goes—"

"It's a bit too late to be tossing it aside. I don't think you realize just how sick you were."

Erich balled the blankets in his fist. Even though he'd lived through it, the leap to believing in holistic medicine was just too much. A few hours ago, he might have been at death's door. Now? His muscles ached, his incision burned, but death's angel no longer loomed in front of him. Did that mean Joseph's treatments helped? Bess's touch had played a role. He was sure of that. As she'd washed him down and cradled his neck, he'd felt the tangible link between them. He stayed because she'd willed it so.

But did that notion devalue Harry's tie to her? Why hadn't Harry's will to be with Bess kept him grounded to this world? How had God, or Satan, or Jaden so easily pulled Harry's soul from her? Of course. Jaden! Erich remained because of their wager. It had nothing to do with Joseph's treatments. "I'm grateful to be feeling so much better, but I really don't think—"

"Mr. Welch has no faith," Joseph said as he gathered up several of the small glass jars Bess had unpacked. "I'll need to use your stove to make the dressing for his wound, and then I'll be returning to the reservation. Make sure he drinks the root tea, even though he doesn't think that is helping either."

Bess's eyes opened wider, and her mouth dropped. "You don't need to leave. You can stay a few more days."

"There is no reason to. All he needs now is rest, the tea several times a day, and for you to change his dressing twice a day. I've already taught you how to make the tea and change his dressing."

"What if the fever returns?"

"I will check on him often, but it's time for me to go home." With that simple declaration, Joseph nodded and left the room, giving neither Bess nor Erich room to argue.

Alone, Bess asked, "Is it true?"

"That I don't believe in voo-doo or witchcraft?"

A scowl tightened her face. "That isn't what Joseph does. He practices a form of medicine that has been handed down for generations. One you should be damn grateful for."

"You're right," Erich sighed. "I'm doing better, but that isn't necessarily because of him." Accepting the worth of the medicine man's treatments proved impossible. He was convinced he'd still be here for the full thirty days even if he went out and jumped off the roof of the house.

She busied herself, smoothing the blanket and trying to arrange his pillows. Wheels turned, and her anger fumed. He could see that she wanted to call him out, debate it all further, and he welcomed the challenge. What words they spoke didn't matter, as long as she stayed by his side and acknowledged him. "Drink your tea and rest."

"I don't know what that is, but it isn't tea. It tastes horrible."

"I don't care how it tastes. You'll drink it anyway. You may not believe in the treatments that are making you well, but I'd give anything to go back in time and have Joseph treat my Harry. Maybe he'd still be here."

Erich grabbed her wrist, drawing her eyes back to him. "You don't believe that." Her bitterness and anger had stirred something in him. At first, her deep mourning seemed like a tribute to Harry and to what they shared, but now Erich realized clinging to Harry held Bess stagnate.

"Yes, I do."

"You can't change what happened to him, and wondering if things had been different is a foolish waste of time." He hated being so harsh, but couldn't help himself. She had to see that one simple fact if he had any hopes of getting her to let go. "And planning this silly séance isn't any better. Dead men can't speak."

"What do you know about the séance?"

Damn his loose lips for spilling something he'd learned from Jaden. But then... "Just what I heard you telling Gail and Martin in the deli the other day. Foolish nonsense if you ask me."

She pulled back and stumbled when he released his grip on her wrist. "You never knew Harry. He never once, in the whole time I knew him, lied to me. If he said he'll come back to me, he will."

"Death is not an illusion!"

Straightening her frame, Bess wagged a pointed finger at him. "Unlike you, I need something to believe in." What little vulnerability she'd allowed herself was replaced with the acidic sternness. "Keep the tea down, and I'll bring you some broth." She stormed from the room in a huff.

Exasperated and more than a little tired, he leaned against the headboard. He had to make her see there was no value in clinging to her past. The moment his eyes closed, his body lurched. His back arched as Harry's soul was ripped from his body. Pulled higher and higher, he tried to get one last glimpse of the world. A white light blinded his sight until he found himself once again in the padded room sitting across from Jaden, who wore white, linen pants and a flowing white shirt.

He pushed his hair off his face as he looked up. The black strands were a dramatic contrast to the surroundings, and those soul-less eyes pierced through him. "Things not going well, Erich?"

"Why do you ask such stupid questions?" Jaden and his sardonic sense of humor was the last thing he wanted to deal with at the moment.

"Do you believe that Bess is in danger now?"

More idiocy! He threw his hands in the air and gave a curt nod. Denying it was pointless. He just wished he had an idea as to how to fix it. "She's lost and the Coopers are taking advantage of her sorrow. They're guiding her down a road paved with gold, but leading to Hell."

"Do you think yelling at her is going to sway her resolve? These are the very people who were there when Harry wasn't."

He jumped to his feet. Proof he'd left his gifted but broken body behind, this spiritual mass reacted as if he were in perfect health. No pain. If this room had a door, he'd have left. Instead, he was trapped with Jaden—the man whose simple truths cut like the sharpest razor blade—and ensnared in a tangled web of his own weaving. But the real world wasn't black and white; shades of gray blurred the lines of truth and happenstance. "You act like I deserted her! I didn't choose to die!"

"Like you didn't choose to overexert Erich's body, knowing full well it carried Harry's scars?"

Erich leaned back against the wall. His head ached as he pushed down the pain and regret bubbling in his throat. "I was taught hard work and supporting your family were virtues not sins. The burden of caring for Bess weighed more than you'll know."

"What would soothe her more at this moment, a simple home and a meager meal with Harry or to continue wandering around that big, lonely house without him?"

Erich cringed against the truth. Of course she'd choose for Harry to still be alive. "I thought you wanted me to change the future, not the past."

"Many think of time as a line, but it is circular. Every event feeds or changes the one to follow. You need to find the right stones to step on if you want her to find peace, otherwise the torment and grief will only grow."

"I'm stumbling around in the dark here. I try to reach out to her and all I do is upset her. I guess if you keep showing up to coach me, it means I'm making things worse."

A wide smile curled Jaden's lips. "So, do you finally accept that I'm here to help and not work against you?"

"I accept that you're using me to help Bess. She's the one that deserves mercy and peace. I'm nothing more to you than a tool."

The last thing Erich saw before his vision began to dissolve to white was Jaden's lips turning up in a sly smile.

# Chapter Thirteen

Erich's return trip to his body was like shoving a size twelve foot into a size ten shoe. He struggled and twisted against the pain crushing in from all sides. Then something snapped and the two pieces—body and soul—fit as one. His eyes fluttered open, and once again he stared at the light green wallpaper of the guest room.

So many selfish choices. Why did Jaden keep giving him more chances?

The reason behind his generosity didn't matter. Not really. Erich accepted it and vowed once again to find the right path.

An overwhelming loneliness for Bess wrenched his gut. He needed to be with her; convince her to stop chasing ghosts and begin living for herself. Pushing the covers back, he used slow, purposeful movements to twist in the bed. With both feet on the floor, he cradled his side and took control of his body, choosing exactly which muscles to use to bring him to his feet. At least something good came from Harry's memories and life experience.

Gripping the bedpost, he measured the distance between himself and the door with his mind's eye. Three solid steps would put him there. A sharp inhale expanded his lungs, putting pressure on the just-bound incision and ramping up the pain. The simple act of moving his left foot forward and shifting his weight felt the same as climbing a mountain. He pushed the pain away using the same controlled breathing that Harry used in his underwater illusions and found enough strength to slide his right foot up to meet the other.

*At this pace it'll take me three hours to get to her.*

A ping in his chest told him she was close. He glanced up. Bess—with her hands on her hips and her chin raised—blocked the doorway. She scowled at him. "You fool! What are you doing?"

"You have been pushing a lot of water and root tea at me for the last two days. What goes in..."

She set a bowl of broth on the nightstand and hurried to his side, putting her arm around his waist and guiding his around her shoulder. "The bedpan is under—"

"I think I have the strength to walk down the hall and back." The little white lie didn't matter if he convinced her he was regaining his strength. He resisted the urge to pull her in and lay his head atop of hers and denied the need to inhale her scent. He'd be thankful for small favors, revel in her touch and make the most of this moment. Besides, if recent history proved to be any indication, she'd bolt as soon as his need for her support evaporated.

No matter how he tried to remain upright, his knees gave way. His strength diminished with each step, taking with it his ego. He always thought of himself as her protector, but now Bess took him under her wing as if she were a mother bird and he her wounded chick. Nothing like the relationship he was shooting for.

She accepted and supported him. As they walked, her feather-light touch caressed Erich's hip in a way that went deeper than skin to skin. Loving and sensual. Maybe Bess didn't consider herself his caregiver. Maybe those lines had blurred for her too.

He should act on it. Do something. Say something. But what? Every time he tried to advance their relationship, it ended in a backward slide.

"I'm sorry," he said. "You invited me here to help you, not be a burden." So close to the truth. His mandate—to save her from herself—had gotten tangled up in all of Harry's mistakes, including his damn burst appendix.

"Don't be sorry, just listen to Joseph and get well." Bess stopped in front of the bathroom, and Erich took a single step alone. He gripped the jamb, lifting from her and bracing the wall for support. The mere inches that separated them seemed like miles; he wrestled with the urge to reach for her again. "I promise, Bess. I'll do what he says."

"I'll wait for you in my bedroom. Just call out when you're finished." She skirted around him, ignoring his attempt to reach for her, and disappeared. The emptiness in her eyes and the tremble to her voice told him she fought her own battle. Did she long for him or was she drowning in a pool of Harry's memories?

No matter how weak his body was, Erich needed to figure out her conflict, find his opening with her and use it. He needed steel resolve to soothe her pain and make her listen to reason. Putting her back on the right life path came first. Once he accomplished that, he could concern himself with finding his way to her side.

A few moments later, he scuffled back into the hall using the door frame to keep himself upright. He wanted to make the walk back to his bed, prove he was strong and able, but the small amount of exertion had left him exhausted. He took a deep breath, ready to call out for Bess, but stopped at the sound of her weeping.

He leaned against the wall and pushed forward until he could see into the room. Tears streaked Bess's cheeks as she looked out the window. In her arms, she clenched his long black stage jacket. Despite her pain, the sight gave him some hope. She *hadn't* removed every trace of him from the house.

Inhaling deeply, she slid the coat against her face. "I miss you, baby."

His instincts told him to go to her, take her tears away and tell her he'd kept his promise to escape death, but knew if he dared to try, he might as well dig his own grave. There was only so much Jaden would forgive before declaring himself the winner of the bet and sending Harry straight to his version of Hell.

Still, he couldn't stand there, watch her cry and do nothing. "Are you all right, Bess?"

Her body jerked at the sound of his voice. She tossed the coat to the bed and pushed the tears from her face with the back of her hand as she walked toward him. "It's been a long couple of days. I'm worn out."

"It's more than that. Something I said or did upset you." He wanted nothing more than to stand tall and be a rock for her. No matter how he fought it, his knees went weak. He couldn't keep himself from leaning on her but she welcomed him. Her arm tightened around his waist.

"Quite the opposite, but never you mind. Save your strength for yourself."

Why was she like this? Every single inch she gave, every glimpse at the soft, tender woman Harry married, became guarded by the stone wall she cowered behind. "Don't hide yourself from me."

"Mr. Welch, it's inappropriate for me to share my personal thoughts with you."

*If she only knew the truth.* "Maybe that was true a few days ago, but you saved my life. You've helped me and now I want to help you."

He watched as the hard façade began to crack again, but she firmed up the flood gates by setting her jaw. "I'll accept your gratitude, but nothing more. Let me get you back to bed."

The accuracy of her words pricked at his chest. He detested feeling weak next to her, loathed that she had to care for him. "I'm sorry to be so much trouble."

"Don't be silly. I like having something to keep my mind and hands busy."

"Lest they become the devil's playthings?" Jaden's words slipped from Erich's mouth. As soon as they hit his ear, he wished he could recall them and cursed the being for putting such a slanderous phrase in his mouth. That was, until he saw her lips curve upward.

"I'd forgotten that adage. My mother used to say it all the time. Busy hands can't get into trouble."

"You have a beautiful smile, Bess. You should use it more often." Part of him expected her to scold him, but he couldn't help saying it. To his heart, there was nothing more stunning.

"Thank you." A blush tinted her cheeks, highlighting the china-paleness of her flesh and the innocence in her heart. Harry's compliments were always met with the same modesty. In his mind, Bess would forever be the prettiest flower in the garden, even if she didn't see herself the same way.

"You're welcome." And there they stayed for the briefest moment. Content. Civil. Meeting her stare, he found the one thing he believed in. The connection that bound them was strong as a steel chain and could never be broken. Trusting they were forever destined on a level neither of them understood, he followed his heart and a hunch.

He twisted his body so they were face to face. He slid his left arm around her waist and wrapped his other around her neck, capturing her mouth with his own. Fulfilling the desire that'd been burning deep within from the moment he'd laid eyes on her again. None of Jaden's manipulations could alter the simple fact he and Bess were soul mates. With the touch of Erich's lips, she'd recognize Harry's spirit. Of this much, he was sure.

He slid his tongue against her mouth, savoring the taste of her, knowing in an instant she was still the love of his heart, his life. Her body softened in his embrace, and she accepted this kiss—the connection that wouldn't be denied. His fingers tangled in her hair as he tried to pull her closer.

Something inside Bess shifted. Her body stiffened, and her hands pressed against his shoulders. The very second he realized she resisted, he released her. She stumbled back two steps, taking with her his heart, now shattered by the realization that every last assumption about bound souls might be a fairytale.

Throwing her arms in the air, her mouth hung agape. Her eyes, huge with surprise, bore through him. "How dare you!"

"But Bess..." Once again, he'd painted himself into a corner. Add another inappropriate misstep to the growing list.

"Why would you even think that was permissible?" Her locked posture and anger tormented his heart. How could Bess not see? Not feel? He struggled for the right words, but like picking the lock in the shed, no excuse would satisfy. "You've been so kind to me."

"I don't know how you were raised, but that is not how you thank a married woman for an act of kindness."

"You're a widow, not married."

"My heart will always belong to my husband. You'd do good to remember that. If you weren't bedridden, you'd find yourself on the street."

As long as she clung to Harry as if he were only away for the time being, Erich would never find his way inside her heart. Backing down might have soothed her. He could—and probably should—surrender the control over the situation that she desired, but he was oh-so-tired of suppressing Harry to appease Bess. The gnawing in his stomach, his need to be the man he'd always been stood tall. "Don't let that stop you. If you want me out, it'll only take a moment to gather my things. God knows I don't have much."

He stepped back from her. Pressing his hand against the wall, he tried to pivot away from her, but she grabbed his shoulders and held him firm. "Stop it! So help me if you rip a single stitch—"

"You'll what? Put me over your knee? I'm not the child you seem to think I am. I'm a grown man and can care for myself." *What am I doing? Saying?* He'd been dim-witted pulling her into that kiss. Instead of apologizing, he defended his actions like a fool.

"Hmpfh. Care for yourself? You can't even walk the length of this hall." Through her stern voice, he could see real concern clouded her eyes.

He needed to figure out a way to get over himself in order to help her. "You've been wonderful to me. Maybe the kiss was out of line, but I just want you so bad, and I thought for sure you wanted–"

"Impetuous! How in the world do I get myself tangled up with men like you? You'd leap into a snake pit without thinking."

"Especially if it were to save you."

His words pushed Bess back on her heels, the confession stunning her. "Before you go off saving damsels in distress—which I'm not by the way—why don't we get you to the point you can keep solid food down." She wrapped an arm around his waist and guided him down the hall. "Let's get you back to bed."

"Don't do this, Bess. Don't ignore what's going on between us."

"The only thing going on is that I'm helping you recover. The least I can do since you got sick while working for me."

Her words might have had more credence if they didn't quiver or if she'd looked him in the eye. He could push harder, try to crack the mask she protected her heart with, but at what cost? Let her deny the kiss meant something; he knew the truth. Leaving her to stew with it for the night would wear her down more than pressure from him.

After helping Erich into the bed, Bess dropped her gaze to the blankets. "Regardless of what you think, I don't need you to save me."

"Yes, you do."

Her body stilled. Erich knew Bess wasn't the knight on a white horse type and doubted that she expected him to answer her, but he couldn't go wrong with the truth—or at least a close variation of it.

Without a word, she left the room. Did he expect that with his declaration, she'd fall to her knees and beg him to rescue her from the quicksand she sank in?

In a way, he had.

****

Back in her own room, Bess let the door slam behind her.

*How dare he? How could he? Why would he?*

Exasperated, she dropped to the bed and picked up Harry's old stage coat. She held it close to her chest and tried to imagine his body in it. "Oh Harry!" The words escaped her trembling lips as tears streaked her cheeks. "I'm so sorry."

How could she betray the love of her life with Erich Welch? The attraction grew from the glimpses of Harry she saw flicker in his eyes. Nothing else made sense. The feelings were not real and oh-so-wrong, for the age difference alone. So, why did her body ache for him?

And his kiss.

When their lips touched, something immense opened up inside. An emptiness that only he could fill. And how she wanted him to kiss her deeper, pull her tighter, and erase the months of pain and tears. In the same way that her desire grew, guilt crept in. After everything Harry had been to her, how could she find pleasure with another?

Standing, she put her arms through the sleeves of the jacket, not caring about how loosely it hung. It comforted her, as if she was wrapped in his embrace. Only God knew what she'd do the day it stopped smelling like him. Wiping tears from her cheeks, she left the room and ambled toward the kitchen.

If Harry would just speak to her alone, going on would be easier. She needed him to do this one thing just for her. And he would, if she just believed enough in him. In the kitchen, she poured a small glass of brandy from Gail's silver flask and took a small sip.

She hoped the bitter fluid would erase the sweet taste of Erich that still lingered. Closing her eyes, she could feel his soft lips and his strong arms. Shaking off the traitorous hunger, she downed the remaining contents of the glass and refilled it.

*This won't work unless you have only Harry in your heart and mind.*

Sitting at the table, she looked at the Ouija board for a moment. She then lit each of the six candles surrounding the board and focused on her heart, pushing aside every other emotion except for the love that tied her to Harry.

Resting her hands on her lap, she focused on the small ivory triangle. Dare she hope Harry could move it without her touch? "Speak to me, Harry. Come back to me."

Staring hard at the piece, she willed it to move until tears clouded her vision.

*Why can't I do this? Is my faith too shallow?*

She laid two fingers of each hand on separate sides of the triangle, keeping her touch light, like Gail had shown her. Closing her eyes and digging deeper, she said, "I believe in you, Harry. I know you can do it. Tell me in our way that you believe too."

*Move, damn it!*

"Talk to me, Harry," she pleaded. No matter how she tried to swallow them, the tears bubbled to the surface and slid down her cheeks. Her voice cracked, but the small piece of ivory lay dead under her touch.

Dead...like Harry.

"Please...Harry...talk to me!" The tears streamed now, and her lips trembled. Yet again, nothing happened. She picked up the ivory and threw it across the room. It hit one of the cabinets and bounced back. If she hadn't darted to the side, it would have smacked her in the middle of the forehead.

Not knowing what else to do, she slapped her hand against the brandy glass, sending it off the edge of the table and enjoying the satisfying crash as it hit the floor. Broken: like her life. Shattered: like her heart.

She stared at the mess, before standing to clean it up. A wave of dizziness crashed over her, tipping her off balance, so she stumbled back up the steps instead. Collapsing on her bed, she wrapped Harry's coat tighter. The room spun, and her stomach heaved.

Guilt over Erich's kiss is what made her so dizzy. So why was it his touch and his kiss that she longed for as consciousness slipped away?

# Chapter Fourteen

The scent of baking bread permeated Bess's sleep. Sunlight streaked through the window, warming her face. The pounding in her head increased. She could almost hear Harry saying the hangover was a just punishment for drinking alcohol. Almost. That voice that had whispered in her ear since Harry's death had been garishly silent since Erich had taken up residence.

Bess got out of bed and shook the cobwebs away, refusing to feel guilty for sleeping in. She'd earned a lazy morning after caring for Erich around-the-clock for two days.

*Erich.*

He'd been alone for hours. What if the fever had returned? What if he'd needed her and she'd not been there? Bess hurried down the hall only to find his room empty and the bed made. She retraced her steps and headed toward the staircase. The warm aroma hit her again.

Was Erich fixing her breakfast? Surely he hadn't gone from lying at death's door to cooking in mere days.

Entering the kitchen, she found him opening the oven and peering in at his work. The muscles in his arms flexed and tightened as he closed the door and stood. The thin, white tank top veiled his chest, failing to hide the ripples of his abdomen. Those arms had felt so good around her, and the lips that now smiled proudly had tasted as sweet as the honey he'd been using to baste the bread.

She bristled at the memories. Erich was not the one she should be focusing on. "What are you doing out of bed? You're going to undo all the progress you've made."

Erich took a step back and lowered himself to one of the stainless steel chairs. "I know I upset you last night."

"You'll get no arguments from me."

"I wanted to make it up to you by fixing breakfast."

She poured two cups of coffee, set one down in front of Erich and joined him at the table. "I appreciate you going to all the trouble, but I don't want you to exert yourself too soon."

"I'm feeling much better today. It only took me twenty minutes to make it down the steps."

They were having a civil conversation and ignoring the big, white elephant in the room—the kiss they'd shared. Did it burn in Erich's memory too? If so, he didn't show it.

He picked up the decanter from the center of the table and poured just a touch of cream into his coffee and then followed it with two heaping teaspoons of sugar. The spoon hitting the sides of her china sparked yet another memory of Harry.

Coincidence. It had to be. Countless men must take their coffee that way and grip their spoon in the same manner Harry did. It wasn't like he was a carbon copy. For each and every similarity between Harry and Erich there were two differences.

She lifted her cup and sipped as if it would drown the smoldering flames of lust. Two days ago Heaven had sent an angel to take him home. Did the fact that she felt such strong feelings for a man who needed her care more than her passion make her a harlot?

Taking the napkin from her lap and placing on the table, she turned from him and her thoughts and toward the stove. She opened the oven and pulled out the loaf of golden-brown bread. "It smells and looks wonderful. You surprise me."

A rich laugh erupted from him. "It's not a gourmet meal."

As she rejoined him at the table, she noticed he was cradling the area of his stomach with the incision. She reached out and grabbed a hold of the cotton tank top, trying to lift it from his body.

His hand closed around her wrist, holding it firm. "What are you doing?"

"I need to check—"

He leaned in so close she could feel the heat of his breath brush her cheek. "Don't get me wrong, Bess. I appreciate everything you've done, but if we're to avoid situations like last night, maybe I should do it myself."

His gruff tone and rough cadence touched her very core, making her stomach quiver like gelatin. Easing away, she set her hands in her lap. Maybe if she clasped them together, she could resist the urge to rub them against his unshaven cheek. She wanted to argue, insist she could remain detached, but he'd know it was a lie.

They both knew she'd experienced all the passion that he'd left unspoken in that single kiss. His feelings were as intense as the ones gnawing at her, and he was right. Physical closeness would only fuel the fire. "The bread should be cool enough to slice. Would you like some lox?"

"Please."

The clanking of the spoon resumed. She busied herself slicing the bread, spreading a bit of Brie and topping it off with the lox, afraid if she turned back to him, she'd submit to the passion.

"I don't mean to sound ungrateful or cold, Bess. I just don't want to overstep any boundaries or act inappropriately. I regret that I upset you."

*Regret.* Somehow that word didn't accurately reflect her feelings. His arms around her shoulders and neck, his fingers in her hair and his tongue dancing against her lips and the roof of her mouth—she'd apologize for none of it. It warmed the cool chill that had consumed her since Harry's death and awoke a hunger in her heart. No, she didn't lament Erich's kiss.

But then there were the vows she'd made to Harry? She'd promised to keep his legacy alive and the first step was this fast approaching séance.

Digging for the strength to face Erich again, she pivoted and found him staring at the Ouija board. Having heard his feelings on the subject already, she expected anger from him. Instead, she saw despair. Or was that disappointment? And why did it matter? She wasn't beholden to him. His opinion should be meaningless, but for some reason it wasn't. It bothered her that he disapproved.

And the broken glass? The memory of sending it to its doom invaded her mind, but there were no traces on the floor. Erich had cleaned it up, but said nothing.

He tapped his fingers against the table and asked, "Aren't you warm in that heavy wool coat?"

She placed the plates on the table and then wrapped her arms around her shoulders, letting the rough fabric scratch at her palms as she took her chair. The oven always made the kitchen unbearably hot, but taking the coat off hadn't even crossed her mind. "I didn't put it on because I was cold. It's Harry's. I feel close to him when I wear it." Her cheeks flushed, and she tried to swallow the blush. But her embarrassment wasn't from wanting to keep her husband close.

Erich picked up the ivory triangle off the Ouija board and slid his thumb over it. "What if there is nothing after death. For how long are you committed to trying to communicate with Harry?"

Good question. Would her need for one more word from him ever wane? "For as long as I believe there's a chance."

"If you just put him to rest, you could have so many good years ahead of you."

"What? With you?"

He shrugged. "Would that be so awful? You deserve a future and some peace of mind."

*Have I ever felt that?* Bess couldn't remember a time of contentment. Even in Harry's company. They lived on the edge, pushed the limits. Wouldn't tranquility be nice for a change? "There will be time for that." The soft words passed her lips, and didn't sound genuine even to her own ears. Why should they? The words weren't hers, they were Harry's knee-jerk response every time she pleaded to leave the road and build a family.

"I'd think if you learned anything from your husband's passing it would be that tomorrow is the one thing you can't count on being there."

"Harry asked for only one thing, and I owe him my best efforts."

"The séance?"

She darted her eyes away from him and the table. He thought she was a fool for clinging to Harry. While other's opinions meant little to her, she wanted Erich to approve of her actions and that frustrated her. "It's going to be a huge event, and I'm so unprepared."

"And that's mostly because of me." Erich pushed his nearly empty plate aside, tapped the triangle on the table a few times. Setting it back on the board, he continued, "I wanted to do something nice for you, fix you a meal. Instead, you served me again. I'm sorry."

Her lower lip curled between her teeth. Just when she thought she had Erich all figured out, he did something to confound her. "That's it? You're going to just drop it?"

"Will anything I say change your mind?"

She shook her head, picked up the plates from the table and took them to the sink. What possessed such a young, handsome man to take her in his arms the way he had last night? And worse, why was she more titillated than offended? "Let me clean up the dishes, and then I'll change your bandage. Joseph said he would stop by today to check up on you."

The chair legs scraped against the floor and she looked to Erich. His hands were braced against the table as he tried to lift himself. "I already told you. I'll tend to myself."

"I don't mind, Erich, and I don't blame you for anything."

A knowing smile turned his lips. "I believe you mean that, Bess, but I still think it's best if I do it myself."

At his side, she put a hand on the small of his back and took his elbow with the other. "You're still weak and I promised to care—"

Their eyes met. As he spoke, she couldn't help but watch his mouth move, the same one that had caressed hers. "You're a very kind and gracious woman, and I took advantage of that. It's unfair of me to ask you to continue."

She should release him from his guilt. Tell him that she enjoyed his kiss and wanted another. Instead, she'd let him care for his wound, grateful to not have the temptation of his flesh. "Can you make it into the parlor on your own? The couch is old, but it's comfortable."

"If we raced, you'd beat me hands down, but I think I can make it." He picked up his coffee cup from the table. "Would it be all right—"

"Of course." She let go of him, but stood close, making sure he was stable, and then grabbed the pot from the stove to refill his cup. She asked, "Would it be easier if I carried it for you?"

"I think I can make it."

She grabbed his elbow and took a step closer, wanting him to feel that she wasn't angry about his kiss, even if she couldn't find the words to express it. "It's not your fault that I've been ignoring my obligations to Harry and this séance. I want to continue to help you get better."

He locked his eyes on where her hand touched his and after a few long seconds, he let his fingers graze her hand. "I'm grateful for that, Bess, but I am getting better and it's important that I rebuild my strength so I can get back to my job and my obligations to you."

Though he moved slowly, with one hand on his stomach, he walked from the room. He didn't shuffle his feet or drag them against the floor. Did that mean he was really doing better or that he was trying too hard to prove to her he was? She went back to the sink and filled it with soapy water to clear away the dishes. How simple it would be if she could wash away her desires for Erich as easily as she would the crumbs.

****

Reclining against the back of the sofa, he pulled the tails of the cotton tank out of his pants and slid it up his body. Lifting the gauze, he peered at the closed-tight incision. It looked neat and clean compared to just a few days ago, and a sigh of relief eased the burden he'd been carrying. He was getting better, but did that really matter? If he didn't accomplish his task, this body would still end up committed to the ground.

He wouldn't give up, but Bess was resolute in her obligation to Harry and unwavering in her adoration. Competing with the memories seemed impossible. Still, there had to be something he could say or do.

Then, there was Martin, Gail and Joseph. They were using her need to contact Harry to form a bond and make a place for themselves in her life, and it wouldn't stop with one séance. He was certain their negative influence and greed precipitated the gnarly road she stumbled down and Jaden foretold. But how to discredit the Coopers and the healer?

Through the door between the living room and kitchen, he could see her descending the steps, dressed for the day. The stage coat gone, he wondered if she'd tucked it back in the chest, hidden it—and Harry—from the outward world once again.

She swerved into the kitchen and reappeared less than a minute later carrying a tray. Setting it on the coffee table in front of him, she said, "Everything you need to clean and bandage your incision is right here. Are you sure you don't want me to help you?"

He gripped the arm of the couch and attempted to pull himself to his feet. "Give me a moment to do this and then I'll go with you. I'm going stir-crazy here."

Her tongue clicked against her mouth twice as she shook her head. "I need to get to town and back this *morning*. Stay here and rest and we can eat dinner out in the yard this afternoon."

Standing toe to toe with her wasn't endearing him and if he was going to get through to her, he needed to stop waging war and start mending fences. "Certainly, Bess."

Her hand went straight to his forehead and a frown shaded her recent warm glow. "Compliance is not your usual mode. You don't feel feverish?"

"It's a new leaf." Erich smirked and raised his eyebrow at her, even though her brief touch was enough to make his body scream for more.

She went back to fussing with her handbag; accepting him at his word, perhaps? "Can I get you anything before I go?"

"No, thank you. I'm fine."

The sound of the back door closing echoed throughout the house. He was alone. He let his hand graze the arm of the sofa and his eyes scan the room. He remembered the first time they walked through the house. So much larger than any other place they lived before, Bess called it a castle. The moment she uttered those words, he knew his queen deserved nothing less.

Those feelings of awe and wonder faded and with Bess's care, the mausoleum had become a home—their home—warm and cozy. But like everything else in her life since Harry's passing, the house had been neglected. And she had gone from being its ruling lady to a grieving captor.

He still had three weeks to affect a change, and he'd also use that time to restore a bit of glory to the house. Another day of rest and he should be good as new.

Careful of how he moved and reached, he washed the incision with peroxide and applied more of the medicine man's magic paste. Despite the fact Jaden gave Joseph's remedies a stamp of approval, Erich still questioned their effectiveness and the shaman's motives. As he re-taped a clean bandage over the incision, there was a knock on the kitchen door. He was tempted to ignore it and save his strength for the picnic Bess promised, but curiosity got the best of him. "I'm coming as fast as I can!" Crossing the threshold to the utility room, he got a first look at their visitor and felt his eyebrows draw together.

*Martin.*

Erich couldn't hide Harry's anger or contempt for the doctor as he pushed open the old wooden door. "What are you doing here?"

"I've come to see Bess." Martin's answer was simple like he didn't owe Erich an explanation. Arrogance. Erich expected no less.

"She's not here."

"But you still are." Martin walked past Erich and laid his long, wool coat over the back of the chair.

"Bess has been a real angel of mercy, helping me when I was sick." Not that it was any of his business.

"I expected to see her in town today. Will said she hadn't been around for a few days. Gail and I became worried."

Why was he worried? If she was in danger, it was from the malarkey they were feeding her—that and the home made brandy she drank and the cigarettes she smoked. But then, his concern was probably a lie too. "Bess told me she called on you yesterday."

Martin leveled his gaze on Erich. "And she wasn't acting like herself."

With Harry's memories, Erich could read Martin's body language and now knew that Martin was on a fishing expedition. He was trying to find out just what Erich knew and how important he was to Bess. "There isn't any reason for you to worry. I'm here to protect her."

Shaking his head and chuckling low, Martin didn't even try to hide his amusement. "Doesn't look like you'd be able to defend her from an intruder right now."

"But I can defend her from the likes of you and that woman you call a wife."

Any fun Martin was having vanished with the insult. "I don't think Bess would appreciate you saying disparaging things to her friends."

"Harry wouldn't want you anywhere near Bess or his home." Erich had no problem declaring that fact.

Martin tipped his head, acknowledging the truth. "But Harry isn't here to think anything at all. If he were,

I'm not sure he'd want you here either. He had a way of scenting out a con."

Laughing wasn't the smartest thing Erich had done, but he couldn't help it. The irony of Martin's words and the nerve he possessed to say such a thing was just too absurd. "Bess asked me to stay and help her care for the house. I think that includes keeping out the vermin."

"Bess isn't in her right frame of mind, and a man who would take advantage of her fragile state isn't much of a man at all."

Wasn't that just Martin's way? Spin the spotlight onto others to avoid being found out. "I couldn't agree more. That's why I'll have to ask you to leave and never come back."

"I might be offended if I believed you had any authority here. This is Bess's home, and my wife and I are quite welcome here. No matter how it would offend Harry or you." There was confidence and an ease to the way Martin spoke, and it burned a hole in Erich's gut to know that there was a truth to what Martin said. Somewhere along the line, he'd earned Bess's allegiance—and once acquired, she rarely wavered from it.

Erich had to wonder if he'd ever be successful in gaining that trust and loyalty for himself.

"I may not have a say in whether you stay or go, but I do know that my heart is pure and my intentions in her life are good. Bess has no business chasing ghosts and pursuing the occult. No real friend would be encouraging her to do so."

"It wasn't my idea for her to call out Harry's spirit. He came up with that scheme all on his own. It pains me to say it's quite brilliant. Not many men focus on their reputation after they've expired." Martin paused, but a hearty laugh shook his body. "Only Harry. Only Harry."

Erich's gut tightened. He'd planned every aspect of the scheme, looking to secure a future and preserve his legacy, and the idea of Martin using that for his personal gain enraged him. "Don't presume to know Harry's mind."

"Like you?"

"I know more than you think."

"You breeze into her life and home out of nowhere and think that gives you the right to run her affairs."

"My place in this house and Bess's life is up to her alone. For as long as I'm here, I'll be doing everything I can to keep the likes of you away."

Martin took a firm step toward him. A dark light burned in his eyes. "Listen here, little boy, I don't have time for this. Don't think for one minute I'm going to let you waltz in here in the final stretch and ruin what I've worked eleven long months to build. Continue to try and discredit me and my wife with Bess and you'll wish you'd never laid eyes on me."

Martin thinly skated around the edges of admitting he'd been plotting against Bess. He hadn't quite said that every interaction with her had been part of a massive scheme, but he'd come close enough to saying that to worry Erich.

What could Martin or Gail possibly gain from the séance? They would never succeed in reciting Harry's message on their own, and he knew Bess would never just give them the message. Even if it were possible for him or Gail to successfully communicate with the dead, which it wasn't, Harry's soul was locked in Erich's body and would remain silent rather than give either scoundrel one ray of the center stage spotlight.

So what was his angle? "What are you hoping to get out of this?"

Martin picked up his coat from the back of the chair, draping it over his arm. "Hopes and dreams are child's play. I planted seeds and tended them well. Now, I just have to wait for them to blossom. Please, tell Bess I checked in on her."

Only after the wood door slammed and Martin was out of sight, did Erich let himself grip the back of the chair and feel the pain still radiating in his side. The length of time he'd been up on his feet was enough strain on his weak body, but Martin's attitude and air of entitlement in Bess's life had frustrated him beyond words. *Did that snake really just threaten my life?*

Erich remembered how Martin strayed from his first wife while she lay on her deathbed. Then, at Gail's request, he cut ties with his children by Louise. So yes, Martin would follow through on his threat without a second thought.

However, just because he now knew Martin and Gail were working a malicious plot didn't give him the ammunition to unravel it. Above all, one truth remained. Saving Bess would be an impossible task if he found himself back in a grave.

****

Bess handed the store clerk the dollar bill and flipped her attention over her shoulder when she heard her name called by a familiar voice.

Gail bustled up the small aisle and came to her side. "What a happy accident to run into you today."

Bess took the change from the clerk and placed the few items into her canvas tote bag, before turning and greeting the woman with a quick hug. "An accident? It seems I'm in town nearly every day as of late."

"Caring for that young man has kept you busy, but you know, the day of the séance is getting closer and we really need to carve out some time to rehearse and to hone our skills."

But how to do such a task with Erich in the house? He'd made it more than clear that he didn't believe in communicating with the dead, and he didn't think she should waste her time with such endeavors. It shouldn't matter what he thought, but Bess couldn't deny that it did. "You're right. Maybe I can come out to your place in the next couple of days and we can make some plans. Maybe try to connect with Harry on our own?"

"That would be lovely. Just wonderful. How about tomorrow?"

"Can we say the day after? Tomorrow is my day to volunteer at the hospital."

"Perfect. You'll come around noon and I will have the cook make a nice lunch for us. We'll make an afternoon of it."

Even though her heart was twisted in knots, Gail's enthusiasm sparked a light in her. "I have to say, it's good to see you so happy."

Gail leaned closer. "And I have you to thank for making my life so much brighter."

"Me? I don't understand."

"Thanks to you and your friend's illness, I no longer have to deal with that Joseph. Not in my home, and not in my life. Between that and having the séance to look forward to, I'm in my own little Heaven."

Bess dropped her gaze to her shoes. Joseph was a wise man and a friend of hers. Bess thought Gail's joy at Joseph's expense was unjust and bordered on cruel, even if she had a reason for it. "He's a nice man and a good healer. I wish him well."

Gail shifted her weight back on her heel and crossed her arms in front of her chest. "I know it's hard for you to understand why I feel the way I do, but you really need to think about it from my point of view. Martin had a life before me, I understand that, but we are ten years past his old life. Why is it wrong for me to be want to be identified as his wife?"

"I've never thought of you as anything but—"

"Not you, Bess. You've always been gracious to me, but anyone who knew Louise holds me at arm's length and blames me for something I had nothing to do with. I didn't get her sick. I didn't wish her demise or do anything to cause it, and despite what most people believe I was no more than Martin's friend until he was free of his marital obligations."

Bess flipped her attention to her purse and the canvas bag carrying her groceries. "I'm sure that is none of my business."

"Can I give you some advice?"

Bess met her gaze.

"I know you don't think so now, but someday, God willing, new love will find you. You're just too kind of a soul to have to live out your days in mourning. When that happens, I implore you to find a balance between your memories and the here and now. If I hadn't been so head-over-heels with my dear Martin I would have given him more time to live in his grief, but it's hard to deny the heart its desire."

Had that time come? Bess wondered if she could embrace a future with Erich and not let Harry's memories live between them. The way her heart broke whenever she considered the question made her doubt she was ready. She stepped closer to Gail and offered her friend another quick hug. "Thank you for your advice. It's hard to imagine anyone else in my life, but if that day comes, I will remember what you said."

Gail tightened her embrace. "Thank you, Bess. I will see you for lunch the day after tomorrow."

# Chapter Fifteen

When Jaden didn't invade his dreams with new messages or warnings, he was faced with an endless stream of obstacles between him and Bess to overcome. The longing to return to her side never faded, and peace never settled in. Knowing she was out somewhere alone was worse than being separated by death. Erich gripped the back of the couch and pulled himself up, calling out to Bess.

Her sweet voice didn't answer his call, so he stood and peered out the window. The sun shone high in the sky and signaled the passing hours—too many for a few quick errands.

Walking out onto the back porch, he lifted his hand to keep the crisp breeze from pushing his hair into his face. Under the large California Live Oak tree, he found her. She'd moved the wrought iron table and its two chairs from the deck. There, she'd laid out a red checkered table cloth and was arranging plates and drinks. Her attention to detail gave him hope. She was looking forward to this meal too. "Let me help you."

His voice caught her attention, and she started across the yard. "I have everything ready and was just going to come get you. Do you think you can make it?"

"Not quickly, but yes." He started down the single step and his balance wavered. "Bess...Can I trouble you for your arm, to steady myself." He prepared himself for her outrage and a lecture reminding him of his proper place, but instead she offered it. Erich fought the urge to reach across his body with his right arm and stroke her forearm as they walked. This moment—so close he could smell her perfume and feel the heat her body radiated—should be enough to ease the fear that haunted his dreams, but a sense of doom twisted his gut, and her touch increased his thirst for her.

"It's so windy. I'm not sure if this is such a good idea, but you said you were getting cooped up."

"It's just what I need. The breeze feels nice after the Santa Ana's a few days ago."

As they cleared the side of the house, Bess glanced toward the front yard. They were now visible to the neighbors across the street, and she slipped her arm from his hand. "Last thing we need to do is give Miss Busybody sitting on her front porch over there a reason to gossip."

Erich chuckled. Every neighborhood seemed to have someone like the silver haired woman. It just so happened this one lived directly across the street. Distant, grainy memories flashed though his mind: images of the woman bending Harry's ear on the subject of this neighbor or that sandwiched between pictures of her grilling him about the latest contraption he'd brought home. Yes, Miss Busybody—Harry's nickname for her—without a doubt had noticed Erich's presence in the widow Houdini's house, and she had probably burned up the phone lines spreading the news.

Lowering himself to the chair, he took in the spread. Simple but magnificent. Any length of time spent in her presence would be. Cheese sandwiches and some cucumber slices arranged with care on small plates and the scent of fresh squeezed lemons rose up from the pitcher. "I hate being so much trouble."

Her laugh floated on the breeze, joining the choir of Rock Wrens serenading them. "Nonsense, it was my pleasure."

He had no reason to doubt her claim. From her eased posture to the almost lyrical tone of her voice, she was the picture of serenity. He flashed her a flirty smile anyway. "I doubt that."

"No. Really. I couldn't tell you the last time I ate outside. It was one of the things Harry and I both loved. That's why I enjoy living here: the weather is often perfect for a picnic lunch."

"Nothing like back east. Instead of a refreshing breeze, the promise of snow would be in the whistling wind, eh?"

Her fork hit the table with a rattle, and she tilted her head toward him. "You lived out east?"

Had *he*? No. But the lingering memories of a past life revealed themselves. He couldn't filter them now, but he could twist them. "Yes, as a child, New York City."

"Hmph. Another similarity. It's like our lives have run parallel to each other's." She shook her head at the perceived coincidence, but accepted it without question. The wind picked up and moved her large curls, begging him to reach out and tangle his fingers in them, but she'd push away the advance as she had every other one. Except for that one kiss.

Erich took a bite of his sandwich, grateful to have something to focus on other than the pulsing need to touch her. He closed his eyes and concentrated on the breeze against his cheek, but it didn't cool the heat burning between them. Fluttering open, his eyes focused in on a large, blue tarp toward the back of the shed and the item he knew must be underneath.

How they loved that automobile!

Harry had never taught Bess to drive. It made sense that she kept it out of sight, but he should have noticed it before now. Another nudge from Jaden? Grateful for the help, he asked, "What's under the tarp?"

The light in her eyes dimmed as she dropped her gaze to the plate. Seconds later, a wistful smile replaced the sadness. "Harry's automobile. I hate that it's rusting away, but I haven't found the strength to sell it."

"Why don't you use it?"

She dismissed the idea with a wave of her hand. "I never learned to drive."

Instead of relying on the memories Harry had created with Bess, Erich realized he could use the car to create their own experiences. Those moments might help strengthen the tenuous bond developing between them. His knee bounced up and down, expelling the built up excitement. "I could teach you."

"That's not a good idea." It was more than her words, her hands crossed in front of her, punctuating her dismissal.

Bess was the most capable person he'd ever known. If she had a want or a need, she always found a way to make it happen. The last eleven months proved her will to survive. So, why was she hesitating? "I'd be happy to teach you."

She took the napkin from her lap, tangling it with her fingers. "It's hard to explain. Life goes on, I know. And there is so much I was forced to handle on my own, but there are some things I cannot bear to change. Some memories are too precious to alter. A long drive on a Sunday afternoon is something I should only share with Harry."

"Do you think learning to drive will change your past? The memories never have to leave your heart."

She tipped her head as if she could hear an answer in the wind. "Time steals so much. It's already getting harder to remember the sound of his voice or how his fingers felt brushing my chin." She shook her head as if she could shake off the loneliness. "We shouldn't ruin our picnic with my melancholy reminiscences."

"I don't mind listening if you need someone to talk to." Maybe a good catharsis would unearth every twisted emotion she'd buried in the last eleven months.

"How boring! You don't want to listen to an old woman's woes." She returned her focus to her plate, reaching for her fork.

Bottling up emotion was a typical defense for Bess. He knew it would take an atypical offense to cross that wall. "I wish you'd quit calling yourself an old woman, it's not how I see you. And I enjoy hearing your stories, even if it seems like your past was so sad."

"There were more good times than bad, but I'm a realist. Another lesson Harry taught me. I don't look at the past through rose colored glasses. It was an amazing adventure to live through, but we didn't plan for the future. We always thought there would be another tomorrow to retire and enjoy everything we worked so hard to achieve. For me, it came last October, only he's not here to share it."

"And that makes you angry?"

"Sometimes. Mostly, it's just sad. I long for lazy picnic lunches where the conversation doesn't drift to the next show or a new piece of the act. I fantasize we're enjoying a cool autumn breeze or taking a drive up the coast without his head being wrapped around his next escape."

Bess's desires shredded his heart. Were her memories of the past accurate? Had he lived his life so focused on the act that he didn't take enough moments to appreciate the way the sun reflected off her hair or to soothe her concerns?

No matter how many times she said it, he'd never accept this view as fact. She'd been the only thing that mattered in Harry's life, and it devastated him to learn she hadn't a clue. "You wish he were here to spend this time with you, but you don't have to stay alone to honor your past with Harry."

She clucked her tongue against the roof of her mouth and shook her head as if he'd spoken the most preposterous words imaginable. "You sound like Martin. He tells me the pain will pass and that love will blossom again in the most unlikely places."

Imagine that! He and Martin on the same side of an argument? At this rate, the next miracle would be ice-skating in Hell. "I should tell you he stopped by while you were in town."

"Oh really? Did he say why?"

"He said it was to check up on you, but I think his real intention was to get rid of me."

"Why would you say that?"

Could he tell her the truth that he'd thrown the first jab in the verbal shoving match? It didn't matter. The story ended the same way no matter who started it. "He ordered me out of your house and your life."

Her eyes darkened and her forehead creased. "I know Martin has grown protective of me, but to go that far?"

Erich's toe tapped under the table as Bess's defense of Martin twisted a knife in Harry's stomach. The ghost jumped up to battle. "Why would I lie?"

"That's not what I meant. Martin can be abrasive. He says things without thinking. What you perceived as aggression, I'm sure he only meant in a protective way."

"Or to guard Gail's seat at the séance table." The words slipped through his mouth with such a sharp edge, he expected to taste blood on his lips.

The single crease in her forehead deepened. She stood and began collecting the plates. "I have no reason to question Martin's intentions, but I can't say the same for you. What, with the way you seem so fixated on the séance, Harry's life, and all of his belongings. Is that why you kissed me? To possess something of Harry's?"

"Bess, sit down. I made it perfectly clear what I'm interested in." Throwing the attraction down on the table as if it were a winning poker hand was probably not the best idea he'd ever had, but damn, what choice had she left him? Spinning their conversation and making him out to be the bad guy, when it was Martin who was up to no good was enough cause to kick good-reason out the door.

She dropped the plates back on the table, and the plastic bounced around against the covered wrought iron. Squaring her shoulders, she said, "A mistake. An improper advance is what it was. I don't want to hear another word on the subject."

"The lady protests too much," he said.

She stepped back. Erich knew he might as well be backing a tiger into a corner; Bess would react the same.

He gripped the edge of the table and pulled himself to his feet, better to have this conversation eye-to-eye. "Look, I'm sorry if I offended you last night, but I'm not going to pretend it was a misguided action. I wanted to kiss you, Bess. I have since the first moment we met. You can stand there and tell me you don't feel the same, but we both know that's a lie. Don't we?"

"I shouldn't feel—"

"But you do."

"It's wrong!"

"I don't believe that."

Her silent stare bore through him. Her lower lip quivered. Erich knew his words had touched something in her, just as he was sure his kiss had done the same. After a moment, she picked the plates back up. "I'm going to clean up."

Watching her walk away again was something he refused to let happen. "Bess!" He called out to her. She ignored him, so he traced her steps and grabbed her arm. "What are you running from?"

"Don't you see? I'm not running away, I'm facing my destiny. I can't forget the vows I made."

"Your wedding vows were absolved with your husband's death."

Trying to free her arm, she pulled harder but refused to look his way. "You and Martin have walked similar paths; you've both lost loves and found a way to free your heart. But Harry and I weren't like most people. I can't forget—"

"Never forget, Bess. Just live for now."

She acquiesced, twisting to him. "How do I start?" In her eyes, Erich saw a meek step of surrender. Tiny, like a baby's step, but a huge leap toward his goal.

"With the automobile."

Her body slumped. "I don't understand how that will help."

"Let me get it running and teach you to drive. You'll see that you can treasure the memories of your life with Harry, while building new ones. Besides, won't it be easier to run errands and volunteer at the hospital with the car?"

She tipped her head, and her chest expanded and fell with a heavy sigh. "Okay."

"I'll get started right away." Her consent gave him another victory, but instead of joy, regret tapped at his heart. Bess hadn't agreed because she wanted him to do this, she'd just caved to his bullying. He could spin it though, right? She'd be happy when they were together on the road, living out the fantasies she clung to for a long life with Harry.

She had to be, he was running out of ideas.

****

As hard as Bess tried, she just couldn't concentrate on the book in her hands. It was just too damn quiet. Funny. When Harry was alive, she used to long for a moment of peace or a day of rest. After he was gone, the silence drove her mad.

With Erich in the house, she was reminded just how much space another person could fill. Just his presence erased some of the loneliness.

Hearing Joseph on the stairs, Bess set her book on the end table and rose from the chair. "How's he doing?"

"Sleeping peacefully. You've done a fine job caring for him."

"I'm surprised at how fast he's recovered. He was out of bed most of the day."

Joseph left cheek scrunched up. He seemed perplexed as he pulled the strap of the large, canvas bag over his head and let it drop to his shoulder. "Pushed too far, perhaps. He fell asleep so quickly. I didn't have to give him anything for pain when I changed his dressing."

"Are there any special instructions?"

He pulled from his canvas tote a brown, paper bag no bigger than the size of his fist and handed it to her. Even though it was taped shut, she could smell licorice. "More root tea, brew him a cup four times a day."

"For the infection?"

"It will help that too, but licorice root helps build strength. Don't wake him tonight, but start with breakfast in the morning." After a quick pause, he continued, "I went to the Cooper estate and fought the new lady of the house to retrieve the root from my garden. Mrs. Cooper assured me it would be the last time I would be allowed on the property, so use it with care. I won't have any to spare for quite some time."

It struck Bess odd to hear Joseph call Gail Martin's *new* wife. They'd been married ten years. With three children, they could hardly be considered newlyweds. "I wasn't aware you had a garden on the estate."

"I planted some herbs on the border of Louise's Seaside Daisies. Now that I've been officially banished from her home, I'm sure the new lady will make it her top priority to turn over the gardens and erase the last remnant of Louise ever living there."

She and Harry had only become acquainted with Martin after he married Gail. Still, since Harry's death, Martin sometimes spoke of his Louise and Bess didn't miss the fact that the same reverence showed in Joseph's eyes that resided in Martin's. "I wish I had known her. To hear you and Martin speak, she was a remarkable woman."

Joseph's hands curled at his side. "What would Martin know? He wasn't the one who cared for her while she was ill. He wasn't there when she took her last breath."

"I know that he regrets that."

Joseph laughed and shook his head. "He didn't even let the seasons change. He just brought that harlot into Louise's home. I don't know how her soul found its ever-after peace, when he treated her memory with such disrespect."

Bess found Joseph's display extreme given the time that had passed, but also knew he wasn't the only one to judge Martin and Gail for the way they treated Louise in her last months. "He's told me more than once how good you were to her."

"I cared for Louise because it was the least she deserved, not for any gratitude or payment from Dr. Cooper."

"Regardless, he's thankful, just as I am for your care of my friend."

"An interesting choice of words." Joseph's smirk didn't escape her attention.

"You suggest a better one?"

Leaning back on his heel, he slipped his hands into his pockets. "My grandmother used to say there were two kinds of lovers. The ones who spent a single lifetime together—joined because of proximity and physical desire. Then there were the older souls—the ones that couldn't be denied. The fates could separate them on different corners of the planet, and they'd move Heaven and earth to be one again."

This was not the first time Joseph had insinuated that she and Erich were lovers, despite how hard she'd worked to maintain a respectable decorum with her house guest, especially in the company of others. If she didn't set him straight now, Joseph might be gossiping about her to others with same disgust he used when discussing Martin and Gail. She drew in her cheeks and felt her shoulders tighten. "If there is one thing I know for sure it's that I have only loved one man, not Erich Welch."

Joseph tipped his head in a way that would make you believe he accepted her statement, yet the slight dimple to his cheek told another story. God help her if the rest of the world could see her lust so clearly.

"Death only happens to the physical, Mrs. Houdini. It what's encased inside the body that lives on and continues seeking love. But you know that. You've chosen to give that spirit that is trapped in between existences a home here."

"Harry was always stubborn, when he's ready to move on he will, but if he's not, I'm not sure either of us could push him to his next life." She couldn't deny the peace that flowed through her, easing the tight muscles in her back and jaw. The idea of Harry's soul not only continued on, despite what he had believed in, but was staying close to her raised hope. The upcoming séance just might bring her the closure she needed.

Joseph sought the same thing, she sensed. One look in his eyes told the story that she had missed in all their other conversations. Louise Cooper meant something to him. And not in the way a doctor grows fond of a patient or the way a friend cares for another, but deeper, as a lover. In the very same way her heart had already come to think of Erich. For the first time, she could picture her future including another man.

But not until Harry let her go.

# Chapter Sixteen

Bess found it easy to slip from the house before Erich could ask her too many questions. All she had to do was hand him a cup of medicinal tea and point him toward Harry's automobile. It was where he'd spent the last three days from sun up to sun down, and he happily crossed the yard, not even pausing to ask where she was headed at such an early hour.

At the time, it seemed best to keep him in the dark about her little chore, just as she had the day before when she'd met Gail for lunch and a séance rehearsal. Now, she stood outside the newspaper office and reread the words scrawled on the paper in her hand, questioning whether or not this was the best move.

The words "séance," "Harry Houdini" and "$10,000 reward" jumped at her. The advertisement she planned to place in the paper this week announced the location of the Halloween event and revealed Gail Cooper as the medium. The perfect publicity stunt, and she knew Harry would be proud of her. There was no better way to fill an auditorium than to have his arch nemesis calling him home.

So why was she hesitant to place the announcement? Was it because she knew Erich would accuse her once again of chasing ghosts? Or did it go deeper than that?

"Is everything all right, Mrs. Houdini? You look troubled." Bess shook off the murky thoughts, surprised to find Joseph standing in front of her.

Was she really so transparent? Harry used to praise her poker face, claimed it was one of her greatest assets to the act. Turns out, he must have taken that with him too when he left. Crumpling the paper, she pushed it into the pocket of her skirt with a sigh. "I need to tie up the loose ends for Harry's séance, but I'm still unsure that I'm doing everything the right way."

"Mr. Houdini would disapprove." Joseph didn't ask a question, but stated his opinion as fact—and with such conviction that for a brief second Bess trusted him.

"No, I'm sure he'd be pleased. The séance was his idea. I just want everything to be perfect. It would mean the world to me to speak to him again, but I've been so distracted."

"The most important element will be your spirit guide. You need someone who truly possesses second sight."

She startled, drawing in a breath. "Gail never mentioned second sight." Neither had the numerous books she read.

"Communicating with the spirit world is a gift. Either you are blessed with the ability or you're not. It can't be learned in a book or accomplished with practice."

If Joseph had meant to comfort her with those words, he'd failed. "Do you truly believe if I am not a spiritualist, Harry will never be able to speak to me?" As the realization began to sink in, her stomach twisted into knots. Maybe that was why, no matter how hard they'd tried the day before, Harry had refused to speak. The séance meant very little to her in the grand scheme of things. It was just another of Harry's shows. What she'd hoped and prayed for—had been working so hard for—was just one more moment with her other half. She wanted to feel him with her in the same way that Joseph claimed to.

She wanted to let go of the past and move forward, but without Harry's blessing that was impossible. She could only get that from him performing his greatest escape. If she failed this time, her loyalty had to remain with Harry. After all, she'd given him her vow.

She began to sway, and Joseph took her elbow. "I did not say you're without second sight, Mrs. Houdini. All I said was it cannot be learned."

"Gail told me that like with any skill, practice makes perfect."

He scoffed and shook his head. "That woman is a cretin. She no more possesses the ability to communicate with the other world than your husband did."

Tears pushed against her eyes, and a lump formed in her throat. Harry used those same words to describe Gail, and she'd suspected her husband was right, but to hear it from someone so close to Gail and Martin made her feel more foolish.

"What do you hope to gain from this?" Joseph asked.

She wrapped her arms tight around herself. No matter how many times she was asked, she'd stick to Harry's script. "I promised Harry I'd protect his legacy and honor his fame. That's why it's important to have a real medium for the séance. Can you do it?"

Joseph's eyes opened wider, and his brow perked up. "Me? I...yes. I could...but Mrs. Houdini..."

"Please. It would mean so much to me."

"I wish I could." Sorrow clouded his eyes. "But it's time for me to go back to the life I lived before Louise, and I can't risk any more anger from Dr. Cooper."

Bess swallowed and pushed away the tears pushing against her eyes. "Of course, Joseph. I understand. Forgive me for asking."

He patted her arm. "Don't apologize. I'm honored you'd ask." He paused to cough. "But...What about...There is a professor that Dr. Cooper used to associate with. Her name is Dr. Wickerland, and she might prove helpful to you. She's said to be very good."

The séance was fast approaching. The last thing she wanted to do was get to know another spiritualist. If she couldn't convince Joseph, she'd have to stay with her first decision: Gail. "Are you sure *you* can't. I've grown to trust you."

"I am sure. There is another option. You could let go of the past and the dead."

"And turn my back on Harry?"

Joseph gripped her hand tight, and his eyes locked with hers. Once brown, they turned into deep, black pools. She averted her gaze to keep herself from falling into them, but couldn't ignore the words he spoke. "The dead walk among the living. Harry's soul breathes in the most unexpected places. How he feels can find its way to your heart without a medium to translate."

Though he'd stopped speaking, his stare was fixed on the wall behind her, only an empty shell stood in front of her.

"Where? How?" Bess shook his shoulder. The words whisked past her lips, caught up in her breath. She must have heard him wrong. Harry walk among the living? Even if she believed in zombies or some such nonsense, she couldn't wrap her mind around it.

But what if she was wrong and he was right? Was that something she could risk?

The man startled and took a step back. "Yes, yes. Dr. Wickerland. She would be a very good choice."

"Joseph. Please! What did you mean by 'Harry's soul breathes?'"

The man's cheeks paled, and he shook his head, "You must have misheard me, Mrs. Houdini. Why would I say such a thing?"

"But you did! You said 'the dead walk among the living. Harry's soul breathes in the most unexpected places.'"

"The spirits, Mrs. Houdini—the restless ones who haven't found the final rest—they are the ones someone with second sight can speak to."

"You've said more than once that Harry's soul is not at rest?"

"I don't believe it is."

She shook her head and waved her hands in front of her face, fighting off the tears that again threatened to spill. She'd heard him right, but now he was twisting the words. Did he feel that threatened by Martin? Or had she just witnessed some sort of possession? Had it been another's words that fell from Joseph's mouth? Harry's perhaps?

What nonsense would she think of next?

Her thoughts flipped to the Ouija board and the spiritualist books Gail had loaned her, and a veil of shame covered her. Harry would be so disappointed. If he were here he'd snap his fingers briskly and tell her the time for moping had passed.

Everyone she knew thought she was on a dead-end road: Will, Martin, and now Joseph. Even Erich had encouraged her to release the past and embrace a sketchy, foggy future. Not one of their opinions really mattered, though. Harry may not want her to wallow in pain, but his instructions had been clear, and it felt so wrong to push forward or even entertain a future with Erich until she fulfilled her obligations. Besides, Harry knew what it meant to chase a dream and wasn't that what she was doing, following her heart back to him?

One last conversation. The real good bye they'd been denied eleven months earlier.

****

Erich slid his hands over the steering wheel and imagined he was cruising down some out-of-the-way road with Bess at his side and the wind blowing through the open windows. Reaching to the passenger side, he imagined his hand falling to her knee instead of the cool, leather seat he'd just finished cleaning. One more day and he could make his daydream a reality. He'd go into town the next morning and get what he needed to fix the brakes, and then he and Bess could start creating memories of their own.

Memories that would make her see they could be happy together.

Stepping out of the car, the strong licorice scent hit his senses reminding him he'd have to keep Bess away or cover it up somehow. If she found out he'd been dumping the tea behind the shed instead of drinking it, he'd soon know the chill of a New York winter again.

As he walked toward the house, the offending odor faded and Bess's cooking filtered through. He could almost taste the meal he knew she prepared with care and walked with a full stride. Only an uncomfortable twinge pinged in his side every so often, proving he was on the road to recovery and Joseph's tea had little to do with it.

In the kitchen, he resisted the urge to kiss Bess's cheek and went straight to his report. "The car is almost done. All that's left is the brakes. I'll go into town for some fluid and pads in the morning. After that, I can take you for your first driving lesson."

Bess didn't look at him, but reached to the back of the stove, picked up the salt shaker and sprinkled some into the pot. "Our arrangement called for you to do home maintenance. That automobile has stolen all of your attention for days."

Erich knew she'd reluctantly agreed to him working on the car, in part, to get out of the conversation, but he hadn't realized she was this upset. "You told me I could work on it."

"I know, and I don't want you to push yourself too hard too soon, but there is still a long list of repairs the house needs." Her words might have been terse, but her voice was toneless.

He rolled the events of the last day and a half through his mind. What had he done to deserve this icy reception? He stepped back and from the corner of his eye saw the box sitting by the back door. Inside was the Ouija board, several books and candles. "Did something happen in town?"

She shook her head. "Dinner is ready. If you want to eat it hot, you'll have to forgo your shower until afterward."

He acknowledged her with a single nod and washed his hands in the kitchen sink as she filled two bowls and took them to the table. He had no doubt she was lying. She hadn't given him eye contact once, and her shoulders slouched as if they held the weight of the world. "Don't shut me out. I thought we'd forged some kind of friendship here."

She pivoted back to the stove, taking the direction that kept her gaze away from him. "I'm just feeling melancholy, I guess." Returning to the table with another mug of that god-awful tea, she took a seat and looked at him for the first time. "Come now, I didn't fix this dinner for you to stand there and let it get cold."

He took his seat, still dumbfounded by her cool attitude. The stew looked good, but he couldn't smell anything over the bitter tea and wrapped his hand around the mug, pushing it across the table.

Her head jerked in his direction. "What are you doing?"

"I don't need it anymore. I'm feeling much better."

"You feel better because it's working. You promised me you'd follow all of Joseph's instructions."

Frustration. Anger. Stress. He couldn't put his finger on what was lacing her voice, but didn't want to aggravate the situation any more. If it would lift this dark veil from her, he'd endure one more cup of tea. He closed his eyes tight as if that could ward off the taste assailing his tongue and swallowed. "I don't like seeing you in such a mood. What's wrong, Bess?"

"Time. There's never enough of it, but I'm under even more pressure than usual to prepare for the big show."

"The show," he repeated in a whisper. Her only desire: for it to go off without a hitch. His only goal: to stop it cold. "Is there anything I can do to help?" The words slipped from his mouth. Stupid words! Helping was not stopping, it was the opposite, but he couldn't contain himself.

What kind of numbskull would offer to participate in his own demise?

"Drink your tea so you can get well. Once you're back to normal we can both move on with our lives."

So, that was it. She wanted him up and out so she could give all her attention to the séance. The thought of leaving here—getting well enough to walk away— tormented him, but it was worse than that. The séance would tear him from this life he'd relearned to cherish.

Somehow in the last week, his life had developed meaning. He hadn't expected that. Maybe it was selfish, but he didn't want to die again, to give up his body and never feel a hot, summer breeze or cool, autumn rain. But it was more than that. The idea of never looking in her eyes again, never seeing her smile, or feeling her arms around him, as they had the night he'd kissed her, made his whole body ache.

But it appeared that Harry spent their entire married life hurting her. Dying was just one of a long list of things he'd done to cut at her very soul. If she wanted him up and out, who was he not to oblige her? Maybe she'd at least smile at him as he walked away.

He gripped the cup and lifted it to his lips, gulping the tea. From the moment Harry had laid eyes on Bess, her happiness had been first and foremost. No doubt, their life had been hard, but as he looked across the table at her now it wasn't only grief that etched her features. Anger and bitterness loomed just below the surface. And he'd already wasted one third of his time trying to erase it, only to fail. Was that all their life had been to her? Pain? He needed to know that wasn't true. "Tell me something happy, Bess."

She looked up at him as if he'd spoke in a foreign language she couldn't comprehend. "Happy?"

"We're both being petulant. I thought maybe if we shared happy memories it would help pull us out of the funk." *Just tell me one thing you loved about your life with Harry.*

She kept her eyes down as if she were studying the meat and vegetables in her bowl. In that moment of complete silence, Erich watched a wide variety of emotions pass over her face. A moment later, she said, "There were so many happy moments. Time we spent on trains, segregated from the rest of the world. Or holidays, the house bustled with family. I think my favorite memory happened just after we bought this house, though. We'd finished dinner and decided to take a walk and enjoy the night air. We became so engrossed in our conversation that we'd walked a dozen or more blocks without even noticing how far we'd gone. Then, it began to rain, an unexpected summer downpour."

The memory she sparked was so real to him he could feel her body tight to his as Harry pulled her close. Once again, it was as if the soaking wet clothes hung from his frame, and he could smell her perfume and taste her sweet lips as they'd stopped running and came together in laughter.

The memory brought forth a chuckle, and her warm eyes met his. "We ran together, holding hands, for three blocks or so, but realizing our clothes were soaked and there was no getting around that, we went back to a nice stroll. It was a warm mid-summer rain, and it just washed away all the craziness of our normal routine. For those brief moments, I felt like he wasn't focused on work. For that one evening in the rain, it was just Harry and me."

Her recount of that day was all he needed to hear to remember why he'd chosen this over an afterlife. Saving Bess from self-destruction and relighting the spark of hope in her was the only choice he could make. "That's a beautiful story, Bess. Wonderful."

"Now it's your turn."

"Pardon me?"

"To share. You said we should share stories. You've told me so little about your past."

What could he share? His only memories were Harry's, and she'd surely recognize them as such. Maybe if he kept it benign they wouldn't offend the terms of his bargain or upset Jaden. "I think my happiest moment was on a train, with the love of my life. We couldn't afford a compartment and were traveling across country. For several days we sat close, arm in arm, but one evening in particular her head lay on my shoulder while she slept. She trusted me to keep her safe and provided for even though we rarely knew where the next meal was coming from."

"When you love someone, it's easy to trust. Not being alone in the world is enough to make you feel invincible, I think."

He could see tears making her eyes glossy and wondered if she'd found her version of that very memory in the recesses of her mind. "I'd give anything to have those days back."

She averted her eyes. Her hand shook as she lifted her spoon to her mouth. Did his story hit too close to home? As well, it should. "How? How did she die?" Her voice rattled the same as the spoon.

He'd told her before that death separated him from his love, and it wasn't a lie. Of course, Bess assumed that he'd had a spouse or lover pass away, not that he himself had experienced death and a rebirth of sorts. But how to answer her direct question? He had no choice but to lie. Jaden wouldn't allow the truth to pass through his lips. Unless, of course, he veiled it. "An illness. The doctors were useless. That's probably why I don't have much use for them."

"That's the way it happens sometimes. No matter what you do to help or how hard you pray, the fates have another idea all their own, and we are helpless to stop it."

"Do you really believe that?"

She shook her head. "But sometimes telling myself that eases the pain. You loved her?"

"With all my heart. We had so many dreams for a home, family and life of our own. You mentioned fate, well, I guess it had a different plan than my lady and I did." He'd tried hard to keep emotion out of his voice, but couldn't stop it from cracking. He only had to look at Bess to know he'd opened up yet another wound for her.

"And now?"

"There's a piece of this worn and tired soul that will always be hers."

"Worn and tired?" she quipped. "You're still quite the young man."

"For all that I've seen, it's as if I've lived twice as long as you'd think." He chose his words with care, staying as true to facts as he could without twirling her into the altered reality or angering his keeper.

Bess picked up the linen napkin from her lap and wiped her mouth, though it was obvious to Erich she was trying to stifle the tears. "Look at the two of us, supposed to be cheering each other up with happy stories, and all we can do is cry in our stew."

A chuckle boiled up from deep inside. "I guess we are a pathetic pair. But I hope my story shows you I know a little more of your pain than you realized."

"It has."

Erich pushed the bowl aside. "The meal was very good. Give me another moment, and I will clear the dishes away."

"You'll do no such thing. You'll sit there and finish your tea." She stood and began gathering the bowls and silverware in her arms.

With an obedient nod, Erich brought the cup to his lips, swallowing the remainder, hoping it would drown the grief. Hoping the new mutual connection would be a bridge to better things. The pungent flavor balled up and closed his throat, bringing on a coughing fit. A moment later, it passed and he shifted his weight. "Would you like to play cards in a bit?"

"That would be lovely," she said.

He watched Bess busy herself with the dishes. Determined to give her a hand, he started to stand, but the room spun away from him. He gripped the edge of the table and called out her name as his vision faded white.

"What is it?"

He heard her long, flowing skirt bustle around her legs. She was moving toward him, but he only saw a blur behind white clouds.

Her voice screeched. "Oh my goodness, Erich, what is it?"

"I feel..." His knees buckled, and Bess's arm came around him.

"Come on, let's lie you down."

His heart thumped against his chest, and he heard ringing in his ears. Life, once again, slipped from him.

Had he given away too much? Angered Jaden for the last time?

Erich blindly reached out. His fingers finding the cotton of Bess's blouse, he gripped it tight and pulled her close. He wouldn't allow her to believe that Harry had abandoned her. When he could feel the warmth of her caress to his cheek and smell her rose scented perfume, he dug deep and whispered. "Forgive, Bess, and believe."

"Believe what, Erich? What are you trying to say?" She tried to pull from him, but he held her. He tried to meet her eyes, but everything was fuzzy and white. He could hear the tremble in her voice, knew the words he'd said had thrown her off balance, but he'd only just begun.

"Harry... Roseabell...answer...tell...pray...answer." His hand slipped from her dress, and his head rolled to the side. The ringing in his ears had subsided and overwhelming weakness had quieted his racing heart.

"Is there more, Erich? Is Harry saying more?"

With slow steady movements he slid his hand up her stomach and rested it between her breasts. "Look...tell...answer...answer." The last word passed through his lips, and consciousness drifted away.

*The code.*

Erich had just recited the message Harry had promised to send from beyond the grave. "Are you still here, Harry?" She called to the empty room. "Say something else. Anything else!"

Bess braced her hands on either side of Erich's face and put her cheek down near his mouth. He was still breathing. "Don't you do this, Erich! Don't die on me."

Feeling the warmth against her flesh, however shallow, she laid a hand to his forehead. It was cool. He looked peaceful.

Emotions knotted in her chest. Harry had used Erich to speak to her alone, just like she'd pleaded and prayed. Was he still with her now? Death had never taken away the feeling that he still walked by her side. She'd been even more aware of him—or lack of his presence—since bumping into Erich on the street. There was a connection between the two men that went beyond the thirst for adventure and the hunger for the limelight.

*Erich.* She had to get him help. On her feet, she grabbed the phone and dialed Martin's number. She'd have called Joseph, but had no idea how to get a hold of him since he'd left the Cooper estate. Maybe Martin did have an agenda when it came to Harry's memory, but Erich needed medical treatment. When Martin's voice hit her ears, she said, "Please, I need your help."

# Chapter Seventeen

The spinning slowed, but white haze still clouded Erich's vision. He pushed and clawed like a drowning man fighting his way to the surface, until he saw Jaden. He had drawn Erich into yet another dream state. Or had he lost the bet and was now sentenced to the cold, wet ground for an eternity?

Jaden tightened the long, leather coat and pushed his soaked hair over his shoulder. Only then did Erich realize the rain and where they stood. It was the very street corner from Bess's memory—where they'd given up on outrunning the storm and melted into each other's embrace. Warm water and the clean, fresh scent of summer assailed Erich's senses. He tilted his head up and let the drops splatter his face, clearing the fog. "What did I do wrong this time?"

"Quite the contrary. You've made your first and only important breakthrough."

Erich rubbed the back of his neck then leveled his eyes back to his mentor. "Then why are we here?"

"For Bess."

"And the rain? Is that for her too?"

Jaden stood firm, his legs at shoulder's width and his hands clasped at his waist. "Every last bit of this has been for her alone. Never for you. Tonight, for the first time, you understood that."

Erich pursed his lips. Despite Jaden's claim, he didn't understand. "Then why pull me away?"

"There are forces working against you. You are even more of a nuisance to them now than before. You threaten their plans. Your delivery of the coded message will stand in the way."

Of course. Giving Bess her message eliminated the need for a séance. He'd accomplished the goal. But with no show, there would be no spotlight for Gail. And when she was upset, Martin became a son-of-a-bitch. "Bess wanted Harry's words. It never mattered where they came from."

"Yes, but it's not just the words. It's the reason you said them. For the first time since all of this began your actions were selfless. You whispered them for Bess alone, for her peace of mind and to ease her heart." A proud smile—something Erich hadn't seen until this moment—crossed Jaden's lips, and his eyes twinkled. "Love, betrayal, comfort and revenge. So much is swirling around you and Bess. You've become unwilling participants in a scheme that has grown larger than it had ever intended. In the name of retribution, you were meant to stop breathing tonight, but nothing is going to mess with *my* plan."

Jaden reached for his forehead, but Erich stopped him. "Is it Martin? Did that bastard try to kill me?"

"The players are many." With those final words the large man pushed his hand past Erich's, and as the fingers touched his forehead, he fell into his body once more, cold and clammy against the kitchen floor. He fought for consciousness, pulling himself back from a murky cloud.

Bess's arms came around him as he coughed and sputtered. "Oh Erich. Dear God, thank you. Thank you for letting him be all right."

"I don't know if I'd go that far." Erich chocked and coughed the words, licking his lips and trying to bring himself to a sitting position.

Bess's arm came down against his chest, holding him firm in her lap. "Wait for Martin."

"You called him? Why? How long was I out?"

"Five minutes or so. How do you feel?"

"Weak. It's that damn tea. I was fine 'til I drank it."

Her arms went tense around him, her voice sharp and biting. "It's a root tea. How could it possibly hurt you?"

"I don't know." He rolled his head away from her, his strength being restored like grains of sand being sifted through a strainer—slow and scattered. Maybe the tea in and of itself was harmless, but that didn't let the person who brought it off the hook. Maybe that voice in his gut that held Joseph suspect from the beginning was accurate.

Touching his cheek, she brought his gaze back to her. "Did Harry tell you anything else?"

Her concern for him—Erich—so fleeting. Of course, it was Harry and an homage to their past that mattered most to her. The realization sucked the air from his lungs as if she'd punched him in the stomach. But why did the distinction matter so much? He and Harry were one and the same. Weren't they?

No. Somewhere along the way—maybe the moment he'd spilled the code—they had fractured, and he'd become disconnected from Harry's past.

Erich needed to make this a catalyst to bring them together, but for the moment he'd hold his cards close to his chest. "What? Did I say Harry told me something?"

"The message that is sealed in an envelope and locked in my safe; you spoke the words before you passed out. Do you remember?"

He scraped his hand across his jaw, and he felt his eyes darting side to side as he decided on the right words. "I remember calling for you and the urge to tell you something..."

Tears spilled down her cheeks, but the smile on her lips gave away her joy, a level of happiness even Harry hadn't seen in many years. The weight of Jaden's labels—cold and selfish—plummeted down on him. How did it happen that Harry had let this light slip from her eyes and never once noticed? "Help me up."

"No. Martin will be here soon. He needs to check you out."

If Martin and Joseph had succeeded in their plan, would she mourn him or only miss the link to Harry? "I don't want that scoundrel laying a finger on me, and if

you were smart you wouldn't have him near you either."
He pushed himself up despite her effort to make him
stay on the floor. "I'm all right, Bess. I swear."

He attempted to square his feet, but the world
gyrated away from him again. He reached for the edge of
the table as Bess slid the chair underneath him. "At
least sit! You're not fine."

Erich followed her orders and looked at the
offending mug sitting in front of him. He'd questioned
that pseudo-doctor from the moment he'd stepped foot
in this house. Why had he been so blind and followed?
The answer was simple: because she asked him to.
"Bess, there's something you should know."

"About Harry?" she asked. The bright, hopeful glean
in her eyes broke his heart as she slid up another chair
and sat so close to him their knees touched. Her hands,
aged by time and sorrow felt so frail as he gripped them
in his. Her eyes pleaded with him, begged for more
words from Harry's lips.

Erich had longed for her to look at him with a pure
adoration since that moment they bumped on the street.
Now that she did, jealousy stabbed at him. She wasn't
looking at the Erich she'd come to know, she was still
clinging to a memory. Not that long ago, he'd have
accepted this as progress, but the man he'd become
wanted Bess for himself. "I don't think Harry spoke
through me, Bess."

A tremble visibly coursed her body, and she threw
her arms up in the air. "How can you still not believe?
You delivered his message! You must be one of those
people Joseph spoke of earlier?"

He shifted his weight in the chair and shook his
head. Always a new twist and something different to
absorb. "What are you talking about? What kind of
people?"

"Someone with second sight."

"A fraud medium?" No use for fancy language, he'd
call a spade what it was, but he didn't mean to push her
buttons and regretted that the joyful glow was already
fading.

Her fingers gripped her skirt, and her lips narrowed. "No, not some phony. Someone who can truly speak with the spiritual world. I'm sure Harry took over your body. That's why you passed out. I wish I knew how to get a hold of Joseph."

She'd made up her mind and that should make his next step easy, but he knew that wouldn't be the case. Nothing so far had come without difficulty. "I wasn't possessed, Bess. It was that damn tea."

"And the tea magically gave you Harry's code for the word believe?"

"The words I spoke stood for the letters in the name Roseabelle. It's the name that is the code word for believe." Harry's words spilled past his lips before Erich could contain them. Damn Harry's ego! He couldn't leave well enough be. Was Jaden right? Did the need to be right matter more to Harry than Bess's heart?

Her whole face lit up as the smile he'd chased away returned. "You wouldn't know that unless Harry told you."

Damn-it-all, he wanted something that belonged to them and didn't involve the past. "You believe in spirits and afterlives but not in poisoned tea?"

She slammed her hand against the table. "Don't tease!"

Pointing out her hypocrisy and fickleness was only part of the reason he'd been so harsh. He knew evil forces were afoot, and he needed her to stop chasing dreams and focus on the here and now. He leveled his gaze. "This isn't a joke. What if Martin was so angry about the things I said to him the other day that he sent Joseph over here to make good on those death threats."

Bess rolled her eyes and exhaled. "Those two had a falling out. Joseph dislikes Martin as much as you do."

"Maybe Martin isn't giving him a choice." Okay, so he was sorting it out for himself as he proposed different scenarios to Bess. Jaden said many people were involved, and those two plus Gail were his top suspects. Erich just needed to figure out the connection.

"Now that's a reach. You're accusing Martin of blackmailing Joseph? Why can't you accept that Harry spoke through you?"

Erich flicked the inside of his mouth with his tongue. It'd be easier to give her the hope, but she'd be devastated later if the truth came out. "It's not possible, Bess."

Her cheeks flushed, and she giggled—like she hadn't in more years than he cared to remember. "How can you say that? You've just done it. Harry came to me tonight, and he used your body as a vessel. You won't convince me any differently."

Bess crossed to the back door and rifled through the box she'd set there earlier. "I wish he could have delivered something personal to me before you lost consciousness, but this was only the first time. Now that he's succeeded, he will surely try again. You'll get stronger, and I'll be able to talk to him next time."

*Next time?* Instead of dousing the need, he'd only fueled the flame. This had to stop. "The séance. He regrets that decision and wants you to call it off."

Her beautiful smile faded, and her eyes scanned him. "Harry did *not* say that."

"He did. Sure as I'm sitting here. He doesn't want you to hold the public fiasco that the séance will become. That's why he came to you tonight. To show you there wasn't a need."

She shifted her weight between her feet. "That doesn't make sense."

"You have your message from Harry. He's proven communication with the dead is possible. There's no reason to hold that carnival side show." His stomach twisted into a knot. Jaden made it impossible for Erich to tell Bess the entire truth, but that didn't mean lying was right. Worse, her life depended on him getting her to trust the fabrication.

Again her expressions changed so fast, it made him dizzy. Her eyes narrowed, and her jaw tightened. "How did you do it? How did you learn the code? Such certainty now. A few minutes ago you didn't remember."

Her tone was biting. Only he could screw this up. In the short span of few minutes he'd gone from her prized possession—a medium with a direct line to her precious Harry—to once again being a drifter trying to con her. If she was going to hold anyone in that regard it should be Martin, but that wasn't Erich's luck. She *knew* the doctor was a rogue and still treated him as a welcome guest and friend.

Why couldn't she just believe in him the way she put her faith in the ruffians around her. "He spoke to me."

"You've studied him. You've picked locks in this house and shown your prowess with sleight of hand. You want to step into his life and use me to gain his notoriety for yourself. That's it, isn't it? You want to walk in Harry's footsteps. You're one of the many he feared, and the sole reason he developed the code in the first place."

Erich's shoulders fell as the weight of her distrust landed on them. "You couldn't be more wrong."

"Did you break into my safe?"

"You said Harry sealed the code in an envelope. See for yourself if it's been disturbed. Whatever happened when I passed out, it wasn't any attempt to con you. I swear."

She averted her eyes, finding a worn spot in the linoleum that demanded all her attention. Her disbelief stung like a slap to the face. She started to walk past him. He was sure she was going to accept his dare and check the vault—at least he would be exonerated from cheating this time around—but a knock sounded on the back door behind her.

"Bess, darling, are you okay? You sounded so panicked on the telephone." Martin's voice filtered in from behind the door. As he rounded the corner from the mudroom to the kitchen, Erich got a good look at his enemy. Martin's clothes, as well as his hair, were impeccable, and his long wool coat was draped over his arm. Slipping the white gloves from his hands, he didn't look like someone who dropped everything to come over on a moment's notice.

Erich clenched his hands under the table as the taste of bile bubbled up. This should be a private moment between Bess and him. Well, as private as it could be with Harry's memory intruding. The last thing he wanted, or the situation needed, was Martin, especially since he topped Erich's list of suspects for the poisoned tea. "We're fine, no thanks to you. Go home!"

"Stop it!" Bess chastised. "This is still my home, and you have no right to order guests around." Pivoting toward Martin she said, "Thank you for rushing right over here at this late hour."

Martin gripped her hands, and gave her an adoring look. "Dear. What's the matter? You look as you've seen a ghost."

"I thought I had, but now..." Her body tensed as she stepped away and looked at Erich. "I think—"

"Stop, Bess! This is between us." The situation would be better handled with decorum, but Erich's temper flared anyway.

Martin interceded with a smooth, calming lilt to his voice. "Whatever is bothering you, I will do my best to help. You know you can trust me. While this scoundrel—"

"Delivered the message from Harry." The words spilled from her, relighting the joyful spark in her eyes. Even though she'd expressed doubts, something inside still believed. "The coded message, Erich spoke it not twenty minutes ago, and then he passed out cold on the floor."

Martin's gaze crawled up and down Erich with such spite it sent a chill through him. "It's impossible. I don't know how, but he's deceiving you. You should have tossed him out on his ear the night you caught him breaking into that cabinet. I told you then it was a sign of bad things to come."

Erich scrubbed his forehead. There was a time when Bess's confidence in Martin would have been expected, but that day had long passed. Now, it confounded him.

Martin's manipulation of Bess—much in the way he and Gail had manipulated Harry—angered Erich. "I would never steal from Bess."

Not even giving him the satisfaction of a response, Martin spoke only to Bess. "Now that the code has been revealed, why don't you tell it to me? Knowing Harry, it was probably rudimentary. Erich merely guessed it once you let him into your life."

Being smug came second nature to Martin, but Erich wasn't going to let him off the hook. "If it was so simple, shouldn't someone with your brains have cracked it?"

"Unlike you, I respect Bess and wouldn't overstep my boundaries. I'm not the one putting a cloud over her reputation by moving in."

"I don't really care what you think."

Martin focused in on Bess, zeroing in on her fears, or so it seemed. "Some in town believe he's smooth talked his way right into your bed." The innuendo in Martin's voice was thick and hit its mark.

"I'd never!" Bess covered her face with her hands, proving that Martin knew how to elicit the desired emotional response.

"Repeating such scandalous lies is *not* a show of respect," Erich said. He wanted to move closer to Bess— take her in his arms and hold her close—but knew it would only give Martin fuel for his indecent accusations. Bess knew it too and wouldn't welcome him now. "Bess can affirm that Harry spoke through me tonight. I delivered his message. There is no need for that spectacle Gail and you are encouraging."

"I don't believe for one moment that really happened," Martin said. "I'm not sure what you did, but I will figure it out."

Erich couldn't help but laugh. "Funny, you claim Gail can talk to the dead, but doubt me."

"Spiritualism is a honed skill. If you've mastered anything in your short life, I'm betting it's treachery. You breezed into town a little more than a week ago, and you're already a mainstay in this house. Harry would be disgusted."

"That's true. It'd make him ill to know you were standing on his doorstep. How can you pretend to be Bess's friend while you're trying to kill me?"

The vein in Martin's temple bulged, and a satisfied smile turned Erich's lips. Seemed he could push buttons too. Martin answered Erich with a sneer, and then spoke to Bess. "Are you going to stand here and listen to him accusing me of such horrible things? Gail and I have stood by your side from the moment you came home from burying Harry."

"I may be a stranger, but Harry trusted me enough to speak through me."

Bess's gaze flickered between the two of them for a moment. Her stare so intense, it warmed Erich's skin. Then, she left the room.

Erick kicked himself. Pride had made a mess of things again. Moments ago she'd been happy, and now, because of his fight with Martin, she'd plummeted to distraught.

Jaden's accusations to Harry had been spot-on, and Erich saw it clearer every time that side of him rose up. Bess might need his protection, but his plan of attack was all wrong. He needed proof to back his allegations, not emotional outbursts that pitted her between the two of them. Set to apologize, he followed her. "Bess, I'm so sorry. I've darkened your joy—"

In the parlor, the sight of her wheeling the large steel safe from the closet stopped Erich cold. He could feel the other man's piercing glare focused on Bess and wished she hadn't shown Martin where her secrets were kept. However, Erich also knew in moments Bess would have her truth.

She picked up the envelope, held it to the light, and then gripped it to her chest. Her eyes closed, and her cheeks flushed. Erich knew since it was still sealed, Bess could believe in Harry's devotion, even if Martin and he had tried to ruin that. Her faith in Harry and his love had restored what Erich had almost ruined. The open wound in her heart was healing. So, why was Erich so jealous?

"Harry used Erich as a vessel tonight. It's the only possible explanation." Her eyes locked on him, studied him for a long moment. "Did he really ask you to cancel the séance? Tell me the truth, Erich."

He could only give one answer. They both knew Harry too well for him to lie. "No, Bess. I only told you that because I'm worried about you and what Martin and Gail are doing."

She nodded once and then put the envelope back in the vault. "I will not let Harry down. For the first time since he died, I feel like I really know what he wants. He's proven to me he can communicate through Erich. We'll hold the séance as planned, but with you, Erich, as the medium."

# Chapter Eighteen

Did Bess really just ask Erich to cause his own death?

"You can't give Gail's spot to Erich. You're smarter than this," Martin pleaded. Erich didn't need to read any minds to know that Martin was Hell bent on protecting Gail's reputation. Only her goals and dreams were important to him.

Erich closed the distance between himself and Bess. There were too many high-strung emotions flying around the room, spinning Bess's head and twisting her heart. In the last half hour she'd made one rash decision after the other and needed time to breathe. She'd think it through and understand there was no reason to push forward. Or so he hoped. "Why have a séance at all?"

"Because I know what Harry wants. He answered my prayer, and I'll repay him by giving his fans the show of a lifetime."

A tremble whisked down his spine as if his blood had turned to ice. If Bess's show ended Erich's life, would Harry's fans be entertained? "What if Harry doesn't come through?"

Bess brushed off his concern with a wave of her hand. All the conviction that Harry demanded from her had taken root and grown to something impossible to trim or contain. It was going to take some quick maneuvering to break through that bond and convince her to defy Harry's perceived will. "Whether or not he appears on Halloween is irrelevant. We'll build the suspense, and just as the audience loses all hope, the message will come to you."

Erich lifted his hands and stepped back, as if he could push everything that had happened since he regained consciousness away. This was the only real excitement he'd seen in her since rejoining this world. How could he fight the passion in her eyes? Did he even want to? Would a fake séance have the same consequences of a real one? Maybe he could flub his way through it without executing himself.

"I see how Erich's rubbed off on you, Bess. You're going to give him the spotlight to rob Harry's fans of their money and leave them with nothing more than a lie?"

"No money. This not what's important."

Bess yanked the attention of both men to her, but Martin appeared more taken aback. "What do you mean no money?"

"Even though the show is for the fans, it will be a small, intimate gathering with only the press in attendance. They will deliver the news to the world: that my beloved is indeed the greatest escape artist ever. Can't you see the headlines: 'Harry Houdini, Man of Mystery, Defies Death.'"

Erich saw a reflection of Harry's soul burning in her. The hunger for the center stage spotlight that she'd accused Erich of possessing twisted his stomach into knots. Maybe it hadn't been a ghost he'd been competing with all along. "You don't need to recreate this scene to get the press's attention. If they even suspect you're lying, it will backfire on you."

"Then we will have to make sure we're convincing," Bess said.

Martin stepped closer to Bess, and he waved a pointed finger between the two of them. "You can't do this with just the two of you."

"Why not?" Bess asked.

"Because if you don't include Gail, I will go straight to the papers and the police and tell them you're orchestrating a fraud: a false victory for a pitiful showman."

Now this was the cold, calculating man that Harry had grown wary of. Martin demanded the reins and expected control despite what Bess might want. She'd let her excitement dig a hole, and Martin was all too eager to push her into it.

Jaden's words rang in Erich's ears. *The players are many...you've interfered with plans long set in motion...*Martin didn't need a piece of the financial pie. Was he still fighting an old feud that should have died with Harry? Bess, having laid her plan out in front Martin, had given him the upper hand. "What is it you really want, Martin?"

"To be part of the notoriety. And for Harry to recant the slanderous things he said about Gail."

Erich couldn't help thinking that was only part of the story.

Interrupting Erich's thought process, Bess spoke through gritted teeth. "I will not lie in Harry's name." Avoiding both men and the brewing argument, she pushed the safe back into the closet.

"Isn't that just what you were plotting with Erich? You are going to clear Gail's name and restore her reputation in the spiritual community. I'm not giving you a choice, Darling."

Martin was right. What alternative did Bess have? The satisfaction ringing in his voice knocked Erich left of center. Giving the Coopers a key role in the charade and recanting Harry's accusations negated the purpose of the code.

Bess reached for the back of the chair and gripped it tight, giving it her full weight. She blinked hard, and Erich could see she was trying to will away building tears. After a moment of quiet contemplation, she nodded and whispered. "Come back tomorrow afternoon. Bring Gail. We have a lot of work to do if we're going to put on a believable show."

A moment later the back door slammed. With Martin gone, Erich expected Bess to explode, angry at herself for giving Martin the upper hand. Instead, she stood still. The color drained from her face. He wanted to reach out, offer comfort or a plan of action, but wasn't sure what words he could say to make any of it better.

Bess lowered herself to the chair. Gripping the arms, she bent over at the waist and the flood gates opened. Her sobs filled the room. "What have I done?"

Erich dropped to his knees and took her in his arms, guiding her head to his shoulder. "Shhh, Bess. We'll figure something out. I won't let them do this to you."

"I've been such a fool." She melted into him and sobbed. Instead of fighting Erich's embrace, she clung to him as if he were an anchor—the only thing keeping her stable in this the newest storm rocking her life. "You're right, you know. Harry would have never allowed Martin back into his home. And what did I do? I handed him everything he needs to rip Harry's reputation to bits."

Damn Harry! And damn his reputation! Why had it taken Erich this long to see that Jaden was right? Everything Harry had lived for was dismantling Bess and her sanity. "Martin will not get away with this."

She lifted her head and slid her hands down his arms. He prepared himself for her to flee, but her contact lingered. "And what are you going to do to stop it? You're still so weak."

Encouraged by her touch, he couldn't control his urges and reached up to brush her cheek with his knuckles. She leaned into the caress, and his breath caught. "I'm getting stronger every day, and you have my word. I know you don't think that counts for much, but you'll see."

"That's where you're wrong. You've given me reasons to doubt it, but your word is the only thing I trust right now." She slid from the chair. The heavy veil she protected herself with fell away, and someone vulnerable yet audacious dropped into his lap and glided her body even closer to him.

His throat went dry, and he swallowed hard. Harry's desire for her was never far from his mind, and his hunger burned in Erich's gut no matter how hard he tried to ignore it. But with her eyes focused on his and her arms reaching for his shoulders, Erich's defenses crumbled. "Bess..."

She put a finger to his mouth; her left arm still draped his shoulder. "I don't know how I got by before you showed up."

He moved his body tighter to hers, dropping his hands to her waist and stopping only when his lips were just inches from hers. "You are such a strong lady. I think you just forgot that for a while."

She exhaled, and her hot breath caressed his neck. "I've been surviving. But since you've come, it's like I have a reason to get up in the morning."

What was she saying? That she *had* felt this connection between them? Even though his gut had told him she did, the confirmation sped up the beat of his heart. So close, she begged for his kiss, but not this time. He couldn't make another advance. If they kissed, it would be up to her.

"Where did you come from Erich Welch? I think you stepped right out of my dreams." She closed the mere inches between them, giving him the kiss he longed for. The right thing might have been to stop her, find out what was driving this sudden change in behavior, but that was beyond him. There was only so much he could do to contain the flames of lust, and the sweet taste of her stoked the embers and gave a new life to the fire.

Was he asleep? Maybe this was one of Jaden's manifestations. If so, he didn't want to wake up. He tightened his arms around her waist and pushed, bringing her to her feet as he stood. He gripped at her back and deepened the kiss, sliding his tongue against her lips and easing its way past them.

When they broke apart, he slid his fingers through her lush curls. "The last thing I want to do is hurt you."

"All you've done is tried to protect me from myself."

He was all too aware of her truth—life with Harry had never been easy, and living without him had been sheer Hell. "I think just being here has hurt you. I've brought up memories you'd rather forget."

She leaned into his touch and reached up to return his caresses. "I needed to let it out. I needed to bleed the pain so I could heal. You've helped me do that. And the desire to touch you like this has been taunting me since that first moment we met."

If he followed his heart he would fulfill their mutual desire, leave the guest room behind and lay with her in their bed—Harry's bed. Struck with the realization that there was really a difference between the man his soul once belonged to and the man he'd become, he took a step away from her. He slipped his fingers from her face and gripped her hands. "I've wanted you too, but I remind you of him, and—"

"The best parts. I don't know what tomorrow will bring, Erich. I'm not asking you to stay forever, just long enough that I can get another taste of you."

Her plea shattered the chains he'd restrained himself with. He enveloped her in his arms and fulfilled her request. More than flesh to flesh, it was as if their bound souls demanded to be reunited.

He leaned over and started to pick her up only to have Bess press against his shoulders.

"No! For Heaven's sake. You'll tear your stitches."

"You deserve to be treated like a princess," he whispered.

A smile and a blush proved he'd touched her. "But not if it further injures you."

To ease her mind, he agreed and followed her up the steps. All the reasons he shouldn't flashed through his mind. If she didn't abandon her plans for the séance, he'd be ripped from this world. He wondered if her future changed if she mourned him instead of Harry.

*All right, Jaden, this would be a really good time to use that magic touch of yours and spin me off the road to destruction.* If this was a misstep, surely he'd stop it.

Maybe. Just maybe. Being with Bess was the right thing to do.

So why did he still have doubts? They reached the top of the stairs and crossed the threshold into the room she'd shared with Harry. She took his wrist and pulled him in. Closing her eyes, she moved even closer, laying her head against his shoulder. As all the rough, hard edges that surrounded Bess began to melt and fade, so did his doubts.

He circled her into an embrace and laid his head atop of hers. His stomach tightened with anticipation. She'd come to him, with an open heart and willing body, with such trust—dare he say love—in her eyes.

Since the moment Jaden breathed life back into his soul, he'd hunted her as if he were a tiger and she was his prey. Now she pursued him, but he was helpless. He wouldn't run. Instead, with trembling knees, he submitted to her.

Bess said, "I've made so many foolish mistakes in the last year, but somehow I don't believe trusting you is one of them."

"You are the only thing in my life that has ever been real and right." He didn't care if the words sounded cryptic or unbelievable. In her mind, they'd only known each other a short time, but his soul had known hers, loved hers, for decades. He'd skirt around that issue, lest she think he insane, but he wouldn't hide his feelings any longer.

He loved her. Always had. Right or wrong, he'd considered her with every decision he made. Whether or not she or Jaden believed it, it was fact all the same.

Her body tensed in his arms, and the familiar shudder told him more than her words could. "You don't need to hide yourself. You can trust me, Bess."

She pulled back just enough to look up into his eyes. An ache coursed him as she pulled her hand from his back, but her touch didn't stray long. She laid it against his cheek. "Forgive me, Harry." Bess whispered and pushed up on her toes, leaning in to kiss Erich.

He drew back. A complete split from Harry's soul might be impossible, but inviting him into bed with Bess was where Erich drew the line. "Don't ask him for permission, Bess. Forgive yourself and decide whether or not it's what you want. I only want this if it's me you're with."

Her eyes flicked side to side as she considered her heart. Certainty came quickly. Her dilated pupils opened the window to her feelings. A slight nod of her head as she moved in to taste his mouth again revealed her decision.

It should have felt familiar, like the thousands of other times Harry had held Bess close, but it didn't. Erich was a new man, experiencing the love of his life as if it were the first time. His fingers tangled in her tight curls, and he mumbled against her satin-soft lips. "Are you sure? I want you to be sure."

"It's been a long time since my body has wanted anyone as much as it wants you." She cradled his face as her body arched to his.

His hand braced the middle of her spine, and it was as if the air had been sucked from the room. The need throbbing within him made breathing impossible. With her body leaning back in his arms, willing and open, instincts fought to take over, but her physical need wasn't enough. He had to know this was more than skin-to-skin for her. "Does your heart want this too?"

"It calls to you as if I've known you for ages and refuses to be denied any longer. I've dreamed of a moment like this since you bumped into me on the street."

Her confirmation of what he believed left him vulnerable to her. He slid his mouth against her cheeks, whispering. "I belong to you and am yours to have or hurt."

She slipped from his arms. "What about...I'm old enough—"

He silenced her concern with yet another kiss. "It doesn't matter. It never mattered." He stroked her cheek, never breaking eye contact. The tight burning low in his gut begged him to give in to his desires this very moment—on the floor if necessary—before either of them changed their mind.

His desire to treat this woman as his queen, with a tender love and consideration he'd forgone in Harry's body, pulsed stronger than the carnal burning. Harry had taken so much for granted, and Erich refused to make the same mistakes. If he was getting another life to spend with Bess, she would always know how much he loved her, and never once question his feelings the way she had Harry's.

Erich squeezed her hand and turned toward the bed, illuminated in the radiant light of the moon penetrating the east window.

A sign from above?

Bess's arms wrapped around his waist, and he could feel her breath against his shoulder. "I've never seen the room like this before."

He gave his focus to her, laid his palm flat against her shoulder. "You should always be bathed in a Heavenly glow, my angel."

She leaned into his touch and then moved past him, undoing the buttons that ran down the front of her blouse. As she spun back, it dropped to the floor, followed by her skirt. She stood in her stockings and slip backlit by the cascading light.

He followed her to the edge of the bed, as he would to the ends of the earth, reaching out. She blocked his impending embrace, guiding him to sit in front of her instead. Pressing each knee on either side of him, she lowered herself carefully to his lap. Trembling fingers worked each button of his shirt. Her eyes never left his as she pulled it from his body and tossed it to the floor.

He danced his fingers all the way down her spine, settling on her hips. Her bottom brushed against his thighs, and passion rolled through him. She pulled the undershirt from his body and then brushed her lips against his neck as she tossed it away.

Bess's eyes burned with hunger, and he had to bite his lip to control his craving. Tugging and yanking, he soon worked the slip from around her hips, and it joined the growing pile of clothes on the floor.

Though time seemed to slow to a crawl, it was a blur of caresses and maneuverings that landed him flat on his back in the center of the feather mattress. She hovered over him. His fingers fluttered over her stomach and then slid up, settling on her breasts.

He started to lift himself to her, needing to taste her mouth, but she pressed on his shoulder, keeping him flat. Leaning over, her tongue lingered against his chin. "You shouldn't be exerting yourself."

He stroked her hair, not able to break from her warm, loving gaze. "I'm stronger than you think." As if to prove it, he clutched the back of her neck, holding her still, and then used the force of his body to roll them, landing on top of her. "Stop looking at me as someone younger or as the person you had to nurse back to health. Let me show you the man I am."

Even though Harry's life had felt foreign to Erich, Bess's body was a familiar place, the only Heaven he'd ever know. Even if he sacrificed himself in the end, it would be worth it for this one moment with her.

He left a trail of feather-light kisses from her neck to her full breasts and then concentrated his efforts, his tongue danced against the supple flesh, teasing the tiny bud and relishing her trembles of pleasure. Too many times this woman beneath him hadn't known Harry's heart. Erich vowed she'd never doubt his feelings.

Clenching her waist, he drew her to him, teasing her neck with his mouth. The sweet-salt taste of her flesh weakened his resolve and augmented his desire. She stroked his hair and whimpered as he moved lower, finding her most intimate place. Her hips lifted, fueling his arousal. His body begged for gratification, but he'd deny himself until her heard her passionate cries, till she knew again the joy missing from her life in the last eleven months.

Her moans hit his ears a second before her body began to spasm. He tightened his embrace and inched back up her body. He brushed his lips to hers and whispered, "Still think I'm too weak to care for you, Angel?"

She hugged his neck, gripping him tight. Her words came in breathless gasps. "Not...weak...need...you..."

His passionate little hellcat. This part of her, the one she'd only shared with Harry, made him feeble with lust. Never again would she be left wondering or wanting. He ground his pelvis to hers and pushed himself inside her. "Is this what you need?"

The answer came to him in her sensual cries.

# Chapter Nineteen

Even after Bess had fallen asleep in Erich's arms, he couldn't let her go. He held her tight, kissed her forehead and inhaled the scent of her hair. His body had hungered for this since the moment he'd first seen her on the street. His heart never stopped burning for her—even in death. With this second chance at life, he'd cherish every minute gifted him.

"You've certainly made a mess of things now."

Erich glanced toward the booming voice and saw Jaden's stare focused on the window. A sense of modesty in the omniscient one? Disappointment was more probable.

Erich leaned back against the headboard and slid his hand down Bess's cheek resting on his lap. "Shhh, she needs to rest."

"She'll sleep through the night. Somehow, I don't think you will." The usual sarcastic bite in Jaden's voice was gone. A heaviness coated each and every word. "Getting her into bed changes nothing. Stopping the séance was and still is your goal."

Erich's stomach clenched. Couldn't he have this one moment, before he had to unravel the mess Martin had caused? "From the way you acted when I gave her the message, I thought she'd give it up. We were both wrong."

Whatever it was that had held Jaden's glare lost its appeal. He flipped his attention and took two steps toward the bed. Intimidation rolled off his massive frame, and the snipped cadence of his speech signaled he'd grown tired of their banter. "Letting go is her only hope."

Pulling Bess tighter, Erich let his hand hover just inches above her cheek. Jaden's outburst should have startled her awake, but she lay still. "She wants to honor Harry. Who am I to tell her no?" He couldn't meet Jaden's stare, knew the truth lay in his eyes. Even though agreeing to perform the séance seemed like helping her, it was really the same as putting a nail in both their coffins

"The idea, *Harry,* was for you to make a choice that benefited someone other than yourself!"

Erich had finally accepted that he was a different person than Harry, so why did Jaden choose this moment to recognize the soul instead of the man? More than just another puzzle for Erich to work, this irritated him. Every time he accepted one of Jaden's truths, the reality was altered. Dare Erich admit that he embraced the man he was now over Harry's past?

"Two entities," Jaden responded to Erich silent question. "I speak to the one who clings to Bess's ultimate demise. And yours too. Don't forget that if Harry's spirit is called forth, it will leave your body, and you'll cease to exist. You may be separate, but your life is still tied to his soul."

Erich's head fell forward. Sacrificing himself for her seemed like an easy choice, but knowing that Bess's pain would continue made it complicated.

"You need to figure out how she can find happiness that isn't dependent on Harry. In the last couple of days you've untangled the man you've become from the man you were. I dare say you've even learned from some of his mistakes. The real gem would be getting Bess to do the same."

Jaden vanished into thin air, leaving Erich and Bess alone. Even though he'd been racing against the ticking clock, this time—alone with her—was something to cherish. She'd sleep through the night, and he would spend these hours holding her and praying she would forgive him for refusing to take part in the séance.

****

The very moment Bess opened her eyes, pain throbbed from her chest and spread throughout her body. Nothing new. After thirty-two years of marriage, waking alone had been the hardest thing she'd had to do. Every morning for the last eleven plus months, the first thing she faced was tears pressed against her eyes.

The scent of *him* overpowered her, and she realized instead of Harry, this morning her body ached for Erich. She wrapped her arms around the pillows and resisted the urge to sob. No matter how she sliced it, or tried to dissect it, she couldn't escape the feelings. Harry had been her whole life; now she longed for another.

The previous night had been a roller coaster of emotions from the moment Harry had used Erich as a vessel right through to her surrender to Erich. Even though her head told her to feel guilty, her heart refused. It was like Erich had told her time and again, Harry wasn't coming back.

But where had Erich gone?

She slipped out of the bed, straightened the blankets and went to search for him. Checks of the other bedroom, parlor and kitchen turned up empty. In the mudroom, she nearly tripped over Harry's old rusty tool box now sitting in front of the washing machine. Laying on top of it was a once white rag, covered in soot and smelling like fuel oil. That blasted furnace must have gone out again, and Erich had already fixed it.

She walked out into the morning sun to be bathed by a cool autumn breeze.

Had he left?

There was no way to tell if he'd taken his belongings; he hadn't arrived with anything of his own. He'd promised to stay by her side and help her out of the mess she'd created with Martin and Gail. Had he changed his mind now that she'd laid down with him? Was that all he'd wanted?

Bess shook off her mind's ramblings. Erich was different than most. Maybe he had given her reason to doubt him, but she knew he was honorable and trustworthy. In the handful of days they'd spent together, she'd come to count on him. Reassured, Bess retreated to the house and started a pot of coffee. Wherever he'd gone, he'd be back shortly.

She plugged in the peculator and moved toward the table, but the large box sitting by the back door caught her eye. Was it really just yesterday she'd packed up all the trinkets and glamor? Her discussion with Joseph and her resulting emotions felt faraway and distant.

Now, she chuckled at the irony.

She still had no use for the box's contents. There would be no Tom Foolery at Harry's show. They didn't need glitz. They could prove to a doubting world that Harry was the greatest illusionist ever—so skilled he could break the chains of death.

His words, the ones he spoke the night he'd scrawled the code on the paper, flashed through her mind. Her stomach flipped, her legs wobbled and she lowered herself to the chair. Who had she been trying to fool? The bigger-than-life persona defined Harry on the stage. He'd spoke of returning to her, but not because he believed he could. The code was an illusion—a means to protect his legacy. No profiting off his death—that was his sole wish.

But his message had spilled from Erich's mouth. Harry had done what he didn't believe in. Shouldn't she share that with the world? His achievement deserved to be shouted from the mountain tops: Harry defied death to declare his love for her.

Now that was the key. Wasn't it?

If Harry really wanted the world to hear that declaration, he'd have waited for Halloween and the stage. His words had been a precious gift to her: a comforting embrace to her weeping heart, and her first instinct had been to shine it up and display it to a crowd.

Her desperate need to hang on to Harry had done nothing but dishonor him. She should have been protecting his legacy. Now, with Martin at the helm, it would all become the circus Harry had plotted long and hard to avoid.

Heavy steps sounded on the wooden step. The rattle of the back door caused her breath to catch. Erich was home. She glanced at him as he came into the kitchen. "Where did you run off to this morning?" A silly question. The white box in his hands gave her the answer.

"I wanted to talk to Will and thought I'd bring breakfast back." He set the box down on the table and hovered over her. She closed her eyes, waiting for his kiss. Seconds later, he fulfilled her expectation, letting his soft lips graze her cheek. "I really hoped I'd make it back before you woke up."

She clasped her hands together, resting them on her lap. The flames from last night still smoldered between them, and she hungered for his touch and his kiss, but also grappled with decency and decorum. The brazen woman who'd thrown herself at him wasn't her true nature, and in the bright light of the morning, she wasn't sure what her next move should be. "Coffee should be ready, let me get some plates and cups." She started to stand, but his hand pressed down ever-so-gently on her shoulder.

"Sit, Bess. Let me serve you just once. You deserve it after the days you've spent caring for me."

She exhaled and acknowledged his request, relaxing in the chair. Still searching for the words, she fell back on an old cliché. "I think autumn has arrived."

"It is a beautiful day."

She caught his gaze as he set a mug and a small plate in front of her. Between that and the inflection of his voice, she could tell he was talking about more than the chill in the air. Her cheeks flushed, but he didn't seem to notice, and he mirrored the table setting and took the seat to her left.

She picked up the napkin and twisted it in her hands. "I've been thinking. Everything got so out of hand last night."

Erich paled. His gaze dropped as if it were in free fall. "Don't do this, Bess. Don't cast away what we shared like it was some sort of mistake."

Insensitive as it was, she laughed and tossed the napkin to the table. Sliding her finger under his chin, she lifted it. "I didn't mean *that*. I'll never regret last night. I meant the argument with Martin and all the threats."

His chest heaved as he exhaled his fears. He wrapped an arm around her neck and rested his forehead against hers. "I suppose I'm to blame for that."

"Oh, there's enough to go around. I let my excitement get the best of me and put myself in a position to let Martin blackmail me. I took what should have been a private moment with Harry and tried to spin it into a publicity stunt."

"You learned that from the master."

She pulled back from him. He'd said the words casually but that didn't make them less true. No, they were dead on. Going for the glitz is exactly what Harry would have done in most situations, but not with this. Not with his good name. "I'm afraid when I tell Martin I've changed my mind, he'll follow through on his threats."

Erich lifted his face to meet her stare, eyebrows arched and mouth agape. "You've changed your mind?"

"Harry gave me what I spent months asking for. We created the code to keep his death from becoming a spectacle. I know this in my heart, but I don't think Martin is going to just accept it."

"If you don't have a séance, it's your word against his, and Martin's doesn't count for much with anyone these days. He can't prove you were going to recreate or fabricate anything if there is no show."

Erich was right, but did she have the strength to stick to her decision? "What of Harry's memory and legacy? It feels wrong to forget it all?"

"You shouldn't forget. You can honor the intent." Erich sat very still, staring at the mug of coffee still steaming in front of him. "I let my temper get the best of me last night. Instead of confronting Martin, I should have been focused on protecting you. I'd still go to the ends of the earth to do that."

It wasn't the first time Erich had made such a claim, but for some reason, she allowed herself to believe him now. The night they'd shared changed everything. "So we fix it just by saying no. And then face the brunt of Martin's anger together."

"For as long as you'll allow me to, I'll stand by your side." His lips curved upward, and his eyes almost sparkled.

A blush warmed her cheeks. Erich's devotion made her feel like the naive, young girl who'd fallen in love with Harry. Where had that girl gone and why had it taken so long for her to return? The answer was simple. She'd been hardened by life's experiences and jaded by his death. She'd become a shadow of herself, lost in her pain, until Erich's light had thawed her heart.

"There's something I should tell you," Erich stammered as he dug his hand into his pocket and came back with a necklace. "Will finished fixing this. He wanted me to bring it to you."

She took it and slid the sterling silver thread through her fingers as if examining every link. "It was an anniversary gift from Harry, you know."

Leaning over the table, she opened the small wooden box that served as a center piece, coming back with his wedding band. Not quite two weeks ago, the broken chain had devastated her, but in the last few days she'd forgotten all about giving it to Will. She hadn't even touched the ring. Opening the clasp, Bess reunited the two pieces of jewelry and set them both on the table.

The first time she placed the band on the chain it'd been about keeping Harry physically close, but not this time. Now, it was as if she was letting him go. A piece of her would always be Harry's, but Erich was right. Harry couldn't consume her anymore. "These are the only two pieces of jewelry he ever gave me. The only extravagance we treated ourselves to...well, except this house."

Erich's hand fell to her knee, but he said nothing. With patience, he offered her quiet support and let her deal with the wave of emotions.

Her right hand went to her left ring finger. She gripped her own wedding band and twisted it to and fro, tugging it free. If she were truly dedicated to moving forward with Erich, it was the very least she owed him. It wasn't fair to either man for her to make love to Erich while honoring her commitment to Harry with the symbol of marriage. After a moment, she slid it on the chain, closed the clasp and returned it to the oak box.

"Are you all right?" Erich asked.

"I am. I feels like it's time." She turned to face him and began to lean forward. As if he could sense what she needed, Erich wrapped his arm around her neck and guided her head to his shoulder. He kissed her forehead and then whispered, "I think we should go away, you and me. Maybe east, to the big city."

She probably should have been offended by the suggestion. A decent woman wouldn't tarnish her reputation that way, but the idea of going away with Erich thrilled her. "You really think we should?"

He paused and slid his hands down her arms. "I think I was pretty clear about how I feel for you last night, Bess. And I think you're starting to feel something for me too."

"But I...but you..."

"You're still grieving, and I'm not anything like what you had in mind for your future, but life's just that way sometimes. I think if you and I got away from here, went somewhere you could get a little anonymity, it'd help you heal. Then who knows what might happen. I'm here to take care of you. I promise."

"You make a lot of promises, Erich Welch."

"And I intend to keep each and every one. You just need to trust me. Believe in me."

*Believe.* The same thing Harry had always asked for. The one thing she'd always given him. Was it right to now turn that faith over to another man? His plan of action did make sense. "My sisters say the same thing, you know, that it isn't good for me to be out here alone, but I wasn't alone. Not really. I had my friends and Harry's memory."

"You'll still have your real friends, and you can carry the memories anywhere you go. We could go back to New York, if that's what you want."

For the first time in a long time her heart felt just a little lighter, and the tightness in her chest eased. Her grief was waning like a phase of the moon, inch by inch. "You're right. We should go."

# Chapter Twenty

Bess didn't recognize the feeling that had settled in her center: contentment. If possible, she'd spend the day with her head on Erich's shoulder, wrapped up in his protective embrace, listening to his slow, deep breathing. The way he kissed her and touched her was as if they'd been lovers for a lifetime, instead of less than twenty-four hours. She twisted her head and looked at his peaceful face, wondering how he could be so different from Harry, yet so similar.

The sun had begun to peek through the west window, confirming they'd burnt off most of the morning making love with each other and building plans for a bigger, better future. Part of her wondered if it was really possible. Could she forget her promises to Harry and go home with a new beau on her arm?

Like it had been extinguished by an autumn rain, the flames of her passion were drowned by guilt. She slid a finger down the length of his nose, across his lips and over his chin. All Erich asked for was her conviction and promised the world in return. And even though every bit of her heart and body screamed to submit and move forward, a tiny sliver of her heart couldn't give up on Harry.

But what was she holding out for? Harry had already delivered his message. Choosing Erich as the catalyst might have been Harry's way of giving this union his stamp of approval.

At least she could try and convince herself of that.

Erich was right. Harry was gone and wouldn't be coming back. Determined to live whatever life she had left, Bess pulled from Erich's clutch and slipped into her robe, returning to the kitchen.

The morning's coffee was now a thick sludge in the bottom of the percolator, and she dumped it down the sink, set on making a fresh pot. Through the window, she saw a familiar car kicking up stones as it pulled into the driveway.

Gail Cooper.

Her final instruction to Martin had been for the two of them to come after lunch, which it was, but only Gail exited the car and walked toward the back door.

Maybe that was a good thing. She'd like to avoid another blow up between Erich and Martin—the last one had almost gone to fist-a-cuffs. It was going to be hard enough to tell Gail that she'd decided to abort the séance. She didn't need inflated and angry male egos making it worse.

Thinking it might be best to keep Gail and Erich separated too, she greeted Gail on the porch.

Gail met Bess's less-than-enthusiastic good morning with a big hug. As if she was the one with reason to celebrate. Not like she'd come to construct a huge sham. "When Martin told me what happened, I was so happy for you. You don't know what it's taken for me to wait for a decent hour to call."

Bess stiffened. Internally, she twisted, but outwardly she returned the hug, patting Gail's shoulder. *Happy?* What exactly had Martin told her? *Blackmail wasn't a cause for this much joy.*

Gail pulled back and sized up Bess with a scowl. "Dear. It's nearly noon. Why are you still lounging around in your robe? After such a glorious event I'd think you and this Erich would be trying to contact Harry again."

So, Gail had been paying attention over the last year. Her prediction was good, but the picture she painted of the two of them trying to call forth Harry didn't thrill Bess, it made her sad.

She only had to think about the man she'd spent the previous night and morning making love with to reconfirm her decisions. "There isn't going to be a séance. I let excitement get the best of me last night. I've thought about it now and decided there is no need. Harry kept his word and showed me death was escapable, and I'm going to leave it at that."

Gail's mouth dropped open, and her eyes bulged. "Don't be ridiculous. You know that wasn't Harry's intent."

"He'd never want to be a part of some spiritualist spectacle. He loathed the thought."

"Harry Houdini never shied from the spotlight."

The truth. It should be a moving argument, but somehow it only proved Bess's point. "In this, I know my husband's heart. Please understand."

"This is that Erich twisting and warping your mind. He's arrogant and sly, that's what Martin said. He thinks Erich and Harry could be brothers, if you only compared their egos." Gail pushed past Bess and stomped into the kitchen.

Bess followed, wondering to herself how she arrived at this place. Only Gail and Martin would have the audacity to claim to know Harry better than her, yet somehow they were the two she'd allowed so close. She sobered, realizing just how much she'd accepted their influence.

Not finding Erich in the kitchen, Gail flipped her attention back to Bess. "Where is he? This spiritual virtuoso?"

Bess grabbed Gail's arm, and kept her from crossing into the parlor. She'd had enough of the woman's condescending attitude and wasn't going to let her attack Erich, even if she had to twist the truth to get her out of her house. "He's in bed, still recovering from his illness. Besides, none of this concerns Erich. It's about me and my Harry."

"So, you're going to stand there and tell me Harry would rather celebrate his greatest escape ever in the privacy of this kitchen than on the stage with the whole world watching."

She dug her heel into the floor. Gail could argue all she wanted. Bess knew she was right on this.

"If he wanted the world to witness it, he'd have waited for the show."

"You're the one who said he liked to practice an act until you both knew it inside and out. You promised Martin you'd give me the glory of being the one. You owe me this. Harry owes me this!"

Harry was beloved by all, and what he said carried weight. If he believed Gail to be a fraud, by God, the free world now believed the same. Gail had a right to her pain and anger, but so had Harry. Bess, however, had no obligation to set right what had happened between the two of them. "I'm truly sorry. You've been a good friend to me this last year, despite what happened between you and Harry, but that doesn't make it okay for me to disrespect his feelings and the gift he gave me. Especially not so that others can profit. It's the last thing he would want."

Gail lunged forward and gripped Bess's shoulder. "You can't think what Harry wants means a thing to me."

"Get your hands off her."

Bess lifted her eyes, looking over Gail's shoulder to see Erich, wearing only his gray wool pants, standing in the doorway. His bare chest and the muscles of his arm rippled as he gripped the door jamb. A shining knight coming to her rescue again. No matter how loudly she protested, when she needed him, he was there.

Gail pivoted to the intruding voice. "What have you talked her into? I won't allow you to save the spotlight for yourself."

Erich compressed his lips, and the vein running down the side of his neck quivered, but—to his credit—he didn't move forward. "The last thing I'm interested in is becoming part of some three ring circus that elevates you and degrades Bess. Why don't you understand? This isn't up to you or Martin. It's Bess's decision."

Gail crossed her arms and pushed her right hip forward. "What right do you have to dictate what Bess does?"

"Every right," Bess answered. The last thing she wanted was the people she felt the closest to arguing—especially over someone who wasn't alive anymore. Erich was here though, and he deserved her loyalty. "Erich knows my heart. He's the only one who's made any kind of sense since Harry died."

"So, is *that* the real story?" Gail asked. "What would Harry's legions of fans think? You're willing to let go of his will, because you've lain down with *that* drifter."

Erich closed the distance between Gail and him with firm steps, stopping short of laying a hand on her. "You are no woman to speak of righteous or proper behavior. How Bess chooses to live from this day forward is no one's business but hers. Not Harry's fans. Least of all yours."

Gail glared at Bess, but the tears cracking her voice said she was more hurt than angry. "This is how it's going to be? After everything I've done for you, and all the help Martin's given you, you're going to cast us out because a virtual stranger told you to."

"It's not like that. Since Harry died, I've been listening to everyone *but* his will. When he sent me the message last night, it all came back into focus. I need to move forward. I'm going home. I'm going back to New York and the people who love and care about me."

Gail's mouth hung agape as the color drained from her face. "You are?"

"Yes. We're leaving as soon as possible."

As if Bess's words had thrown Gail off balance, she shifted her weight to the opposite hip and crossed her arm in front of her chest. "I won't stand for that."

"You really don't have a say in the matter," Erich said, "and neither does your know-it-all husband or his faithful sidekick."

The double assault from Bess and Erich rustled Gail's feathers even more. She blinked her glossy eyes and whisked past Bess without another word. The screen door slammed. A moment later the sound of her wheels spinning in the drive, spitting up as many stones as she disheveled coming in, could be heard.

Erich's jaw set as he paced to the window, watching as the car pulled away. "I wish you hadn't told her we're planning to leave."

"What can she do?" Did it really matter if Gail was disappointed or angry? It ended there.

"I don't think that bunch is going to let you or the séance go without a fight. It's something they were willing to poison me over."

Like a dog with a day-old soup bone, Erich refused to let go of the notion. "This again? You have no proof."

His spun toward her and leaned back against the counter. "I trust my gut, and it's telling me those three are up to no good. Your séance was only one step in a master-plan."

"I think you have a vivid imagination." Bess dug her heels in, ready for another argument; instead he walked the length of the counter and back like the caged tigers at the zoo. Something about channeling Harry had changed him, sharpened his focus.

Stopping in front of the window, he stared out a moment. "Go pack a bag."

"What? Why?"

He tapped his knuckles against the counter. "Damn. I wish I'd finished the brakes on the car. We're leaving. Right away."

"You want to go now?"

"This minute. Pack a bag. I'm going to go talk to Will, ask him to give us a ride to the train station and keep an eye on the place until we can get settled. We can come back to deal with the house after everything blows over."

Bess reached for the back of the chair to steady herself. He was pushing things too far too fast. "Just up and go? Right now?"

"I think it's best."

She shook her head and planted her hands firmly on her hips. "You're over reacting, Erich."

"I don't think I am."

"What are they going to do?"

"I don't know."

"Like you said, they have nothing over me if we don't do the séance. They only have power if I try to recreate or fake something." Still, Harry *had* come to her once. Maybe he'd do it again. Especially if Erich's and her reputations were on the line. "What if we could do it for real? If Harry crossed the boundaries for me, he'd certainly be able to do it for his fans."

Erich walked toward her, his head cocked and his posture soft. "Are you having second thoughts, Angel? Because you can't call this off *for* me. You have to know in your heart it is the right thing to do."

Bess looked away from him. Why was it so hard to let go of Harry? He'd kept his word and in the process set her free. Given how she'd spent the previous night and this morning, she should be able to let Harry rest in peace and give herself completely to Erich. Somehow it just wasn't that easy.

His hands gripped her shoulders, and she knew Erich's stare was bearing down on her, demanding an answer to his question. She gave herself over to his touch and the way he made her feel—calm and at peace. It was too soon after Harry had delivered his message of love and faith, too soon after meeting Erich, and even too soon after Harry's death. She was his widow, and she was acting like a teenager, crushing on the gorgeous new man in town. How in the world had it come to this so fast? Was she really willing to pack a bag and run away?

"What will it be, Bess? Are you going to let go of the past and live your life, or stay here, abide Martin and Gail, and drown in it?"

She inhaled slowly, and her body trembled as she exhaled. His mouth against her neck comforted her as much as it thrilled her. When he held her close in the darkest part of the night, it sated her.

Besides, Harry had chosen him.

"You, Erich. I'll leave with you."

# Chapter Twenty-One

Erich walked toward the deli for a second time in a matter of hours. He couldn't shake the blaze of anger he'd seen in Gail's eyes. He recognized that driving need—to not only succeed, but do one better than before or anyone else. It gnawed at one's gut and could only be quenched with the sweet nectar of victory. She'd burned Harry with it when grief blinded his instincts, and now she was after Bess.

Gail wouldn't rest until she was the star of Bess's séance.

Maybe he shouldn't have left Bess alone? With a slow, measured breath, he tried to expel the nervous quiver in his stomach. Gail had just left; it would take her time to get home, complain to Martin and for the two of them to form some sort of plan.

After gaining Will's help, the two of them would return together to collect Bess. He would take her out of this god-forsaken place and on a train to a simpler way of life within the hour.

Once they were back east, he could cement the relationship they had begun to build.

The bustle of the lunch crowd inside the deli grabbed Erich's attention. He ignored his first instinct—to push himself behind the counter and demand Will's attention—and instead got in line behind the owner of the hardware store and his wife. Erich tapped his foot and struggled against the urge to scream as the woman reviewed the menu over and back and then placed the same order both Harry and Erich knew to be her usual. She stepped away, and he approached the counter. "The more things change, the more they stay the same, huh?"

Will cocked his head. Of course, the statement sounded odd from someone who'd only spent hours in the shop. "What can I do for you, Erich?"

"I took your advice and talked to Bess. She's agreed to go back to New York. Can you drive us to the train station?"

"Sure. When?"

"Right now."

Will laughed, like Erich had just told some epic joke. "It's the middle of the lunch rush. I can't take you right now."

Why did everyone react like he was an over-dramatic school girl or a small child afraid of the boogieman? The danger was more than a figment of his imagination, and he'd save Bess from it, no matter how many laughed in his face. "I wouldn't ask if it wasn't important."

"I'll come by after the shop closes at 3:00."

He slammed his hand against the counter. "We can't wait. I have to get Bess out of town before Gail and Martin hurt her."

"What? Erich, I know you're suspicious of their motives. Heck, everyone is, but you're taking this too far."

"I don't believe I am."

Maybe it was because of his determination, or Will's own fondness for Bess, but the portly man posture softened, and he weighed the issues. "Do you have proof?"

"No."

"Well, then, I have a business to run. If you're not going to order something, please step aside."

Erich reached across the counter and grabbed Will's arm. "I'm begging you." *Where had that come from?* Harry would rather die than surrender his pride to anyone for any reason. But, to Hell with Harry and his arrogance. Erich wasn't about to stand idly and let that group of vultures prey on his Bess.

Will's jaw set. "The line is stacking up behind you. If you're so worried about Bess, go back to her place and stay with her. I'll come by after I close."

He slumped back from the counter. If he still had Harry's face, Will and Bess would believe the threats, and they'd be acting on them. Instead they thought he was delusional. Frustrated didn't even begin to cover the well of emotions pooling inside him. If he couldn't get Will to come now, then his advice was second best. Erich would keep watch for the enemy in the interim.

Stepping out of the diner, he bristled against the cool breeze blowing up the street. He was used to extreme changes in the weather, but that was back east. Southern California endeared itself as the state of non-changing weather. Drastic shifts like what they'd experienced in the last twenty-four hours were rare and only added to his discontent. Erich rounded the corner and hit a brick wall.

A tall, brick wall wrapped in black leather. Jaden stood in front him, a long, black braid draped over his left shoulder. Not hidden by dark glasses, his eyes sent a chill down Erich's spine.

"For every step forward you take, you slide back two."

Games and puzzles. Erich was sick of them, especially now that something sinister permeated the air. The scent of evil was so powerful it twisted his belly into knots. Reading a situation: a gift from Harry? Perhaps. "I got an idea, Jaden, either help me out or step aside."

"Have you wondered why things have gone from bad to worse since you convinced her to call off the séance?"

"Let me guess. It has something to do with my selfish love for her."

Jaden tossed his head and chuckled. "Love. Surprisingly, that isn't the gaffe in the plan this time. How well do you know your Proverbs?"

Erich tried to push his way past Jaden, but that was like trying to wrestle a draft horse to the ground. Jaden held him at bay without any effort what-so-ever.

Erich said, "I don't have time for Bible verses. Bess is in danger."

"If you don't remember them and soon, the waiting will be over."

Pulling his arm back, Erich prepared to ram it into Jaden's chest, even if it doing so didn't clear the path. To his surprise, Jaden evaporated, leaving the street empty. Erich shook off the ominous warning and started running toward Bess's house. He focused his mind to his body and paced his breathing. The scent of smoke rode the breeze. Maybe someone burning leaves. Another sharp inhale and it became apparent that wasn't the source. Nor was it the scent of burnt bread or pies put on the sill to cool. This was thicker, heavier, like a campfire accelerated with an igniter and contaminated with plastic and rotten eggs.

He stopped and scanned the horizon and found the black, billowing smoke rising above the trees and houses. The image of Bess passed out in the chair while the pan burned dry on the stove flashed in his mind.

Had she tried again to contact Harry? Maybe drank more of that home-made brandy? She wouldn't. Not after all his warnings.

Who was he trying to fool? Of course she would.

Erich's stomach did a back-flip, but even with its contents pushing upward, he quickened his pace, dashing into the street without looking. A searing pain flashed in his gut, and he cradled his would with his hand. The sound of a fire engine in the distance bore down on him. Wheels squealed, but he didn't even glance back to see how close he'd come to being run down. His life meant zero in the grand scheme. Bess had to be safe.

*Why did I leave her alone?* Why had Jaden stolen precious moments that could have been used to prevent...

As he came up on the corner of her street, the sight ahead froze him in his tracks. Bess's neighbors were assembled on the lawn, gawking at the same truck that had whizzed past him two blocks back and was now setting up in the driveway. His lungs burned and hands trembled. He'd never forgive himself if Bess was caught inside. Sprinting up the street, he called her name.

He joined the crowd as a stream of heat billowed over him. The entire house was engulfed in angry, orange flames. He tried to ignore the thought too horrible to consider and shoved through the neighbors he'd never taken a moment to know in this body. A large fireman blocked his progress. "Where do you think you're going, Bud?"

"In the house. Bess is in there."

The hard, mask-like veil that draped the man's face didn't shield his emotions. Erich knew the firefighter's thoughts mirrored his own. No one was inside that house and still alive. "I'm sorry, sir, but as you can see, there's nothing left to do."

Something in Erich's gut told him Bess wasn't caught in the house. Or maybe he just hoped. He'd rather give Jaden back this body in this fire than go on without Bess. He tried to push past the fireman again. "I won't stand by and do nothing."

He never should have left her with such a heavy heart and so many questions. He knew her resolve to contact Harry still lurked, but chose to ignore it. Instead he clung to the notion they had all the time in the world, despite the fact he knew better. Time is fleeting, and fate is a mean-spirited bitch.

The fire roared again, and a flash of heat smacked him in the face, forcing him to look away. The smell of fuel oil permeated the air. Maybe the fire wasn't caused by Bess's carelessness, Martin or one of his cronies. Maybe it'd been that damn furnace.

"Whoever started this fire intended to leave nothing in the aftermath," a firefighter said to the one standing next to Erich.

"You think Mrs. Houdini is still in there?" His partner answered.

"If she is, God rest her soul."

Hope rose above the anguish. Martin and Gail would have no use for a corpse. They needed Bess to repair

Gail's reputation. They'd probably taken her and set the fire to force him into compliance.

But what to do? Rush to the Cooper's? That's what they'd expect, probably want, and it would get him nowhere.

"Are you sure Mrs. Houdini is in there?" Standing square in front of Erich was the firefighter who had held him at bay.

Erich almost hadn't heard what was said. The snapping and cracking of the beams of the house giving way under the stress of the fire held his full attention. Words caught in his throat, and he shook his head while swallowing the lump that blocked his voice. "I left her here half an hour ago. She didn't mention going anywhere else."

"I saw her leave. Ten minutes later I noticed the flames," the elderly woman from across the street said. If anyone knew the goings-on in the neighborhood, it would be her. "Shortly after *you* left, Dr. Cooper drove up in the driveway. He and Bess exchanged some pretty heated words out here in the yard, but then she settled down and got in the car with him."

That was all Erich needed to confirm his suspicions. He spun away from them but the firefighter grabbed his arm and held him back. "Did the doctor go into the house?" The fireman asked the neighbor.

"Not that I saw," Miss Busybody answered. "I went in my house a moment later and didn't come back out until I heard the explosion. Do you think it was the furnace?"

The firefighter turned to Erich. "The neighbors say you've been living here."

"I have. To help Bess."

"Or help yourself to Mrs. Houdini's money?"

Erich's fingers curled up tight, just like the muscles in his stomach. *Is this what the neighbors think?* "I don't need to listen to this. I'm going to the Cooper's and check on Bess."

"If Dr. Cooper never went into the house, then you were the last one in there besides Mrs. Houdini. It's a little convenient that you were out of the house at the time the furnace exploded. Wouldn't you say?"

Erich fought the fireman's hold. "Why would I do such a thing? Let me go! I need to check on Bess." Another hand gripped his shoulders, and Erich pivoted to see Will.

"I came soon as I heard Bess's house was on fire. Is she okay?"

"Apparently she left with Martin, but this clown thinks I started the fire and won't let me go," Erich said.

"Come on, Frank. Erich's been a good friend to Bess, doing work around the house. He wouldn't do this."

"You smell the sulfur? This fire was started with fuel oil. And enough of it to burn down every house on this block. It didn't happen by accident."

"He was up at the deli talking to me. It wasn't him."

Erich wanted to speak in his own defense, but Stanley, the police chief he'd served at the deli, approached and addressed the man just identified as Frank. "What's going on here?"

"This is the guy the neighbors have been talking about. The drifter whose been sponging off Mrs. Houdini."

"Excuse me?" How dare these yokels accuse him of using Bess? Or starting their house on fire. "That's just idle gossip."

"Bess is a friend of mine," Will said, "and I know Erich. He worked in my shop for a few days. Remember? It wasn't him."

"Didn't you just repair that furnace about a week ago?" Stanley asked.

He couldn't lie. Stanley had been there when he'd offered his services and Bess accepted.

*Good God, was this my fault?*

Had Martin done him a favor pulling Bess away before the furnace exploded?

"I fixed it then, but it took a lot of work. It's seen better days."

"So, you must know a lot about fuel oil furnaces. Maybe how to make them explode when you're not around to get your baby-fine, blond hair singed."

"That's ridiculous. Look, Gail Cooper came by earlier and argued with the two of us. That's why I went to town, to ask Will to drive us to the train station. I was worried the Coopers would do something...something like this."

Stanley eyed him up and down, seemed to be weighing the facts. He then gave his attention back to the house and the flames that the firefighters appeared to be controlling. "Has anyone seen Mrs. Houdini?"

"The neighbor from across the street saw her leave with Martin Cooper. Ten to fifteen minutes later, they heard the explosion and saw the flames," Frank answered.

"Martin Cooper is a respected doctor. You're a drifter. I'm taking you back into town." Stanley grabbed Erich's arm and used brute force to spin him around. Metal handcuffs clamped down on his wrist. A sensation burned in Harry's memory.

Though stunned, he knew it best to just cooperate for the moment. It wasn't like any pair of cuffs could *really* hold him anyway. "You're not seriously going to arrest me?"

"Not yet, but I'm suspicious enough to hold you until we find Mrs. Houdini and can talk to her." Stanley addressed Will, "I'll send Lou out to the Cooper's. See if she's there."

Will patted Erich's shoulder. "Just hang tight, guy. I'm not going to wait for them to mess around. I'll go and fetch Bess now, and she'll straighten everything out."

"Thank you." Though not in his nature, Erich decided patience was probably the best course of action. For now. Causing a scene would only make him look less stable. As the second cuff clicked into place, he couldn't help but laugh out loud.

"Something funny?"

Stanley would never understand the irony. "It's kind of an inside joke."

Erich shook his hands up and down once, feeling the weight of the metal against his wrist. They were light, and Stanley had not closed them as tight as he could have. At least he didn't consider Erich a threat.

Harry's knowledge told him he didn't even need a pick to get them off. If he folded his hands just right, pushing the joints out of place, the cuffs would fall away. Arrogance bubbled up, and Erich was tempted to use the know-how just to show he could. As quickly as the thought came to him, he dismissed it. What would it prove? Where would it get him?

Will was a good friend, and he could trust him to get to Bess. She would explain everything to Stanley. He needed to forgo his pride, and embrace some patience. Anything else would complicate matters more than they needed to be.

*Pride goeth before a fall.* Wasn't that a Proverb?

As Stanley pushed down on his shoulder, directing him into the back of the car, Erich spoke to Will. "Go to Bess, please. Make sure she's okay."

"I'm on my way, Erich. Just sit tight. I'll get her to town."

# Chapter Twenty-Two

Why was it that clear decisions only stayed that way long enough for something to happen to muck up the picture? Not ten minutes after Erich left for town, Martin showed up full of apologies and petitioning for one simple request. Not for him, but for Gail.

Now Gail sat across the table from Bess, each with a mug of tea. Before Martin left the room, he insisted they talk through the issues. She hadn't needed Martin to tell her that Gail had few friends. Gail had been all too willing to say just that a few days earlier, and most people in town would gossip about her when given the chance. But, when he said he'd be damned if his arrogance cost his wife the one friend she most valued, that touched her heart. All the scandalous chitchat was just that.

True love was selfless. Like Martin's. Like Erich's.

"Everyone thinks it was easy for Martin." Gail wrung her hands as she spoke. She never lifted her eyes from the centerpiece on the table. "They believe our relationship was sordid. They see him as unfaithful and me as disrespectful. They fault him for needing a shoulder to mourn on, and me for providing it. Erich might think he's right to cast stones, but he doesn't know. No one really does."

The pain radiating in Gail's voice couldn't be faked. Bess knew how hard it was to live by the community's moral compass and that they would assess her by a harsher code because of her celebrity status.

She'd made choices in the past few weeks based on how she would later be judged. Now, she regretted giving anyone else that kind of power. "I've always maintained that was none of my business. Other people's feelings on the matter is not why I am canceling the séance. This isn't about your relationship with Martin or past events between you and Harry. It's about me and being able to live with myself. Harry didn't write his code, or ask me to hold séances because he believed in any of that."

Gail drew in her cheeks as she nodded.

Bess knew facing the truth was hard for Gail, but there was no way she could argue with facts. Harry let it be known how he felt about spiritualism. "I didn't realize until after he communicated with me how much I was clinging to him. Erich showed me that Harry is gone. He didn't want his name or his legacy drug through the mud. It was for the exact opposite reason he made these plans. If I go to the press and tell the world he's been in touch, I'm opening the door to everything he despised and fought so hard to protect his name from. The best thing I can do for Harry is to let him go."

"But he was the one who gave credence to the notion I was a liar and a cheat. Martin and I were already being condemned for being in love. Harry made it worse by calling our characters into question."

"I'm sorry about that."

"It's not *your* fault, Bess. You didn't have anything to do with it."

"I regret it just the same." She'd stood by when Harry's temper flared, comforted his grief, but didn't call him out on the anger. He was entitled to his emotions, but threw too many stones, way too hard. "Gail. I believe wherever he is now, he's sorry too. His mother was just so dear to him."

"I only tried to help."

"I know that." Who had Harry been to judge? It made Bess nauseous to think of the time they spent running their own spiritualist con, especially now that she'd lived the aftermath. She remembered the pain in Harry's face when he spoke of his mother and had, herself, spent too many nights crying and even more days drowning her pain in Martin's brandy, longing for the comfort of his voice or the warmth of his touch.

Faking communication with the dead was a cruel hoax and misguided game. She saw that with crystal clarity.

"Contacting Harry would restore my reputation, and you have the power to do that. All you have to do is help me make people believe that Harry talked to me from beyond the grave."

"I won't lie in my husband's name."

"It would make things easier for Martin if people didn't malign us. Don't you owe us that much for all we've done for you in the last year?"

"Don't you understand what you're asking, Gail? You want me to dishonor my husband's memory—"

Gail pounded her fist against the table to accent every word. With each strike, she spoke louder. "To restore the reputation that Harry ruined. I don't think it's too much to ask."

"Ladies, I'm sorry to interrupt, but Will's here, and he needs to talk to you, Bess."

She turned her chair and saw only one thing on both of Martin and Will's faces: disaster.

Will took cautious steps until he stood in front of her, then squatted down and touched her knee. "Sweetie, something's happened."

A pang vibrated through her, as if a rock had free fallen to the pit of her stomach. Was there anything left to go wrong? "Is Erich sick again?"

He tightened his grip. "No, he's fine. It's...I hardly know where to start."

She didn't have patience for side-stepping and kit-glove handling. If there was more pain to be had—and the look on the men's faces told her there was—she just wanted to hear it. "Tell me."

"There's been a fire, honey. At your house."

"Oh my God. Bad?" Tears pushed against her eyes, but she swallowed hard. No more crying for things she couldn't control.

"They're still fighting the flames, but I doubt there will be much left." With a long exhale, Will shifted his weight and looped a thumb through the belt loop of his pants. "Bess, there's more. It's Erich—"

She leapt to her feet. "You said he was fine?"

"He is, but..."

Her chest tightened. "Just spit it out!"

"He's been arrested. The fire chief thinks the fire was set on purpose, and he suspects Erich."

"That damn furnace went out again this morning. Erich just relit it."

"He didn't say anything about that. He's a stranger in town. No one knows him and many suspect he's up to no good because of the way he latched on to you."

Bess took her handbag from the table. "That's ridiculous. Please, take me to him."

"Let's go."

As they crossed the threshold, Martin grabbed her arm. "I'm so sorry, Bess, about your house. If you need anything at all, let me know."

A tenderness shown clear in his eyes, signaling sincerity and concern, but grateful words balled up in her throat. She merely nodded.

"You can stay with us until you work something out."

She squeezed his hand. No matter what other's thought, Martin and Gail were true friends, despite Gail's need for fame. "Thank you, Martin, but the only thing I can focus on now is helping Erich."

****

*Give me your best. I'll escape any confines.*

In the early days of their careers, Harry would dare the police officers in the cities they performed in to try and restrain him. Every station sounded the same: ringing phones, clacking typewriter keys and the static from the car radios. Walking into this one took Bess back to all those nights and every challenge.

Each and every one brought a foreboding sense of agony. The lawmen took the challenges to heart, getting more cruel and demeaning in the attempts to contain Harry, at times endangering his life to protect their delicate egos. She knew if Erich's anger got the best of him and he provoked the police, they would retaliate. She'd seen it time and again.

Bess shook off her fear and approached the desk. "Erich Welch, please. Can I see him?"

The officer looked up. Recognition flashed in his eyes as he stood. "Mrs. Houdini. The sergeant wants to talk to you about the fire." He shifted his weight. "I'm sorry, ma'am."

She waved her hands in front of her. "Mr. Johnson told me that you folks arrested my friend Erich. I want him released."

"Mr. Welch hasn't been charged with anything. The sergeant wanted to talk to you before he assumed innocence." The officer tried to offer comfort by reaching out—to touch her arm perhaps—but she pushed it away.

The only thing that would console her now was to see Erich. "Innocence is what you're supposed to presume, not guilt. The only place I'm going is to the cell where you're holding Erich. You can tell the sergeant if that old fuel oil furnace caused the fire, it was an accident."

Stanley showed his face from behind a closed office door. "What's going on out here?" His gaze locked on Bess, and sympathy softened his chiseled features. He crossed the room and offered his extended hand. "Mrs. Houdini, I'm so sorry about your home."

The gentle way everyone was handling her told Bess the damage to her house must be devastating, but she wouldn't let that veer her from what was most important.

"The officer says you have questions, and I'll be more than happy to answer them, but not until you release Erich. He is my friend, and I know he didn't cause the fire."

"Ma'am it's my understanding he's only been in town a week or so and that he showed up out of nowhere."

"That doesn't make him an arsonist. Take me to him now!"

Stanley's head bowed. "Okay, okay, but I'm not releasing him until you both answer some questions."

She conceded to the deal, anything to get to Erich and make sure he was all right. The next step she needed to focus on was getting him out of jail. "Can you wait for me, Will?"

He motioned her over to him, and she reluctantly obeyed. Now that Stan had complied, she didn't want to waste minutes.

"I told them Erich was with me," Will said, "I mean, he was with me—at the diner—and I told them that."

In the quiver of Will's voice she could hear just how scared he was. She closed her eyes and dug deep for the strength to fight for Erich's honor. "I'll make them understand."

"I'll wait right here while you get this taken care of."

Stanley led her through a door into a large cinder block room. There was an aisle that ran between two rows of barred cells. All but one sat empty, half way back and to her left. She could see Erich lying on the small cot, his left arm shielding his eyes from the harsh florescent lights. As the heavy door shut, he let the arm slide over his head and glanced in their direction. When he saw her, his face lit up with a smile.

He stood and gripped the bars. "Bess. I was so worried."

At the sound of his voice, restraint disintegrated. The heels of her shoes clapped against the concrete floor as she ran down the small aisle. When she was in front of him, she reached through the bars and gripped his hair, pulling him down until she tasted his lips. The scent of him circled and calmed her, even if he was doused in smoke.

"When Will first told me about the fire, I was so scared you were caught inside." She'd mourn the house later. It was just a building. Looking into his eyes, she knew her home existed anywhere that she could lie in his arms.

Erich stroked her cheek. "I'm okay. Don't you worry. We'll get through this."

She leaned into his touch. "I know we will. I trust you. I just have to figure out how to convince them you didn't do this."

"They just want to protect you. It's okay. Answer their questions."

She hadn't expected humility. For some reason she imagined him pacing the cell like an animal and roaring his anger like a tiger, but that would be Harry's reactions to such an event, not Erich's. The dichotomy confused her almost as much as it touched her. "I know you'd never hurt me."

She tipped her head and kissed his palm, before turning to the officer. "Okay, Sergeant, I'll answer your questions."

"Why don't we go back up to my office? You'll be more comfortable."

"I want to do this right here and now." Bess knew Erich was right; the poor man only wanted to do his job. She didn't mean to stand in the way, but wouldn't be whisked away or hide anything from Erich.

Stanley rubbed his eyes. "Okay. How long have you had trouble with that furnace?"

"Since the day Harry bought that house, he talked about replacing it, but there was never time."

"What happened this morning? You said Mr. Welch worked on it."

"This morning? No, I didn't."

Erich's words knocked Bess back a step. "Then why did you leave Harry's tool box out in the mud room? And the oily rags that were lying on top of it?"

The color drained from Erich's face, making him even paler than normal. "When do you think I did this?"

"This morning, before you went to town to get breakfast. I saw the tool box. I meant to ask you about it, but we started talking about other things as soon as you came home."

"Bess. I didn't touch that furnace this morning." He turned back to Stanley. "But the issues with the furnace weren't the kind that would cause it to blow up. Usually the pilot light would go out for one reason or another. That fire was caused by an explosion."

"That's what the guys at the fire department said." Stanley gave his attention to Bess. "Is there anyone you can think of who would want to destroy your home, maybe hurt you or Erich?"

Bess knew Erich had a short list of suspects, but she refused to believe her friends would do this. It had to be an accident. "I don't associate with people who harbor that kind of hate."

"Gail and Martin," Erich said.

Bess spun on her heels. "You shouldn't accuse. You don't have any proof."

He stared right through her and curled his lower lip up between his teeth. He gave his attention to the officer. "Martin's threatened to 'make me go away,' and Gail was furious because Bess called off the séance. We fought. Less than an hour later, the house was on fire."

"But Martin came over after you left. He drove me out to his place so Gail and I could talk it out. They were with me when the fire started." Even if the timing did work, she'd never accept they were capable.

"What about Joseph?" Erich asked.

"That guy from the reservation?" Stanley asked.

Bess leveled her stare on both men: Erich for even mentioning his suspicions and Stanley for his attitude. "He's a respected healer who was learning traditional medicine from Martin. He did a marvelous job managing Louise's pain in her final days, and he treated Erich's infection. He might be dead otherwise."

"The teas he gave me were laced with a drug."

Bess knew Erich believed his accusations, but she'd seen the altercations between Joseph and Martin and rejected the idea they were working together. There wasn't a single good reason why Joseph would want to hurt either of them, and she refused to cause problems for a man who had taken care of Erich and hadn't charged a single penny. "You of all people shouldn't condemn him. His medicine cured you."

Stanley no longer looked irritated or bored. He leaned in closer to Erich, his eyes wide. "Tell me more about these teas."

"Bess is right. My infection cleared up. Quickly too, but I'm not sure the credit belongs to the teas. There was also a homemade ointment he used to dress the wound, but he insisted I drink the tea at least four times a day. When I did, I couldn't get out of bed. Then I stopped."

"You didn't stop. You were drinking it right up to the moment—"

"No, Bess, I'm sorry, but I started dumping the cups out by the shed. That's when I got my strength back. Bess made me a mug with dinner the other night. Since she was watching, I drank it and almost immediately passed out." Erich shifted his weight and looked back to Bess. "Then there's that brandy from Martin."

"Brandy?" Stanley asked.

Would Erich keep anything to himself? With everything else going on between she and the Cooper's and all the damage Harry had done to their reputations, she didn't need Erich getting Martin in trouble for manufacturing brandy. The officers in this town were known to look the other way instead of upholding prohibition laws, but it was just the type of thing Stanley could use to bring Martin in for questioning. "Cough medicine. It's Martin's family remedy. I haven't been feeling well."

Erich gripped the bars. "Why do you protect him?"

"You think the Br— cough medicine was tainted?" Stanley asked Erich.

"It was very strong."

Bess laughed. "The good stuff usually is."

Stanley pulled a set of keys from his pocket and opened the cell. "I'm going to let you go for now, Welch, but don't do anything stupid like skipping town." He then turned to Bess. "I'm sorry, Mrs. Houdini, but I need to ask where I can get a hold of you should we need you to answer more questions."

*Where can we go?* Martin had made a generous offer, but she couldn't take Erich there, especially after he'd put the police on their trail. Between the two men, she'd much rather spend the evening with Erich—couldn't imagine spending it without him. "I guess we'll get a room at the hotel, but first I want to go back to the house and see it for myself."

Coming out of the cell, Erich wrapped his arms around her, pulled her in and kissed her forehead. She eased into him and let go of the stress that had clenched her stomach since the moment she'd heard of the fire. "That's not a good idea, Bess. I've been there-"

"I'm a big girl. That's my home, and I need to see it for my own eyes."

"I think maybe your friend is right." Stanley said. "Last I knew, the fire was still smoldering."

"I didn't say I wanted to rummage around in the ashes, but I do need to see it. Please, Erich, will you take me?"

He tightened his grip. "If that's what you want."

*What do I want?* The answer should be easy. But she didn't even have a clue.

# Chapter Twenty-Three

"You know what I think we should do?" Erich asked, but didn't wait for an answer. "Go straight to the train station and get on a Brooklyn bound train."

Bess twisted around in the car seat to look at him. "Don't be ridiculous!"

Even without the glare, he knew she was angry and why. His eyes darted back and forth between her and Will, who drove the car toward what remained of the house. "It made no sense to lie to the police. Someone burnt your house to the ground, and instead of being angry at them, you're upset at me for being honest."

"You pointed the police to Martin and Gail with no real evidence."

"I didn't make anything up."

She threw her hands in the air. "You are just like Harry. He condemned the two of them for his version of the truth, and for something that he was guilty of doing himself."

Will raised his hand between them and then touched her shoulder. "Bess. You're upset."

"Damn straight I am."

"And for good reason, but lashing out at Erich doesn't fix anything. If Martin or Joseph really had nothing to do with this, then the police won't find anything. But they can't do their job if you don't cooperate. You and Erich should stay with me and the wife."

"We can't."

"Of course you can. Not a good reason in the world why you can't." Will parked the car in front of the lot and twisted his body so he could look over the seat.

Erich watched as Bess's eyes scanned the devastation that was once her home. Tears streamed down her cheeks unchecked. The fire department had nailed a sign to one of the trees—condemning the property—and everything on the lot from the shed to the outlying flowerbeds was singed black. It was pure luck the fire hadn't spread to the shed or the neighbor's homes.

Bess sighed and gripped Will's hand. "It's not the house, not really. The things...Harry's things. I only kept a few choice items, but now, even those are gone."

*Like that old wool stage coat she wears.* Erich watched Bess step out of the car and then slid across the seat. Coming up behind her, he laid his arm over her shoulder. "I'm sorry, Bess. You've lost so much...it isn't fair—"

"Life rarely is." She pushed her hair back over her ear. "There's the cabinet in the shed with the last few things for the museum. The key was in my bureau drawer. You picked the lock once, do you think?"

He laid a finger against her cheek and nodded. They said their goodbyes to Will and promised to call him in the morning. Then, Erich gripped her hand and led her across the yard to the shed. Inside, it took less than a minute to work his magic.

The lock slipped away, and he reached for the handles, but the feel of the cool metal snapped something in his brain. None of this was his, not really. Not the way he'd assumed in the beginning. Stepping back, he waved his hand toward the cabinet, allowing Bess to claim whatever she needed.

She ran her fingers over the wood and then pulled the door open. Looking over her shoulder, Erich got a first glance of what she'd hid away. Chains, locks, shackles and his ring of master keys: one to open each and every lock made. She reached out, picked up a plastic bag from the middle shelf and opened it, removing a straitjacket. She held it in her hands and fingered the nylon ties. Bringing it to her face, she inhaled deeply. As she exhaled, he saw her upper lip quiver, but she regained composure and steeled again. She slipped it back in the bag and returned it to the shelf. "Come on, we should check in at the hotel and stop by the department store since everything we own is ash."

"All right. Let me lock this up."

Bess took the lock from him and tossed it to the corner of the shed. "Don't bother. The rats and thieves can have it for all I care. If anything had to burn why couldn't it have been that?"

With her open hand she pounded the front of the cabinet so hard it fell back against the wall, but Erich didn't take his tear-filled eyes off her. He pulled her tight and laid his head on hers. "I'm sorry. So sorry."

She pulled out of his arms and started across the yard, but at the midpoint the draw of the devastation turned her back. Her eyes scanned the remains, and he thought she teetered on the edge of a complete breakdown. Instead, she laughed, quiet at first, but soon her chest heaved and she bent at the waist.

"What's so funny?" Erich asked, fearing she'd snapped.

"It's just Harry's way. Take that damn book to the grave with you!"

The range of emotions Bess displayed didn't surprise Erich. How much tragedy was she expected to bear? "What are you talking about?"

She leaned back, giving him her full weight. Erich accepted it, and wrapped his arm around her chest. "Since Harry died I've been trying to find his stupid little black bible with all his contacts, addresses and notes. I never did. It's been driving me nuts. Now, I guess the fire has taken that from me too."

He gripped Bess tighter. Harry's book contained information on every person they'd ever met as well as the businesses to contact for supplies for the act. If she'd had that, it would have served as a road map to normal. Without it, he could only imagine the confusion she faced with every detail of their life.

He left a kiss on her forehead, released his grip and walked to the car. Opening the passenger door and popping open the glove box, he saw it laying there: right where Harry had put it after they'd driven up the coast to meet with a prop company. After talking to the salesman for two hours, they returned to the car. Harry immediately filled a page with notes and then put the book there for safe keeping on the trip home. It was still there three days later when they boarded a train for the last round of shows. A trip Harry never came home from.

The book had never been returned to the house.

Erich picked it up. Heavy in his hand, he drug his fingers across the soft brushed leather. Gripping it to his chest, he walked back to Bess. Inside, Harry wept for her pain, but Erich felt nothing but anger. So many little things had been stacked against her, too much to endure. Her pain needed to end.

He offered the book to Bess. "Is this it?"

She took it and ran a hand over the cover. "Oh my. Yes. But how?"

Something to hold onto. That was all she'd wanted, and that book—the only thing left—would become even more treasured. How he hated lying, but there was no reason to even try to tell the truth. Jaden wouldn't bend the rules now. "While I was working on the car, I stumbled across it. I had no idea or…"

"It's okay. Thank you, Erich." She flipped it open and slid her hand down a page.

He stepped closer and opened his arms. The anticipation of her coming to him made his insides tremble. Maybe they were past her hot-and-cold reactions to him, but he wasn't willing to risk it. He wanted to comfort her, but it was also possible she needed time alone with Harry's memory. She stepped into his embrace and buried her head in his chest. As he closed his arms around her, she whispered, "Get me out of here, Erich."

"Can you walk into town?"

"Do I look like an invalid?" That sharp, snappy tone

was back to her voice. The emotional moment passed, she was back to being the pillar of strength he and everyone else was used to seeing.

"No, love, the furthest thing from it."

\*\*\*\*

Erich's every muscle cried out from fatigue, but standing in the hotel lobby his mind rattled with questions. Was it presumptuous to get one room? If he requested two would she feel slighted? It angered him to be dependent on her and Harry's legacy to pay the bills, but his illness had put a quick stop to earning a paycheck at the deli.

They'd followed up their investigation of the house with a stop at the department store to buy some essential clothing and toiletries, and then dinner in the hotel's restaurant. As tired as he was, Bess seemed to be carrying her anguish on her sagging shoulders. She responded to his nervous rocking by tugging on his sleeve. "What's the matter, Erich? Can we get the room? I need to lie down."

*The room? One?* Deciding it best to be clear, Erich asked, "Should I only get one?"

She stepped closer to him and looped an arm around his waist. "I don't know what would become of me, if I didn't have you with me." Her words came so soft, he strained to hear them, but they lifted his heart all the same. He stroked her hair and kissed her forehead. Moving to the reception desk, he gripped her hand.

Moments later they were alone in the hotel room, and Bess's walls crumbled. She lowered herself to the chair and peered out the window at the small town. He dropped to his knees in front of her and laid his hands on top of hers. He searched for the words to comfort, but knew they'd be inadequate and disproportionate to her pain. Instead, he sat in silence and stroked her arm.

Several moments of silence passed, and then she let her gaze fall back on him. "I want the investigation stopped. The fire was an accident. If anyone is at fault, it's me."

"Trust me, that fire was set."

"I could smell the fuel oil. Harry should have replaced the furnace, but he didn't. When he died that responsibility became mine."

"It's not your fault, Bess!"

"Then whose? I knew it needed to be repaired or replaced and I did nothing. I'm going to tell Stanley to call off the investigation."

Guilt bubbled up in Erich's stomach for everything Harry had left undone, from fixing the furnace to not preparing Bess for a life on her own. Sure, he hadn't expected the damn appendicitis to take his life, but every night that he went on stage, he tempted the gods and bargained with the fates for his life. Just because he'd always emerged victorious, it was asinine of him to believe it would always end that way. "Do me a favor, Angel. Get a good night's sleep before you make a final decision."

"You really think someone maliciously burnt my house down?" From the rasp in her voice and the way she squeezed her forearm with her opposite hand, Erich knew it was just too horrible for her to accept.

"I think it was someone who knew the furnace was bad and tried to use it to cover up the sabotage. I know you don't want to think Martin or Gail would do something so awful, but I can't think of anyone else with an ax to grind."

She shook her head and sighed.

Erich stood but let his touch linger on her arm. "You look so tired, Bess. Why don't you let me run you a bath? Try to set it all aside tonight and we'll examine everything tomorrow."

She leaned into his touch. "You spoil me."

"That's the point."

# Chapter Twenty-Four

Bess set the brush on the vanity and pushed her still damp curls to and fro. She cursed herself for the places on Erich's body her mind was undressing and for craving him the way a man would crave water in the desert—as if her very life depended on another kiss or graze of his hand.

From the bathroom she could hear the pipes clanking and the water shutting off in the shower. It was replaced by the water running at the sink, and her thoughts jumped to him toweling off his rippled abs and lean-yet-strong calves. The fantasy continued and she imagined him slipping on the cotton robe she'd just bought him.

When the door knob started jiggling, she stood and pivoted toward him, adjusting the tie to her housecoat to maximize her cleavage.

"Angel, would you like me to order up some tea before we go to bed?" he asked as he emerged into the room.

She straightened her back and squared her shoulders. "No. What I need is to crawl into this bed next to you and for you to hold me tight. I need for you to make all of this go away."

He wrapped her in his embrace and kissed her deep. As she hoped, his arms blocked out the rest of the world, and she surrendered herself to these new feelings. Desire and adoration for Erich lived side by side with her love for Harry.

"I know Harry will never fade from your mind or heart," he whispered against her quivering lips, as if he could sense her conflicting emotions.

"But Harry's gone, and you're here. It's not his arms I want right now, it's yours."

Erich responded by capturing her mouth again. With each passing minute her need had pulsed and grown until she was sure she'd die without his touch, yet when his lips caressed hers, the desires weren't squelched; they grew.

His hands stroked her back, cradled her head and intensified her longing. Her fingers tangled in the collar of his robe with a passion she'd never known. She needed him closer, wanted him to possess her.

As recent as a few days ago, she never would have believed anyone but Harry could own her heart. Now she was lusting after the flesh of a man who might be gone tomorrow, a man who felt like a life-long companion, even though he was closer to a stranger.

His strong fingers separated the robe, letting the sash fall away, as his mouth clamped down on her neck. A shiver rode her spine, drawing a gasp. His hand slipped beneath the white cotton, and the touch of his bare flesh sent waves of electricity pulsing through her.

"Please, Erich." *What am I begging for?* All she knew was his touch made her weak.

His lips brushed her ear. "All in good time, my pretty little angel."

*Pretty little angel.* Harry's pet-name for her, and she swore it was his voice, not Erich's. She shook off the thought and stepped back. Dropping her arms and letting the robe glide off her body, she refused to let those memories destroy this moment.

*Standing nude before a man who's not my husband.*
*What am I doing?*
*He's gone.*

Erich's eyes caressed her body same as his hands, flowing over every inch and curve. "You're so beautiful, Bess."

"And you..." She reached out to him. What could she say? So young, so strong. If she thought too much about what a perfect specimen he was, the doubts would resurface.

His fingers fumbled with the tie to his own robe, but soon it too fell to the floor. The sight of him stole her breath, let alone the ability to form words.

Everyone today, from Martin and Gail to the firefighters and policeman to the clerk at the clothing store all questioned what this handsome, young man would want with a widow. They doubted the validity of his affection so much that they accused him of burning her house down—or worse—trying to kill her.

Foolish, vengeful accusations; not all that different from the ones Harry'd made against Gail. Bess now knew what others thought didn't mean squat. She could trust Erich to care for her, maybe even love her.

Only that was relevant.

Before he touched her again, Bess had to let the past go. Just as the fire had burnt the last of his belongings, she needed to put his spirit to rest. Erich had been right from the very beginning.

No séance. No calling Harry back. Not forget. Never forget. He'd been her whole world, and he would always live in her heart. But if she spent her life pursuing his memory, there'd be no room for Erich.

And she needed Erich.

"Is something wrong?" he asked.

She must look like a fool, the way she'd stood there staring at him while letting go of her past. "No. Just admiring how perfect you are."

He stepped closer, let his knuckles slide against her cheek. "I'm nothing without you, Bess."

"I don't want to talk."

A playful smirk danced across his face. "You don't?"

"No. I want to make love with you again."

That was all the encouragement he needed. Two quick steps and his arms came around her. She buried her head in his broad shoulder and let him lift her feet from the ground. Mere seconds later, she was in the middle of the bed with the weight of his body on her. He nibbled at the lobe of her ear, and his hot breath caressed her neck as he pulled her tighter to him.

It would never be close enough.

She locked her arms around his neck, lifted her hips from the bed to meet his. Soft moans mewed from somewhere inside, involuntary. She leaned her cheek into his, just shaven soft and the clean, powder scent of the shaving lather made her head light. He tipped his head, his mouth searching for hers. His eyes closed; he was the picture of sheer bliss. She hesitated, and then let her fingers trace his hair line, the fine blond hair against his pale skin.

This moment couldn't be faked, even by a masterful conman. More than physical nakedness, he laid himself out bare straight to his heart. He declared his needs and desires, and she knew she could take it as gospel.

She pressed against his shoulder, and his eyes flittered open as he rolled to his side, bringing her with him. "What is it? Something wrong?"

"Not as long as you're with me." She gripped his chin between two fingers, smiling at him, and then drug her nail the length of his throat.

His body shivered in her arms, but he tipped forward, pushing his forehead to hers and gasping in pleasure. "The things you do to me, Angel."

His reaction. His words. His tone. Martin had said he could be one of Harry's brothers, but it was more than that. The differences were many, but the similarities that existed were eerie.

And the address book. Easily explained, but still.

His lips caressed hers again as his strong fingers danced along her spine, his arousal pulsating against her thigh.

The air in the room sparked, and her skin tingled. She guided him to his back and straddled his waist. His eyes widened and his lips parted as his hands slid up her thighs to her stomach.

Their connection, too intense for the short time they'd known each other. Star crossed-lovers? Or what had Joseph said—bound souls?

There was a time that she believed her soul was bound to only one other. But *that* just wasn't possible.

*Was it?*

She circled her bottom against his pelvis. His body shuddered beneath her, thrilling her. His back and neck arched, and his eyes closed as his fingers inched their way up her body. "Bessy," he cried.

*It couldn't be.*

"Air-iec," she whispered, purposely drawing out the syllables and accenting the vowels. If it were true—if her Harry was somehow inside Erich—he'd find a way to answer her.

Erich startled, and his eyes popped open. Her beautiful brown eyes locked to his, as if she was searching deeper than the surface.

Harry's parents and siblings pronounced his given name with the heavy accents from their homeland. The name the neighbors thought they heard—Harry—stuck. Bess knew the story, and in their most private moments would call out for the man behind the celebrity. But only one man—or one soul—would know that.

Had she just identified him? If so, Jaden's binds would be lifted, and he could explain everything to her, but the part of him that had grown as an individual stared down Harry's soul with jade eyes. He didn't want the ghost to be the one she loved.

"Did you just call me Harry?" He tipped his head, averting his eyes from her. The last thing he wanted was for her to see the confusion and pain. If she could feel Harry in him, he'd won his bet with Jaden. Yet, the words cut him hard and deep. "I can't do this, Bess. I want to be with you, baby, but I can't be a stand-in for him." His hands gripped her hips, and he tried to lift her from his body, but she ground back down against him. He acquiesced, not willing to fight.

"No, please, Erich. I didn't say his name."

"That's sure what it sounded like."

"Er-ich," she repeated, less drawn out, but keeping the focus on the "ah" and "eh" sound.

He held her gaze, despite the fact he could feel tears rimming his eyes. "Promise me this is about us, and the here and now. Not some way to hang on to—"

"I swear it, Erich. It's you I want."

With her declaration, his arm came around her hips as he pushed himself up, leaning against the headboard. Face to face and eye to eye, his fingers dug into her as he lifted his hips, burying himself deeper inside her. He could see her let go of the notion, and his opportunity to be honest with her slipped away. They couldn't build a future on a foundation of lies. But how could Erich ever live in Harry's enormous shadow?

She gripped his shoulder and gasped as he bucked up against her with an unbridled passion.

His right hand slid up her spine, resting in her hair. He pulled her tighter and pressed his lips to hers, kissing her as she was the only one who could quench the thirst that threatened to take him down.

"Say it," he mumbled against her mouth and then clenched her bottom lip between his teeth playfully.

"It's you, Erich."

Unsatisfied with that answer, he grasped her waist, pulling her down as he thrust up. "Say it," he pleaded.

His passion crashed against her like the ocean's waves. So close to succumbing, she groaned. "I need *you*, Erich."

He fell back, hitting his head against the headboard as if her words had weight and they'd delivered a sucker punch, but he didn't still—couldn't stop. Sliding his hands against her flesh, he teased her breasts and tantalized her neck. Ever closer he pushed her toward the abyss of ecstasy. Sweat dripped down his face and neck. She was on the edge of enraptured bliss, but he wouldn't know release until she said the words he longed to hear. It had to come from her first. "Say it, Bessy."

Spasms of pleasure raked her body, and the words she'd held behind defensive walls spilled from trembling lips. "I love you, Erich."

His spine tightened again, and his neck rolled back.

He groaned through parted lips and pulled himself back to her, enveloping his body around her. He brushed his cheek to hers and whispered in her ear. "Me too, Angel. I love you too."

# Chapter Twenty-Five

The heavy odor of sulfur and charred wood still permeated the air. The sun hadn't even cleared the trees yet, and the grass was still wet with dew. They were serenaded by the wren's chorus as Erich lifted the fire department's rope that circled the house, giving Bess access to what was left of her property. She'd been asked to consider the house and all its contents a loss by those in charge, and Erich had advised her there was nothing to be found except more pain, but Bess—with a renewed strength—insisted she look for one item.

What item, she wouldn't say.

Again, Erich examined the structure, charred girders, holding up pieces of crossbeams. Very little kept the whole thing from collapsing to a pile of rubble, and he knew walking among the remains was begging for another tragedy. "Bess, please, tell me what you're hoping to find and let me go look. I don't want you to get hurt."

"What I need is my responsibility not yours." She walked toward what used to be the back door when she could have just as easily stepped into what was once the kitchen through the large gaping hole.

He grabbed her sleeve, holding her back. "Whatever it is, it's worth your life?"

She averted her eyes. "I don't know that you can understand this, it's just something I have to do."

He understood all too well what it was like to hold something so tight and dear, but what could he do? He couldn't break her conviction. As close as they were, he knew Harry and his memory would always remain between them in some way.

Since his rebirth, he'd come to recognize Harry's faults, embraced his strengths, but understood that the only thing Erich shared with that soul was memories, and now Bess's heart. But the guilt of carrying the truth was pressing on his chest like a two-ton elephant. It wasn't only that he kept an important fact from the woman he loved, but the actuality that he'd told her a lie.

Yes, it was Harry's code delivered from Erich's tongue—and even though he knew now they were two different people, the memory came from within, it wasn't a message from beyond and, if anything, it had been Erich giving Bess the solace she so desired, not Harry answering her plea. Now, with the time, distance and lessons learned; he was beginning to question just how the man he used to be would react to all of this.

He tapped his toe against the ground and bounced his knee. She'd been in there too long with her memories—spent too much time in a structure that wasn't sound, tempting the fates to deliver yet another blow. Against his better judgment, he entered the rubble, determined to pull her back to safety.

Bess stood in the same place the kitchen table had twenty-four hours earlier. As if trying to place things in her mind, she took careful measured steps to her right and then began pushing the ash and chunks of burnt wood around with her feet. Scorched, bare wires hung just above her head, reaching toward her like tentacles of an octopus. Not knowing what else to say, he whispered her name.

She flipped an acknowledging look over her shoulder, but then dropped her eyes back to the search. "Don't ask me to leave, Erich. Not 'til I feel like I've really looked."

He stepped up behind her and squeezed her shoulders. "What are we looking for?" Under his grip, her muscles hardened, her posture firmed and she exhaled a little whimper of self-disgust. He pulled her closer, trying to show support, and she melted into him.

With her movement, his eye caught the faintest glint of silver sparkling amongst the black soot and realized the item she searched for was Harry's wedding ring. The same small piece of metal that had bound Harry and Bess had been an introduction tool for her and Erich. Now, it lay amongst the ruins, symbolic in a way. Maybe another man would have been jealous, but Erich knew putting Bess on the road to living didn't mean breaking the bind to Harry's long-gone presence, but helping her find a way to honor her past without losing herself in it.

He was all too aware she knew that, but also realized the process of letting go while embracing the memories was the near impossible task she faced. Taking slow, conscious steps around her, he bent down and picked up the two bands and the chain that kept them bound. He rubbed the ring in his fingers, amazed that the tarnish wiped away and the silver sparkled underneath.

Bess's arm came around his hip, and her head fell to his shoulder. "You found it! Thank the Heavens."

Her words tightened the ropes of guilt clenching his heart. He needed to tell her some sort of truth, find some way to make her understand, but how with Jaden's restrictions? His pride had let a golden moment pass last night. Despite her explanation for calling his name in the way she had, somewhere inside she accepted the truth. She'd recognized him and vocalized it. Instead of embracing the opportunity, he'd turned her away from it and hid behind his new face like a coward.

He'd find a way to make her believe, but first things first. "You have what you came for. Let's get out of here before what's left crumbles around us."

She nodded and squeezed his hand, leading him out through the once-was door. Once outside and away from the disaster zone, she twisted toward him. "I know I'm being disrespectful given what we've shared, but please, can I have Harry's ring?"

He dropped his chin and closed his eyes. "I know your heart, Bess. And I'll give you the ring, but I want to take you somewhere first."

She accepted his words and looped her arm through his, no longer concerned with what the neighbors thought. Her new-found comfort taxed his heart until it felt heavy as a rock.

Receiving her weight, he led her away from the house, the past. If they were going to face the future as one, they needed to face the truth, but Erich couldn't help but question his decision. If history was an indicator, every time he followed his heart, the results were disastrous.

Jaden warned him Bess's path had been altered the very moment she'd met him on the street, and his charge—his whole goal—was to change it for the better. Was he unburdening his heart for her or was this another selfish move?

The moment he'd seen the shimmer of silver among the ashes, he knew where they needed to go so he could make her see the truth: the park Bess had mentioned to him a few nights earlier, the one where Bess and Harry had shared a passionate embrace and soul-caressing kiss in the pouring rain. Their love hadn't been doused that night, and the fire didn't have the power to destroy them either. Their souls had reclaimed each other. Despite what Jaden had warned—that she'd never believe—he was all too aware she felt it. She had called out to him, and he'd been too afraid to answer, or too proud to accept the man she longed for, the one he'd left behind.

"Erich, what are we doing here?" she asked as he guided her through the arbor at the park's entrance.

"Just indulge me for a few minutes." He led her straight to the tree she and Harry had taken refuge under the last time they were here. Stopping, he gripped her hip and spun her to him. He then took her hand and laid it flat against his chest. His heart pounded until he was sure it could burst through his flesh. "Feel that?"

She nodded, her eyes wide. "What's wrong? You're scared?"

"My heart beats for you. I'm right here, right now, because wherever you go, I'll be right beside you." He dropped to his knees in front of her, hugging her waist and laying his cheek against her stomach. "Harry should have done *this* more, Bess. He should have said out loud that it was always you. You were his strength. You made him weak. The only spotlight he ever craved was your loving gaze. It filled him with pride. *That's* what he lived for."

She slid her hand under his shoulder, tried to lift him. "What are you talking about? How would you know what Harry felt or wanted?"

"You know the answer to that, Bess. You feel it in your soul, and I see it in your eyes."

Her fingers touched his temples and traced the lines of his jaw. "Is Harry speaking to you again?"

"No!" He covered her hand and held it against his cheek, leaning into it and closing his eyes to the tears pressing against them. "No, it's not channeling. I'm not a medium, a spiritualist, or anything like that."

Compassion and confusion faded from her face, and her fingers stiffened on his cheek. Her touch went cold. "What are you trying to say to me?"

He straightened his back so he could look up into her face while still holding her hand tight. "It was always you, Bess. Without you, he was nothing but a wayward dreamer with no plan, no motivation. And I know when you look in my eyes, you see the soul inside me."

"I don't understand."

He gritted his teeth and pushed the words out. "Yes. You. Do." *All you have to do is believe.*

"I'm tired of games, Erich. I don't want to play anymore. Just tell me."

He pushed himself to his feet and walked by her. If he could he would, but the simple truth was tied up in a tight ball at the back of his throat. Forbidden words for him to speak until Bess said them first. "I can't. You have to say it and believe it." He spun back to her, reached for her hands. "Just think about it, Bess. Think about the two of us and you will know."

Her eyes lit up, but a tear slipped down her cheek. She raised a trembling hand to her cheek and spoke in short, clipped speech. "The similarities...the code...the address book...the way we are in bed together."

He stepped closer and reached out, touching her arm. "Yes."

"Harry? He's inside you somehow." Her voice quivered, and her hands trembled.

As the words slipped from her mouth, the force that was constricting him slipped away. He took a deep breath, letting his chest expand fully. On the exhale, the words spilled from him. "From the other side, Jaden—I think he must be your guardian angel—made a bargain with Harry's soul. He gave him a second chance at a life with you if he— No. If I could convince you to stop the séance you had planned and save you from a life of pain, heartache and loneliness."

She rolled her eyes and shifted her weight. "Guardian Angel? I think your fever is coming back."

"You've felt Harry's presence in me. I see it painted on your face."

"There are similarities. And he used you to talk to me." She spoke the words in an even cadence. Slow. Rhythmic. Who was she trying to convince? What was she trying to talk herself out of?

"It's more than that, Bess. You just have to summon that rock-strong courage you have and believe with all your heart, no matter how outrageous it seems."

She shook her head and wiped a stray tear from her cheek. "You've absorbed yourself in his life, and he communicated with you. You feel like you know his heart."

"I didn't channel Harry, Bess. I could speak the code, because I wrote it. Or I have Harry's memory of writing it."

She furrowed her brow and stepped back from him, wrapping her hands tight around her waist. Closing herself off from him and the painful words. "Why are you doing this, Erich? If you're through with me, just leave. Don't stomp on my heart before you go."

There was only one way to make her accept the truth. "Harry came up with the scheme a week after Gail pulled her stunt with the letter from his Mom. The two of you were getting ready to leave for a set of shows back east the following morning. He sat at the desk in the parlor. You'd made tea and sat in that old chair that belonged to your mother."

She lifted her trembling hands to her cheek, pushing away the tears. "How? Why? It's just not possible."

"Jaden told me if I didn't convince you to give up chasing Harry's ghost, you'd live your remaining years devastated and alone. He said it was Harry's fault you were so miserable, and he's right. You deserved better, baby. He set you up for that future. Can you ever forgive me for all the mistakes I made in that life and this new one too?"

Flames flared in her eyes, as bright and strong as the ones bursting from the house yesterday. He stepped closer, but she threw her hands up between them, holding him at bay. He hesitated, but decided it better not to push another step closer.

"Stay away from me! I trusted you! Gave you my heart, my body, and to you it was all some super, slick game? What's your ultimate plan here? You *do* want to replace Harry, take his spotlight and steal his life. Martin was right!"

Her words stabbed at his chest like a pointed dagger. He wasn't sure what hurt worse, the idea that she was no more than a game to him, or the fact that in the end, Martin held more trust than he did? "Listen. I exist for one reason. You! Only you."

She dug her heel deeper into the soft grass and said, "How is this possible?" Pivoting away, she started toward the park entrance, but stopped after only a few steps. With her back still to him, she continued, "Harry didn't believe in an afterlife. So, if one exists, he would be denied it. This is what I *know* in my heart, but I still hoped. I wanted to believe that the stupid coded message was more than a means to an end."

"Bess." No matter how he tried, keeping the tears from his voice was impossible. "What do I have to say for you to believe he loved you above all else?"

She spun back to him. "Cease this shill! You can't work over a master. Harry taught me well the art of illusion and the game of the con. I may be a pitiful, heartbroken widow, but I'm no one's fool."

"I never said you were. Never thought it. Not for one single moment. You are smart, sophisticated and intuitive. I need you to look in my eyes right now and just believe." He spun his fingers around the silver band, and he then handed it to her. "The inside of yours is engraved with Roseabelle. Harry chose that—because like the message in your safe—it was a code. Remember?"

"There is nothing to believe in. It has to be some kind of fairytale. How can you be Harry resurrected?"

"You had faith in the two of you, trusted your love when there was barely enough money to put food in your stomachs or a roof over your heads. When far away cities called asking the Houdinis to perform, you never once lost confidence that the two of you could—and would—succeed. You never lost that devotion to you and him, no matter how bumpy the road got. Look in my eyes. I know you see his soul. You know it's true, but you're just afraid to accept it."

Bess bowed her head, pinching the bridge of her nose between her thumb and forefinger. Her body slumped; she looked broken. "I'm losing my mind, every last bit of it."

"No. You're not."

"It's true," she whispered, crossing her arms in front of her chest. She may be accepting the truth, but that didn't mean she was ready to welcome him home with open arms. "His spark, his soul, lives and breathes inside you, maddening me and stealing my heart." She paused. He waited for joy to fill her eyes, for her to embrace him and kiss him, but she stumbled back. "So the great Harry Houdini has escaped death. Bravo!" She waved her arms as if she were announcing him to the stage.

Was shock stealing her joy? Surely she understood the truth. "We have another chance at life and happiness."

"By whose definition? I'm too old to go back on the road and perform for my supper, and I'm just too broken to stand stage-side every night and wait for the reaper to steal Harry from me again. My heart couldn't bear mourning him a second time."

*What was she doing? Now that she knew the truth, she was breaking up with him?* "No, Bess. No more spotlight. No more quest for glory. Just you and me, a second chance at the happiness he promised and failed to keep."

"Not failed. I loved that life while we lived it. Yes, every night you tempted the gods to rip you from my arms—"

"It was never that dangerous. An illusion, baby."

"To the crowds it was a show, but it was my reality. Death broke our bond and not even the great Houdini can repair that."

He stepped closer to her, reached out, but she swayed to the right, avoiding his touch. "In this body Harry's soul has learned how much pain he's caused. I started this journey thinking of Harry and me as one and the same, but I have grown as Erich. And my touch has begun to heal your pain."

A smile curved her lips, and her body softened. "It has. You've shown me that no matter how beautiful the past was, Harry's dead and I need to live for tomorrow. The irony is with you, I would be living for yesterday." She stepped closer to him, touched his cheek with a trembling hand and lightly brushed her lips against his. "Thank you for the guidance, but I can't go back to Harry, and with his soul that's who you'll always be." She looked deep in his eyes. Was she looking for one last glimpse of Harry or memorizing Erich's face for her dreams? "Good bye."

*No.* They hadn't come this far for her to just give up now. She tried to walk by him, but Erich took her elbow and guided her back. Gliding that hand up her arm and over her shoulder, he pulled her body to his and left a chaste kiss on her cheek. "Before you walk away from what we could be, think about these last couple of weeks. Haven't I been good for you?"

She laid her head against his shoulder. This wasn't easy for her; he could see the pain of her choices clearly etched on her face. "For years I watched you flirting with the Angel of Death. No! Not flirting. You two were caught in a torrid love affair, sharing passionate kisses right in front of my eyes. The whole world watched you make love to her night after night in the bright, white spotlight of the stage. In the end, you chose her over me."

"That's not true."

"Don't you see? If I stay, I know how this story ends. With Harry's soul it would only be a matter of time before you would be called back to danger's arms. I can't stick around for the encore, my love. It would be too damn painful." Her body tightened as she pulled away and walked toward the street, never once looking back.

For Erich, it was as if she took Harry's soul with her, leaving him an empty shell. His flesh went cold, and his knees weak. He'd anticipated anger or tears, but for her to walk away? *That* was unthinkable.

Theirs was a love for the ages, one that couldn't be broken. Or so he'd thought. Bess said she was leaving him now, because she couldn't relive that past. Harry had lived a fantasy. While painting illusions for the rest of the world, he'd thought his wife was happy and their love for each other was enough to conquer the worst, but it hadn't been. No, love hadn't eased her fear. And trepidation kept her from his arms now.

He stumbled to the park bench and sat, focusing on the gentle breeze pushing around the leaves on the California Oak Trees. He locked his gaze, knowing if he allowed his heart control of his emotions, he'd dissolve. Living without Bess was unthinkable.

"You did it, Erich. You saved her." Jaden's voice rang in his ear with none of the pompous flare or righteousness Erich was used to. Quiet, sullen, as if Jaden mourned too.

"From Harry," Erich whispered, realizing now that he'd been the real demon in her life.

"From drowning in the memory. From clinging to a past that was dead and buried."

"I might have won the bet, but in the end I've lost." Erich looked to Jaden, who was dressed appropriately for the time period, his hair braided and tucked beneath his shirt. He almost looked normal as he approached the bench and sat next to Erich.

"I can't imagine a life without her." There was no containing his pain. His voice cracked, and his hands shook with it.

"Why don't you go to her?"

"Because the last thing she wants is to relive a life with Harry. I know you don't believe me, but it was always for her. She was all that ever mattered to him. And she's all that ever mattered to me. What good is winning our wager if in the process I lost her?"

"Then why do you sit here mourning the loss when there is still fight in your body and soul?"

"She won't take me back as long as I carry Harry's soul." Saying the words sparked an idea, and Erich slowly turned his gaze to Jaden's icy eyes he often tried to avoid. "But there is something you can do about that. Take back Harry's soul, it's no longer a part of me anyway."

Jaden shook off the confusion and twisted his body toward Erich. "If I did that, you, Erich would cease to exist."

"No! I don't believe that. At first, maybe it was true, but something happened in my time here. I'm completely separate from him. You controlled this game, moved us around like pawns for your amusement. You say I won, reward me with my own life."

The large man shook his head slowly. "You are right that things have changed. I had the power over Harry's soul in the beginning, but that changed along with your transformation. It doesn't belong to me anymore. Harry and Erich may have started this journey one and the same, but you—Erich— have taken his past and created a new future. One that you control. You've become a man that has learned the value of putting other's needs before one's own."

Was he still doing that? "What's better for her, Jaden? A life with or without me?"

"What do you think? Does she deserve a life with an unconditional and all-consuming love or one that she lives alone?"

# Chapter Twenty-Six

*How could I turn Harry away?* Yet, she stopped short of following her heart and running back to the park and his arms. She couldn't. Erich had taught her not to live in the past, just before asking her to reclaim it.

That was Harry all right. A living, breathing dichotomy.

But now, the crossroads had made her stop. What she was running from...and to? She could go to the hotel, but he'd come looking for her there. Same for the deli, but she needed to talk to someone. Martin and Gail were biased against Erich. How could she tell them about Harry?

She couldn't tell Will about that either, but she could think out loud and express to him the jumbled mess of emotions twisting her stomach into knots. He would give her honest, evenhanded advice. He'd also toss Erich out on his ear if he showed up and she asked.

Given it was late morning, it didn't surprise Bess to find the deli empty. Will ambled into the dining room, wiping his hands on his apron.

Her strong facade crumbled.

"Bess, what wrong?" He rounded the counter's corner and took her elbow, leading her to the booth and helping her sit. "Coffee?"

She nodded. Will's heavy steps sounded as he rushed back, but she focused on the torn upholstery of the seat across from her and gripped the table with both hands. She shoved the brewing tears back down; too many had already been shed. Will grabbed her attention by dropping the coffee mug and small plate with a flakey pastry to the table in front of her. He slid into the booth and covered the tear she been studying to keep from dissolving to a puddle of tears. Reaching across the table, he laid his hand on top of hers. "What happened?"

"How much am I supposed to bear, Will? At what point is okay to just give up and crawl in some hole?"

"Never, sweetie. You always have to keep moving forward. Even with all the bad things, life is still worth living. I think you'll see that when Erich takes you back east to your family. Things will look a lot brighter."

Just the mention of Erich caused a thumping in her temples. She took the grief and did the only thing she knew to do: held it at bay with anger. "You won't catch me crossing the street with that reprobate."

Will's posture softened, and a smirk played across his face, only escalating her anger. "So when did you realize you were falling in love with him?"

She hated being transparent as glass. She'd worked so hard for so many years to learn how to shield her emotions from the crowds and the fans, and she had fallen out of practice so fast. "Love him? I can't stand him. He's done nothing but manipulate me since the moment he stepped foot in this town."

"Funny thing about love and hate, they're both rooted in passion. It's pretty hard to feel one without the other. Whatever he's done now wouldn't have irritated you so much if you didn't care." The smile evolved into a hearty laugh that poked at her, stirring the flames, forcing her to ask the question: what had Erich done that was so wrong? Admitted that Harry's soul was trapped in his body?

When he said that was something she already knew, he'd been dead on. Maybe it was that he knew her so well that upset her the most. Explaining to Will that being with Erich was impossible because of Harry's soul would earn her a one-way ticket to the funny farm.

The facts? The idea of starting a new life that would become the same as the old not only frightened but enraged her. "He insinuated that we might have a future together."

"That scoundrel!"

Will's mock shock did nothing to soothe her anger. She wasn't being silly, even if he saw it that way. "I can't do it, Will! He has this spark, this light, just like Harry. He thinks the world is his to own, and I'm just too tired to be chasing grandiose dreams. I should be settling in to rock grandbabies, but because of the life I led with Harry, I don't even have a child to care for me in old age."

"Have you seen the way he looks at you? I was with him when he thought you may have been caught in that fire. He loves you."

"It's Harry's old life that he's wanted all along."

Will simply shook his head. "I can see where you think there are similarities, Bess, but I don't believe he wants to be with you for any amount of fame or fortune. His heart is in the right place."

"He says that now, but in time that would fade."

"Hmf," Will muttered and cocked his head to the right as if he were studying the words she's said. "Is it time that worries you? Are you afraid of what ten or twenty years will bring you? On one hand is a man who says he loves you and wants to stand by your side, accompany you down whatever road you want to walk, but instead you'd rather go it all alone because you fear what might happen? How he *might* change?"

"What do you want me to do? Believe in him?"

"If you love him, you have to. That's what love is: giving another person blind faith, trusting that they will keep their word and never leave you behind. It wasn't Harry's choice to do that. Despite the fact he took risks every day, he didn't want to die. He didn't mean to leave you alone. You need to forgive him for that so your heart can heal. And you can't hold Erich accountable for Harry's mistakes. Just because Erich has the same hunger for living a full life, doesn't mean he'll fulfill it in exactly the same way Harry did."

Was it really that simple? If she only believed in Erich, it would all be okay? Will's words were gospel; she knew that leaving her alone wasn't Harry's intent, but still she blamed him. And what did she do after learning he defied the laws of life and death? She'd refused him again. Opening her billfold, she dropped two dimes to the table as she stood.

Will asked, "Where you going?"

"To find Erich."

On the street, she repositioned her purse on her arm and pointed herself toward the hotel. Coming across the street, waving an arm to get her attention, was Edwin with his wife on his arm and their three children in tow.

Her life had been so full in the past week plus, that she hadn't much thought of her favorite patient at the hospital. Part of her was disappointed in herself. She painted on a smile and greeted the couple with a cheerful hello.

"Mrs. Houdini," Edwin said after they'd closed the distance. "I'm so glad we ran into you. I'd been meaning to come by your place since I was released from the hospital—"

His wife elbowed his ribcage sharply. "Edwin! We were so sorry to hear about your home and the fire, Mrs. Houdini. Is there anything you need?"

The kind offering from the couple who barely had enough to make their own ends meet touched her. "The damage to the house and its contents was complete, but I'll be just fine. Possessions can be replaced. I'm lucky that my friend Erich and I were not injured or worse."

"We really do want to help, in any way we can," Edwin said. "After all, what you did for us by paying my hospital bill was such a generous blessing."

Bess stepped closer to Edwin and gave him a loose hug. "I don't want you to mention it again. I was glad to help. What's important is that you are back with your family." She turned to the three kids, looked into each of the round faces. "You have such a lovely family, Edwin. Take good care of them."

"I will ma'am."

As she watched them continue up the street, Bess's decision to go back to Erich reaffirmed itself. Whether it was because of Harry's soul or despite it, she was in love with him, and it was worth any risk to have him by her side.

****

Erich stopped in front of the hotel and questioned his choice again. Who was he doing this for? And why? Bess didn't think she could live with him, and Jaden—and his previous views on love—almost convinced him that it caused far more pain than pleasure. Still, Jaden orchestrated this whole journey and had just declared the only future in which Bess found real happiness included Erich.

With a new found courage, he entered the lobby and started for the elevator. When the doors opened, he moved forward, but a strong hand grabbed his shoulder and spun him back, bringing him eye to eye with Martin.

His brows were furrowed and his jaw locked. "Me? That's what you told the police to save your own sorry skin? That I started Bess's house on fire? Forget the fact I can't be two places at one time, I'd never do such a thing."

"I didn't say you did."

"That's not what Stanley Fisher said. He came out to my place and said you accused me and Gail of trying to poison you and starting the fire."

Erich could hear the elevator door close again behind him. Harry wanted to lash out, shove Martin away and continue on his search for Bess, but Erich resisted. It'd do nothing except anger Bess, and she was mad enough at him.

"Look, all I said to Stanley was that you were upset with Bess because she canceled the séance."

"And you told him that I gave her homemade brandy? He could have arrested me for that alone." Martin lowered his gaze. "I don't understand what I ever did to make you hate me so."

Erich's jaw dropped. "You threatened to make me disappear!"

Martin slid his hand through his cropped hair. "Not one of my finer moments."

"You admitted to me you had laid seeds and were waiting for them to take root."

"To help my wife! Not burn down Bess's home." He exhaled and looked to the ceiling for a moment. His angular chin quivered a bit as he leveled his gaze. "Rumors and speculation about what *really* happened between Gail and I while Louise was still alive have ruined her reputation. That's on me, but Harry gave the gossips more fodder, and they pushed her down the social rungs of the spiritualist community. I had hoped that through this stupid séance, she might regain some respect from them. Not that it matters all that much to me, but it's very important to her. I've worked very hard to mend the bridges with Bess that Harry had burned."

All of Martin's guilt and pain lay open on his face. And he had a point. Harry had lashed out in anger and set part of this wheel in motion long before his death. "Bess's house is gone along with every possession that was in it. I had to tell the police what was happening."

"Stan was pretty hard on Gail before he turned his investigation on me, but that isn't anything new in this town. After all I've done for this community, all my years of service to the hospital, in their eyes I'm nothing more than a womanizer, and she's no more than a home wrecker."

How was that Erich's fault? He'd only been in Martin's life for a little more than a week, and he couldn't be held accountable for Harry's actions. "What am I supposed to do about it?"

Martin shrugged. "Feel a little guilty maybe."

Erich sighed. "I don't have time for this right now. I need to find Bess."

"Well, that's why I'm really here. Gail was pretty upset after being questioned. She took off in her car. I don't know anyone she'd go to except for Bess."

Erich pivoted and pushed the button to recall the elevator. "Bess and I had words at the park, and she's in a bad mood. I bet the two of them are up in the hotel room, cursing me."

As the doors closed, Erich stood alone with Martin in the small compartment. In some ways it felt so familiar; in others it was damn awkward. Despite his protests, Martin might be responsible for burning down Bess's home and trying to poison him, but the piece of Harry who considered Martin a good friend missed the kinship. Erich had become good at squelching Harry's voice recently, but he found himself listening to the longing in Erich's soul and hearing the pain over Gail's actions that Harry buried.

Sometimes anger isn't a mask for other things, he realized.

The doors opened, and Erich led Martin down the narrow hall. In the room, he called out Bess's name.

"They're not here?" Martin asked. "Maybe they went to the deli for some coffee?"

"I looked there before I came here. Will said I'd just missed her."

The mild concern that had tempered Martin's irritation grew and deepened. Hard lines framed his eyes and mouth. "Where could they be?"

"Bess is angry at me right now. I'm not surprised she's hiding out. Did Gail have a favorite place to go when she was upset?"

"Yes. To Bess."

*Bess. Not just his angel, but a true angel of mercy.*

Martin paced the room, as if he expected the woman to jump out from behind the closet door. "Where ever they are, I'm sure they're together. Do you think Bess went to look through the rubble at the house?"

"She already got the only thing from there that mattered to her. All that is left, besides destruction, is painful memories."

Martin gave him a quizzical look, like he expected Erich to explain, but that was something he couldn't do.

Was there anything else these two had in common? Only one that Erich held suspect. "Maybe it *was* Joseph all along."

"What are you saying?"

Bess's faith in Joseph had been just as unwavering as it had been in the Coopers, but she knew Martin and Gail longer, spent more time in their company—too much time to be wrong.

Instead of fighting her on this for his own satisfaction, Erich should have been listening to her. "Would Joseph try to hurt Gail?"

Martin stepped back and dropped his head, as if he could hide behind a veil of shame. "Joseph helped me by caring for Louise in her later days. I could have kept her comfortable with Morphine, but she wouldn't have been as alert as she was with the herbal and Indian medications he used. Watching her die was the hardest thing I'll ever do, Erich, and I'll be the first to admit I handled it like a rotten S.O.B. Joseph grew quite fond of her. How could he not? She was so kind to everyone. So, to answer your question, he didn't care for Gail at all. Like the rest of this town, he blamed her for my lack of attention to Louise in her final days."

That had to be it. Erich had put blame in Martin's direction, because that is where Joseph led him. "Where did he go when you kicked him out?"

"To the reservation, I guess. He's always had a small cabin out there he'd retreat to at times."

"But he used to live on your grounds?"

"I gave him lodging in the servant's quarters while he was studying medicine. One of the last things Louise asked of me was to make sure I treated him well, just like Joseph had treated her. I gave him everything I could, until he pushed me too far."

The entire premise that all Joseph had ever wanted was to learn traditional medicine had always seemed fishy to Erich. He'd done nothing but praise his people's herbal treatments and run down hospitals and doctors as the ones who practiced witchcraft. It seemed to him, Joseph would be insulted by Martin's teachings and demeaned by a room in the servant's quarters. Add that to his dislike for Gail and suddenly there was a mound of evidence—albeit circumstantial—piling up against

Joseph for everything that had gone wrong, including the disappearance of two women. "I think both Gail and Bess are with him, and I'm not thinking it's for a good reason."

"Joseph? He may dislike Gail, but he's very serious about his role as a healer. He wouldn't hurt anyone."

"Love can make a man do things he never thought he would before."

"Love? That doesn't make any sense."

"Sure it does."

Martin shook his head. "Joseph has gone back to the reservation. I think you were right about Bess and Gail being together though. If Bess isn't at the deli or with you, then my money is on her being at the hospital, volunteering. I bet Gail is there talking to her. That's where I'm headed."

Erich shook his head. "I told you we had a fight. Why would she go on to the hospital?"

"The same reason she's been there twice a week for the last eleven months, to get her mind off Harry. Are you going to come with me?"

"No. I don't think she's there."

"Do you have another idea?"

"Actually, I do."

****

Erich turned from Martin and left the hotel. He started walking toward the far edge of town, the opposite end from where Bess's house used to stand.

The more he thought about his conversation with Martin, the more Harry's memories came crashing down on him: good memories of time spent with a dear friend. It seemed like Erich's new understanding of recent events had given Harry's soul some clarity and regrets.

Would they be in a different place now had Erich not used Harry's memories as a barometer of Bess's life? She'd insisted time and again that Martin and Gail were true friends and innocent of trying to hurt either of them. Of course, she'd felt the same way about Joseph.

He was sure that the root tea had been tainted, and Jaden had confirmed it. If it wasn't Martin who'd tried to poison him, then it had to be Joseph. The idea that Joseph may have tried to hurt Bess, like he had Erich, drove him to break out in a full run.

From the time he'd been gifted this body, Erich hadn't been well enough to exert himself as he was, but as he sprinted toward the Cooper estate, the pain that had never really left his side evaporated. His chest heaved, and his lungs burned, but it only took a few blocks for him to tap into Harry's memories and remember how to control his breathing and pace himself.

The further he ran, the more he reflected over everything that had happened. His heart broke for Bess. He cursed himself for ever letting her walk away from him and turned onto the road the Cooper's lived on. With the house in sight, he dug deep and pushed harder, running even faster.

As he neared the house, he saw Martin's black Studebaker—the one Gail had driven to the house the other day—sitting back by the servant quarters. It made no sense, and seemed to confirm Erich's worst fears.

Erich sprinted across the finely manicured lawn, jumping over a patch of daisies to land on the concrete pad. He pushed the door open, screaming Bess's name. He stumbled into the room, gasping for breath and bending at the waist. He scanned, hoping to see Bess visiting with her friend; instead he saw Gail sprawled out on the couch, very pale.

He fell to his knees at her side and put his cheek down near her face. Feeling a light exhale against his skin, he forced himself to his feet and slipped one arm beneath her neck and the other under her hips. Erich picked her up and carried her toward the car. One of the servants, a gardener Erich would guess by the way he was dressed, met him at the car and opened the back door. "Is Mrs. Cooper okay?"

"No, her breathing is really shallow." Erich rounded the car and slipped behind the wheel. Relieved to see the keys in the ignition, he called to the man who had helped him. "I'm taking her to the hospital. Martin is there already. Call ahead and tell them I'm on the way with Gail."

# Chapter Twenty-Seven

Bess tried to ignore the knots twisting in her gut as she walked into the police station. Erich hadn't shown up at the deli or the hotel. She'd even gone back to the park, thinking he might still be waiting for her on that bench. For a moment, she wondered if the awful argument had put him on an east bound train without her, but realized neither Harry or Erich would leave her. The only logical conclusion she could draw was Stanley had arrested him again.

"I need to see Sergeant Fisher. Right away."

"I'm sorry, Mrs. Houdini. He's with a suspect in connection to your fire. If you'd like to have a seat, I'm sure he'll give you an update as soon as he's done."

Her suspicions proved right, she said, "I told him yesterday not to waste any more time with Mr. Welch. He's innocent."

"It's not Mr. Welch, ma'am."

"No?" Where in the world was Erich?

"Ma'am, take a seat. Sergeant Fisher should be available soon."

She nodded and walked toward the bench in a fog. The idea of losing Erich ripped through her and shredded her heart. Her weakened knees dipped, and she lowered herself to the bench, cursing herself for sending him away.

*He wouldn't leave me. Only give me time and space.*

But then, she'd said such nasty things about Harry. She'd been brutally honest and directed all of her anger on the man who'd defied death to return to her side.

"Okay, Joseph," Stanley's voice came from the back of the room. Bess looked up to see the two men coming toward her and met them in front of the desk. Stanley addressed the officer who'd helped her. "Send two units out to the Cooper estate. I want Martin brought in and Gail taken into protective custody."

She couldn't be hearing this conversation right. Had everyone in town lost their mind? "Joseph is innocent. He's a healer."

"I agree with you, Mrs. Houdini." Stanley then spoke to Joseph. "Thank you for talking to us. You're free to go."

Joseph nodded, pushing his hands into the pockets of his pants. "Ma'am, if I may offer some advice? Take that old soul who's made a place for himself in your life and run. Get as far as you can from here before Dr. Cooper finds a way to destroy you too."

As she contemplated his words, Bess watched him fidget, shifting his weight from heel to heel. His worn pants, the same pair he always wore, were now adorned with white spots, as if he'd tried to bleach away some stains and in the process had ruined the fabric. *That old soul. Harry within Erich.* "You've known the truth about Erich from the first moment, haven't you?"

He nodded. "True love, my dear, comes your way but once, and when two souls bind, they are each other's for an eternity. They'll always find one another no matter the flesh that encases them."

Her teeth clenched as she tugged on the collar of her blouse. Joseph had told her old souls were walking among the living and still she couldn't listen to the voice in her heart that knew. "I've pushed him away."

"He'll be back."

Bess smiled and leaned in hugging the man. "I don't know how to thank you for everything you've done."

"It's not necessary." Joseph answered, before leaving the station.

Only then did it hit Bess what Stanley had said. "Did you say you want Martin arrested and Gail taken in for her own protection? From who?"

"Her husband."

Bess's jaw dropped, and her lips parted. "That's crazy. Martin loves Gail."

"Like he loved Louise? According to that Joseph fellow, Martin hired him to administer a lethal dose of painkillers to Louise to clear the way for Gail, but now their love has faded and Martin didn't think his reputation could take another hit like a divorce."

"That's preposterous. They are my friends."

"I think a lot of people have been fooled by Dr. Cooper, Bess. Don't feel bad. Why don't you go back to the hotel. When this is all over, I'll come and talk to you and Mr. Welch and let you know what's going on."

Bess nodded and watched Stanley walk away. She thought about all the pieces of the puzzle; she slid them around in her mind and tried to make them fit. Erich—or was it Harry's soul inside of him—had accused Martin of trying to kill him. Just like Joseph said Martin had done with Louise, but that couldn't be true.

She'd sat with Martin while he talked about his first wife. He wouldn't hurt either woman, and she didn't believe he'd hurt Erich either. Martin loved Gail. Maybe it wasn't the same soul-consuming love Bess had shared with Harry, but it wasn't any less real.

Joseph was blinded by his anger, because he loved Louise too.

*He loved Louise.*

He hated Martin for falling in love again so fast, and Gail for the way she took over Louise's home. Hate and revenge can be as powerful a motivator as love. Martin hadn't laced the brandy or tea. He hadn't burnt down her house either.

Joseph had. All to frame Martin.

It was a good fifteen miles to the reservation, but Bess doubted he was headed there. The look in his eyes and the words he'd said about love and final resting place told her Joseph wanted to be with Louise, and he believed she'd gone on to her ever-after. Now that he'd exacted his revenge, Bess was sure Joseph believed his soul could rest too.

But where would he go to be close to Louise? She knew his faith wouldn't look to a rotting body for physical closeness. He wanted a spiritual connection.

The Seaside Daisies.

When Gail threatened to turn over his herbal garden and Louise's flowers, she'd pushed Joseph over the edge. Like Harry's ring had been for her, those daisies were a physical connection to the woman he loved. It had to be where Joseph was headed.

****

It was a short two block walk to the cab company, and a fifteen minute wait for an available driver. Now, as the car rolled through the gates and rounded Martin's house, she saw Joseph moving through the flower garden on his knees.

*Thank Heavens I'm not too late.*

Bess paid the cab driver and told him there was no need to wait. As she crossed the short distance to Joseph, she forced herself to act calm and collected; knowing anything else might upset the other man.

"What are you doing here, Mrs. Houdini?" he asked as she approached.

"After you left the police station I started thinking about what you said the other day. You've done so much for Erich, I wanted to do something for you and thought I'd come care for Louise's flowers."

"That's very kind." A wistful smile graced his lips, and he moved his hands through the flowers, stopping to pick weeds. He used a gentle touch, like a lover's, and paused every so often to lower his face and inhale their scent. "I've taken care of everything. Nothing's going to happen to Louise's flowers now."

"Louise was lucky to have you, Joseph. You're a good man."

"I told you Gail would turn up her gardens. I came by earlier and she'd just given the order to the gardeners. I couldn't stand by and let her do that. I had to stop her."

Bess could see fragility in him that she'd never noticed and lowered herself to the grass, kneeling there. "Gail can be insensitive at times."

His lips curled. "She's a whore and has no right in that house."

"She's Martin's wife."

"Louise was his wife first. Martin broke his vow to love her alone until death and left the sweetest woman in the world to suffer alone while he desecrated their marriage bed with that trollop."

Such anger. Such passion. Bess suppressed a tremble and laid her hand on his arm. Joseph trusted her, and if she handled this right, she'd get a confession for everything out of him. "Martin tried to help her. He took her to all the best doctors and then found you to help her with the pain."

"God must have been watching out for her," he answered as he continued to finger the flowers surrounding him. After a moment, he pulled a silver flask from his pocket, unscrewed the lid and drank long from it.

"Where is Gail? She let you stay and changed her mind about digging up the gardens?"

He shook his head, laughing under his breath. "She cursed me and tried to throw me off the property herself." He closed his eyes, inhaled deeply and turned his head toward the sky. "I'm sorry, Louise. You would have wanted me to just let her be. But it was grand, watching her eyes roll back in her head, knowing she'd never say another reproachful word."

Something inside Bess seized as if her heart had stopped beating. She couldn't show her pain and confusion to Joseph though, even if he'd just admitted to killing Gail.

She'd been such a faithful friend over the past year, and Bess had acted ungrateful in the past few days. But she wouldn't allow herself to grieve until she had the proof the police needed. "I'm sure Gail was jealous of Louise, felt like she had huge shoes to fill among Martin's friends and the people in town."

"She never aspired to be anything like Louise. Couldn't have. The only way that woman could ever have anyone's respect is to have a man like Martin and his money. But you put a pig in a Sunday dress and it's still a pig. People knew better, and she hated them for it. That's why she tried to hang her name on Mr. Houdini's star, but he saw through her too."

"When Harry's mother passed away, he was lost in his grief for quite some time." Ironic. Joseph and Harry had done the same thing. "He said things to Gail he probably shouldn't have. Probably wouldn't have if he let some time pass and his heart heal."

"Gail had no right to try and use Mr. Houdini's reputation in such a self-serving way."

"Who am I to judge? Harry and I—"

He turned his gaze to her and reached out, taking her hand. "Mrs. Houdini. The two of you may have made mistakes, but your heart is good. You saw the errors and changed your ways. Mr. Houdini even warned others. The new lady of the house had a coal-black heart filled with envy."

"Did she have to die for that?" Bess waited for an answer, but his stare was vacant, as if everything inside him was gone. She'd sensed pain and torment before, but now, he was numb.

"With her gone, the trouble that's surrounding you is going to lift and go away. Your soul's mate is back. He will stand by you, protect you and love you. You'll never have to be alone again, not in this existence or any other." He looked away from her and toward the flowers.

Maybe Bess should have been scared. Here she sat with a man who'd just admitted to killing her friend in the name of everlasting love, but all she could feel was overwhelming sadness. Maybe Joseph had a point. Maybe Martin should have honored Louise a little every now and then. Gail certainly should have allowed him to. They both should have realized the heart's capacity for love.

Joseph moved from his knees to sit in the grass next to her. He folded his legs and drank again from the flask. Bess let her eyes wander to the flowers, but her attention was caught by the dark, oily stains on his shoes.

Just like the rags on her back porch the previous morning.

"Did you burn down my house?" she asked.

"No one was paying attention to the little things, Mrs. Houdini. I had to do something big, something that would cause everyone to suspect Martin."

She had to lift her hand to her face to block the strong odor on his breath—licorice. Like the tea Erich accused Joseph of tainting.

"I don't know how that man of yours survived the poison, but that proved to me he was here for you. I couldn't make another attempt on his life after the angel came to me."

"An angel?" *The same one that Erich spoke of?*

Joseph nodded as he brought the flask to his lips again.

The image of Erich collapsing in her kitchen flashed, and she slapped her hand against the flask, knocking it to the ground. "Is the tea tainted?"

Joseph fell forward on his hands, coughing so hard she thought he might tear himself in two—like Erich had the night he whispered the code to her. "The angel. The one who reminded me love is more powerful than hate. I can see him, coming to take me to Louise." He crawled into the flowerbed, rolled onto his back and reached toward the sky with open arms. As his eyes rolled back in his head and his arms dropped, Bess realized a moment too late exactly why it'd been so important to Joseph to give his own soul peace.

She went to him, pushed his long hair away from his face and slid her fingers down his clammy skin. His lips were already turning blue; his breathing had stopped. "Don't do this!" She shook his shoulders, hoping to make his lifeless body gasp for air. "No more senseless dying!"

****

As Erich pulled up in front of the hospital, he saw Martin waiting out front with another doctor and nurse and a gurney. As soon as he stopped the car, Martin pulled open the back door and lifted his wife from the seat, laying her on the cot. "What happened?"

Erich jumped from the car and rounded to the opposite side. "I found her like that on the couch in the servant's quarters."

Martin pressed a stethoscope to her chest and leaned over the woman. "She's still breathing."

The other doctor leaned over the gurney. "Let us take her inside, Martin."

He nodded and stepped away.

"Joseph poisoned her. I know you don't believe me, but he laced the brandy you gave to Bess and the licorice root tea he prescribed to me."

"With what? Unless we know the poison, treating her is like a game of Russian roulette."

"I don't know. No clue." He walked from Martin, pushing his fingers through his hair, screaming internally to Jaden. He would know. Maybe, just once, he'd disseminate information simply—and not in the form of a puzzle—to save a life.

Erich leaned back against the hospital wall and pressed his hand to his side. He was expecting a shot of pain, and was surprised when there was none.

"I need to get inside to Gail. Come in and I'll have a doctor look at your incision. Make sure you didn't reinjure yourself."

Erich nodded and waved Martin ahead, hoping that once he was left alone, Jaden would bring him the information they needed to save Gail. As the hospital doors swung closed, Erich lifted the tails of the flannel shirt he wore.

Where his skin had been once marred by the incision Jaden gave him and Joseph's repair, it was now smooth. No stitches. No scars.

*You are free of Harry's chains.* Jaden's voice flitted through his mind. *His thoughts and words no longer influence you. Other people are your first concern.*

"What did he poison her with?" He asked his question out loud. "Help me make this right, Jaden."

*Their live's courses are not up to me.*

Erich spun away from the wall and went into the hospital, walking past a door that led to back to the examine rooms, he found Martin and the other staff members treating Gail. He called Martin's name and then said, "I want to go back out to your place. See if I can figure out what Joseph used. Maybe I missed something. Can I take the car?"

"Of course," Martin said, not looking up from their care of Gail.

As Erich turned to go, he was turned back by Martin calling out to him.

"Thank you, Erich."

****

Bess checked her watch and walked away from the police officers who surrounded the bed of Seaside Daisies. She'd answered all their questions, more than once, but still they searched for answers where she doubted they'd ever be found.

She'd asked Stanley to try and find Erich for her, and he'd radioed the request in. As of yet, he hadn't shown. Hearing stones being kicked up in the drive, Bess looked over her shoulder to see the Cooper's older, black car coming up the drive. Expecting Martin, she was shocked when Erich jumped out from behind the wheel. She called his name.

He'd been on a bee-line to the servant's quarters, but when he heard her call, Erich turned and ran to her.

He opened his arms, and she ran to him, gripping his waist. "I'm so sorry," she whispered into his chest.

He slid his fingers under her chin, lifting it so he could look down into her eyes. "What for?"

"For turning you away, I shouldn't have."

"You were shocked. I don't blame you." He looked over her shoulder at the garden. "What's going on?"

"I thought you knew. Joseph is dead."

Erich stumbled back out of her arms. His lower lip slipped between his teeth, and he pushed his hands into his pockets. "I'm here to try and find a clue as to what he poisoned Gail with."

Bess wrapped her arms around herself. "He told me he killed her."

"No." Erich pulled her back into his embrace. "She's very ill, but she's still alive. Martin came to the hotel looking for Gail and you. We talked and I figured out it must be Joseph..."

Even though she was still confused about him and the part of him that was Harry, she clung to his shoulders and buried her face against his chest, needing the comfort. There had been too much pain, too much death, in the name of love. Erich continued talking, bringing her up-to-date on everything that had happened, but she focused on his arms pulling her tight to his chest.

Erich released one arm, but still clenched her with the other. He twisted his body so he could get a look at the scene behind him. "What in the world was he thinking?"

"That he owed it to Louise to ruin Martin and Gail for the way they behaved during her final days."

"He was in love with Louise?"

Bess nodded. "He was drinking from a flask while we talked, I could smell the bitter licorice tea he taught me to make for you."

"Martin says there must be something other than licorice root. Until they know for sure what they're dealing with, they don't know how to treat her."

"I need to go to them. They're my friends, Erich, and I need to be there for Martin." Maybe Erich—and Harry—were entitled to their anger and resentment, but she had to honor the way they'd treated her since Harry's death, and she wasn't going to let any man decide her actions.

He nodded once. "I was wrong, Bess. I see that now. Gail may have made some mistakes, but she didn't deserve what Joseph did."

"Can you take me to them?"

"Of course, but I need to talk to the police first, see if

they've found anything that might be able to tell Martin what Joseph poisoned her with." He clutched her hand tight and led her back toward the daisies.

She followed him, but inside she wrestled. She loved Erich, wanted to be with him, but there was still so much lying between them. "When this is all over, we have to talk."

# Chapter Twenty-Eight

Erich stayed at Bess's back—close enough for comfort, far enough to give her room to breathe—as they entered the hospital room.

Martin sat at Gail's bedside, caressing her hand and his eyes locked on her creamy pale face. Bess recognized the pain and the irony. She'd cared for Erich with patient compassion, but cursing the gods. No one deserved this pain of losing their heart's love twice in a single lifetime. "Is she going to be okay?"

Martin's body sagged at the sight of Bess. "Thank Heavens Joseph didn't hurt you too."

"Erich explained everything," Bess said and then rounded the bed. Standing behind Martin, she squeezed his shoulders.

He reached up and laid his hand on top of hers. "It looks to be some sort of overdose. They're trying to figure out just what so they can give her an antidote. Nothing they've tried has seemed to make a difference."

"Stanley brought the flask he was drinking out to the lab, but we have no way of knowing if he used the same mixture to poison himself that he did Gail," Erich said.

Martin craned his neck sharply, meeting her eye. "He's dead?"

"Yes," Bess whispered.

Erich would have expected to see some sort of vindication flash in Martin's eyes, but his expression didn't change. Maybe vengeance didn't thrive in his heart the way Harry had accused. Instead, Martin scratched his forehead. "Licorice root is not a poison. It has healing properties, but it has such a strong distinct odor, so it would cover up any number of poisons. If I'd been paying closer attention, I might have been able to prevent him from hurting her, or you and Erich," Martin said. His voice sounded heavy.

"You have no reason to feel guilty," Bess said. "You treated him well. Gave him opportunities. He fell in love with Louise."

"Is that what he told you?" Martin asked.

Bess could only nod.

"But that doesn't explain why he drugged me or burned your house down," Erich said.

"Because everyone—including you—would believe it was Martin, especially since I started wavering on the séance. Joseph felt he owed it to Louise to exact some sort of revenge."

"Hmph." Martin's gaze fell back to Gail. "Louise didn't know what revenge was. She would have never wished another person harm and would have hated vengeance in her name."

Erich reached out and briefly touched Martin's back. "There are no words I can say that will offer any comfort, but I'm here—same as Bess—if there's anything you need."

Bess leaned over and hugged Martin's neck, while eyeing Erich. This kindheartedness he offered Martin puzzled her. Harry knew compassion, but he held it close, only gave it to those he deemed most worthy. He would have declared that Martin and Gail had brought this house of cards tumbling down upon themselves. Was Erich doing this to impress her? Trying to prove that Harry's soul was only a portion of the man he was now?

No. Bess couldn't accept that she drove his actions. Not when it came to something like this. Either he was acting from his heart, or he wasn't any kind of man at all. Either way, the time had come for them to have that talk. As soon as they left the hospital. "But Erich got her here in time, right? That's what's important. She'll be okay."

He shrugged and sighed. "We're treating her in the best way we know. She seems to be stable, but only time will really tell." He gave Bess an insincere smile. "But there's no reason for you and Erich to sit here waiting."

The misery on his face caused Bess to look away. "We're here for you. For as long as you need us."

"And I appreciate that, sweetie, I do. But you've been through a lot these last couple weeks too, and I'd feel better if you let Erich just take you back to the hotel so you can rest. I'll send word if anything changes here."

She patted his arm. "If you're sure?"

"I am."

****

Erich reached out to take Bess's hand as they walked toward the hotel, but withdrew it before he touched her. He pushed it into his pocket and let the words she'd said—we have to talk—play over and over in his head.

"What made you go to estate? To talk to Gail?"

As they continued their walk, Bess recounted each and every event from the moment she'd left him standing in the park, until he'd found her at the Cooper's. She waited until they were alone back in the hotel room to ask the question that he guessed weighed the heaviest on her mind. "How and why are you here?"

He supposed she wanted all the complicated details. Ones he didn't know how to explain. The kernel of truth was simple, though. "I'm here because of Harry's will."

She fidgeted and then paced the room for a moment. He suspected she was taking time to choose her words instead of letting her heart spew. "Why do you say Harry's? Aren't his and your will the same?"

Erich lowered himself to the edge of the bed. "No. It was Harry's desperation to get back to you that instigated his deal with Jaden. He put Harry's soul in my body, animated it and set it down next to you. Even with all his memories and feelings, from that first moment, it was like there were two different people inside of me. I'm not Harry, but I've learned from his mistakes, his success, his time and these experiences."

"But you thirst for danger."

He shook his head and pushed his fingers through his short hair. "I enjoy the skills he mastered, but I don't crave a spotlight. I do understand his hunger. His memories are as real as my own, and you've misjudged him."

Bess twisted her heel into the floor and crossed her arms in front of her. "Don't stand there and say Harry didn't yearn for the crowd's applause."

"I won't lie to you. Not ever. But you don't understand what drove his desires. Both of you knew great struggles. He went to work at a tender age, to compensate for what his father couldn't provide and never wanted to fail you like that, Bess. He took the stage when he was bone tired—or deathly ill—because not doing so put *your* future at risk. He loved you from his heart to the bottom of his soul. Your welfare and succeeding for you, was always at the forefront of his mind. Always."

"His mind? His soul? Don't you share these things?"

"Yes. No. I don't know." Erich exhaled and stood. He could really use Jaden's help now. Reaching out, he hoped she'd give him her hand. She complied, and he kissed her knuckles. "I guess our souls are one in the same, but his memories are a distant past, one I feel removed from."

Bess hesitated, eyed him up and down, and he couldn't blame her. The last year had been Hell, and she used the time for careful examination of her life with Harry. A moment passed, and then she inched closer and slid her arms around his waist. "You were so kind to Martin at the hospital."

"We've reached an understanding."

"Forgive me if I'm confused."

He smiled, leaned in and brushed her lips with his own. "At first I harbored all the ill will Harry died with. I clung to it. His suspicion that everyone would want to cash in on his fame breathed within me, and finding out

Martin was so much a part of your plans confirmed those fears. Watching you mourn and understanding your pain, I began to see inside Martin's. He explained to me Gail's need to make a place for herself in this town. I understand Harry's anger and hurt, but time has passed—a lot of it. And I've also learned that life is just too short for resentment and hate, especially when it's misdirected."

"Grieving is hard. I hope it isn't something Martin has to endure again."

"We have to have faith that Martin and the other doctors can help her." Erich laid his hand against her cheek. "Can you love me, Bess, now that you know the truth?"

"As hard as it is to imagine going back, there's no way I can move forward without you."

"I've learned from my mistakes, and that's the truth. You are the only dream I want to chase. No spotlights. No screaming crowds."

"Just go back east and what?"

"Live the remainder of our days together. And maybe open a little diner of our own?"

Bess laughed. "You always hated manual labor."

"Harry did. Don't get me wrong, I wasn't thrilled at first, but I like the interaction with people, and I like the idea of working together. Face it, we do it well."

Her whole face lit up with her smile, and even though her eyes were glassy with tears, he had no doubt they were tears of joy. "I love the idea."

He leaned in, laying his forehead against hers. "But we should wait and see what happens with Gail. Martin may need some of the same support he's shown you this past year."

"It's going to take a while for me to get used to all the changes," Bess said.

He brushed his lips to hers and wrapped an arm around her shoulders. "I plan to spend the rest of our lives surprising you and keeping every single promise I've made."

# Chapter Twenty-Nine

When Erich escorted Bess into Gail's hospital room this time, he held her hand and tried to ignore they were being escorted by the police. From the moment Stanley had said Martin sent for them, Erich feared the worst. If Gail had lost her battle, it would devastate both Bess and Martin, neither of which deserved any more pain. His reunion with Bess would be tainted if they celebrated in the shadow of Martin's grief, and Erich would forever regret his actions if he never got the chance to make amends for the things he'd said to Gail because of Harry's memories.

In the room, they found Gail semi-alert. The weight lifted from his shoulders, he smiled. Bess's hand slipped away, and she went to the other woman's bedside. "Oh, thank the Heavens. You're doing better."

Gail's eyes fluttered as she opened her mouth and reached to Bess. However, no voice emerged.

Martin touched his wife's cheek. "It's okay, honey, your voice will come back." He turned to Erich. "You were right about the licorice root tea. Its taste is strong enough to hide Oleander."

"You found it in the sample from the flask?"

"Eventually, but we had to work in reverse. It would have taken forever to test the sample for everything it could have been. We sent a lab technician out to the estate to make a list of poisonous plants on my property. They started by searching the garden shed and found a small jar of dried Oleander. It's highly toxic, but has a very distinct odor and taste. That's why he needed something with a unique smell—the licorice root."

"Dear Heavens," Bess said. "I still can't believe it. He was so kind while caring for Erich."

"With Louise too. He had all the components of a good doctor: smart, resourceful, caring."

Erich watched Gail. Her eyes filled with sadness, and she tilted her gaze away from the conversation. He had more in common with this woman than he'd ever realized before. They both would always share the heart of the person they loved with a ghost. Erich had somehow made peace with that in the last day; maybe he could help Gail do the same.

He sat on the edge of her bed and laid his hand on the blankets covering her legs. "You don't need to feel threatened by the fact he's loved before, Gail. All that shows is that he has the capacity to do so."

Gail lifted her gaze, meeting Erich's eyes for the first time since he'd walked in the room.

"I know it's hard. You sort of feel like you have to compete with a ghost, or at least that's how I felt at first. But I realize now I was wrong...about a lot of things. Just because Bess loved Harry, that doesn't mean she can't love me too. Martin loves you, Gail, I've seen it with my own eyes."

Her lips parted as if she was going to try and speak, but she clamped them shut and covered his hand with hers, squeezing it tight to show her appreciation.

"There's something else. I owe you an apology. I judged you—and your husband too—and for no other reason than idle gossip and misrepresented tales. I've said some pretty nasty things to the two of you, and I had no right."

Martin said, "I think there's plenty of regret to go around. We've all let ourselves be guided by past angers and hurt. I'd like to try and let it go and move forward, start anew if that's possible." Martin extended his hand, and Erich hesitated before he gripped it.

As his fingers closed around the other man's hand, a pang from the past tapped his heart and his mind. It was that piece of Harry that still tumbled around inside him, remembering the touch of a dear friend.

****

Erich fought to keep his eyes open as the clickety-clack of the train rolling down the tracks lulled him toward sleep. It had already worked its magic on Bess, and she slumbered against his chest. This moment—one Harry had experienced time and again as they had crisscrossed the country—was now somehow sweeter. Moments like this would not be ignored. Life. Love. Family. They were the precious moments.

In the days after her ordeal with Joseph, Bess found peace. Together, they shipped the remainder of Harry's stage props to the founding museum, and upon her insistence, they sold the car to a young couple just embarking on a life together. As the two of them drove off in what had been a part of her past with Harry, Bess commented that the young lovebirds reminded her of the two of them.

He had a second chance at life with Bess. There were no regrets.

One by one the other passengers who had shared the car got up and moved.

*Were he and Bess the only ones who thought the expense of a sleeper car was too lavish?*

He dismissed it, blessed to have this time alone with his bride-to-be. His heart still beat like mad when he recalled the moment she'd agreed to a private, family ceremony once they arrived in New York.

From the corner of his eye he saw a man wearing an all-white suit push himself to his feet. The great height and long black hair registered, it must be Jaden. Erich shifted his weight and readied himself to welcome one more conversation, but surprisingly Jaden knelt in front of Bess and touched her knee. She startled awake, and his voice came soft and reassuring, unlike the brash thunder it had been for Erich.

"It's all right, Bess. I didn't mean to wake you, but there is something I need you to know."

She stretched her back and rubbed her eyes, as if she couldn't quite discern whether or not this was a dream. Her glance shot to Erich then back to the man in front of her. "You're Jaden? My guardian angel?"

He laughed, full and rich—this was the entity Erich was used to. "Yes, I'm Jaden, but I'm not an angel—guardian or otherwise. I'm the gatekeeper between purgatory and a soul's ever-after. I bended a few rules so the two of you could reunite, but that's my prerogative. Harry's soul still had too much to learn to be put to rest."

"I guess I can't argue with that," Erich said as he looped his arm through Bess's .

Jaden let the remark slide without comment. He was here for Bess. "You've been on a rough road, but it wasn't in vein. Your soul learned several lessons too, but I hope with Erich's help, you comprehended the biggest one."

"That I can be self-sufficient."

Jaden nodded. "But thankfully, you won't have to be." A sly smile played across the man's face. "I don't think he's going anywhere."

"He better not," Bess said with a chuckle.

Jaden let his hand brush her stomach. "No. The child you carry needs two parents, and it will have them both for quite some time."

"A baby...but I'm beyond—" Her hands began to tremble, and Erich wrapped his arm around her shoulder, pulling her tight to his.

"No, you're not," he whispered. "You're going to be a wonderful mother, and I'm going to be right by your side."

Jaden spoke again. "These last few weeks have been a journey, and I hope the road taught you that hatred stirs up dissention, but love covers up all wrongs."

"Where have I heard that before?" Erich asked.

"The book of Proverbs," Bess answered.

"That's right. And with that knowledge you won't fail, not as a union nor a family. There was no point in any of this, Bess, if we couldn't address your one regret.

What Erich says is true. Only a piece of Harry remains within him, and that will be passed on."

"Thank you, Jaden," Erich said. "For another chance, the lessons learned and the new life to live. None of it will be lost on me."

For the first time since appearing on the train, Jaden met Erich's eyes. "I know." Jaden then turned back to Bess. "Are you happy?"

She wiped a tear away and leaned forward, kissing Jaden's cheek, "Beyond words."

"Then I think I'm done here."

As he righted himself and walked up the aisle and through the door to the next car, Erich squeezed Bess tighter. "I can't find the words to express how happy I am. I promise this time around I won't fail you or our child."

"So many promises, Mr. Welch," she teased.

"And I intend to keep every single one."

"I don't doubt it for a minute."

Bess closed her eyes again and curled into his shoulder. He held her tight and watched the lights of the city beyond his window whiz by. A lifetime was a brief moment in the grand scheme—a single grain of sand on an expansive beach. Not everyone would be as lucky as he, and he'd never again take for granted the lessons learned or the second chance that came from resurrecting Harry.

# Acknowledgements

Thank you to everyone who encouraged and supported me with the book from conception to publication: My husband, Brad Phillips; my children, Josh and Katelynn Phillips; my fellow MVRWA members and the B-I-C crew.

Thank you to Sloan Parker and Tracy Madison, for their time spent critiquing the manuscript and encouraging me on my path.

Thank you to some of my biggest cheerleaders, your support has meant the world to me: Shay Lacy, Jill Kemerer, Jenna Rutland, PM Kavanaugh, Kristina Knight, Jayne Kingston, Ray Wenck, Josh Hathaway, Justene Adamec, Cathy Stein, Sagan Arp, Mackenzie Bensch, Geri Call, Gloria Hakala, Mom, and Dad.

Thank you to my editor, Sheldon Reid, for helping to make it the best book possible.

# Author's Biography

Constance Phillips lives in Ohio with her husband, daughter, and four canine kids where she writes contemporary romance novels and paranormal romance novels.

When not writing stories of finding and rediscovering love, Constance and her husband spend the hours planning a cross-country motorcycle trip for the not-so-distant future...if they can find a sidecar big enough for the pups.

News and information on Constance can be found at her website (Constancephillips.com). She also blogs regularly at www.blog.constancephillips.com. You can also follow her on Twitter or friend her on Facebook.

# Other Books By Constance Phillips

**<u>Fairyproof Series</u>**
 Fairyproof
 Council Courtship (Novella)
 Chasing Power (Coming in 2015)

**<u>Resurrecting Harry Series</u>**
 Resurrecting Harry
 Liz's Legacy (Coming in 2016)

**<u>Sunnydale Days Series</u>**
 All That's Unspoken
 All That's Unclaimed
 All That's Unrealized
 All That's Unforgiven (Coming Dec. 2015)
 All That's Unforeseen (Coming Jan. 2016)

**<u>Anthology</u>**
 One Lucky Night (Lexi's Chance)

**<u>Boxed Set</u>**
 Sweet But Sexy Boxed Set (Inc. All That's Unspoken)

**<u>Single Titles</u>**
 The Ultimate Catch

# Liz's Legacy

*An Excerpt from Resurrecting Harry Book Two*
*Coming in 2016*

Liz stumbled to the bench and sat, welcoming the silence of the nurse's locker room and letting the door swing closed behind her. A deep, cleansing breath released the scents of disinfectant and urine that seemed to play in equal parts in the patient's rooms. And the blood. How could she forget the scent of blood?

With a slow inhale, she focused on the modest hygienic scent: soap and water minus stringent, sanitizing solvents. When her stomach stopped sloshing back and forth, she reached up, pulled the brown band from her hair and let it fall around her shoulders. As she stretched out her legs and kicked off the ugly-yet-sensible white oxfords, all she could focus on was getting home, crawling into bed with her cat, and pulling the covers over her head.

Blessed sleep. When she woke up, it wouldn't be Halloween anymore.

Two notes were taped to the outside of her locker. One on a regular piece of notebook paper, the second was on Dr. Davis Steven's personal stationary—ivory with a family crest. She peeled off the other one first: an invitation to a Halloween party from one of her fellow nurses. She crumpled it into a ball, tossed it toward the garbage can and mock-cheered when it ricocheted off the wall and landed in the can.

Opening the other, she read the words and wanted to send it to the same destination as the first.

"Lizzy, nice work today. Please, come to my office after your shift. I have something to discuss with you."

Throwing away a note from her boss and perspective benefactor wasn't the smartest thing to do, but she wasn't in the mood for good news, especially when it came with a price. When he gave her the open position in his nurse-to-doctor program, it would close a door for Ren. One more missed opportunity might be a fatal blow to his battered ego and the idea of being part of his pain wrenched her heart.

She folded the paper in half twice and slipped it into her duffle bag. Unbuttoning the front of her dress and pulling it off, she imagined the cost of ignoring the summons. "I'm so sorry, Dr. Stevens. No, I didn't see any note from you."

Not today. Not on Halloween. Tomorrow she'd shoulder the world's burdens. Tonight, she just wanted a cup of hot chocolate and her cat.

Slipping on her coat, she padded toward the front entrance. Near the revolving doors, Ren leaned against the brick wall as if he'd melt into the ground if it weren't there to hold him up. His eyes were closed, so she couldn't see the brown pools that were a clear window to his mood, but she didn't have to. The slack in his shoulders and tremble in his knee told her he was defeated. The difference: he probably had a reason that made more sense than the date on the calendar.

When she called his name, he looked to her and straightened his posture. She stepped in to give him a hug, even though a tight squeeze from him better fit her agenda, but he dodged to the side, brushing off her advance. To go back six weeks and erase that single action that changed everything between them: she'd do it in a heartbeat. But, she knew better than anyone that the past can't be changed and it has a way of haunting you.

"Have you talked to Dr. Stevens?" he asked.

"No. Well, not since rounds."

His eyes fell, focusing on the black mat in front of the revolving doors. "I'm surprised." When she didn't respond, his eyes met hers again. "Congratulations."

Her biggest hope and greatest fear was true, yet... "For what?"

"I just came from his office. I've been eliminated as a candidate for the program. You're the only one still in the running, Lizzy."

She'd expected as much when she'd seen his note, but somehow thought delaying her good news, would also delay his bad. "I'm sorry."

"Why?"

Her fingers curled tight into fists, bouncing against the side of her thigh. Ren wallowed in disappointments. She couldn't blame him. He'd suffered enough in his short life to justify the sullen face he showed the world, but his inability to accept comfort from her angered instead of encouraging more sympathy. "Because the program was important to you. I know you're let down."

He shrugged his shoulders. Her initial reaction was to offer a comforting embrace, but seeing as he'd just brushed off one, she didn't dare open herself up to more rejection.

"I knew it was a long shot. You should go talk to him."

"I'd rather walk home with you. I can talk to Dr. Stevens tomorrow."

"I'm not going home, Liz. You should call your dad to come get you."

"I am twenty-four years old. I am capable of seeing myself six blocks. I just like spending time with you. You used to like being with me, too."

"You know I do. It's just different now. Besides, I really do have an appointment. I'm not even going in the same direction."

"Fine. I'll see you tomorrow." She threw her duffle bag over her shoulder and started for the doors. The black metal was within reach when she heard her superior calling after her.

"Lizzy. Lizzy Welch!"

She could feel her shoulders drop as she turned around.

"I'll talk to you later," Ren said as he went by, leaving her alone in the entry with the doctor.

"Didn't you get my message?"

"Message? No. Sorry." She hoped her pasted-on smile wasn't transparent and her lie wasn't blinking in her eyes like a bright, neon sign.

His arm slid around her back as he guided her into the waiting room. Going to the quiet corner, she took a seat adjacent to the one he chose. His blond curls and sky-blue eyes were only two of the reasons most of the nurses in the hospital longed to spend time with Dr. Davis Stevens, but not Liz. Not that he wasn't kind or an expert, it wasn't like she disliked him. She just didn't see what all the fuss was about.

"What did you want to talk to me about?"

"The nurse-to-doctor program. It's starting next week."

She nodded, waiting for the inevitable.

"I've decided to award the last opening to you, Liz. You've earned it."

She should be excited, but she couldn't shake the look on Ren's face. It was bad enough for him to lose the position, but the fact that she won it made this tangled mess between them even more complicated. "Thank you, Dr. Stevens. I look forward to it and am grateful for the opportunity."

Polite and gracious, the words didn't even feel like ones she'd normally say. Of course, she was appreciative and her parents would be so proud. If only Ren could be too.

He smiled and patted her knee. "And I know you're going to be my little shining star. There's a lot of paperwork to be done and information for me to tell you. How about I come by your house tonight—"

"Not tonight! I'm sorry." Was her harsh refusal over the top? Probably.

"Is something wrong, Lizzy? I expected more excitement."

"It's just a bad night, Doctor. Halloween is always so busy at my parent's restaurant. A lot people come in to commemorate—" The words and the emotions balled up and filled her throat, forcing her to swallow before continuing. "My mother's first husband—Harry Houdini—it's the anniversary of his death."

"Oh, yes. I almost forget your mother is Bess Houdini."

"Welch. Bess Welch."

He paused and smiled at some internal recollection or maybe a memory. "None-the-less, it's really important to get a jump on this. Your classes will begin in just a week and there's much to be done. I'll wait until after dinner and come by the restaurant."

Before she could argue, he patted her knee again, stood up, and walked away. Liz shuddered and added "hot shower" to the list of things she wanted when she got home.

Dr. Steven never crossed any lines: a touch here or there, but always in a friendly or encouraging way. Still, coupled with the three previous invitations to dinner, she knew the good doctor had more amorous thoughts on his mind, and she was running out of polite ways to refuse him.

This was a Halloween for the record books. Not only was Ren so angry he could barely look at her, but now she had to spend this evening with Dr. Stevens.